W9-BYX-953

A Time of Change

Also by Aimée & David Thurlo

ELLA CLAH NOVELS

Blackening Song
Death Walker
Bad Medicine
Enemy Way
Shooting Chant
Red Mesa
Changing Woman
Tracking Bear
Wind Spirit
White Thunder
Mourning Dove
Turquoise Girl
Coyote's Wife
Earthway
Black Thunder
Never-Ending-Snake
Plant Them Deep

LEE NEZ NOVELS

Second Sunrise
Blood Retribution
Pale Death
Surrogate Evil

SISTER AGATHA NOVELS

Bad Faith
Thief in Retreat
Prey for a Miracle
False Witness
Prodigal Nun
The Bad Samaritan

A TIME OF CHANGE

OF CHANGE

Aimée & David Thurlo

A TOM DOHERTY ASSOCIATES BOOK

NEW HANOVER COUNTY
PUBLIC LIBRARY
201 CHESTNUT STREET
WILMINGTON, NC 28401

This is a work of fiction. All of the characters, organizations, and events portrayed in this novel are either products of the authors' imaginations or are used fictitiously.

A TIME OF CHANGE

Copyright © 2013 by Aimée and David Thurlo

All rights reserved.

A Forge Book
Published by Tom Doherty Associates, LLC
175 Fifth Avenue
New York, NY 10010

www.tor-forge.com

Forge® is a registered trademark of Tom Doherty Associates, LLC.

Library of Congress Cataloging-in-Publication Data

Thurlo, Aimée.
    A time of change / Aimée Thurlo and David Thurlo.—First edition.
        p. cm.
    "A Tom Doherty Associates book."
    ISBN 978-0-7653-2452-8 (hardcover)
    ISBN 978-1-4668-1458-5 (e-book)
    1. Navajo Indians—Fiction. 2. Businessmen—Crimes against—
Fiction. 3. Trading posts—New Mexico—Fiction. I. Thurlo, David.
II. Title.
PS3570.H82T56 2013
813'.54—dc23

                                                          2012042845

Forge books may be purchased for educational, business, or promotional use.
For information on bulk purchases, please contact Macmillan Corporate and
Premium Sales Department at 1-800-221-7945 extension 5442 or write
specialmarkets@macmillan.com.

First Edition: April 2013

Printed in the United States of America

0 9 8 7 6 5 4 3 2 1

To Jennifer Purdy—may you always walk with blessings before you.

—ACKNOWLEDGMENTS—

With special thanks to Michele Kiser for her help with the Navajo language.

To Sergeant Ryan Tafoya, who has amazing patience answering all our questions.

And to Steve Henry, attorney-at-law, for sharing his legal expertise once again.

A TIME
OF CHANGE

—ONE—

Josephine Buck walked in beauty. She attended school two nights a week at San Juan College in Farmington, New Mexico, and held a part-time job at The Outpost, a trading post adjacent to the Navajo Nation. At age twenty-six, she was also the youngest apprentice to one of the tribe's most revered *hataaliis*, medicine men. Though it would take years, someday she hoped to become a Navajo medicine woman—a rare profession for women of her tribe.

Her schedule was impossibly demanding, but through the traditions of the *Diné*, the Navajo People, she'd found the strength to honor all her commitments. She started each morning by offering her Prayers to Dawn, a ritual as old as the sacred mountains.

Standing on the sage-covered hillside behind her home on the Navajo Reservation, she waited for the first rays of light to peer over the horizon. The moment Sun greeted her, Jo began to chant. "Dawn, beautiful dawn." Her voice rose, each line reverberating with the power of conviction. The prayer was as much a part of her as the beating of her heart.

At long last, she finished. *"Hozhone nas clee,* now all is well," she said, then took a pinch of pollen from her deerskin medicine bag and threw it into the air. The tiny particles danced like yellow glitter in the early morning light, catching in a gentle breeze and dispersing before drifting down to Mother Earth.

Filled with energy, Jo hurried back downhill. She was going to work early to meet with Tom Stuart, the trading post's Anglo owner. For the past two months, something had been bothering him, but the store was a busy place—she worked thirty-five hours a week there now—and they hadn't had time to talk about anything except business. Then he'd asked her to stop by his house before work this morning to discuss an important matter. His tone was so grim, he'd scared her a bit. She'd spent a long sleepless night speculating on the reason, each new scenario worse than the last.

Tom was more than her boss; he was the father she wished she'd had, and her friend. When her own father became sick, the former marine turned storekeeper had been there for her. He'd allowed her to keep flexible hours and done everything in his power to help her through that difficult time.

As a good Navajo, Jo believed that balance was the way to harmony. Tom had helped her, and now she'd do the same for him. Jo hurried to her truck and set out, wondering what lay ahead for them today. As she steered into the long curve around the south end of the Hogback formation, the ridge that ran north and south along the Navajo Nation's eastern boundary, she could see the trading post off in the distance, just off the Rez.

A white van, probably a delivery vehicle, pulled out onto the highway from the turnoff and headed east toward Farmington. The van reminded her of the vehicles used by bank and business couriers, or those extra rental vans used by FedEx around the holidays, except this one had no markings. The odd thing, though, was that it was awfully early for a shipment or food delivery to come in.

Tom's trading post was a private operation, not affiliated

with the tribe. It was modeled after early nineteenth-century businesses, the kind most Navajos had often used to trade or purchase supplies. Painted in a light turquoise blue color, the building contrasted with the surrounding coal-rich countryside that supplied fuel to two major power plants.

Jo drove straight to the big metal gate that led to Tom's home behind the trading post. His white Chevy pickup stood just inside, parked in its usual spot. Jo pulled up next to the enclosure and walked to the gate. Tom had given her a key to the padlock months ago, but she didn't have to use it this morning. The chain and lock were nowhere to be seen.

Tom was a man of settled habits, and this change in routine surprised her. Jo strode quickly up the flagstone walk and knocked hard on his front door. Tom was an early riser. A widower, he'd turned what was once his wife's sewing room into a gym, and worked out every morning. She figured that he'd probably be there now.

Her knock went unanswered. Maybe he'd finished and stepped into the shower. She went to the front window, open about eight inches, and listened for the sound of running water.

"Morning, Tom. It's me, Jo," she called out. She expected to catch a whiff of the eye-opening pitch black brew Tom called coffee, but an entirely different scent came wafting out to meet her.

It wasn't strong, but it was distinctive. For a moment, she struggled to identify it. Then memories of family gatherings and freshly butchered sheep came rushing back. Blood—that was the scent. Maybe he'd been butchering a side of beef someone gave him last night, or possibly a freezer had broken down. If meat had spoiled, he would have arranged to get an early delivery from a butcher shop.

She shivered, not from the cold, but from the thought that niggled at the back of her mind. Something felt . . . off.

Jo brushed away the big blowflies that had gathered on the

window screen, but they came right back. Uneasy, she circled around to the front door. As she reached into her shoulder bag for the emergency key he'd given her, she noticed that the door wasn't completely shut. She pushed it with the tip of her boot and it swung open without a sound.

"It's me. I'm coming in," Jo called, her skin prickling.

There had been a time people around here didn't bother to lock their doors, but modern life had ushered in many changes. With thieves and drug crimes more prevalent now, caution had become a fact of life. Yet she'd seen no signs of a break-in, just a door that shouldn't be open and a missing lock and chain. And there was that white delivery van. . . .

Though she hated the thought of intruding on anyone's privacy, Jo forced herself to go inside. As she stepped into the living room, the scent of blood grew stronger.

Her entire body began to tremble as she took the room in at a glance. The shelf on the wall that had held antique salt and pepper shakers had been rearranged. The pair of brightly colored parrots she'd often admired were no longer there. Everything else appeared to be in order. But that scent . . . Maybe he'd fallen and bumped his head, or cut himself while slicing meat or chicken.

Jo poked her head around the corner into the kitchen. Nobody was there, and the place was immaculate, as usual. No coffee was brewing either. Strange.

"Where are you?" Her mouth was dry and her heart pounded in her ears as she crossed the living room and went down the hall.

A sudden heart attack wouldn't explain the heavy scent of blood. She took another whiff, trying to pinpoint its location. Maybe he'd slipped in the shower, or cut himself shaving . . . badly.

Seeing the light was on in Tom's study, Jo hurried toward it and looked inside. Her body turned to ice and for a moment horror kept her frozen to the spot. Tom was slumped across his desk, his forehead resting in a pool of dark blood. All that was left of his temple was a mass of red, gray, and black tissue. His face was turned toward the door, toward her, and his open eyes, opaque and totally lifeless, stared into eternity. With a strangled cry, she looked away. On the floor on Tom's right side was a revolver. His lifeless hand dangled a foot above the weapon.

Grief and shock raged a battle inside her. This wasn't happening—it couldn't be. She opened her mouth to scream, but no sound came out.

Finally something inside her snapped. Panic surged through her and she ran outside as fast as she could. By now her entire body was shaking so hard, she could barely function, but she managed to fumble through her purse and find her cell phone. It took her three tries, but at last she was able to call 911.

As she tried to describe the scene to the emergency operator, she kept having to stop in midsentence and suck in air. Tears were streaming down her face. Finally, inevitably, she tasted the bile rising in her throat. Mumbling she was going to be sick, Jo dropped her purse and phone on the floor of the porch and ran out onto the gravel just in time. Her stomach turned inside out, emptying its meager contents, followed by the dry heaves.

After several moments, Jo stumbled back to where she'd dropped the phone. Wiping her mouth with a tissue, she managed a weak "I'm back."

Remembering something her *hataalii* teacher had taught her, Jo forced herself to slow her breathing. Little by little she regained a measure of control and was able to finish speaking to the emergency operator.

Jo was just putting the phone away when she felt a hand on her shoulder. Startled, she spun around.

"What's wrong, Jo? You sick?"

Jo stared at Regina Yazzie. Like her, the young Navajo woman worked nearly full-time at the trading post. Mother to a two-year-old, Regina was about her age, but they were nearly opposites in every conceivable way.

Regina's close-cropped black hair was highlighted in shades of brown and gold. Jo's hair was long, thick, and ebony, and at work she usually wore it in a single braid that fell almost to her waist. Regina was also tall for a Navajo woman, standing around five foot seven. Jo was five foot two—if she stood up really straight.

Yet the biggest difference between them went beyond looks and family. Regina was a Modernist Christian, and Jo, an apprentice medicine woman, treasured the traditional beliefs of the *Diné*.

"What's going on? Is it Tom?" Regina pressed, turning her head toward the front door of the house. "Did he have a heart attack or something?"

"Don't use his name," Jo said, her hand on the medicine bag tied to her belt. Navajos believed that the good in a man merged with universal harmony, but the evil found in every person remained earthbound. That force was an ever-present danger to the living unless the proper cautionary steps were taken. The small drawstring bag contained flint, said to be powerful medicine against the *chindi* because of the way light reflected off its surface.

"Oh, my God . . . he's *dead*?" Regina whispered, crossing herself.

Jo nodded and tried to swallow, but her mouth was too dry and her throat tasted foul.

"What—?"

"I don't know," Jo said, her voice trembling. "He was shot—in the head."

Regina stared at her. "Shot . . . an accident? How? That shotgun he keeps behind the counter?"

Jo shook her head, not wanting to answer any more questions. "Here comes the county deputy," she said, taking another unsteady breath.

The sheriff's car that pulled up was unmarked, but the flashing light on the center dashboard told them what they needed to know. A tall, middle-aged Anglo woman in civilian clothes wearing a dark blue SJSD jacket approached. "I'm Detective Wells," she said, motioning toward her belt, where a gold badge and handgun were attached. "I'm responding to a call. Which one of you is Josephine Buck?" she said, looking from face to face.

Regina crossed herself again, took a step back, and pointed to Jo. "I just got here."

Were Navajo Christians afraid of the *chindi*, too, Jo wondered, watching Regina's reaction. Or maybe some Navajo traditions were too deeply ingrained for any *Diné* to ignore.

"I'm the one who called the sheriff's department," Jo said, still gripping the medicine pouch tightly.

As she told the detective what she'd seen inside the house, Jo saw Regina's face turn pale and her eyes grow large.

"Did you see any sign of an intruder—maybe a door kicked in or an open window?" Detective Katie Wells asked.

Jo told her about the open front door and the missing chain and padlock on the gate. Then she remembered the delivery van. "I saw a white van coming out of the drive and onto the highway as I slowed for the turn, but I think it was probably an early delivery. The van drove off toward Farmington—east."

Katie's eyes narrowed. "Did you see a company name or get a look at the tags?"

"It was a plain white van. I didn't see any name or logo on it. It had yellow New Mexico plates, I remember that. I can check the delivery schedule, or call our vendors, if you'd like."

"Later. Right now I'm going inside to take a look. You two stay put," Detective Wells said.

As Jo watched, the detective stepped up on the porch, placed her hand on the butt of her handgun, and opened the screen door.

While Regina moved to speak into her cell phone, Jo tried

to recall all the conversations she'd had with Tom yesterday. Nothing had been out of the ordinary—except his request to meet with her this morning. She was sure he hadn't mentioned any delivery.

Five minutes later, Detective Wells came out of the house and, removing latex gloves, walked over to Jo. "Ma'am, are you familiar enough with the interior of the house to know if anything is missing?"

Jo remembered the rearranged shelf and missing parrot salt-shakers and mentioned those to her. "But they weren't particularly valuable, I don't think. They were mementos that belonged to the man's late wife."

"You and your coworker need to stay back. A crime scene team will arrive soon along with the medical examiner, but the wound appears to be self-inflicted."

"No . . . that can't be," Jo said in an agonized whisper.

Detective Wells reached into her pocket, brought out a packet of antacids, then popped a couple into her mouth. "What was your relationship to the victim?"

"He was my boss, and my friend. Regina and I both work for him at the trading post. I came in early today because he wanted to talk to me. He'd said it was important. I . . ."

"You're thinking that something was troubling him and you weren't fast enough to pick up on it. People associated with the victim often do that, but you're not to blame. He made his own choices."

Jo looked up at her, startled. "That's exactly what I was thinking."

"I'm not psychic, I've just seen this before. When people are upset, they tend to blame themselves for things they had no control over. Do you know what he wanted to talk to you about—what was so important?"

"No, but something had been bothering him."

Hearing the sound of a siren, Detective Wells turned to

look. A white county sheriff's van with the words CRIME LAB on the side turned onto the lane leading to the trading post.

"Stick around," the slender detective said. "I'll have more questions for you in a while."

A three-person crime scene team climbed out of the big van and came up to the porch. As they and Detective Wells went inside, Regina joined Jo. "Esther and Leigh Ann will be arriving before long. Do you want me to head them off and leave the store closed for today?"

Jo looked at her blankly for a second, still trying to process everything that had happened. "Yes, closed," she said at last. "Can you make the calls?"

Regina nodded. "Do you know where Mr. Stuart went to church? He always wore a cross around his neck. His pastor will want to know. . . ."

"Church . . ." Jo felt as if she were stuck in slow motion while the world around her revolved at a normal rate. "I . . . don't know." She took a breath. "Yes, wait, I remember he used to go to the Good Shepherd Church in Kirtland until his wife passed on. After that, I think he and his son stopped attending."

Jo thought about Ben, Tom's son, and a crazy mixture of feelings, everything from tenderness to anger, swept over her. Ben was her boyfriend back in high school, and their relationship had been an exciting, stormy one that ended badly. Ever since Tom gave her the news that Ben would be coming home on leave from the army in a few weeks, she'd been counting the days, looking forward to seeing him, but a little worried, too. It was Ben's first visit home in years, and a lot had changed.

Now tragedy had struck, and all Tom's carefully laid-out plans were at an end. Although Ben would have to be told about Tom's death immediately, Jo had no idea how to get hold of him. Before she could organize her thoughts, Detective Wells came back out of the house. As she approached, the detective popped another white tablet into her mouth.

"The salt and pepper shakers you mentioned are in the kitchen trash, broken. There are no signs of forced entry, nor anything that indicates a fight, so the victim may have been responsible for the breakage," Detective Wells said. "Killers rarely pick up after themselves."

"Did you happen to find the two-foot chain and the padlock to the gate?" Jo asked.

"I didn't, but I'll keep looking."

"What about the delivery I saw? Did you notice any mailers or shipping containers inside?" she asked, still troubled about the van.

"Not a one. I checked every room."

"Is it possible his killer didn't break in but, instead, snuck up on my boss and forced him to open the gate?" Jo said, searching for the answer.

"Maybe, but at this point, the evidence suggests it was suicide, so don't jump to conclusions. Why don't you and I go to the store and look around? If there was a delivery, maybe the merchandise or paperwork is in there. We can also check the front and rear entrances in case something was left outside."

Jo led the way, noticing that Regina had caught up to Esther and Leigh Ann in the parking lot. All of them had been scheduled for the morning shift today. Focusing back on Detective Wells, Jo walked around to the trading post's front entrance. Not finding any sign of a delivery, she punched in the entry code on the keypad on the top lock. Using her copy of the store key, she opened the sturdy original lock just below the electronic one.

"No one tampered with this door, from the looks of it," Detective Wells said, studying it. "There are no marks that suggest someone tried to force their way in."

"It would take a lot more than a kick to break this down," Jo said. "This is an industrial-grade door set in a steel frame. The rear door at the top of the loading dock is exactly the same. There are bars on the windows, too, and they can only be opened using locks on the inside. To get into the trading post, you need both the key and keypad code. You can't ram the doors with a vehicle either, not with those concrete parking barriers."

Jo waited by the entrance while Wells turned on the lights and searched the storeroom, office, break room, and the main business area.

"Look around," Wells told Jo, waving her forward. "Besides looking for parcels or shipping containers, see if any merchandise is missing. Check for your most expensive items, like jewelry or cameras. I assume that no cash is left in the registers at night?" Seeing Jo nod, she continued. "Try not to handle anything, at least not until after you've done a general survey."

Jo pointed to an interior door in a short hallway. "I'll check the safe and see if someone tampered with it."

The safe appeared untouched, so Jo continued to search, even looking in the freezer and produce locker. Sorrow was eating away at her and demanded she find a reason for Tom's death.

At long last, she came back to the front register, where the detective was waiting. "I don't understand it," Jo said. "There's no sign of a delivery, and nothing seems to be missing or even out of place. Our high-ticket items, art sculptures, paintings, and Navajo jewelry, are behind locked glass cabinets, but no one's touched them or tried to force the locks. Same with the cameras and electronics."

Detective Wells nodded. "As I said—suicide. I know it's hard to accept, particularly when it's someone you know, but it happens," she said.

"No, my boss was a fighter who faced trouble head-on. The Navajos called him Tsélgaii, 'the white rock.' "

"Earlier, you suggested that something was bothering him. What kind of problems did he have, business and/or personal?" the detective asked, bringing out a small notebook and pen.

"Business has taken a hit because of the recession, but no

one's been laid off. I know he's been worried about something, but I have no idea what the problem was."

"Maybe whatever was worrying him became too much for him to handle. These things happen even to the strongest among us," Wells said, reaching for a small tube of white tablets and taking two more.

"How many of those do you take?" Jo asked.

"Too many. Acid stomach—comes with the territory."

"How about herbal tea?"

"Puts me to sleep. Coffee is my lifeline."

"Detective Wells, do you think the driver of the white van saw something?"

"Probably not. My guess is that when nobody answered the door, he took off."

"Without leaving a note or a package?"

"Maybe it was fresh food. You can't leave something like that on the loading dock or front porch."

"All right. I'll check our records and also ask the others if they knew about a delivery scheduled for this morning," Jo said.

"Do that and let me know what they say." The detective gave Jo a sympathetic smile, then headed back to Tom's house.

Jo saw the trading post's three morning employees standing together, waiting for her on the porch. As she tried to figure out what she'd say to them, she remembered the horrific scene in Tom's study.

She'd missed something, and the realization rocked her to the core. "Detective Wells," Jo called out, jogging down the steps and into the parking lot. "Wait! The gun was by his *right* hand, but my boss is left-handed. It couldn't have been suicide."

TWO

Jo saw the surprised look on Detective Wells's face as she stood in front of the officer. "I'm right. Ask around," Jo insisted.

"Maybe he was ambidextrous?"

"No. I've known the man for over a decade, and I've worked for him almost daily for the past seven years. He was left-handed. There's something else you should know," she said, her thoughts clearer now. "He wouldn't have killed himself now. He was really looking forward to seeing his son. That's practically all he talked about lately."

"Okay, then. We'll take a closer look at the evidence—and follow up on that white van." Wells saw one of the crime scene techs coming out of the house and hurried over to meet him. "Did you find a note anywhere?" she asked him.

"No, but that's not conclusive, you know that. The OMI will have the final say, but even without a note, it sure looks like suicide to me."

"According to Ms. Buck, the vic was left-handed, and unless his right hand was injured, it's doubtful he would have used his weak hand to pull the trigger. That means there's a possibility the scene was staged and we're looking at a possible 187. Go back inside and recheck everything with that possibility in mind. And see if you can find any sign of a chain and padlock on the property or nearby. There was supposed to be one on the gate. If the chain or lock were cut . . ."

Though she continued to listen, Jo tore her gaze from Tom's house and focused on the sacred mountains off in the distance. They were said to be the forked hogans of the gods, and in them resided the strength and power of the *Diné*.

With renewed energy, she pushed back the darkness that had weighed down her spirit. Suicide was no longer a possibility she needed to either fear or dread. Yet if Tom was murdered, the killer had been here last night. What if he came back? Should she be worried? And what about that white van?

When Jo turned back to the woman detective, the officer was looking directly at her. No . . . looking *through* her was a more accurate description.

Uncomfortable, Jo turned her head and saw Leigh Ann Vance standing off to the side. The tall, leggy, blond ex-cheerleader was wearing a white blouse and turquoise skirt. She was a West Texas native from Amarillo and had worked their front register for almost a year now. Leigh Ann, in her mid-thirties, was always flawlessly made up, with her hair sprayed into immobility.

Directly to her right stood Esther Allison in her flowery, long burgundy dress. The short, bony seventy-something Navajo woman was a Modernist and a Christian, like Regina. She was clutching her ever-present Bible to her chest. Actually, she appeared to be holding on to it for dear life.

"If you need to question all of us, please start with Esther, the lady in the burgundy dress, then let her go home. A shock like this could be hard on someone her age," Jo said.

Wells nodded, and glanced around for someplace suitable to conduct the interviews. "Open up the trading post for me again. I'll use one of the back rooms to interview each of them in private." She glanced at the group. "Is that everyone who works here?"

"No. Del Hudson, our stock boy, is in class right now—Kirtland Central High School. He won't arrive till school is out this afternoon."

"All right, then. Let's get started," Wells said.

As Esther Allison entered what had been Tom Stuart's office, Detective Wells introduced herself. As a detective, she'd learned to always talk about something ordinary and non-intrusive at first. It helped put people at ease.

"This is terrible business, just terrible," Esther said immediately, getting straight to the point. "I heard someone say it was suicide. Is that right?"

"That was our first impression," Katie said, "but there's also evidence that suggests it could have been a homicide."

"Tom Stuart, *murdered*?" she whispered, her eyes wide with shock.

"How long have you been working here, Esther?"

"A little over two years now. This job's been a huge blessing to me and my husband. It's hard for someone my age to find work where you actually get a decent paycheck. I'm not full-time, but almost."

"Would you say that you knew Tom Stuart well?"

"Not personally, no. He was a good man and an excellent boss. But we didn't socialize. I was just one of the staff. I work in the housewares and fabric section and fill in elsewhere, if needed. Whenever he and I spoke, it was usually about business."

"Did Mr. Stuart seem worried or upset lately?" Katie watched her eyes, and even listened to her breathing.

"He seemed a bit more impatient, but I assumed it was because his son was coming home and he had a lot on his mind. If you ask me, Tséłgaii was just plain excited."

"Tom Stuart's nickname," Katie said, nodding.

"I'm Christian," Esther said, "so I believe in souls, not the *chindi*, but it still feels wrong to call him by name, at least here at the trading post. It makes our Navajo brothers and sisters uneasy."

"So I've heard," Katie said with a nod. Esther was as sharp as a tack and diplomatic. She was easy to interview, too, because she was straightforward. "I'd like your professional opinion on the way business was going here at The Outpost. How much has the recession affected sales and the trading post's bottom line?"

"I'm not the bookkeeper, but it's no secret that most retail businesses have seen less traffic these past two years," Esther said. "We've all had our hours cut from thirty-eight to thirty-five, and two of the former employees had to find full-time jobs elsewhere since the recession kicked in. But I'm sure sales will pick up before long. Things go up and down all the time. It's all part of life—cycles, you know."

"Were any of the current employees afraid of losing their jobs because of the economy?" Katie asked.

"If they were, killing their boss would have only guaranteed their unemployment," Esther said. "In fact, with him gone, we all may end up looking for new jobs."

Katie watched her for a moment. At first glance, Esther appeared to be a frail senior, but Katie sensed the core of steel just beneath the surface. Instinct told her the woman had gone through some tough times in her life. "Can you think of any reason why anyone might have wanted your former boss dead—maybe another employee, a business contact, or even a customer? Take your time."

"Don't need to, the answer is no. That's even more so when it comes to my fellow workers. Most of us here at The Outpost really need the money. Our salaries pay for food, schooling, and other necessities."

"You're speaking for yourself as well?"

"Yes, absolutely. My work also gives me a reason to get up every morning and keeps me active and useful. One of my jobs is to make display garments using our fabric and patterns. When people see how pretty the finished product is, that gives them more of a reason to buy. Once a month, I change all the displays and the garments I made go to my church, where they're given to families in need. It all works together for a common good and gives me a wonderful sense of purpose," Esther said. After a beat, she continued. "That's what makes The Outpost so special. We each bring something unique to it."

"Someone wanted your boss dead. Can you think of any reason for that?" Katie pushed once again.

Esther considered it for several moments before replying. "People are always more complicated than they appear to be. I knew only one side of my boss, but maybe the others will have more to say."

Katie nodded. "A white van, maybe a delivery vehicle, was seen exiting the grounds earlier this morning. Do you know anything about that?"

"No, I'm sorry, I don't. Mr. Stuart and Jo kept track of shipping and deliveries. You might want to ask her," Esther said. "Anything else?"

"No, we're done for now, but I may want to talk to you again later," she said. "Do *you* have any questions?"

"Yes, I do," Esther said. "If it turns out that our boss was murdered, does that mean the rest of us are in danger now? Is it safe here at The Outpost?"

"I don't know of any connection between Mr. Stuart's death and The Outpost, Mrs. Allison, but until we have all the answers, it might be wise to remain extra careful for a while."

Esther nodded. "All right. And if you think there *is* a threat to the employees—"

"I'll let everyone know right away," Katie said.

As Esther left, Katie made some quick notes, then stared vacantly across the room, lost in thought. Esther appeared to be a religious woman who lived by certain principles. She, too, was that way once, but over the years, her religious beliefs had fallen by the wayside, and her principles had become more . . . adaptable to the situation.

Katie stared at the badge clipped to her belt. Esther was right about one thing: No one was ever what they appeared to be.

Katie felt her cell phone vibrate and lifted it from her belt. The display showed the caller's name was blocked. Already knowing who it was, Katie brought the phone to her ear.

"Make this a private call," a familiar male voice ordered.

Roberto Hidalgo, the biggest drug dealer in the Four Corners, was used to giving orders and having them followed, but that wasn't why she hated him so much. Katie felt her stomach tighten.

"I'll be a few minutes," she told the store employees waiting their turn, then closed the door.

"Now what?" she snapped. "I'm at a crime scene."

"I know, that's why I'm calling. Listen up. The store owner died by his own hand. That's what you'll say in your report. Understand?"

Katie's stomach lurched, and not just because it was clear someone had followed her here this morning. "That's going to be a tough sale. Not all the facts fit."

"Then change the facts or do what's necessary to make this blow over quickly. If my name comes up, so will yours—and your son's. *¿Me comprendes, mujer?*"

She was trapped—again—and her stomach hurt. "The Office of the Medical Investigator determines the cause of death, but I'll do what I can," she said, deciding not to ask if his men had been in the white van. Anything she might be able to eventually use against him was best kept secret.

"Make it happen. Don't disappoint me," Roberto said, ending the call.

Katie put the phone away, took a deep breath and another antacid, then opened the door and signaled the next person to enter. It was going to be a very long morning.

⁂

Forty-five minutes later, Leigh Ann Vance stood in a corner of the store talking to Regina Yazzie. "What did she ask *you*?" Leigh Ann whispered.

"She knew that Tom had been upset lately and wanted me to tell her why. She also wanted to know how well I knew him, and like that." Regina glanced around the room. "Apparently a van was here just before Jo arrived, and the driver might have seen something. Or maybe he was the one who killed our boss. Nobody knows, and that's part of the problem. I'm so scared right now, Leigh Ann, and it's not that I'm afraid of getting shot. This job is what's buying our groceries. Pete hasn't had a good construction job in months. He's been hired for day jobs here and there, but my paycheck's the only regular money we've got coming in. I don't know what'll happen to us if this place shuts down."

"I hear you," Leigh Ann said. "I've been working hard, too, hoping Tom would hire me full-time. Now this happens."

"At least you don't have kids," Regina said.

"I also don't have a husband or family I can count on. When Kurt died, all he left me was bills. I've already sold everything I can except the house. If I lose this job, I'll be out on the street," she said, her drawl somewhat softening the fear in her voice.

Regina gave her an apologetic smile. "I'm sorry. I know you've been through a lot."

"Kurt never took out a life insurance policy, and that's made things hard." Leigh Ann ran her fingers through her shoulder-length blond hair, pushing it away from her face. "I'm not sure what I'm going to do if this place closes down. I have no real job training except with that cash register."

"You're tall, beautiful, and still young enough to attract any man. That'll get you in the door almost anywhere."

Leigh Ann smiled bitterly. "Thank you, hon, but my looks will never get me the kind of job I need—or could live with."

"You know the boss's son is going to inherit the trading post. If he doesn't sell it, maybe he'll hire someone to run it for him and we can keep our jobs," Regina said.

As Detective Wells came out of the office, Jo alongside her, Leigh Ann and Regina turned away and pretended to be busy.

Leigh Ann glanced back furtively at Detective Wells and saw the deep lines of weariness etched on her face. That all but assured her that even tougher times lay ahead.

✹

Jo watched the detective work with the crime scene people inside the yellow tape line surrounding Tom's home. Knowing that there was nothing more she could do out here, Jo went back inside the trading post. The second she stepped through the door, all eyes turned to her.

As it often happened in her life, everyone seemed to expect her to take charge. Even as far back as high school, people had looked to her for answers. Maybe they'd sensed her almost in-stinctive need to make things better for everyone. That was what she'd always done at home, trying to defuse her alcoholic father's unpredictability by covering all the bases and leaving little to chance. That need to make things better was one of the primary reasons she'd wanted to become a medicine woman.

She'd wanted to offer those who turned to her for help something more than words of comfort or leadership without foundation.

"Let's keep the trading post closed today. We all need time to say good-bye in our own ways," Jo said.

"His son will have to be notified," Esther said.

"The police will be handling that," Jo said. "I found his address and telephone number and gave them to Detective Wells. There's nothing else we can do for now, so let's lock up."

"What about that white van you saw? Was there a delivery scheduled for this morning, Jo?" Leigh Ann asked.

"Nothing was in the log, and when I called our vendors and couriers, I got zip."

"Maybe it was just somebody who got lost and went to the wrong address," Esther said.

"Could be," Jo said, unconvinced. She saw her uncertainty and fear mirrored on their faces, her heart going out to all of them. She turned away, determined not to let them see the apprehension she shared.

Something was up. Sergeant Ben Stuart had seen it in the eyes of the corporal who'd come to get him. To make things worse, the secretary who sat outside his battalion commander's office refused to look him in the eye.

Instructed to sit rather than stand across from his commanding officer's desk, he waited, trying to remain cool and calm.

"Sergeant—son—I have bad news. Your father was found dead in his home earlier this morning," he said.

Ben stared at Major Johnson and shook his head, the words refusing to sink in. "That can't be. I just spoke to him yesterday on the phone, sir."

"It happened last night, apparently. One of his employees found the body at his home early this morning. I spoke to the investigating officer, a sheriff's department detective. She said he died from a bullet to the temple."

Ben leaned forward, certain he'd misunderstood. "Sir, are you saying that my father committed suicide?"

"The medical examiner has yet to make that determination, but that's what it appears to be," he said in a quiet voice. "I'm sorry for your loss, Sergeant."

Ben felt as if he'd been sucker punched in the gut, yet oddly enough, he felt no pain, just a numbness that seemed to go right to his brain. "It's got to be another Tom Stuart—not my father. It's a mistake," he said, then quickly added, "sir."

"No mistake, son. Employees at his business—The Outpost—made a positive ID, and the fingerprints match those in your father's service record. You'll be granted twenty-one days' emergency leave as soon as the orders are cut. Check with my clerk before you leave so the paperwork can be processed. Again, my condolences to you and your family. You're dismissed."

Ben nodded, dazed, then rose to his feet and saluted before turning to the door. There'd be forms and a million steps to follow. There always were. He reached for the door handle, functioning on automatic now.

A half hour later, seated on his bunk, Ben was still shaking his head. This had to be a mistake. It just didn't make any sense. Former-marine Lance Corporal Tom Stuart offing himself? Impossible. His father would never have taken that way out.

Memories came flooding back to him. Eighteen months ago, Ben had been driving drunk, trying to run from memories of combat. He'd wrecked his car, nearly killing himself. His father, a man of few words, had come to the hospital to see him. There'd been no pity in Tom Stuart's eyes as he looked Ben straight in the eye. "Only a gutless coward would kill himself, son. If you want to die, die like a man. Don't hide behind a bottle," he'd said.

Simple and to the point. No sympathy, no coddling. Tom Stuart had been capable of neither.

Yet that meeting became a major turning point in Ben's life.

Now they were telling him that the old marine had shot himself? No way, it had to have been murder. He'd go home and find out what really happened. He'd have three weeks, including travel time, to figure things out. Somehow that would have to be enough.

—THREE—

TWO DAYS LATER

Jo tried to remain calm, but these Anglo memorial ceremonies were *not* natural, that is according to traditional
Navajo thinking. Speaking of the recently deceased could
be dangerous. At least, with the body still at the Office of the
Medical Examiners undergoing an autopsy, there was no actual
physical presence to worry about.

Jo stayed in the back of the chapel, avoiding the Anglo
mourners. Honoring her own beliefs, she hadn't said a word, not
joining in prayer or song.

Jo adjusted her long, traditional skirt as she half listened to
the preacher speaking of the god the Anglos worshipped, her
mind miles away. She and the other employees had been working their regular shifts at the trading post these past few days—
five hours a day, seven days a week, with split shifts and long
lunches. Business had always been slower on weekday mornings, but even in the afternoons and evenings recently, traffic
had been almost nonexistent. Most of the customers were non-

Navajo regulars who stopped in to pay their respects and maybe buy one or two items.

All during that time, whenever a white van entered the parking lot, all of them focused on it. Del, their high school stock boy, had tried to joke about it, looking out for Casper the Van, he'd said. Nobody was amused, though Leigh Ann smiled the first time he'd said it.

Fear cast its long shadow over everyone at the trading post these days, leaving little room for humor. Everyone's future was at stake, including Jo's. Without her job, things would get tough in a hurry. She had very little money set aside, so she'd have to scramble to get another job fast. More important, she'd also be unable to continue her training to become a medicine woman.

She'd already spent many months memorizing Sings, and learning what each god would accept and how to present her prayers so that the gods would honor the requests. Stopping now would result in a serious setback. She'd lose the continuity of her lessons, and her teacher would undoubtedly take on a new apprentice. His list was always long. There'd be no guarantee that she could continue her training with him at a later time either.

"I know a memorial service is hard for Navajos to attend," Leigh Ann, who was standing beside her, said. "But at least there's no body here and it'll be over soon, hon. Try to think of how pretty it is outside. There couldn't be a better place anywhere for him to eventually be laid to rest."

Jo glanced out the window. It *was* pretty. The small graveyard, with all its crosses and statues, was bordered by a tall hedge of rosebushes laden with hundreds of red and white flowers. "I'm told he'll be buried next to his wife. That's good."

"I arrived late and didn't get a chance to offer my condolences to the boss's son," Leigh Ann said. "I know he's in uniform, but which one is he?"

"He's in the army uniform, standing by the reverend," Jo whispered without looking up.

Sitting in the back of the chapel, Jo caught a glimpse of Ben earlier, but hadn't spoken to him yet either. He'd changed a lot from the kid she knew back in high school. The boy whose name had been perpetually associated with trouble had turned into a tall, confident-looking soldier with strong, broad shoulders. She'd never seen him look more handsome.

"Honey, if that's him, he's older than his dad."

"Ben's only twenty-five, what are you talking about?" Jo looked up then and saw a WWII vet in an olive drab uniform and garrison cap. "No, not that white-haired gentleman. He's *old* army, one of the honor guard." Jo glanced around and spotted Ben a second later. "Our boss's son is behind the large wreath, just out of our line of sight."

"You trying to hide from him back here?" Leigh Ann asked.

Jo almost choked, but managed to clear her throat instead. "No. I just didn't want to be in the middle of those speaking about the deceased so freely."

"Of course. I'm sorry, hon. I know this is difficult for you," Leigh Ann said softly. "We all have our own demons to face."

Jo knew Leigh Ann hadn't meant any disrespect. To her, the *chindi* were nothing more than ghosts used to scare children.

"If you want, I'll give him our condolences," Leigh Ann said.

"Thanks, but no. This is something I have to do."

As the service came to a close, Jo watched the handsome sergeant in his dark blue uniform jacket, white shirt, and black tie. His trousers were light blue with gold braid down each outside leg seam. He was wearing a dark blue service cap with a black brim, and stood with his broad shoulders thrown back, his spine ramrod straight. There was just something about a man in uniform.

Ben shook hands and exchanged a few words with each of the people who came up to greet him, but there was little sign of emotion on his face. The only thing that betrayed the pain beyond the mask was the way he'd curled his left hand into a tight fist. Somewhere beyond the polished gold buttons, medals, and campaign ribbons that covered his chest beat the heart of a son in mourning for his father.

As she drew near, Ben's eyes met hers at long last and Jo felt a deep stirring that almost took her breath away. Memories, good, bad—and overwhelmingly confusing—crowded her mind. She'd intended to say something comforting, but somehow the words got lodged at the back of her throat.

The stranger gazing back at her didn't seem to need them. He looked tough, hardened by the life of a soldier.

"Jo," he said simply.

"I'm sorry you had to come home to this," she managed at last. "You were all your father spoke about these past few weeks. He couldn't wait for your return."

A flicker of pain crossed his eyes, but it was gone in a flash. "You've suffered your own loss, too. I was sorry to hear that your dad passed away."

She nodded slowly in acknowledgment, but it was hard to give voice to what she felt. In the silence of her mind she told him how much she'd miss Tom and how hard it was to say good-bye. She couldn't even count the many times she'd fanta- sized about Tom being *her* dad. Her own, in comparison, had always come up short in a multitude of ways. Alcohol had been her father's only interest, but Tom's steadfast loyalty to those he loved, his unflagging sense of right and wrong had made him a man who stood out among men. Yet those simple sentiments remained unspoken. Giving Ben a shaky smile, she moved on.

Mentally exhausted, Jo walked back to the parking area. She'd make it a point to go see Ben later. She wanted him to know how much his father had loved him and how badly he'd wanted things to work out between them. Tom's badass marine exterior had effectively hidden the inward feelings of a man proud of his son.

As she reached her truck, Leigh Ann caught up to her. "Do you think we should keep the trading post closed the rest of today?" Leigh Ann asked.

"Yes, but we'll have to show up again tomorrow," Jo said. "Our boss's attorney made it clear that he wanted us to keep the business running. That's why we've stayed open."

"I'm really worried that we'll all end up out of work once Tom's son takes over," Leigh Ann said, her voice barely a whisper. "He probably doesn't want anything to do with the trading post, particularly now."

Jo could see the fear in her eyes. Everyone at the trading post lived from paycheck to paycheck, and there was no health insurance, just shared commissions on sales of big-ticket items. Even Del Hudson, the high school boy who worked afternoons and weekends, had more responsibility on his shoulders than anyone his age should have. His mom, a teacher's aide, had been let go by the financially strapped school system. As a result, the entire family lost their health insurance coverage. Del's medications and those of his dad would be nearly impossible for them to fill without the money Del earned at The Outpost.

With luck, Ben would decide to keep the trading post open and hire one of them to manage the business while he was deployed overseas. Even in good economic times, there weren't many job openings in the Four Corners area.

Tom's lawyer, Mike Broome, had been mum about the estate, so Jo was planning to speak to Ben as soon as possible. Tom hadn't been wealthy, but The Outpost made a good, steady profit, and that said a lot for the small retail operation. If Ben allowed it, they could run the place for him while he continued to serve his country. Everyone would come out ahead.

As Leigh Ann walked away, Jo remained beside her truck a moment longer, hoping for a chance to catch Ben alone. Since there was still a crowd around him, she'd have to wait awhile, but she was prepared to do that. Her eyes were still on Ben when she heard footsteps.

Turning around, Jo saw Mike Broome approach. Tom's middle-aged Anglo attorney was over six feet tall and carried about forty pounds too much for his frame. His short cropped hair had turned a premature shade of silver that contrasted sharply with his black suit.

"Morning, Jo. How ya handlin' all this?"

Mike had been a regular visitor at The Outpost for years. In reality, he was just a cowboy in a suit. Though he had an office in Farmington, he and his wife lived on an old farm in mostly rural Kirtland and owned a half dozen or so miniature donkeys.

"I'm fine. How's Rosie doing?" she asked, referring to his wife. Raising the donkeys had clearly been her idea, but Jo had never quite figured out the attraction. The tiny donkeys were incredibly cute, but they served no purpose that she could see. They couldn't be ridden, and they certainly weren't used as pack animals.

"She's still showing her little guys at county fairs all around the Southwest. Expensive pets, but she sure loves those animals."

"Do I detect a touch of jealousy?" she teased.

"Maybe," he admitted grudgingly, "but they make her happy, and when I get tied up with a case, I'm lousy company." He followed her gaze. "Ben's taking this a lot harder than he lets show. Don't let him kid you."

"His dad had so many plans for them once Ben was out of the army," Jo said sadly.

"Yeah, but deep down, Tom also had doubts that things would work out between them in the long run. Tom wasn't big on compromise and his son always had his own way of doing things, too," Mike said, then shrugged. "No sense in couching the truth with me. I know how Tom's mind worked."

"You two practically grew up together, didn't you?"

"Oh, yeah. We went to the same schools, served in the same marine battalion, married our childhood sweethearts while on leave, and lived within twenty miles of each other all of our lives. I'm sure going to miss that old so-and-so," Mike said quietly. "He was too young to die."

Jo took an unsteady breath. "You told me to keep the trading post open for business this week and I have, except for today, of course, but what now? If Ben decides to close down the trading post, I'll need to give everyone as much lead time as possible—two weeks at least."

He gave her a long look. "You really don't have any idea, do you?"

"About what?" His look was oddly penetrating and made her feel uncomfortable.

"I'll need to see you in my office tomorrow at around one thirty." Then, as if answering her unspoken question, continued. "Ben will be there, too, of course."

"Is there a specific reason you want me there?" she asked.

"It's business. Tom's estate needs to be settled, and he specifically requested you be present for the reading."

"Me? Why?"

"You'll find out." Hearing voices nearby, she turned her head and saw the trading post's staff gathered by their parked vehicles. From time to time, they'd shoot a fleeting glance in her direction.

"They're scared," she said.

"Try to remain calm. The wait will be over soon."

As Mike walked away, Esther hurried over. "That lawyer, did he tell you anything?"

Though Esther hadn't mentioned the trading post, Jo knew precisely what was on her mind. "I'm going to meet him tomorrow. Hopefully, I'll find out more then."

"Why don't you come over to the trading post this afternoon and have a bite to eat with us? We all need to talk."

"Talk?" Judging from Esther's tone, Jo didn't think she meant a casual get-together.

"We need to settle a few things among ourselves, and while we do, we'll finish up those leftover deli sandwiches. Otherwise, we'd just have to throw them out."

Jo nodded slowly. To Esther, waste was a sin. She'd heard it a million times before.

"This isn't about not letting food go to waste, dear," Esther said softly, almost as if she'd read Jo's mind. "Fear's knocking on all our doors at the moment, but we don't have to let it in. Together, we can come up with a proposal to offer Tom's son, and hopefully we can persuade him to keep the trading post open even if he has other plans."

She looked at Esther and smiled. "That's a great idea."

"Good. Then we'll see you there."

Navajo Way teachings echoed in her mind as Jo watched Esther join the others. To walk in beauty, particularly now, she'd have to honor the connections between all things and find her place within the pattern. Harmony would then follow.

J o left for the trading post before the others did, hoping for a few minutes alone. There were no vehicles out front, and the lights were still off inside when she arrived. She heaved a sigh of relief. She just needed time alone to grieve, to cry, to be angry at life.

As she turned the corner, Jo saw an old dark green pickup backed up against the small loading dock. Two men in baseball caps were at the back door, and as she came into view, they turned and looked at her.

Seeing the taller man carrying a crowbar, she realized instantly what they were—burglars. Jo leaned on the horn and took a hard right, spinning around and away from them. She had to call for help. Jo came to a stop about a hundred feet from the men and fumbled for her cell phone. If they came at her, she'd be gone in a second.

Suddenly a white sedan came to a sliding stop next to her, raising a cloud of dust and throwing gravel everywhere. Ben, still in full uniform, jumped out the driver's side, then yelled across the top of the car at her. "Stay in the truck!"

"Wait for the police!" she called back, but it was too late. Ben was on the move and looking for a fight.

The third man, the driver, was still inside the green truck. Movement caught her eye, and Jo saw him extend his arm and point a pistol at Ben.

"Gun!" Jo yelled out.

Ben must have seen it first. He turned away and dived across the hood of his car, hitting the ground, rolling, and coming up in a crouch.

As he looked up at her, she threw open her truck's door. "Get in!"

As the burglars piled into their own vehicle, Ben ran over. "Slide over, I'm driving."

She moved without thinking, and as she took her foot off the brake and clutch, the old pickup lurched, then the engine died.

Ben slid behind the wheel, restarted the engine, and pushed the stick shift into reverse. "Fasten your seat belt. We're going after them."

They chased the fleeing pickup around the side of the trading post, sliding as they cut the corner and barely clearing the concrete barrier. Despite that, the green truck had gained ground and was almost at the highway, too far away for them to read the license plate.

"Call the sheriff," Ben said, not taking his eyes off the road.

Jo nodded, fumbling for the phone again. Ben's dress uniform, covered with campaign ribbons and medals, was dusty now, but he was all self-confidence. All she felt was sheer, unadulterated panic, but Ben was totally focused on catching the men ahead of them. Fear wasn't part of his equation.

The pickup turned out onto the highway, running the stop sign. She heard tires squealing; then a car ahead swerved sharply, fishtailing as the tires left a cloud of blue smoke.

"Damn fool," Ben muttered, slowing as they reached the main road.

Jo glanced left, hoping Ben wasn't going to take a chance like that. They were lucky. There was a gap in traffic and they were able to turn right onto the highway with a move that strained her seat belt as she was suddenly thrown to the left.

Ben floored her pickup as they raced past the car that had just escaped a collision. The elderly woman looked terrified, her hands clutching the steering wheel like they'd been welded in position. She didn't even look over as Ben raced past her at high speed.

They'd gained ground on the green pickup, which was now blocked behind two slower vehicles driving side by side. "Now we can catch up," Ben said. "You make that call?" he added, glancing over for a second.

"No, I was just trying to hang on," Jo said, looking down now to dial 911.

As they closed the gap, Jo saw the license plate clearly and she read it to the dispatcher.

Trying to escape, the driver of the green pickup leaned on his horn, but the yellow pickup on the outside lane was keeping pace with the sports car on the inside. Teenagers in both vehicles were carrying on a back-and-forth conversation, and the pickup driver flipped him off without a backward glance.

The burglar on the passenger's side reached out, gun in hand, and fired a shot into the side of the yellow pickup's bed. That got the teen driver's attention. Panicked, he pulled to the right too quickly and nearly lost control.

The gunman then turned and aimed the gun right at Jo.

She ducked below the dashboard, clutching her medicine pouch and uttering her secret name, a source of power in emergencies.

"Hang on!" Ben yelled, swerving back and forth as he tapped the brake.

Jo grabbed the door handle to steady herself as her old pickup rocked and swayed. Hearing a rumble to her right, she looked up. The yellow pickup had gone off the road into the shallow drainage area and was bouncing along, barely maintaining control.

The red sports car carrying the three teenaged girls had veered left almost to the median, clearing a gap in the center of the highway.

The green pickup shot through, accelerating away at high speed. Ben followed through the gap but was unable to gain any ground. Her old pickup was outclassed.

She looked over at Ben, her heart thumping against her chest. "Ben, even if we catch up, we don't have a gun—*they* do. This isn't a tank. We can't fight them."

He cursed softly. "Yeah, you're right. I've put you at risk and I'm sorry. We'll let the cops handle this." Slamming his hand against the steering wheel in frustration, he veered away.

Jo heard a woman's voice, looked down at her cell phone, and remembered the 911 operator was still on the line. As she continued to explain the situation, Ben slowed, then eased off into the shoulder.

Jo asked to speak to Detective Wells. As she waited, hoping they could transfer the call, she glanced over at Ben. He wasn't even breathing hard, but she was shaking like a leaf.

"Please let her know what's happened as soon as possible," Jo said when the operator came back on the line to tell her Detective Wells wasn't available. "This must be connected to Tom Stuart's murder."

By the time Jo put the phone away, Ben was turning onto

the driveway leading to The Outpost. "You pulled in just ahead of me over here, so I guess I didn't miss much," he said. "Do you have any idea who those guys were? I know you told the police you thought this was connected to Dad's death. I got a pretty good look at the guy who did the shooting, but I didn't recognize him. Of course, I've been out of town."

"I have no idea who they were, but I'm sure there's a connection to what happened to your dad. First there was that white van nobody could track down, and now this."

"Back up, there. What white van?"

Jo quickly told him what she'd seen just before arriving at his father's house that morning. "No one's been able to figure out what it was doing here so early."

He listened closely, nodding, then finally spoke. "So you think there's more to my father's death than I've been told."

"Yes, look at the facts: Three guys commit a burglary in the middle of the day. We're used to shoplifters, but not armed gangs. These guys looked older, too, like professional criminals, and they never panicked," Jo said. "Somehow I don't think they were here just to steal jewelry and cameras."

"You could be right, and that detective needs to locate the van you saw, if only to rule it out. But only one thing seems obvious about today's attempted break in. The guys we chased were professional thieves, probably hoping to cash in on Dad's death. I've heard that the pros often scan the obituaries, looking for information that indicates people will be at memorial or funeral services and not at the home or business they plan to burglarize," Ben said.

"Well, whatever the case, I'm glad you showed up at just the right time, Ben. Who knows what they would have done if they'd found me here alone? But I wish you hadn't been so ready to take them on. You scared me half to death," she said with a hesitant smile.

"I'm sorry about that, but I would have protected you," he

said. "And just so you know, if you hadn't been with me, I wouldn't have backed down."

"There's a difference between backing down and knowing when to pull back."

"You sound like my lieutenant," he said with a ghost of a smile. "I would never have let them hurt you, Jo. Know that."

She nodded. Giving up the chase hadn't come easily to him. Though he was an adult, the Ben she'd known was still there—never afraid of anyone and willing to stand up for his friends. That was what had drawn her to him back in high school, and even now she could feel the familiar tug on her senses. The one big difference was that as a teen, he'd been trying to prove his own worth, but now as a soldier, his strength and courage had matured and were a measure of the man he'd become.

"What made you drop by when you did?" she asked, wondering if he'd heard about the staff's planned meeting.

"I just wanted to drive over and take a look around, to see how things had changed. It wasn't planned, I thought I'd have the place to myself. Were you going to reopen today?"

"No, that would be disrespectful. The staff was just coming over to talk about our jobs, our future here," Jo said. "Why don't you join us? After all, we're going to be in your hands."

"No, thanks. I'll be getting the details about the estate tomorrow, but until I talk to Mike Broome, Dad's lawyer, I'd hate to unintentionally make any promises I might not be able to keep," Ben said.

"Do you have any idea what you're going to do with The Outpost?" she asked.

Ben started to speak, then glanced in the rearview mirror. "Better hold on to those questions for a while. Here comes the law."

※

Since Detective Wells hadn't been available, the department sent over a young deputy. He listened to their description of the men and their vehicle and took down the license plate. He then walked around with them and took a few photographs of the back door. All the burglars had managed to do was scrape the paint and bend the metal just a little. No break-in had actually occurred, and no repairs were necessary.

Thinking ahead, Jo suggested that the deputy check Tom's house and shed. Ben agreed, and the three walked over together. Neither building showed any signs of a break-in attempt—the doors were locked; the crime scene tape was still intact. The deputy saw no reason for them to check inside, so they returned to the parking lot.

The Outpost employees arrived while they were still talking to the deputy and signing their statements. As soon as she was finished, Jo went over to join them. She wrote down the keypad code and gave Leigh Ann the key so the others could go inside.

When she returned to where Ben and the officer were, Ben had just agreed to go to the station to look at mug shots. Saying a quick good-bye to her, Ben followed the deputy down the road.

A few minutes after Ben drove off, Jo joined the trading post staff. She quickly explained what had happened, sharing Ben's theory that it was a well-timed robbery.

"If you ask me, that's pretty low," Regina said as they sat on high stools around the large display table near the front of the store.

"Which is why they came when they did," Leigh Ann said, setting out sandwiches. "They steal stuff they can sell fast, then use the cash to buy drugs. There was an article about it in the paper." She shook her head. "Times sure change. Drug-related crimes were no part of daily life in these parts a few years back—well, except for a few pot busts and a meth lab or two."

"Today's incident will be on the television news tonight and all over the local papers. Customers will stay away in droves," Regina said. "I'm not sure how long The Outpost can weather that kind of slowdown."

"You're assuming this place will stay open," Del said. "We may not have jobs by the end of tomorrow," he said, voicing what was on all their minds.

"You're the only one here who actually knows Ben," Esther said, looking at Jo. "What's your take on this? Do you think he'll want to hang on to his dad's store?"

"I knew him a *long* time ago when we were teenagers. There's no way I can second-guess him now," Jo said. "I did ask him about his plans and even invited him to join us for lunch, but he wanted to wait until he spoke to the lawyer. He's been out of touch with his dad for years, so we know more about the business than he does."

"He's obviously career military, but maybe he'll want to keep The Outpost as an investment," Regina said.

"I'm hoping you're right," Jo said, "but we all have to face the possibility that this place is part of a past he's left behind and he'll want to put it up for sale."

"So let's show him that it's to his advantage to hang on to The Outpost," Esther said. "When he comes home for good, he'll have a business that's established and filled with people who know how to keep it running. All he'd have to do is allow it to stay on track and collect the profits."

Jo glanced at Tom's now-empty office. She missed her friend. He'd always been there for her when she needed him, but had also been willing to stand back when she had to work things out on her own. Ben never realized how lucky he'd been to have a dad like Tom.

"I miss him, too," Regina said, following her line of sight.

"It feels as if someone broke the lead rope that kept us all together," Del said.

"That's exactly what happened," Leigh Ann said.

"We'll all miss him, but we should honor and celebrate his life, not just mourn his passing," Esther said. "He's in heaven now. It's all part of God's plan."

"Traditional Navajo beliefs see someone's passing in a different light. According to Navajo teachings, death is a friend we don't always recognize," Jo said, then saw Leigh Ann and Del looking at her, curiosity alive on their faces. Not wanting to offend, Jo looked at Esther and Regina, both Christians, but seeing them nod, began, her tone soft and entrancing. "At the time of the beginning, the Hero Twins, the sons of Sun and Turquoise Woman, were sent to defeat all the monsters that preyed on mankind. One by one, their enemies fell before them until only four remained—Cold, Hunger, Poverty, and Death. The Twins wanted to kill Cold, but she warned them that if they did, there would be no snow or water in summer. That's why they had to let her live.

"Hunger then introduced himself. He told the Heroes that if they killed him, no one would ever take pleasure in eating again and that's why he was allowed to continue.

"Poverty was an old man dressed in dirty rags. He begged them to kill him and put him out of his misery, but he also warned that if he died, old clothes would never wear out, and people wouldn't make new ones. Everyone would be as dirty and ragged as he was. That's why he was allowed to live.

"Finally they turned to Death. She was old, and frightening to look at. The Twins wanted to kill her immediately, but Death warned them to reconsider. If she ceased to be, old men wouldn't die and give up their places to the young. They needed her so young men could marry and have children, and life could continue its endless cycle of renewal. She assured them that she was their friend, though they didn't realize it."

Jo paused and looked at the others gathered around her. "Our boss's time came to an end. Now his son will take his place. It's all part of life."

They finished eating in somber silence, and afterwards, Jo helped them clear up. "Ben said he'd let me know as soon as he decides what to do. I've been asked to attend the reading of the will tomorrow, so maybe I'll have at least part of the answer by then."

"We'll open up as usual and wait to hear from you. Hope you'll bring us good news," Leigh Ann said, then glanced at the others, who nodded.

"All right, then," Jo said. "And in the meantime, everyone keep an eye out for a green pickup."

"And the white van?" Del asked.

She nodded. "Stay safe, all of you." Jo handed Leigh Ann the door keys, and left.

The next morning, Ben drove his rental car east down Farmington's Main Street toward Mike Broome's law office. It was north of Main and within sight of the old clock tower that had chimed the hour since Ben's childhood.

Five minutes later, Ben stepped into a quiet, pleasant office, noting the faint scent of something flowery, roses maybe. He instantly surveyed the room, an ingrained habit that stemmed from threat-assessment training. From left to right, there was a leather sofa, the nearly mandatory Southwest landscape painting on the gray white wall, and a closed wooden door. To his right, against the window, was a low coffee table with, appropriately, a coffeemaker and several ceramic cups with Broome's name written on them in gold.

An attractive black woman in her early twenties sat behind a large oak desk. She rose as he entered. "Sergeant Stuart? I'm Liz

Walker, Mr. Broome's legal assistant. Can I get you something? Coffee or a soft drink?" She gestured to a small refrigerator against the wall just to her left.

All he needed right now was to spill coffee or Coke on his only civilian suit jacket. He'd nearly trashed his dress uniform yesterday rolling around in the parking lot, and dry cleaning ate up his pay in a hurry. "No thanks, ma'am. Am I early?"

"Not at all, just on time, as a matter of fact," Ms. Walker said with an easy smile. "Let me show you into Mr. Broome's office."

Ben followed the long ebony legs into the office on his right. As he went in, he saw Jo seated on a chair next to the window. Her beauty was the kind that sneaked up on you, with those big, expressive, almond-colored eyes and silky black hair that fell down nearly to her waist.

Michael Broome, his dad's attorney, was standing beside her, coffee mug in hand. He'd taken off his suit jacket, revealing a gray vest.

Ms. Walker passed by him, leaving a rose-scented breeze in her wake, then closed the office door behind her.

"Have a seat, Sergeant," Broome said, gesturing to the chair beside Jo's.

"Just call me Ben," he said, taking the seat.

Ben gave Jo a polite nod. "We meet again," he said, keeping his tone neutral, then turned to the attorney, who'd stepped behind his desk and was now easing into his chair.

"Okay, Mike. We're here as you requested," Jo said. "Are we it, or are more people scheduled to be here?"

"It'll just be the three of us," Mike replied. "By the way, I heard about yesterday's incident on the news. You two okay?"

Jo nodded. "I'm still shaking and looking over my shoulder, but other than that, I'm fine. Ben got a good look at the man with the gun, and went to the station afterwards to help try to identify the guy. How'd that turn out?" she asked Ben.

"I couldn't ID anyone in the photo array, but I worked with

one of their techs and she came up with a good computer image. It's going to be splashed across the news tonight," Ben said. "Hopefully someone will recognize the guy."

"And make an arrest," Mike said. "I'm sorry that had to happen on the same day as the memorial service," he said, looking at Ben then Jo. "It must have made for a long day."

"Not as long as some," Ben said. "I'm used to the unexpected. As for Jo . . ."

"I've had enough excitement to last me a lifetime. I don't see how anyone copes when they're stationed in a war zone."

"They say you get used to it—but that's a lie," he said, looking down at his hands, which were tanned and rough. "It seems like home is just as dangerous these days."

Jo tried to read his expression, wondering if he was also trying to connect the dots between his father's death, the van, and those men in the green pickup. After several seconds she gave up. It was impossible for her even to guess what he was thinking.

Mike cleared his throat, then glanced down at an open folder on his desk. "First, I'd like to point out that what we're going to be discussing is actually a trust, not a will in the traditional and legal sense. I was designated his trustee, and as such, I'm responsible for ensuring that his estate is divided and assigned according to his wishes. With an active business as his primary asset, Tom wanted to avoid probate, which would have put daily trading post operations in jeopardy."

Jo nodded. "His life, outside his family, was The Outpost. He always referred to the trading post as his legacy."

"Yeah, the business was dad's life, all right," Ben said. He wanted to add *so let's get on with it,* but instead decided to let things go at their own pace. He had plenty of time to decide what to do with The Outpost—sell, or hire someone to run it for him until his enlistment was up.

"I'd like to point out now that Tom and I discussed the

distribution of his estate more than once, and he made his wishes crystal clear. My job now is to carry those out to the letter."

"What's the problem, Mike?" Ben asked, sensing hesitation. "Did my dad leave everything to charity or some church group?"

"No, not at all. Your father knew that, combined, the entire estate—business, land, and home—was worth in excess of a million dollars, at least on paper. That would generate a sizable tax bill," Mike said.

"So Dad broke it up just enough to keep that value under the minimum for his benefactors," Ben said, nodding. "Makes sense. So I get the house, the trading post, and the Expedition, and Jo gets, what, his Chevy pickup?" Ben asked. He was anxious to put an end to the dog and pony show Mike seemed determined to put on for them.

"Actually, Ben, *Jo* gets The Outpost, the business property, the Expedition, and all monies included in his business accounts. His salary will now go into payroll, to be distributed by the new owner. Ben, you receive the house, the residential land and right of way, his pickup, and all his personal property, including a substantial life insurance payout and his 401(k). That's about a sixty–forty split, when you consider the money flowing into your account."

Ben stared at Mike, still trying to process what he'd heard. "*Jo* gets The Outpost?" Seeing Mike nod, Ben stared in disbelief, his fists clenching into balls. As he glanced at Jo, Ben saw her shocked expression—or maybe she was just a good actress. Yesterday, she'd been so innocent and . . . frightened as well. He was sure that hadn't been an act. But today?

"What the hell?" Ben managed at last. There was no reason for his father to have divided things up like this with someone who wasn't real family. This didn't make any sense.

As he looked again at the beautiful woman Jo had become, an answer slowly came to him. Of course. It was obvious that she'd used her looks and maybe her body to manipulate his old man. It wouldn't be the first time a middle-aged guy had been played by a savvy gold digger—flattery, manipulation, and sex in exchange for a big payoff in the end.

"I know this comes as a shock to you, Ben, and to you, too, Jo, but Tom wanted this detail kept between him and me." Mike looked at Ben. "Keep in mind that you two had a history that was still unresolved at the time of Tom's death. Your father also knew that you'd never been interested in the business. That's why he decided to make sure The Outpost went to someone who had sweat equity in it—those were his words, by the way, not mine."

Ben sat up even straighter than before. "This isn't just bullshit, right? You have a copy of the trust?"

Broome nodded, handing each of them thick white envelopes. "Witnessed and signed. Being a living trust, there won't be any public proceedings," Mike said. "I understand the reasons for your surprise and confusion, so why don't you both take a few moments to read this over. Then I can answer any questions you might have."

Jo took the envelope offered, then turned to Ben. "Ben, I—"

"Skip it," he snapped, staring at the envelope in his hand. He'd come up with a battle plan and fight her in court. Jo had always been a presence in the Stuart household, and there'd even been times when he was sure his dad secretly wished she could have been his kid instead of him. Now, a woman, Jo had clearly manipulated his dad into giving her his inheritance. He wouldn't rest until he set things right.

"Jo, until the paperwork passes through the county clerk's office and becomes public record, I'll retain control of the accounts and dispersals. If you need to purchase anything or make payroll, I'll have to cosign."

Ben watched her take in the news. She never spoke, just

nodded, her eyes as wide as saucers. She was good. Her reaction looked so real, he was almost convinced.

Mike looked back at him. "Ben, the police have released the house, and I paid a housekeeping service to clean things up for you. I understand a deputy was there yesterday, so you weren't free to roam around inside. Why don't you let me give you a ride over there now? After all that's happened, it may be easier to have someone tag along the first time you go into the house."

Ben nodded. He didn't need a babysitter, but he wanted more time to talk to Broome—alone. The man had known his father better than anyone else he could think of at the moment. Maybe he'd open up a little more once Jo wasn't around. If his dad had been having an affair with Jo, he had a feeling Mike would know.

Jo stood, holding up the envelope. "I'll read this later. Right now, I'm going back to the trading post," she said in a shaky voice. "The staff has a lot of questions that they need answered. Their futures are tied to what happens to The Outpost, and they're waiting for news. We all assumed you'd be inheriting—"

"So did I," he shot back, then looked at Mike, dismissing her completely. "Ready when you are."

Ben avoided talking to Jo as they left the law offices. It was clear to him that she couldn't be trusted. His own past with her should have told him that. Jo used people. She always had. He'd been a fool to think she might have changed. All time had done was allow her to refine her skills.

Five minutes later, they were in Broome's Mercedes, heading west out of town. Not wanting to drag things out, Ben decided it was time to speak his mind.

"Was Josephine Buck my father's lover?" he asked.

"I'd say no, at least not to my knowledge," Broome answered after a beat. "If anything, I'd say he loved Jo like a daughter. But you know your dad, Ben. He was harder to read than a cell phone tech manual."

Ben nodded, his response automatic, nothing more.

"You and Jo dated back in high school, didn't you?" Mike asked.

"Yeah, we were together for about a year, more or less. Then we broke up." Jo had been his first real love, and though they said good-bye a lifetime ago, he'd never really gotten over her. She'd been a pretty teen with a sexy smile and soft, kissable lips. He'd wanted her so badly, it hurt, but she'd always played it cool. She'd been a year older than him and out of his reach at first, but somehow they'd come together for a while. They'd never been really close, not as close as he would have wanted, but the constant challenge to break through her shell had only added to the heat. Then one day when he really needed her support, she'd said good-bye and never looked back.

Her rejection stung and had left deep scars, but he eventually put it all into perspective. Now here she was in his life again. As undeniably attractive as Jo had been back then, she all but sizzled now. If his father had fallen for Jo, he couldn't really blame him.

"I know the terms of the trust took you by surprise, son, but don't go thinking that Jo somehow manipulated your old man. You knew him well enough to know that he had a mind of his own. Nobody conned Tom Stuart—not ever."

"Jo's hot, and smart, too."

"Yeah, but your dad wasn't the kind to be seduced by a sexy voice and some well-placed curves. Your mother was *the* love of his life, and in his eyes, nobody could ever match her."

"True enough, but maybe . . ."

"Face facts, Ben. You aren't really interested in running the trading post, are you? Your career is with the army. So what difference does it make that he left it to her? He left you with a paid-for home and a sizable financial legacy. You've got more now than most men have at fifty."

"I'm not reupping this time, Mike. I was planning on returning home for good."

"To become a shopkeeper?" Broome shook his head. "Maybe I'm still remembering the boy who manned up and enlisted, what, five—six years ago? That kid wouldn't have settled anyplace for long. Are you really that different now?"

"Yeah, I am," he said, nodding slowly. "Back then I had to enlist—it was either that or possible jail time, but all things considered, the army was just what I needed. I'd wanted to know who I was and test my own worth as a man." He paused. "I found out, times two."

Broome glanced over, but didn't ask. "Lessons learned in the military usually come the hard way."

Ben nodded slowly. "Hard work, sacrifice, and accomplishment all go together. Each step demands a price."

Ten minutes later, as they approached the trading post, he felt the tug on his gut. This had been his father's world—the place he'd retreated into after the death of his wife, leaving little or no room for his son.

As memories and old hurts rushed back, Ben took a breath. That was then—this was now. Adding emphasis to that conclusion was the county police cruiser just pulling up in front of his father's house.

For a few hours today, he'd somehow set aside the main reason he was here—to uncover the facts behind his father's death. That goal was now at the top of his list again. It was time for action.

—FOUR—

Mike glanced over at Ben. "The sheriff's department investigation of your father's death is still active and ongoing, so let me stick around. It's always a good idea to have an attorney present when you talk to the police."

"Thanks." Ben went up to the front porch, where the sheriff's department officer in the blue San Juan County jacket stood. The not-unattractive dirty blonde in her early forties looked tired. He recognized that close-to-burnout look. It went far beyond not getting enough sleep. It was the weariness that came from having seen too much of human nature.

"I'm Ben Stuart," he said, offering his hand. "This is my attorney, Mike Broome."

"Detective Wells," she said, shaking hands with both of them. "I'm sorry for your loss—Sergeant," she added, clearly having done a background check on him.

He gave her a curt nod. People meant well, but it was difficult to keep hearing condolences. The constant reminders just reopened the wound.

"I understood the scene had been released," Broome said.

"It has, Counselor. I just came by to speak to Mr. Stuart," Wells said.

"Good, because I have some questions for you, too." Ben walked to the entrance, then after pausing for a heartbeat, went inside.

He'd expected to drown in memories the second he stepped in, but the home he remembered and what the house had become were two very different things. Everything in here smelled of pine disinfectant and had an odd, flat feel, like a home up for sale. The rooms seemed smaller, too, the walls, closer now that he was an adult.

He walked to the shelf where his mother's treasured salt and pepper shakers had once been. She'd find them at garage sales and antique shops and had sworn some dated back to the early 1900s. They'd been her own prized collection, but the shelf was half empty now, with some of the pairs missing their mates.

"Several of the shakers were broken and in the trash when we arrived on the scene," Wells said, volunteering the information.

He snapped his head around. "Pardon me?"

She repeated what she'd said.

"Something isn't right. Dad wouldn't have thrown them away. If he'd broken one, or half a dozen, he'd have still saved the pieces and glued them back together. He'd have never given up on something Mom had treasured. Look at the owl salt-shaker. I broke it with a Transformer missile when I was nine. My dad reconstructed the left wing with Spackle and repainted it." He held it up for her to see.

The detective nodded. "Maybe this time they were beyond repair."

"Even so, he wouldn't have just tossed the pieces into the trash. He would have picked them all up, and put them in a plastic food container for safekeeping."

Yet even as he spoke, he wondered how much his dad *had* really changed, living alone all these years. Maybe he'd just snapped one day and had lashed out at the memories. He'd seen that happen often enough in combat when a soldier reached the boiling point. Or sometimes they'd be as tough as stone out in the field, then crack up after being dumped by a wife or girlfriend ten thousand miles and another world away.

Ben examined the room slowly, carefully, studying everything around him with a practiced eye. Some familiar things remained untouched, like his name, the pencil marks, and the dates on the door trim where his mom had kept a record of his height over the years.

Ben stepped into the kitchen and saw that the embroidered rooster his mother had worked on years ago still hung on the wall. It was only three inches by four and badly faded, but it was a permanent fixture, like the chipped willowware teapot beside it. "If my dad had been cutting his ties to the past, that old blue teapot would have been long gone, too."

Katie followed him. "You have an eye for detail."

"That skill has kept me alive the past few years." He circled the counter and finally faced her. "Check for fingerprints on the broken salt and pepper shakers found in the trash. They won't belong to my dad. My father undoubtedly fought his killer, and that's why some things were broken."

"What makes you so certain he didn't commit suicide?"

"In his book, only a coward would go out that way—and that's practically a quote."

"Sometimes circumstances can alter the beliefs we hold most dear," Katie said. "People change."

"No, ma'am. Once a marine, always a marine. My father was never the proverbial bull in the china shop. He did everything with precision. That defined him. His trading post was always immaculate, and so was this house. He wouldn't tolerate it otherwise. No drill sergeant was more exacting than my dad when it came to order. Ask any of his employees or just look around the store."

"Have you been told the circumstances of your father's death?" she asked.

"He was found at a desk in this house, shot to death."

"One bullet to his right temple, the mark of a suicide," Katie said softly.

"Did you say *right*?"

She nodded and waited.

"There were no cuts or injuries on his left hand? Bruises?"

"None I could see."

"If I'm reading you correctly, you know what I'm about to say."

"I've been told by several witnesses that your father was left-handed. But is it possible he was ambidextrous?" she asked. He was nearly sure she'd asked the others this same question before. "No way," he said, verifying it for her, then smiled, recalling a memory. "When I turned sixteen, I found out that old traditional Navajos were bothered by people who ate with their left hand— something only ghosts do, they say. So I decided to scare my Navajo girlfriend by training myself to eat with my left hand. I made one hell of a mess that night because we had soup. My dad was left-handed and laughed like crazy at me, so I dared him to try eating with his *right* hand. He spazzed out, just like me."

"All right. I'll keep looking into this, but the ME has to make the final call. They can usually tell handedness by the degree or lack of muscle development, and by calluses left by pencil or pen use over time. Stuff like that."

Ben walked into the den, his eyes focused on the scuff marks on the hardwood floor. "My father would have never allowed those marks to remain there. He would have rubbed and sanded them out, then refinished the floor. Offhand, I'd say that there was one helluva fight in here. Somebody got bounced against the wall, or off that shelf, which would explain the broken shakers on the opposite wall."

"Sometimes when we're too close to things, we end up seeing what we want to see," Wells said. "There was no clear evidence of a fight when I came on the scene, and I was the first officer to arrive."

"Then where did the marks come from?"

"Anyone can forget to push back a chair or move it against the grain. Maybe the cleaners were clumsy or inattentive. I can compare these marks to the crime scene photos. But I have to point out something else here. There were *no* signs of a break-in."

"Maybe the person or persons walked in while my dad was in another room, before he locked the house. Or the lock could have been picked earlier in the day and his killer or killers were already inside."

"There were scratch marks on the door," Katie admitted, "but those could have been caused by a misdirected key in the dark." As her cell phone rang, she stepped away from them and walked outside.

Ben went into his father's bedroom, then walked directly to the nightstand. That was where his father always placed his watch when he came home in the evenings. It was the same handcrafted silver and turquoise watch Ben and his mom had given him one Christmas, and he always kept it close. Ben opened the drawer and looked inside, but it wasn't there either.

Ben checked by the sink in the bathroom next, then walked to the kitchen and found Mike looking through his dad's old mail. "My father's silver watch, was it on him when he died?"

"Not that I know of. You want me to ask the detective? If it was, you probably won't be able to get it back for a while."

"That's fine. I just want to know where it is," Ben said. "It has special meaning to me."

"All right. Give me a moment."

While Mike went outside to talk to the detective, Ben looked around. This kitchen had seen some happy times, though most of those memories were part of his distant past. He'd just reached his teens when his mom died, and after that, everything changed.

"I asked," Mike said, coming back in. "No silver watch. He was wearing one of those multifunction Casios with a plastic band."

"The cleaners, could they have taken it?" Ben asked.

"No way. I sent my assistant to keep an eye on things. I was protecting my client's assets," he said, by way of explanation.

"Dad never left it in the trading post, and he certainly never would have sold that keepsake. So where did it go?" Ben asked, mostly thinking out loud.

"After the detective leaves, go take a look in his office desk anyway," Mike suggested. "Check the safe as well. Maybe it was broken and he hadn't had time to take it to a jeweler."

Just as he finished speaking, Detective Wells came back in. She sat on one of the kitchen chairs across from Mike and glanced up at Ben, who was standing at ease in the doorway at the opposite end of the room.

"Let's say that you're right and your father was murdered. Do you have any idea who might have wanted to kill him and why?"

"I've been out of touch too long to answer that accurately, but I'm not going to be sitting on my ass. I'm going to find out everything I can about my father, who his friends and his enemies are. I suggest you do likewise."

"I will, because that's my job. What you need to do is step back and let us handle the investigation, Sergeant. We know what we're doing."

"Then you better get with the program. I have a limited amount of time here, and I intend to find the answers before I rejoin my unit."

Katie Wells met his challenging gaze with one of her own and stood. "Don't get in my way, Sergeant. If I find out you've compromised or mishandled evidence, I'm going to come down on you like a ton of bricks. Back off and let me do my job."

"So do it, Detective—I'm not stopping you. How about tracking down that mysterious white van, the delivery vehicle that apparently didn't make a delivery? Where are you on that?"

"Every courier and company that does business with The Outpost has been contacted. Only a few of them operate white vans, and none of them made any deliveries or stops by this location on that day," she replied. "My guess is that it was a lost tourist or business vehicle, and it's not connected to your father's death."

"Assuming that's true, what's next?" Ben said.

"I'd like to check the trading post's security system and take another look around inside the store," she said.

"We don't have cameras here, so the security system is non-existent except for the good locks, the steel doors and frames, and the outside lighting. If you can tell me what you're looking for, maybe I can help," Ben said.

Wells shrugged. "I'm trying to find connections—any link between your father's death and the break-in attempt the other day, which, of course, may also be unrelated. I'll just take a look around and try to stay out of the way of the staff. Do you or your attorney have a problem with that?"

"Not at all," Ben said.

She looked over at Mike Broome, who shook his head.

"Let's go," Ben said, and followed Detective Wells out the door.

Jo sat in the break room just down the narrow hall from Tom's office. The trading post was hers now, but she couldn't quite force herself to use Tom's desk and chair. The *chindi* were often attached to personal possessions like those. She'd be giving away Tom's things to an Anglo charity soon; that is, unless Ben wanted them for some reason. Once that was done, she'd make the larger office her own.

Jo walked to the window and, lost in thought, stared west at the long sandstone ridge of the Hogback. She'd always dreamed of owning her own business, one that would give her the freedom to offer her services as a medicine woman at a cost even her poorest patient could afford. Yet now that the trading post was hers, she felt no joy, just a deepening sense of responsibility and fear. Someone had killed Tom, and yesterday they'd tried to break in. That suggested they had unfinished business, and as the new owner, she could easily be their next target.

Hearing footsteps, she turned her head and saw Ben at the door. "Now that the detective is gone, I need to go into Dad's office and look inside his safe for something. I won't be long."

"Sure, no problem, but—" Before she could finish the sentence, he was gone.

Jo stepped out into the hall just as Mike and Ben entered Tom's office. She joined them a few seconds later and watched Ben check his dad's desk, then go to the safe.

"I can help—," Jo said, but seeing Ben hold up one hand, fell silent.

He punched in a series of numbers onto the combination lock, but when he tried to turn the handle on the door, nothing happened. Frustrated, he looked up. "Something's wrong. The combination has always been my dad and mom's wedding anniversary."

"That's not the same safe. It's the same brand, but a newer model. It's got a different combination," Jo said.

Ben drew back, studied it, then nodded. "Where do you think he kept the combination, Mike? Under the desk pad?"

Broome shrugged. "I hope not."

"No need to search." Jo made her way around Mike, knelt beside Ben, then turned the dial while he watched.

"The day, month, and year I enlisted," he whispered, shaking his head.

"Exactly," she answered, reaching for the handle and turning it clockwise. The heavy metal door opened a crack.

Jo stepped aside, giving Ben access.

Inside, Ben found several DVDs and flash drives marked ACCOUNTING, photos of the trading post's high-end merchandise, tax records, and a long, carved wooden box. When he opened the lid, he discovered some of his mother's jewelry. "I didn't realize he was so . . . sentimental."

"He loved your mother very much," Jo said softly. "He told me once, that as the years went by, pieces of her disappeared from his mind. To him, that was a bit like losing her all over again, so he kept the things he associated with her most—her wedding ring, her favorite earrings, her necklace. He said that when he looked at those, he felt closer to her."

Ben stared at the box, fingering the items there.

Jo stepped back, feeling uncomfortable around personal possessions so closely connected to the dead.

"I can almost see Mom when I look at these, too," he said, his voice low. Then he cleared his throat and looked directly at her. "I'm searching for my father's silver and turquoise watch. Any idea where it could be?"

"No, but he wore it all the time. Maybe you should ask the police," she said, taken aback by the abrupt change in his tone.

"It wasn't with him when he—" He stopped speaking and stared at an indeterminate point across the room for a second or two before glancing back at her. "I also looked at home, in the place he normally kept it, but it wasn't there."

She forced herself to concentrate. Tom had always worn that watch to work. He'd loved the beautiful silver and turquoise band, so appropriate for a man doing business beside the Navajo Nation. "I don't know what to tell you. It wasn't one of those electronic watches, so sometimes he took it in for

cleaning. Check around the house, or here in his office for a re-
ceipt from a jeweler. I'll ask the others to keep an eye out for it
too. You're also welcome to search the rest of the place if you
want. Maybe he took it off for some reason and it's still where he
left it."

"Good idea. I'll start here. Going through Dad's things will
help me reconnect with him," he said, glancing around.

Mike placed a hand on Ben's shoulder. "I've got to get back
to my office, but if you need anything at all, let me know. I can
have your rental car brought here for you right away. It's still in
my parking lot."

"Okay, thanks."

"Your father kept a duplicate set of keys to his pickup here in
his desk," Jo said. "The Chevy belongs to him now, right?" she
asked, turning to Mike, who nodded. "And your dad's insurance covers you as a driver," Jo added.

"Thanks," Ben said, opening the middle drawer and taking
out the keys. "Same place as always. See you later, Mike."

Leaving Ben alone in his father's office, Jo accompanied Mike
to the front entrance. Only two customers, tourists judging
from the way they were dressed, were in the trading post now.
They were looking in the jewelry case while Leigh Ann waited
to bring out their selections.

"I've never seen the place so empty," Mike commented in a
whisper.

"These aren't ordinary times," she said. "Certain things will
have to be handled before traffic here resumes."

"You mean like holding a Sing to ease Navajo concerns?"

"Among other things," she said with a nod.

"If you need me, Jo, just call," he said, handing her one of his
cards.

Broome went to his Mercedes, parked at one of the concrete
barriers just beyond the full-length wooden porch. As Jo watched
him drive away, Leigh Ann came up behind her.

"I don't think Ben trusts us," Leigh Ann said. "He's locked himself in his father's office."

"No, it's not that. He's mourning his father . . . and trying to come to terms with the loss of all those what-might-have-beens if things between him and his dad had gone the way he'd hoped."

Jo returned to her office and, as always, took care of what had to be done. A proper ceremony like the Evil Way would have taken days and been prohibitively expensive, but maybe a short purification rite could be done. The need was urgent, judging solely by the absence of customers inside the store.

Yet a Sing would only be the beginning. They'd have to reassure their Anglo customers, too, that it was safe to return. Unfavorable publicity connected to a business, especially the kind involving murder or a threat of danger, tended to repel everyone but the morbidly curious.

Jo logged on to the store network, then accessed the trading post's business account. The numbers told her that even a short purification rite would strain The Outpost's limited budget.

She paced around the office for several seconds, trying to figure out what to do. Her options were limited. The only thing she could do was speak to her *hataalii* teacher and see if he'd allow her to pay him in installments.

She was on the phone, making arrangements, when Ben knocked on the open door. She waved him in and he took a chair.

"Did I hear you mention a ceremony?" he asked after she placed the phone down. "Are you going to have a Navajo Sing here?"

"We've got to," she said. "You've noticed the lack of customers, I'm sure. It's only been a few days since your father passed on and over half of our regulars are members of the tribe. Most of them will continue to keep their distance until we do what's necessary. For the Navajo customers, a Sing is absolutely essential. The Anglos will need a different kind of reassurance."

"Like what?"

She considered it, then smiled. "Good publicity, like a Grand Reopening. I'll call the radio stations, television studios, the local press, and invite them. We'll have the Sing first, then officially reopen The Outpost for business. We'll have a ribbon cutting and everything."

His eyes captured hers, and for one brief moment, she remembered the boy who'd awakened her body to the pleasures of his touch. Echoes of their stormy teen love, of feelings too powerful to fight, whispered from the back of her mind. Then, as he spoke, the illusion vanished in a flash.

"Sound business decision," he said, his voice cold and hard. "Know your customers, come up with a plan, conduct the operation, then follow through. Very professional."

She blinked. "There's a lot more involved in this than just Retail Sales 101. Ceremonies are the way the *Diné*, my people, establish order and replace chaos with harmony. They're part of who I am," she said, hoping to make him understand. "I also know our Anglo customers and understand what their fears can do to both The Outpost and all who rely on it to make a living." She stopped and took a calming breath. "I have to protect this trading post just as your father would have done." She paused, then added in a quiet voice, "You may not believe this, but I love this place almost as much as he did."

"I'm sure you worked hard to convince him of that," he said, anger boiling to the surface. "He and I were ready to bury our past and start over, a clean slate. We both wanted that father–son relationship we'd lost somewhere along the way. Things had never been better between us. Yet now I find out that he's left the one place he considered his legacy to you. What's wrong with that picture?"

"It's not that simple, Ben. That trust was signed over two years ago. Had things worked out between you two, he probably would have changed the terms. As it was, he wasn't sure what would happen once you two got together—no more than you were."

"So what will you do with the place? Are you going to run things the way he did?"

"I have some plans of my own, but I'll do my best to make sure everyone who's working here now can hold on to their jobs."

"For how long? Are you going to wait until the economy turns around, then find a buyer?"

"That sounds more like what you'd do if the choice was yours," she snapped, then regretted it. Anger served little or no purpose. She wouldn't give in to it. "My plans are for the long term, and they entail helping this trading post continue to grow."

"Count on me looking over your shoulder. I'd like to see how you're going to pull that off."

There'd been no touch of humanity in his voice, and that coldness chilled her spirit and filled her with sadness. She'd hoped they could be friends. "You've already passed judgment on me, Ben. Nothing I say is going to convince you differently, so stop wasting my time. I've got work to do."

Jo picked up the phone and started making calls to the people she needed to contact. Turning away from Ben, she ignored him completely. After a moment she heard him leave.

Alone again, she finished her conversation and breathed a sigh of relief. She was beyond tired. What she felt was that bone-deep weariness that came from being under constant pressure. She closed her eyes for a moment, and when she opened them again, Leigh Ann was there.

"Ben's getting hard to handle, isn't he?" she said.

"He doesn't get it. The trading post was entrusted to me for a reason. It was a gift, but it also came with important, unstated strings attached."

"After all those years estranged from his father, you'd think

Ben would understand why Tom didn't just leave everything to him. Do you think greed's popping up its ugly head?"

"No, it's that he resents my relationship with his dad. He always did."

"He's a complete bonehead," Leigh Ann said, then with a slow mischievous grin, added, "but he's also droolworthy man-candy. Enjoy that part and ignore the rest."

"Be careful around Ben—he's got some very hard edges," Jo said.

"Yeah, the kind that beg to be gentled by a creative woman's touch," she said, giving her a wink.

Jo laughed for the first time in days, and was surprised by how good it felt.

A few minutes later, with no customers in the main room of the trading post, Jo assembled everyone together for an impromptu meeting. "The trading post's in trouble, so we've got to come together and turn things around." She told them about the reopening. "A lot of work will need to be done in a very short time, but we can do it. I've made a list and we'll split the work up among us. We'll be having the ceremony here first thing tomorrow. A *hataalii,* a Navajo Singer, who in this case happens to be my teacher, was able to make himself available to us on very short notice. He understands the urgency, so he's agreed to come and do a blessing for us. I've also invited our newspaper, and our local cable TV and radio stations to attend our official grand reopening. They're used to moving fast, so they'll give us coverage."

"A Sing will help us with the *Diné,*" Regina said, "but the Anglos . . . I've heard the talk. They're saying that too much has happened and it's dangerous to shop here now. I'm not sure a reopening is going to change their minds."

"It's true. At first we'll attract the curious who saw this place on the local news and want to know more," Esther said, "but what will eventually save us is that people's memories are short. Shopping at a country store is more convenient for the locals, so, before you know it, things will return to normal."

Jo saw all of them looking at her expectantly and knew they were counting on her to lead them, and The Outpost, out of trouble. No matter what it took, she wouldn't let them—or herself—down.

FIVE

Early the following morning, Jo stood next to Leigh Ann as the reporters began to arrive. News had traveled fast in their small community, and the crowd of onlookers and press was much larger than Jo had expected. Esther had been right. Curiosity trumped reluctance.

"Make sure no one bothers the *hataalii*," Jo told Leigh Ann. "I've assured him that no photos would be taken of him or the ceremony without his permission."

Seeing a cameraman going toward the Singer, Jo went to intercept him.

"I'll get that," Leigh Ann said. "Take care of the medicine man and the ceremony."

"Thanks," Jo said, and rushed off. The last thing she needed was for Rudy Brownhat to get upset right before the ceremony. Calmness, clarity, and peace of mind were required for a successful Sing.

Jo joined Rudy, who was standing beside his pickup. "What can I do to help you, Uncle?" she asked, using the word to show respect. They weren't related.

"Help me bring out what I need and put things away afterwards. That's all you can do. You can't actually take part in the ceremony, because you're the one who requested the Sing," Rudy said, reaching into the bed of his pickup and bringing down a big wooden trunk.

"I'll help any way I can. I'm really grateful that you came on such short notice." She bent down and took one of the trunk handles.

He grabbed the other handle. Together, they carried it over to the trading post. "The prayer won't be a long one, but it'll require care and concentration," he said, noting the reporters around them as they set the trunk down. "These onlookers will need to keep their distance and show respect for the proceedings."

"They won't interfere," she assured him once again. "I've already spoken to them. They'll stop filming and lower their cameras as soon as we ask."

"You want the Sing done here, not at the man's home?" he asked, opening the truck and bringing out a large Navajo blanket.

"That property is not under my care," she said, helping him place the blanket on The Outpost's wooden porch, a spacious veranda that ran the length of the entire storefront.

Jo brought out the medicine bags Rudy had filled with pollen and other collected substances, and placed them on the blanket. Along with those, was a bead token that would be hers to keep at the end of the blessing. That would become a symbol of the rite and, as such, carry the power and blessing of the ceremony.

Feeling her cell phone vibrating, Jo stepped away and pulled it out of her pocket. The display listed a private caller. Curious, she moved even farther away from Rudy and brought the phone to her ear. "Hello?"

"Listen carefully, I'm only saying this once. Gimme back my property or you'll end up like your boss. When you're ready to deal, park your pickup in front of the trading post, then wait for my instructions. Act normal. I'll be watching. If you tell anyone, I'll make sure your death is slow and painful."

The caller had a heavy Spanish accent, but his words were clear, and terrifying. Her mouth went dry and her heart had lodged at her throat. "Give back what? Who is this?" Jo said, looking around for anyone using their phone. Soon she realized that her caller was no longer connected.

It took a minute, but she forced herself to stop shaking. As she drew in a breath, she saw Rudy motioning to her. Blinking back tears of frustration and fear, she put the phone back into her pocket and walked toward him, head held high.

Tony Gómez, a slender, wiry man in his early forties, slipped the phone back into his pocket and raised his binoculars again. He could see the trading post clearly from where he was standing, hidden among the dark shadows of a cluster of cottonwoods near the bosque. He tried to steady his hold by bracing his left wrist against the bark, but got some smelly liquid on his wrist.

Moving quickly, he wiped it off his new silver and turquoise watch. It beat the hell out of his cheap Timex. Now he had a *caballero*'s watch, not the dollar-store crap ones he'd worn most of his life. Feeling his cell phone vibrating, he brought it out of his shirt pocket. Sap had stuck to that as well.

"Smelly shit," Tony muttered, wiping off the phone.

"What'd you say?" Roberto said.

"Sorry. Stepped in something, boss. I just made the call. Now I'm watching the store," Tony said, keeping his voice calm and collected. "It looks like there's an Indian ceremony of some kind about to start up."

Tony knew Roberto well. All that counted to Mr. Hidalgo

was getting the job done, and he'd blown it twice already. The first time was when he shot that asshole shopkeeper too soon. Stuart had turned out to be a good liar even when bargaining for his life. Waiting until the memorial service to search the store for his boss's property had been his second mistake.

Although Stuart gave them the key, he'd lied about the key-pad code for the electronic lock. Then, just when they'd given up punching in numbers and brought out the tools needed to break in, their luck had evaporated. Thanks to his idiot helpers, they got a late start, and the Navajo clerk and Stuart's son had shown up. Roberto's orders had been clear—don't get caught—so they'd had no choice except to take off.

None of them had worn masks that day, because they hadn't expected anyone to be at the trading post. Then after the entire operation had turned to *mierda*, Frankie poked his head out the window and started shooting. Now that idiot could be identified. Too bad for him and his brother. Their days were numbered.

Tony continued watching the Indian prayer ceremony, trying to figure out what was next. The young woman he'd called hadn't left the grounds or used her cell phone. There were police from three agencies standing around, but she hadn't run to the cops either, so she must have gotten the message. There were also some TV people with cameras, and a crowd of mostly Indians, but so far, she hadn't talked to anyone.

"There's a Navajo guy over there wearing a headband and beating a drum, boss. I guess he's a medicine man and they're praying for the dead store owner."

"It's more likely a blessing to chase away evil spirits. The Navajos are jumpy around the dead. What else can you see?" Hidalgo asked.

"A half dozen agency cops, a couple of TV vans and guys with cameras, but they aren't filming anything right now. No-body's gone inside the trading post yet."

"Good. Keep watch. If one of those crime scene vans comes

up, or the police get excited, or the Navajo woman talks to the cops, call me back. If they find it before we do . . ."

Tony knew what Roberto meant. Despite the many years of loyalty and service he'd given Roberto Hidalgo, he'd be dead in a matter of hours if the police got their hands on what he'd failed to retrieve. It was already too late for the brothers now. A third screwup would mean the end of Tony Gómez.

"I'll be here until they're done, boss," he said, blindly reaching into his shirt pocket for a cigarette, no longer caring about the tree sap.

Roberto grunted, then hung up. Tony, cigarette dangling from his lips, focused on the Indian wearing the white headband and carrying a leather bag. He was clearly in charge now.

Pushing back her fears, and trying to concentrate on the blessing, Jo followed Hosteen Brownhat as he went to the center of the store and continued the Sing. His monotone voice, filled with power, rose as he scattered pinches of corn pollen to the four points of the compass.

She remained close, concentrating on the words he intoned, and repeating them precisely. As the petitioner, this was her part of the ritual, to support the prayer. Repetition carried compulsion. The gods had no choice but to grant a properly worded prayer. She couldn't slip up now, her spiritual protection was at stake, and boy did she need it now.

The chant continued flawlessly as the Singer demanded that the deities give their blessing and protectively encircle the trading post and those therein. At long last the Singer went outside again and, giving Jo a flint arrowhead to hold, threw bits of turquoise into the air. As the *hataalii* pronounced harmony restored, the rite came to a close.

The *hataalii* handed Jo the small medicine bag and her

bead token. "Allow nothing to happen to the bead. It is now a part of you."

She nodded, remembering that if the bead broke or was destroyed, misfortune would surely befall her.

"Thank you, Uncle," she said.

While she helped him put away the ceremonial items that remained, the other employees brought out folding tables to place along the porch. Esther and Regina had prepared a big batch of mutton stew, fry bread, and punch. Food would be served to everyone, Anglo or Navajo, who'd come to watch and benefit from the power of the Sing.

The medicine man was served first; then Jo led him to a small shaded picnic table where he could sit and enjoy his meal. As she walked back to the entrance, ready to officially open the trading post, she saw Ben out of the corner of her eye. He'd taken Del aside and was clearly trying to speak privately to him, though Del was supposed to be busy helping with the food. Now what?

Annoyed, Jo started to go over, but before she could reach Ben, Esther came up holding a bright turquoise and white ribbon. "Don't forget. You said I could tie this across both front posts, ask the Good Lord for his blessing, then cut the ribbon."

"I remember. Are you going to need some help?" Jo asked, not objecting to the Christian prayer. They all had different beliefs, and honoring that was part of walking in beauty.

"I could use an extra pair of hands to get the ribbon up. I've already selected a blessing," Esther said.

Jo helped her tie the ribbon; then Esther, holding her Bible, read a brief prayer.

After the final amen, Jo motioned for the reporters and public to come even closer. "Today we officially reopen The Outpost. It's a new era for all of us."

Jo reached for the scissors, then cut the ribbon. The employees all clapped enthusiastically, and most of the people joined in. Stepping out of the way, Jo invited their visitors to come and eat.

Jo studied every man within view while at the same time avoiding eye contact. She didn't want to send the wrong message, like she was flirting or checking them out, but she had a feeling the caller was close by, maybe in the crowd. He'd had an accent, Spanish or Mexican, and sounded mature, maybe middle-aged.

She'd been standing there for less than a minute, watching the activity, when two reporters came up to her.

"The sheriff's department continues to call Tom Stuart's death suspicious. Was it murder or suicide?" one male TV reporter asked her, holding up his microphone. "And do you think it might be connected to that burglary attempt and the high-speed chase you were involved in yesterday?"

"Those are questions the medical examiner and local law enforcement officers will have to answer," Jo answered, sticking to her planned script. "Today is a day to celebrate life. The Outpost will continue to be a vital part of our rural community, and as in the past, we'll do our best to serve our guests, friends, and neighbors."

Rather than take more questions, worried that she might slip up and say the wrong thing, she invited the reporters to enjoy some of the traditional foods that had been prepared for the event. As she glanced past them, Jo caught a glimpse of Ben, dressed in casual slacks and a knit shirt, talking to Esther now. Esther's focus was clearly not on him. She was in the process of moving fry bread from a big plastic storage container to a warming tray.

The elderly woman looked over at Jo, then focused back on her work. Ben finally moved away, and although he hadn't looked in her direction, Jo suspected that he knew she'd been watching him.

Something was up. As Jo went to help with the food, she saw Ben approach Mike Broome, who was standing near the door, eating a steaming bowl of stew. The two men spoke briefly, then Broome strode away,.

Rather than drive herself crazy wondering, she decided to confront Ben right now. She'd already had one death threat today so far. How much worse could it get? As she crossed the porch, she felt a different kind of excitement. After learning he was coming home on leave, she'd spent days wondering what it would be like the next time they met. Deep in her heart, she'd clung to the dream that he, too, woke up in the middle of the night, tantalizing what-ifs teasing him with endless possibilities.

Now reality was forcing her to give up those fantasies. As she met his gaze and held it, she felt the power of his personality probing for any weakness in her. He was no longer someone she could trust. Yet that muscled chest and those gorgeous hazel eyes made her wish . . . for what couldn't be.

"I saw you speaking to my staff," Jo said in a soft voice, not wanting to be overheard. "Exactly what are you doing here today?"

He gave her a smile that didn't quite reach his eyes. "Worried?"

She glared at him, then took a breath, refusing to take the bait. "Your father trusted me to keep his dream alive. Why can't you?" Jo turned and walked away.

"Why the hell should I trust *you*?" he said, following her around to the side of the building, away from the crowd. "You tell me that you want to honor Dad's wishes, then all but admit that he would have eventually changed his will and left the trading post to me."

"The terms of his trust were clear, and I have to honor that," she said. "But even if I were to give the trading post to you, what then? You're not staying here, right?"

"I have to go back to the army, yes, but my enlistment will be up soon. Ten months, ten days."

"And afterwards, are you telling me that you'll be coming home for good, and you'll be perfectly happy running The Outpost for the rest of your life? Face it. You're don't really care about The Outpost. You just don't want *me* to have it. What is it, pride? Or maybe it's good old-fashioned greed?"

"Straight talk—you ready for it?" he snapped.

"Bring it." Nothing could scare her now, not after that phone call.

"Game on, lady. You mentioned greed? That's what I see when I look at you. What makes you think you have a right to my dad's business in the first place? You're . . . a glorified clerk. How far did you have to go to get what you wanted?" He looked down her body slowly, undressing her with his eyes.

The implication was unmistakable. She swung her arm to slap him, but he caught her wrist a foot from his face. She countered by kicking him in the shins.

"You're a pig, Ben. What you're accusing me of doing dishonors *him*, not just me. He was your father, not some dirty old man." She walked away, too angry to speak.

Wanting to put some distance between her and Ben before it got really ugly, she circled around the far corner to the rear of The Outpost.

Finally she reached the west corner and hearing running footsteps, turned around. "Now what?"

Ben caught up to her, though she kept walking. "If I'm wrong, I'll apologize," he said, his tone reflecting his lack of sincerity.

"*If?*" She put her hands on her hips. "That's the height of arrogance, but I'm through arguing. The Outpost is mine, get used to it."

"You've scored a temporary victory, Jo. That's all. Once I find a lawyer, I'm going to contest the trust. Mike Broome refused to take the case, I asked him just five minutes ago. I'll get someone else."

"And if by some miracle you end up with the trading post, then what?"

"You called it, Jo. I'll either sell or shut it down if I can't get a quick enough offer. I haven't decided yet."

The news sucked the air from her lungs. She'd given Ben nothing but the benefit of the doubt, but inside, he was still the same selfish boy who screwed up, then abandoned those who'd loved him.

As she looked away, trying to swallow her rage before she faced the public again, she saw Esther and Del seated at the picnic table, speaking to the *hataalii*.

This wasn't just about her. She had to do *something*. "You see that elderly Navajo woman and that boy talking to the medicine man? They *need* their jobs to take care of their families. That teenager is carrying more responsibilities than you can even imagine. You think it'll be easy for them to find any job during this recession? A seventy-year-old woman and a kid with health issues? Your father *cared* about his people. That's why he left The Outpost to me. That decision wasn't about *you*, it was about keeping The Outpost going and protecting his trading post family."

"Family?"

"You're a sergeant. In your unit, squad, or whatever you call it, there are men you're responsible for, aren't there? I would imagine you watch out for them, and they watch out for you. Don't you think of them as family?"

He nodded slowly. "That's generally how it works."

"Your father was a military man, a proud marine, a man of *honor*. He always acted according to his highest sense of right. If you sue me now, it'll undermine this place and The Outpost will lose maybe half its value before a judge makes a final decision.

And let's say you finally win, then what? You'll destroy what your father loved and ruin the lives of people he cared about. Think about what you're doing. This isn't just about *you* or your pridc. It's bigger than that."

As Ben stood there, his expression changed from hostility to one of grudging respect. "You can sure argue your point, I'll give you that."

She walked away without another word, but by the time she stepped inside the trading post, she was shaking all over.

Rudy Brownhat came to join her. As they stood in the far corner of the room, he spoke in a voice meant for only her to hear. "I can see hurt in your eyes, and more. The troubles you face are many, but you can't win a fight unless you walk in harmony with your surroundings."

"You're right, but the owner's son is being completely unreasonable. What he wants . . . is just plain crazy."

"Our way teaches that everything has two sides. Are you seeing both?"

His serenity was unassailable. For the first time since she'd started her apprenticeship almost a year ago, she questioned her ability to maintain that same state of calm control. Unable to answer him truthfully, she looked away.

"There's more that's troubling you, isn't there? Before the ceremony you were ready to face the world. Now you look . . . frightened. How can I help?"

"There've been too many changes in my life these past few days. That's all. Thank you for coming and for caring enough to offer to help," Jo said. Rudy was very perceptive, but she couldn't afford to let anyone guess her secret, not until she'd figured things out first.

"Come see me again when you're ready to talk."

Jo left the *hataalii*'s side and went to mingle with the customers and guests, inviting new faces to return and greeting her regulars. As she walked down one of the aisles, she noticed

Mrs. Todacheenee, one of their oldest customers, placing cans of Spam into her shopping basket. Carlene was raising three grandchildren by herself, and Jo knew she was living on a tight budget.

"Good morning, Mrs. T.," Jo said, coming over with a smile. "I'm glad to see you today. Are you finding everything you need?"

"Yes, I am, dear. I'm so glad you're still here, and after the blessing, I know it's safe to shop here again. I'm sorry for all that's happened. Your boss was a good man." Mrs. Todacheenee looked frail in her long thin dress and scarf, but she still had prance in her step and a strong voice.

"I appreciate that, ma'am. Did you know that our tortillas are on special today, half price?" Jo knew that the woman always purchased the same items together, Spam and the tortillas. She already had a brick of cheddar cheese, the third food on her usual menu.

"No, and thank you, dear, for pointing that out. I'd better hurry, I've got to be back home before my ride leaves without me." Mrs. Todacheenee laughed at the joke. Her ride home was a small scooter parked out front, with two baskets astride the back tire.

Jo said good-bye and moved on. Slowly, her spirits lifted and her mood improved. *This* was what she did best—connect to people and bring supply and demand together. She'd made a place for herself here, one that filled a need and helped many walk in beauty.

She'd fight Ben if she had to, but not out of anger. She'd fight because it was the right thing to do, and he'd left her no other choice. In the meantime, she had an even greater danger to face.

※

The following morning she arrived at the trading post a little after six and spent the first fifteen minutes just looking around, trying to find out what, if anything, could be considered someone else's property, something worth killing Tom for. Nothing at all came to mind.

Surprisingly enough, she wasn't tired, though sleep the night before had come only in spurts. She'd had continued nightmares of a faceless man chasing her through the store, through Tom's home, and down the empty highway. Those were followed by long wakeful periods trying to figure out what the caller wanted returned.

Finally, she'd come up with the only answer that made sense. It had been a crank call from some sicko, like those Internet trolls who tormented people just for fun.

Long after The Outpost opened for the day, Jo remained in her office. She'd paid all the bills—some which Tom had uncharacteristically put off to the last minute—and now she barely had enough to make it through to the end of the quarter.

Most important of all, she'd discovered that she didn't have the funds to cover a legal battle if Ben actually took her to court. She left a phone call for Mike Broome, and was waiting to hear from him when her stomach growled loudly.

Jo stared at her cold cup of coffee and realized she was hungry. Preoccupied, she hadn't bothered with breakfast this morning. Almost as the thought formed, Esther walked in.

"I had a feeling you'd need a little extra fuel today," she said quietly, then placed a small basket of homemade cinnamon rolls in front of her. These were Esther's specialty, her mother's secret recipe.

"I know why I'm here," Jo said with a wry smile, "but what on earth brings *you* here so early? You have the afternoon shift today."

"I've been thinking of a conversation I had with Ben yesterday.

He's going to bring trouble down on us, isn't he?" Esther said, sitting down by the desk and reaching for a roll.

Jo nodded slowly, taking one for herself. "He said he's going to contest the trust and try to take over the business. Unfortunately, he's not really interested in the trading post," she said, and explained.

Esther listened, then considered things in silence as they ate. "I know you're angry, Jo, and it's human nature to strike back as hard as you've been hit," she said at last. "But that only escalates the problem. You have to remember that, deep down, Ben Stuart *is* a good man."

"I thought he was, once, but how can you say that now?" Jo asked.

"How can you *not* see it?" Esther countered. "That young man's suffered a hard public blow to his pride and he's feeling betrayed. He's in pain. He's facing the loss of his father and the end of a dream. He was coming home hoping to earn his father's love, and doesn't realize that it was his all along."

"But in his bitterness, he's turned against all of us."

"He's hurting because some people still think his dad killed himself—the ultimate act of a weak man. But you can help change things if you refuse to see him as your enemy."

"Turn the other cheek? That's Christian thinking, my friend, and I'm not Christian."

"It *is* Christian, but it's extremely practical, too. What sense is there in continuing to harbor resentment? See him as someone who's hurting and striking out because of that," Esther said. "That doesn't mean you have to accept wrong behavior from him, but you'll get farther if you help him see that you both have one thing in common—you want to honor his father's memory."

"I can't get through to him. I've tried," Jo said in a weary voice. "And if he wins and gets The Outpost, he's thinking of selling or closing it down."

Esther closed her eyes as if in prayer, then after a moment opened them again. "Invite him to the trading post and encourage him to get involved in our daily operations. Use whatever reason you can think of to persuade him to come, then let him get to know all of us. When he sees all the lives The Outpost touches daily, he'll be less likely to want to destroy what his father spent a lifetime building."

"Ben seems to do best in a disciplined, structured environment—like the army. I'm not sure he'd be able to cope with the daily challenges here," Jo said.

"You'll be making the decisions and there's structure in that," Esther said. "Let him be part of the operation. I'm sure that's what Tom intended on doing when his son returned—get Ben involved. By following through, you'll be honoring our old boss's memory. You'd also be helping the rest of us in another important way. If trouble comes to find us again, it can't hurt to have a man around who's trained to fight."

Especially if someone is out to kill me, Jo thought instantly. It was a good idea, even if that caller was just a crank. After Esther left, Jo nuked her coffee in the small microwave on the credenza. Everything Esther had said made sense, but she still hated the thought of going to Ben now.

Jo returned to her desk and picked up another roll. Just then, Leigh Ann came in and smiled. "Esther mentioned she might be bringing in some cinnamon rolls today," she said, looking hungrily at the basket.

Jo laughed and pushed it closer to her.

Leigh Ann took one and sat in front of Jo's desk. "I can't resist these, even though I know I might as well just glue them to my hips."

"You're not fat," Jo said.

"That's because I fight it every day." After several happy bites of the roll, she looked at Jo again. "Esther and I were talking earlier, and for what it's worth, I agree with her approach to the Ben Stuart problem. There's an old saying, 'Keep your friends close, and your enemies closer.' Let him come see for himself how much work goes into running the trading post. Then maybe he'll understand why it was left to you, not him."

"I have no other choice," Jo said. "I'm going to have to give it a try."

—SIX—

It was midmorning when Jo dialed Broome's office again. This time Mike's secretary put her through immediately.

"I was just about to call," he said. "This is about Ben, isn't it?"

She gave him an update on the situation. "Ben said you wouldn't represent him."

"That's true. It would be a conflict of interest. I can't work to break up a legal document I prepared and represented for his dad. There are also ethical considerations. I won't go against what Tom clearly wanted. Before you ask, I shouldn't represent you either, but I'm your best witness if it comes to that. Would you like me to recommend another attorney who may be able to help you?"

"Hold that thought. I'm hoping we won't have to take things that far."

"Ben can't win in court. He doesn't have a leg to stand on and I've already told him that. He'd only be wasting everyone's time and money."

"I really don't want to turn this into a war," she said, then gave him the highlights of her plan. "What's your opinion on this?"

Mike considered it for a while, then spoke. "Give it a try. As they say, it may not help, but it can't hurt."

"Thanks. Do you happen to know where Ben's staying? I didn't see any cars at his dad's place when I drove up, and the pickup is still at The Outpost."

"He's not staying at the family home. I don't think he really sees it as his yet. Unless he's changed motels, he's at the Desert Inn on Farmington's west side."

"Isn't that the motel that's been in the news recently because of all the criminal activity there?" she said.

"Yeah, prostitution mainly. I warned him the place had gone downhill in the past few years, but he didn't care. He said he could handle it. As a kid, he'd sometimes go there with his dad to meet out-of-town vendors. Those were good times for him, and he wanted to visit familiar ground and rekindle those memories."

Jo thanked Mike, picked up her purse, and headed out. Seeing Leigh Ann at the front register, she took a moment to fill her in. "I'm going to need you to handle things here while I'm gone. Are you okay with that?"

"Of course. There are three of us here, and we'll keep the back door double-locked."

Esther came up to Jo before she could leave. "Are you going to see Ben?" Seeing her nod, Esther continued. "Just remember, don't react in anger no matter what he says. Keep your guard up and don't lose the real fight—the one against yourself."

The drive to the motel took less than twenty minutes. Jo saw a rental car that could have been Ben's parked in the lot, but it wasn't in front of any particular door. Rather than disturb someone she didn't really want to meet, she went to the office to confirm the number with the clerk.

A greasy-haired man in his fifties with an armful of tattoos eyed her closely, then checked the information.

"You're just visiting, right?" he asked, his voice dripping with sarcasm. "How long you plan to stay?"

The odd question surprised her. Then she remembered the last time she'd read about this place in the Farmington newspaper. Hookers had made a deal with the former desk clerk to rent by the hour.

Jo found the possibility that he'd assumed she was a prostitute annoying. Was it her age, the clientele, or what she was wearing? She looked down at her blouse, a simple linen camp shirt. Nothing revealing or formfitting, and the only attention-getter was her purse—a woman thing men wouldn't give a rip about. She'd always had a thing for handbags. No drab black or brown leather types, thank you. She liked vivid colors, ones that made her smile. Today, needing a pick-me-up, she'd chosen a tomato-colored one with silvertone accents.

Tom had always teased her about her color choices. As an apprentice medicine woman, she should have considered earthtones, he believed, or a leather tooled handbag that looked Southwest-y. She'd had to point out that a medicine woman wasn't like a nun. It was perfectly all right for her to choose the bright cheerful colors she loved.

Jo got the room number, thanked the man without looking him in the face again, then drove the long way around the one-story building and parked next to the rental sedan. Beyond the closed door she could hear a television set going. She knocked, but no one answered.

Jo knocked again, this time louder, and heard someone call out.

"Hold your horses, will ya?" A second later, Ben came to the door. He was wearing jeans, and his hair was damp as if he'd just stepped out of the shower. As he stood there, revealing his wonderfully broad, bare chest, his scowl faded into a half smile.

"Sorry. I figured it was just another . . . woman . . . wanting to do business. GI on leave and all that . . ."

Uncomfortable, she entered the room at his invitation but remained standing. "I came with a proposition."

His eyebrows shot up, and she cringed. "Sorry. That's *not* what I meant."

"I'm disappointed, but you've sure got my attention."

"Finish getting dressed and let me take you for coffee," she said, glancing down at his bare feet to avoid any further distractions.

"Sounds good. Let me grab a shirt," he said.

"I need to talk to you about the trading post," she said as he reached into the nylon carry-on atop the luggage rack.

"I'm listening," he said.

It was hard to think clearly, seeing him half-dressed like this. The man before her was all roughness and muscle, unlike the boy she'd seen shirtless years back. Back then, he'd been a lanky sixteen-year-old kid. They'd gone wading in a ditch, despite the dangers of sudden currents that could trap you beneath debris in the water. He'd almost convinced her to take off her wet T-shirt when they heard a woman with two kids and a dozen or so sheep coming along the embankment. They'd scrambled up the side of the ditch bank at lightning speed and raced back to his pickup, laughing.

Focusing, she cleared her throat. "I came to invite you to join us at The Outpost. Take a look inside your father's world and get a feel for the business he worked so hard to build. Take part in the operation and help us deal with our customers. Be there when we open and when we close up at the end of the day. That's what your father had planned for you. Would you like that?"

"What if I still don't change my mind about taking you to court?" he asked, slipping a tan knit shirt over his head.

"Let's take this one step at a time. First, come see how your dad spent his days. Work side by side with us."

He nodded. "I'd like that. The trading post holds a lot of memories for me," he said, sitting on the bed and putting on a pair of brown leather boots. "I used to love watching my dad speak the little Navajo he knew to make connections."

Jo smiled. "People automatically liked your father. He treated everyone like family."

"Except for me. One of the reasons you ended up with the store, no doubt," he said coldly.

She took a deep breath, determined not to react. "I know you've spent years in harm's way and it's hard for you to lower your guard, but you're home now. People really do want to be friends with you and give you a break. Can't you lighten up just a little?"

As she looked into his hazel eyes, she saw no emotion there. Somewhere along the way, Ben had acquired the ability to completely shut down his feelings. Or maybe it was just one heckuva poker face. She wasn't sure which.

"Let's go to the trading post," he said, checking his pockets and producing a rental car key. "I'd like to start right away."

"Why don't you ride over with me?" she asked. "We can talk on the way."

"Sounds like a plan," he said as they stepped out the door.

※

As she drove west out of the city, tension shimmered in the air between them like the sun off the river to the south. "Your father was my friend," Jo said after a while. "I owe him more than I can ever put into words."

"The Outpost is easy enough to pronounce."

As difficult as it was, she forced herself to ignore Ben's smart-ass comment. "As great a gift as that was, it was the least of what he gave me. Whenever I needed help, your dad was there. Without him, I don't know how I would have coped after my father got diagnosed with cancer. Dad refused to go into an assisted-care facility, so I took care of him at home."

"From what I remember, you never got along with your dad," he said, looking down the road, then back in the side mirror. "Taking care of him must have been tough."

"Yeah, sometimes it was almost too much for me. Becoming my dad's caretaker turned into an exhausting, thankless job. My job at the trading post is what kept me sane."

"And now you're the owner of The Outpost."

There had been no recrimination in his tone. It had simply been a statement of fact. "Yes, I am."

"Do you like your new title?"

She wasn't sure if he was baiting her or not, but she decided to give him the benefit of the doubt. "I hope it won't be my only one. As soon as things settle down a bit, I'll also be continuing my apprenticeship as a medicine woman."

"Wait—you, a Singer?" He looked down at her purse.

"Not you, too," she said, and laughed. "Your father thought that meant I should start looking like a cleric or a missionary."

Ben smiled. "Back in high school, you used to carry around a huge, bright orange canvas purse. You took a lot of teasing for it, too. Some of the guys called it your orange barrel."

"Actually, it was a tote," she said, chuckling. "I'd made it out of some fabric I'd found at a yard sale. I was proud of that bag, no matter what everyone else thought."

"You always did go your own way," he said. "I don't know why I was so surprised when you dumped me." His face hardened. "You ripped my guts out, did you know that? I was going through all kind of shit, and when I needed you the most, you bailed."

"Ben, I gave you plenty of warning. The real problem was that you'd stopped listening to anyone but yourself back then." She clamped her mouth shut. "No. Let's not go over the past like this. It serves no purpose. We're different people now, and that's all that really matters."

"I know who I am, but who are you?" he asked quietly.

"A woman who has worked hard all her life and, now, thanks to a gift from a friend, owns her own business, one that will continue to take care of a lot of other people." She paused. "I trusted your father and he trusted me."

"But neither of you were willing to trust me, is that it?"

"Stop trying to put words in my mouth," she said, raising her voice. Drawing in a breath, she forced herself to calm down. "Your father loved you—unconditionally."

"No, that's not the way it was between us."

"You're wrong. He wasn't one for flowery speeches, that's for sure, but his feelings for you were strong. You should have heard the way he spoke about you. He was really looking forward to seeing you again. He'd bought two new fly rods so he could take you fishing for trout up by Navajo Lake. He knew you'd love that. He also bought a treadmill for his office and one of those weight benches. He remembered how you loved to work out."

Jo saw him staring ahead, silently digesting her words.

"Tell me about the trading post," he said at long last. "I've noticed some changes, like the expanded grocery section and snack counter. The inventory now also includes a lot more Native American arts and crafts and several new glass display cases. What else goes on there these days?"

For a second, Jo wondered if there was something in that particular inventory that the threatening caller had been referring to. Had Tom cheated someone, or more likely, had a former customer felt he'd been cheated somehow? She'd put that research on her to-do list, but right now, she had to play it cool and stick to the current problem—Ben.

"I'd rather you see things for yourself. Talk to the staff and the artisans who come in. The Outpost has a heartbeat all its own." She slowed and made the left turn across the median into the long driveway.

"I'll do that," he said.

She circled around the trading post and parked in one of the employee slots. "Your dad's Chevy is still parked in its spot. Why aren't you using it?"

"When I saw your truck, I figured you and The Outpost could use it more, so I put the keys back in Dad's desk drawer."

He looked around the cab of her truck, noting the duct-taped seats. "How old is this bucket of bolts, anyway?"

She laughed. "Hey, it's still running, and even if it's older than we are, it's got a new engine and it's reliable. It handled pretty well the other day, didn't it?"

"Yeah, not too bad, but I've seen faster tanks," he said with a straight face.

They went inside through the loading dock using her key and the touchpad. Esther, at the rear counter folding some clothing atop it, was the first to see and greet Ben. Hearing them, Regina looked over her shoulder from her position at the front register and waved.

Since he'd already been introduced to everyone, Jo gestured around the shop. "Where would you like to start? Out here? Or would you prefer office work?"

"Let me stay out front. What can I do?"

Esther spoke first. "I have some clothing samples I made using the fabric and patterns we stock—a blouse, a skirt, some pants. Once people watch me sewing a garment right before their eyes and see the possibilities, it encourages them to try it for themselves. Why don't you help me find the best places to put them up on display? I'd like to hang them up."

"Lead the way, ma'am," Ben said.

Jo watched him walk away with Esther. She couldn't have picked a better companion for Ben.

Leigh Ann came over to join her. "I know you've been handling a million details lately," she said in her soft drawl, "but I just have to ask. Do you have any idea when we can expect our checks? I'm scraping the bottom of the barrel right now."

"Payroll's done. All I need to do now is print the checks and get Mike to cosign."

She smiled with relief. "Phew! Up to now, I had no idea how I was going to pay this month's electric bill."

Hearing Esther laugh from halfway across the room, Jo glanced over and saw Ben with a big smile on his face. "I'd forgotten how charming he can be when he wants," Jo said softly. "When it comes to dealing with the public, he may be a chip off the old block."

"Maybe, or maybe not," Leigh Ann whispered. "As my mama used to say, 'Just 'cause a chicken has wings don't mean it can fly.'"

Jo laughed softly, then returned to her desk in the lunch/break room. Calling up the business spreadsheet on the computer, she studied the numbers before her. Business was starting to pick up again, but things were moving so slowly that cash flow had reached a critical level. If she lost the ability to purchase inventory, their retail sales would continue to decline, especially in the grocery section, where foodstuffs had expiration dates and needed to be rotated constantly.

She'd have to find ways to grow the business, but that meant getting back all their lost customers, and more.

The trading post had assets, of course. She knew that other area merchants would scoop up their jewelry and saddles in a second if she offered them a good deal, just above wholesale. Their nonperishable merchandise could also be used as collateral for a bank loan, but there was no comprehensive list of the store's inventory. The tax records contained the minimum information required, mostly the cost of acquisition and estimated value, but nothing more specific than that. Tom had insisted on keeping a lot of information in his head or on handwritten lists. His distrust of computers had been almost legendary.

At least payroll, at Jo's insistence, had been set up in their systems. Jo had taken the checks from the printer and begun placing them inside a manila envelope when Regina came into the office.

Jo greeted her with a smile and gestured for her to have a seat.

"I'm in trouble, Jo. My whole family is," Regina said.

"What's going on?" Jo asked.

"Pete broke his arm at a construction site yesterday. I didn't even find out about it until I got home. The company paid the medical bill, but no one's going to hire a carpenter with only one working arm. It could take weeks for him to receive unemployment, and he's not going to get that much with his work history. We've been living from paycheck to paycheck as it is. I need more hours, Jo—badly. Without those, I won't have enough to keep food on our table."

Jo exhaled softly, noticing the bank account balance still on the screen. Under different circumstances, she might have been able to extend Regina some credit here at the store, but as it was, it simply wasn't an option. Without a positive cash flow, the business couldn't operate.

"We haven't had much traffic here lately. Funds are very tight for us right now," Jo said.

"Maybe I could stock and clean the place at night—anything—please. My mom's taking care of the baby, so it's all on me now. I've got to pull in some more money. I'd get a second job, but no one's hiring. I've asked around."

Jo remembered a time when her paycheck was the only thing that had kept her dad and her going. Although she should have said no, she just couldn't do it. "I'll give you as many hours as I can, if you can be flexible. Start by coming in on the next morning you usually have off, tomorrow, I believe, and we'll work it out from there. I'm going to have to inventory absolutely everything the store has on hand. You can help."

"That's going to be a big job."

"Exactly. While most of our groceries, hardware, and wholesale purchases are already computerized, I need to bring the rest of the trading post into the twenty-first century," Jo said. "After that's done, we'll want to drum up new business by contacting all our special-order customers, the ones who've commissioned artwork and jewelry from us in the past. We need to let them know we're still here and running strong."

"Leigh Ann's already on that, I think," Regina said.

"Really?" Jo said, surprised.

Regina nodded. "She said that we all had to look for ways to get business going here. Otherwise, we'd be on the street before Christmas."

"She's got a point," Jo said, pleased by Leigh Ann's initiative. "Could you ask her to come into my office?"

"Sure, and thanks for the extra work. I'll take as many hours as I can."

Regina left, and Leigh Ann came in minutes later. "What's up?"

Jo thanked her for taking the initiative contacting previous customers.

"I'm not very far along," she said, "and I haven't got any new orders yet, but I'll keep at it."

"I really appreciate what you're doing, Leigh Ann."

"This is your store now, Jo, but we all have bits of ourselves here, too. This job became my lifeline after Kurt's hunting accident. Knowing that I was needed and valued kept me going. Now I'm ready to give back. Don't y'all call it balance?"

Jo smiled and nodded. "It's how we walk in beauty."

"There you go, then," she said with a happy smile. "One more thing. I think you should call our biggest customers yourself. Everyone likes to feel important, and getting a call from the new owner would hit just the right chord. The day before Tom passed on, I remember Herb Matthews called. I took the message. Herb—he likes the first name basis—always places substantial orders."

"The man who owns the art school up by the community college?"

"That's him," Leigh Ann said.

"His special orders can be a challenge to fill, but he pays us well for our efforts. Last time, he wanted a special rug woven in certain colors for his wife. He also insisted that it be done by a Traditionalist who'd do all the work the old way—never weaving during storms, and never sketching the design first. He told me that he wanted someone who worked from the heart."

"I remember. Tom called you in on that because you have a knack for matching the right craftsman to each job," Leigh Ann said. "Which begs the question, how on earth do you do that each and every time?"

Jo smiled. "When I was much younger, all our artists seemed larger than life to me. They had the ability to create something tangible and beautiful out of nothing more than a picture they saw in their minds. I wanted to be just like them, so I started going to their studios, galleries, and every art event or show I could find. I studied and worked in every medium that appealed to me, but soon it became painfully clear that I had no artistic talent whatsoever," she said, laughing.

"But that's how you got to meet so many local artists," Leigh Ann said.

"Exactly."

Just then the phone rang. Jo answered, holding up her hand, signaling Leigh Ann to wait. After a quick hello, she put the caller on hold. "While I take this, would you go ask Ben to drive over to Mike Broome's office in Farmington and get these payroll checks signed?" Jo held out the big manila envelope.

"My pleasure," Leigh Ann said, taking the envelope.

As Leigh Ann went to find Ben, Jo picked the phone back up. It was a vendor, and she knew it was going to take a while.

By the time she looked up again, Leigh Ann was at her door, looking as pale as a ghost.

"What's wrong, Leigh Ann?" Jo stepped over to the door and found Esther was also there, gripping her Bible tightly. Right behind both women was a tall, slender, Hispanic-looking man wearing large, dark sunglasses and a baseball cap.

Jo gasped as she saw the gun aimed at the backs of her women employees. Instantly she thought of the caller—the one who'd shot Tom. Was this him, and were they all about to die?

"Sorry, Jo. I walked over to help him and he pulled a gun," Leigh Ann mumbled. "Then he got Esther."

"No more talking, and don't look at me. Just do what I say and you'll stay alive," the man ordered in a thick Spanish accent. "Put your cell phone on the counter, then move over to that big door," he said, pointing toward the produce locker with a gloved hand.

As Jo got rid of her cell phone, she took a quick glance around the big room. At least no customers were in the store. If they could just survive a few minutes, or she could get to Tom's shotgun below the counter. . . .

The man with the gun waved it in her direction. "Stop looking around, Indian. Get inside there before I shoot the old lady."

Leigh Ann took Esther's hand, then Jo's, and they walked together into the produce locker.

"We'll freeze to death," Esther pleaded.

"Hush," Leigh Ann whispered. "We'll be safer in here."

"Listen to the bitch," the man with the gun said. "If you try to come out, I'll kill you all."

He slammed the door shut on them and the light went out, plunging them into total darkness.

Jo fumbled for the inside switch. When it came on, she saw Leigh Ann hugging Esther tightly. "We're still alive," Jo whispered. "Don't do anything to attract his attention. He can have whatever he wants as long as it's not us."

She looked back at the heavy galvanized steel door. There was an emergency knob to push and open the door—a safety measure—but it would be stupid to try that now. If this man was

Tom's killer, he'd finish them off without a thought. She had no doubt he was out there now, trying to find whatever it was that had caused Tom's death. If only she knew what it was, she'd gladly give it up right now.

Jo looked around, trying to think of a way to keep the door shut if he tried to open it . . . and shoot them. If there was a rope or wire, they could attach it to the bolted-on shelves and hold the door shut. Unfortunately, there was nothing like that where they were, and nobody was wearing a belt. They'd need more than one anyway to reach.

"Well, if we're going to be in here for a while, why don't you turn up the thermostat?" Esther said, her voice finally back. She pointed toward a control a foot above the light switch.

"Of course. What was I thinking?" Jo said, turning the temperature wheel with her finger up to fifty degrees. "At least the cooler and fan won't come back on."

There was a sliding sound on the floor outside, then a couple of loud thumps at the base of the door. A sliver of wood poked through the rubber seal at the floor.

"He's jammed a wedge into the outside. We'll have to force our way out," Leigh Ann said. "At least we're not locked in."

And he'll be less likely to come after us, Jo thought, somewhat relieved.

"Let's huddle together to stay warm," Esther said, reaching out for Jo and Leigh Ann.

"We need to keep listening, too. Maybe we can track his movements. As soon as he leaves . . . ," Jo said, her voice trailing off.

They remained quiet for several minutes, but couldn't hear anything whatsoever. Finally Leigh Ann spoke. "Should we assume he's gone?"

Jo shook her head. "I just heard footsteps. It sounds like he's coming from Tom's office."

"Think he's trying to break into the safe?" Leigh Ann asked.

"That's where the money is . . . what we have of it," Jo answered, nodding. "I just hope Regina doesn't come back from lunch early today. I don't want her running into this guy."

Esther nodded. "Amen."

As they waited, Jo considered moving the cold produce boxes off the shelves and stacking them in front of the door, then realized it would only restrict their own movements if they had to try to race past their captor. All they could really do now was wait.

After another twenty minutes, the only sound they could hear was that of their own breathing. Then Jo heard a faint call.

"Hey, anyone here? Where are you guys? Jo?"

"It's Ben," she said, smiling and nodding to the others. "Ben! We're in here."

"Help!" Leigh Ann yelled, and Jo and Esther joined in.

"Jo, you in there?" Ben's voice much closer now.

"Yes, but the door is jammed at the bottom."

"I see it. Wait a second."

There were two thumps, then a loud click and the door swung open.

Ben met her halfway, throwing his arms around her in a big hug. "What's going on? You're as cold as an iceberg. Ladies, come out and get warm," he added, seeing Leigh Ann and Esther still inside.

"A robber with a gun. He locked us in here. What did he take?" Jo said, looking around his shoulder but not letting go of his warmth.

"No hugs for me? I'm getting a jacket," Esther grumbled, stepping past them and grabbing a freezer coat from a hook on the wall.

"Me, too," Leigh Ann added.

Jo reluctantly broke free from Ben's warm embrace, turned the refrigerator back on, then shut the big door. Ben handed her a third jacket, and she took it gratefully.

"So that's why the entrance was locked," Ben said, stepping

back and looking around the big room. "I had to use my key. And I found this out on the front steps." He held up the pistol. "It's a toy. Shoots plastic bullets."

"That's . . . it? Damn! I should have kicked the bastard in the balls, then beat him over the head with that thing," Leigh Ann said. "We've been conned."

"Tell me about it." Jo suddenly felt a lot better, in spite of what they'd just gone through. They hadn't faced a killer, just a low-life thief taking advantage of their current situation. "Let's go see what he stole. Esther, check the registers first, and Leigh Ann, the high-end cases. Make lists. I'll check in Tom's office."

"We need to call the sheriff's department," Ben said.

Jo picked up her cell phone, which was still on the counter, and walked to Tom's office. A chair was tipped over, and drawers were open. The computer hardware appeared to be intact, but the safe door was wide open.

"How'd he—?" Jo said, crouching by it and looking inside. Her stomach was turning flip-flops. Her hope that the robbery was unrelated to Tom's murder had just been crushed. She tried to remember the man's voice. Was he the same guy who'd threatened her over the phone? Maybe.

Ben glanced at the safe's inside shelves stacked high with ledgers and records on disk and paper. "Dad must have been forced to give up the right combination the night he—"

"Yeah, but the inner box, the one with the store's cash and checks, is still locked tight. He didn't get in there, and I don't see anything missing. What the hell was he looking for?" Standing, she looked around. "He didn't even ask for my keys."

"You three either just laid eyes on my dad's killer or someone who works with him. Call Detective Wells," Ben said.

Jo nodded, looking up the number. Maybe it was time to let the detective know about the caller and his threats, too. Next time, the gun might be for real, and she couldn't risk everyone else's lives.

"The robber was probably watching the place, then moved in as soon as the coast was clear—no customers in the store," Ben said. "I should have been here."

"That would have only changed his timing. He may even have staked us out for a couple of days, looking for the best time," Jo said, looking up as the back door opened.

"Back from lunch," Regina said. "What'd I miss?"

While waiting for a deputy to arrive, Jo confirmed that nothing appeared to be missing except for the cash from the one register that had been opened—less than two hundred dollars. Leigh Ann and Esther confirmed that the Navajo rug display had been sorted through, and that the unlocked storage drawers had all been rifled, but nothing else was missing. He hadn't even tried to force open the display cases, enclosed in clear Plexiglas and virtually unbreakable.

A deputy arrived—Detective Wells was on another call—took their report, the physical description they had of the robber, and left with the plastic revolver. He promised to pass his report to Detective Wells.

Jo encouraged everyone to go back to work, and their routines were reestablished quickly.

Moments later when Leigh Ann appeared at Jo's door, she had a smile on her face. "I just found the checks. Ben must have set them down by the register when he came in. You want me to hand them out?"

"Go ahead."

Leigh Ann seemed to hesitate, and that caught Jo's attention. "What's wrong?"

"It's just something I overheard earlier today, before all the excitement. I've been wondering if I should say anything. . . ."

"Does it concern the trading post?"

She nodded. "And Ben Stuart."

"Come in and shut the door behind you," she said. "Now what's up?" she added, after Leigh Ann took a seat.

"I overheard Ben asking Regina if you and Tom had a thing going," Leigh Ann said.

"A *thing*?" Jo took a deep breath, trying to calm down, but it wasn't working. "How did Regina react?"

"I didn't hear what she said, but Ben walked away looking really embarrassed. You want me to tell him to get his sorry butt in here?"

"No. He and I will step outside and have a talk. I don't want anyone else to overhear what I've got to say, especially any customers."

Leigh Ann nodded once. "Go ahead, hon. I'll hand out the paychecks while you're busy reaming him out."

Jo found Ben standing behind Regina, who was busy checking out a good-looking Anglo cowboy near the roping saddles.

"Ben, a word, please?"

He followed her outside through the storeroom and down the steps of the loading dock. "Where we going?"

"Why are you being such a bonehead?" she said, spinning around to face him.

"*Bonehead?*" His mouth twitched, but he stopped short of cracking a smile.

"Listen up. I thought we'd settled this. I was *not* having an affair with your father, you dumb-ass."

He blinked, but said nothing.

"I adored your father, but not in the disgusting way you're trying to suggest. Your dad was my *friend*. After my dad became bedridden, I stopped having a life. My entire day revolved around his needs, and I spiraled into a depression that nearly destroyed me. Your dad stepped in just in time. He helped me see that I didn't have to stop living because my dad was dying, and that sometimes when we're doing all we can do, it has to be enough. I owe him for that and all the other times he was there for me. That's why I'm not punching you in the nose right now."

"Oh, now I'm really scared."

She glared at him, took a step away, then whirled and slammed her fist into his jaw.

—SEVEN—

S he should have aimed lower. "Ow, you dirtbag!" she said, stepping back, cradling her injured hand. "You have a chin like a rock wall."

"Are you okay? You should have just slapped my face or punched me in the gut. At least you wouldn't have risked breaking your fingers."

"Don't you *dare* patronize me! The only reason I invited you into *my* trading post is out of respect for your father. You, I can do without. If you ever go behind my back again, you're out of here. Clear?" She strode back to the loading dock.

He caught up to her on the steps and placed a hand on her shoulder, stopping her. "I'm sorry. I really am."

His eyes held hers with an intensity that took her breath away. She turned away, glad for the pain in her hand that demanded her attention. It was a much-needed distraction. As she looked down at the redness already there, she gritted her teeth.

"Put some ice on it, sooner the better," he said.

"No time, I need my hand. I have to make a call. There's a patron of ours who wants a special order . . ." she said, then winced as she glanced down at her knuckles. Her index finger was starting to swell.

"Get some ice on that or you won't be able to use your hand for a few days. While you do that, I'll make the call for you. I can be one helluva salesman. Trust me."

"Trust is in real short supply between us right now."

"You're right, so let me redeem myself."

As she looked into his eyes, she remembered the boy with the penetrating gaze that had always made her heart beat faster and her brain go blank. She looked away, refusing to dwell on memories. That was then; this was now. Too bad that he looked better than ever. Thinking of appearances, she looked at her hand and tried moving her fingers. Another knuckle was starting to swell and her whole hand felt stiff.

"I've had that same problem, slamming my hands into something—or someone. Like I said, a little ice, the sooner the better, and you'll be as good as new. You didn't hit me that hard."

"Thanks. That just makes me want to try it again."

"I'll give you one free shot when your hand heals. How's that?"

There was a contagious grin on his face, and she had to bite back a smile. "Next time I'll aim for your balls."

As they went inside, Esther glanced at her, then at her hand, but didn't comment. Leigh Ann's focus was instantly on Ben's face.

"Somebody needs some ice," Leigh Ann said without asking for an explanation.

Moments later, Leigh Ann walked inside Jo's office carrying a plastic bag filled with ice. Ben had gone directly to his father's old office and was already on the phone.

"You socked him in the jaw, didn't you?" she said, then seeing Jo nod, continued. "I've got to teach you a few things. Before I married Kurt, I served drinks in an El Paso titty bar, and it seems like every shift some cowboy or roughneck tried to grab my ass. I had to haul off and slap my share of drunks and horny morons. Rule number one is never aim for something as hard as your fist. Slap them across the cheeks, or punch them in the package if they're standing. You can also stomp their toes. Knees or heels are the weapons of choice."

"I just wanted him to shut up."

Leigh Ann chuckled. "I hear you, but sometimes it's better to just walk away. You're not really going to change anything. Fight the battles you can win and forget the rest."

As Leigh Ann left, Jo continued to hold the ice bag over her hand. Minutes ticked by, and after a while her hand began to improve. This time when she tried to flex her hands, her fingers actually cooperated. The swelling had gone down by half. Maybe it was just the cold numbing things, but either way, it helped.

Hearing a knock on her door, Jo glanced up and saw Ben.

"I spoke to Herb Matthews," he said. "I'm not sure we can fill his order. To be honest, I'm not sure anyone could."

She waved him to a chair. "Tell me what he needs."

"He's been working with some special art students— elementary school kids. Herb wants them to learn to see with their hearts and their imagination, not just try and copy what's before them. To that end, he wants to commission a special sculpture. He wants something that shows perception, imagination, and spirit, not just a statue, 'no matter how beautifully rendered'—and those were his precise words. Herb's going to keep it hidden in a box so the students won't be able to see it at all. They'll only be able to reach inside and touch it. Then they'll have to draw what they're able to visualize from that limited exposure."

Ben handed her a sheet of paper. "That's what he's willing to pay, but finding an artist for a job this difficult to define is going to be nearly impossible. And if Herb isn't happy with the results—"

"That won't happen. The trading post has dealt with him for years. Call him back and tell him we'll accept the project. Once we confirm that fee with the artist, he'll need to pay half up front, as usual."

"Okay," he answered with a shrug.

She stared at the figure Matthews had quoted Ben. Their portion of the sale would carry them nearly a month, and that would buy them vital time. Hopefully, between now and then, business would pick up.

While Ben left to make the call, Jo used another line to try to track down the one artist she knew would be ideal for the job—Melvin Littlewater. The Navajo sculptor was legally blind—the result of an accident with a drunk driver—and not easy to work with at times. Yet his creations were unique and highly sought after because they seemed to have a life of their own. What he'd lost in sight, Melvin made up for in perception and heart.

There was only one problem. She'd been trying to get hold of Melvin for days now, hoping to touch base now that she was the new owner, and hadn't had any luck. She'd tried everything she could think of, but Melvin's cell phone appeared to be turned off. She'd also tried the secondary numbers she'd been given, including his relatives and suppliers, but still hadn't been able to contact him.

That usually indicated that Melvin was in one of his dark moods, which meant locating him would be all but impossible. Since his accident, he'd occasionally go into what Jo thought of as his isolation periods. Yet during those times, his work never suffered—in fact, it was just the opposite. Whatever he produced would show real artistic genius.

Ben came back in. "That money's as good as in the bank. Matthews is already convinced that we'll find the right artist for the job, so he's going to hand-deliver his check by the end of the day."

Jo invited him to look at the screen. "This is why that was so important to us," she said, showing him the account after the payroll, and less the $203 taken by the robber.

"I'm no business major, but I'd guess there's only enough money there to pay bills and payroll through the current quarter. Isn't that cutting it pretty close?"

"Unless business picks up at least to last month's level, and stays there, we won't be able to make it through the fall. That's why it was so difficult to let Regina work extra hours, but she's in a tight spot and needs help. We don't really have the money to spare, but she's part of the trading post family."

"Their personal lives aren't your problem. You're giving them a job. That should be the extent of your involvement with your employees," Ben said.

"No. Everything is connected, and what affects one, affects all. Without honoring those connections, there's no harmony and no one can walk in beauty."

"You're a small business owner now. Maybe it's time for you to shift your priorities and focus on the bottom line. If you can't stay in business, nobody will have a job, not even you."

"I'm Navajo, and I'd like this business to reflect the values I've been taught."

"How would my dad have handled this situation?"

"First of all, he wasn't Navajo. I also can't speak for him, but I can tell you this. Your father had his own set of values and never put profits ahead of people. He treated everyone fairly and lived in harmony . . . until this past month, that is. Something had been bothering him."

"What do you think the problem was?"

"I really don't know," she answered. Technically, she wasn't lying. She still had no idea what Tom's killer was after. "Your father and I worked together, but to him, any conversation that dealt with feelings was just 'girl talk.'"

Ben laughed. "That was him, all right."

"I miss him," she said softly.

"Yeah, me, too."

Neither said anything for several long moments, silently mourning the man who'd been such a huge part of their lives. Jo looked around the room, then sighed. "All that's happened since your father's death leads me to believe that he was killed because of this trading post—either the place itself or something inside here. I have no idea what it could be, but it's possible everyone who works here may be in danger," she said. "First it was the burglars in that green pickup, then today another robber confronted us in broad daylight. This time we got off lucky. Next time, his gun could be real and the stakes higher."

"My father may not have confided in you, but you might know more than you realize. The way I see it, nobody alive knows more about this place than you do."

"Maybe so, but I still haven't come up with any answers," Jo said.

"Could be that the robber found what he wanted and has no reason to come back," Ben said.

"I hope it's true, but we can't afford to assume that." Her stomach growled loudly, and she reached for the candy bar at the corner of her desk.

"Is that all you're having for lunch?"

"Yeah. This'll give me fast energy. I need to make some calls and get some paperwork done."

"Sounds to me like you could use a good dinner and maybe a dependable bodyguard to share some downtime with," he said. "How about I take you out this evening for a decent meal? I'm good at guarding and eating."

"Dinner . . . I'm not sure that's a good idea."

"Why not? You have to eat, and it's not like we don't have a lot to talk about. Besides, I'm tall, strong, and handsome. Well, taller and stronger than I was. The handsome part, well, that's nothing new."

"Since when did you become so humble?"

"I'm twice as good-looking as I say. That's humble. So how about it?"

"Okay," she said, laughing. "As long as it's not a date."

"It's dinner. You can call that whatever you want."

"Afterwards, I'll have to come back here. I need to work late tonight."

"No problem, just keep the doors locked tight."

As her phone rang again and she answered, Ben slipped out of her office. She spent the next twenty minutes calling various places and leaving messages for Melvin, but so far, no one had seen him.

Frustrated, she began pacing. She wasn't at all sure what to do next. They'd already accepted the commission, or soon would. She *had* to find Melvin. They needed the money, and Melvin's skills made him the perfect choice. She'd go to his home, but unfortunately, she had no idea where he lived.

Leigh Ann came in holding a cold soft drink and placed it on her desk. "You look worried. Is there anything I can do?"

"I've been trying to track down Melvin," she said, filling her in. "At first, I was just going to ask him if he had any new sculptures we could buy and put up for sale, but now I have a special job for him. The problem is I can't seem to make contact."

"I may be able to help. Melvin and I . . . have a special connection."

"I had no idea you two were involved."

"No, it's nothing like that," Leigh Ann said quickly. "He and I understand each other, that's all. Have you noticed that he gets gruffy when anyone else tries to help him through the store? Yet if I'm here, he'll ask for my hand and let me lead the way." She smiled. "He makes me feel beautiful in all the ways that really count." She gave Jo a hesitant smile. "I don't think he means anything by it, but I'd like to believe he and I are more than just business acquaintances."

"Then how about locating him for me? Tell him about the special order, and see if he's willing to take it on," Jo said, giving her the notes she'd taken and the details. "I'm between a rock and a hard place right now, Leigh Ann. We need some positive cash flow for a change. I could really use your help."

"I'll get started on this, then," Leigh Ann said.

Jo worked hard for the rest of the day. Unfortunately, sales remained unspeakably slow. By the time the trading post closed for the day, she was worn out, but her work was far from done.

"Where do you want me to pick you up for dinner?" Ben asked as she checked the front door locks one more time. The rest of the staff had already left, and only the storeroom lights were on.

"Why don't we keep it simple, Ben? The sandwiches in the cooler are fresh, and we can grab a couple of Cokes and eat in the break room."

"No, I think we should both get away from here for a bit," he said. "Let me take you to the Steak-Out. It's not fancy, just a family place, but the food's great—according to Del, your stockroom guy."

"Sounds good." Jo accompanied him out the back, then double-locked the door and checked the knob. The outside security lights would be coming on soon, since the sun had already set. She looked anxiously down the road, wondering if they should have a gate put in and keep it closed after hours.

As they walked down the steps of the loading dock together, Ben glanced over at her. "Tell me something, Jo. If you become a medicine woman, what'll happen to the trading post?"

"First, becoming a Singer takes years and years, so that's not going to happen anytime soon. When it finally does, I'm hoping The Outpost will also be running on track and providing me with a steady income. That way I'll be able to hold Sings for patients who can't afford the regular fees. Many of our people just don't have the means to pay a Singer anymore, even in trade," she said. "When my dad was sick, he really wanted to have a Sing done, but we never had any money left after paying for medicines and food. I could have worked something out with my teacher, but Dad wouldn't allow it. It was pride, but at the time, that was all he had left."

"Sometimes that, and honor, are enough."

His simple words touched her. "Who are you these days, Ben?" she said in a soft voice. "It's been so long, but from what I can see, the boy I knew is gone."

"Yes, he is," Ben answered in a low, deep voice. "Fighting a war changes a man. It pulls you apart piece by piece, and if you're lucky, time puts you back together again. But you're never the same afterwards."

She waited for him to continue, but he never did.

Before long, they arrived at the roadside restaurant in the old farming community of Kirtland. The parking lot was about half full and they found a parking space up close when a patron pulled out. As they walked inside, Jo hoped that over dinner he'd tell her more about himself, maybe talk about what his life had been like as a soldier. Yet balance was part of walking in beauty. If she wanted to know more about him, she'd have to share something in return.

There was no hostess at the moment, so Ben led them to a seat toward the back of the dining area, facing the window and main entrance. "Most people like seats by the window," she said. "Why did you choose this spot?"

"Habit," he replied, checking out the room and the diners. "Overseas I learned the hard way not to make myself an easy target. Since we don't know what the situation is regarding my father and the trading post, I'm keeping my guard up. From this spot we can see what's going on outside, and check out whoever's about to come inside." He paused, then smiled at her and continued. "It's all part of the new me, but from what I've seen

so far, you haven't changed much. You're still the most organized person I know."

"It's up to me to get everything done, but I don't make as
many lists as I used to," she said, and smiled. "You used to hate
that."

"I was a jerk back then. I hated a lot of things—including
myself."

She was surprised by the comment. "I never knew that. You
were always so sure of yourself."

"I was being defensive. It was the exact opposite of the way I
felt inside."

"And now?"

"I outgrew all that. What you see is what you get, pretty
much, at least while I'm in civilian clothes."

His quiet confidence appealed to her on a multitude of lev-
els. Ben was all tension and hard edges that softened only when
he smiled. That hint of danger that had always drawn her to
him was still there, but it was kept under tight control now. It
teased her imagination, making her yearn to touch him, to go
past all those walls and see the unguarded side of the man she
was just beginning to know.

Twenty minutes later, they were enjoying a really nice dinner, and she took advantage of the moment to try to get
him to open up. "After all you've experienced as a soldier, normal life must seem unspeakably boring," she said, enjoying the
mesquite-grilled steak she'd ordered with broccoli and a side of
fries.

"Back in high school, I thought living an ordinary life would
be like dying one inch at a time. Now, the side of me that was
looking for adventure found all it could handle and was laid to

rest out there in the mountains of Afghanistan. Normal—even downright boring—appeals a lot to me these days."

"For a while, or for the duration?" she asked quietly. "You're going back into combat within a few months, right?"

He nodded. "Yeah. That's why I don't like making long-term plans. When you focus on tomorrow, you can lose track of today, and that's all we really have. We kid ourselves, thinking we'll be around forever, and try to plan for every contingency, but that's just a waste of the time we do have."

"I *have* to plan ahead. Becoming a medicine woman will take time and effort, but it's my way of connecting my tribe's past to my own future. That circle will someday complete and define me," she said. "That's how I'll run the trading post, too. I'll build on your father's dream with an eye on tomorrow."

"From what I've seen of the bottom line, you have your work cut out for you. It's not going to be easy."

"Speaking of that, you really helped me out today by nailing down that special order."

"Have you considered cutting staff to stay afloat? Businesses do that all the time. Those who want to keep their jobs will pick up the slack," he said. "Or you can reduce salaries or hours."

"Never happen. Once you get to know the others, you'll understand why neither of those is an option. Look at what happened today. Esther, Leigh Ann, and I stood together and that helped us face the danger. It's not company loyalty. It goes beyond that. What I will do is cut my own pay."

"Will you have enough to meet your own expenses?"

"Not if you're not going to pick up the tab tonight."

He laughed. "Don't worry. I've got you covered."

As they were finishing their meal, Jo told him more about her plans for the trading post. "I want to phase out the tourist-type trinkets and specialize in Native American crafts." She leaned back and sipped the last of her coffee. "For years, your father has ordered cotton Navajo look-alike rugs from Mexico.

There's another big order scheduled pretty soon, but after those sell out, I'm thinking of cutting them out completely, or at least way back."

"Why? Do they take forever to sell?"

"No, actually it's just the opposite, at least for the past six months or so. The last order was gone in a few days and, this time, all the rugs woven in the Chinle style have already been presold. As soon as I get word they're ready, I'll be going to Juárez to pick them up," Jo said.

"Chinle. Those are the rugs with repeating geometric designs and alternating bands of solid earthtones. Am I right?"

"Yes, you've got a good memory. The rugs can also use natural wool and come in red, white, and black. They're very popular and usually don't take a lot of time to weave."

"So, if they sell like hotcakes and you're making money, what's the problem?"

"It undermines the work of our local weavers," she said, then paused and smiled sheepishly. "Hey, I've been doing all the talking. There has to be balance between us, so why don't you tell me about what's going on in your life? Your father told me once that you'd become an exceptional marksman in an infantry company. Then, more recently, he said you'd transferred to a medical unit. Why the change? Seen enough combat?"

"Sniper school was something that appealed to me at first," he said. "Dad had taught me how to shoot, and when I enlisted, I figured that getting the bad guys should be at the top of my list. I wanted my contribution to count."

She recalled the medals he'd worn on his uniform at the funeral, then later in the lawyer's office. "I have a feeling you did just that."

"I accomplished my missions."

As the waitress refilled their coffee cups, Jo noted the tiny scars on the back of his hands, and the way he was gripping his cup. Although Ben had lapsed into a long silence, waiting for his response wasn't hard for her. She was used to long pauses. It was part of the way Navajos normally spoke.

"Snipers usually work in two-man teams except in urban combat," he said at last. "One day my spotter and I ran into some trouble." He stared at his coffee, lost in thought. "Things got bad in a hurry, and some that shouldn't have died, did. The army conducted a full investigation and my partner and I were cleared, but I requested a new mission after that. Eventually I transferred out and ended up working with a medevac unit."

His words had been simple, but the total absence of emotion in his voice told her a different story. Whatever horror he'd lived through still haunted him.

Uncertain of what else to say, she waited, finishing her second cup of coffee. "Did your partner transfer out with you?"

"No. After that deployment, Paul and I returned stateside with our unit. He went home to his family and a month later ate a bullet," he said quietly.

She sucked in her breath.

"I faced my own crisis, too, but at least I came out of it with a pulse. Dad helped me, mostly by being himself."

"What do you mean?"

"He told me to man up and learn to deal." Ben gave her a wry smile. "It was a far cry from all the psychobabble I was hearing, and precisely what I needed."

"You two had your ups and downs, but he was very proud of who you'd become."

"Did he say that to you?"

"In his own way," she said. "It was a while back, but I remember him telling me that the army was starting to make a man out of you. He then said that it was too bad you hadn't signed up as a marine, 'cause the job would have already been done."

Ben laughed. "Thanks for sharing that."

She wanted to see him laugh more, to soothe the pain that lay just beyond her reach. Suddenly realizing the direction her thoughts had taken, she sat up straight. "I've got work to do. I better be getting back to the office."

"Are you sure you have to go now?" He placed his hand on hers.

His palm was rough, his gaze compelling. It drew her to him, tempting her to lean on him, to surrender control, if only for a little while. Knowing the danger and the heartbreak that would inevitably follow if she yielded to those emotions, she pulled her hand back. "Don't do that."

"Do what?"

"That look, that voice. Your hand on mine. You're hoping I'll turn into a puddle of goo, but you're wasting your time. I'm not sixteen anymore."

"So let's act like adults. The evening is still young and you're the absolute center of my attention."

She glared at him, though it took an incredible amount of effort to even appear mad. Out of all the emotions raging inside her, anger wasn't even in the running. "Forget the line, it won't work. Let's get going."

"Yes, ma'am."

"A snappy salute would be nice," she said, noting his tone.

"So, you're into discipline now. . . ."

She ignored his comment, hiding her smile as they walked toward the exit.

As they stepped out onto the sidewalk, his playfulness suddenly vanished and his attention shifted away from her. She could feel the tension thrumming through him, and in his strides the coiled edge of a trained soldier.

—EIGHT—

Ben looked in the side mirror of a parked car as they walked past, studying the reflection of a dark-colored sedan at the outside row of the parking lot. That same sedan had remained several car lengths behind him all the way to the restaurant.

It could be nothing more than coincidence, and his wariness a leftover knee-jerk reaction from his days overseas. Just the other day, his heart started pumping overtime when he'd seen a vehicle with an upraised hood parked by the side of the road. His first thought had been *suicide bomber;* then he realized it was just a guy with a split radiator hose.

He had to start thinking stateside, but some habits were too ingrained into him now, and he couldn't afford to lose his edge. Two months from now, he'd be back in a combat zone, watching for insurgents, IEDs, and ambushes. Even a dead animal beside the road could conceal a bomb.

Throughout dinner, he'd kept looking out the window, but he never saw anyone exit the dark sedan. Had the guy who'd arrived just after them changed his mind, or maybe gotten involved in a long conversation on his cell phone?

"I don't think you're listening to me, so let's test it out," she said as they reached the truck. "I'm going to join the Marine Corps and offer to become a medicine woman for them. Think it'll work?"

"Huh?" he asked, the last part sinking in.

"Welcome back," she said.

"I was distracted," he said. "Sorry. I think we may have been followed."

"You mean from the restaurant, or from The Outpost?" She turned and looked back toward the entrance, which was only fifty feet away. "Maybe it's the same guy who robbed us."

"It's possible. Just don't make a show of looking around like that. I don't want him to know we're on to him. If I'm right, he followed us all the way from The Outpost."

"Where is he?"

"On your right, out toward the highway in the last row of parking spaces, is a dark-colored Chevy. The driver is still in his car and looks to be talking on a cell phone. He never came in, but he drove down the highway behind us for several miles."

Jo forced herself not to look. "Maybe he just pulled over to have a long talk with his wife or whomever—a salesman far from home. Driving and talking on the phone at the same time can be distracting," she said. "Not to mention illegal in some places."

"Too coincidental for me. He could have pulled over a dozen places farther back, or at that gas station," Ben said, gesturing with his head to the business a few hundred yards down the road.

"I'm going to call the sheriff's department."

"Call if you want, but I'm going over to see what he wants."

"No, don't. What if he pulls a gun?"

"If this guy wanted to kill us, he would have been hiding somewhere close to our ride, knowing we'd be coming back after dinner. My guess is that once he sees me heading his way, he'll stay cool and drive away as casually as possible, pretending nothing's going on. If that happens, we'll follow, get his license plate, and turn that over to the cops."

"I was told by the sheriff's department that the plates on the green pickup at The Outpost were stolen. These could be, too."

"At least I can get a closer look." He handed her the keys. "Stay here, but if he drives off, be ready to move." Before she could argue, he strode confidently toward the sedan.

The man, who'd been looking their way, started his engine and pulled out of the slot, heading straight for the highway and never looking back.

Ben broke into a run, wanting to look at the plates, and spotted the tag just as the sedan raced out into traffic. He'd just finished keying it into his cell phone when Jo pulled up next to him in the Chevy.

"Jump in," she said.

"No, let him go. We've got his license plate. The cops need to take it from here," he said, unwilling to expose her to additional danger. "The fact that he was watching and wouldn't let me get close makes me think he was up to something."

"Or maybe he thought *you* were," she said after he'd phoned in all the information. "You can be pretty intimidating at times, and you were obviously going straight toward him."

"Nah. He followed us and made it a point not to get too close, like he'd done it before. That's what a pro would do."

"When did you spot him?" she asked as they waited for the police.

"Over by Waterflow, more or less."

"And you didn't think it was important enough to tell me?"

"At that point, I wasn't sure. What's a signal of danger overseas isn't necessarily one away from the war zone," he said.

"For whatever the reason, The Outpost has become the center of a war zone right now. And we've already lost a man," she added in a whisper.

Just then, Detective Wells's car pulled into the lot. Ben got out and walked over to her open window. He filled her in quickly, then pointed east. "Let me ride with you. I can spot him," he said.

"No. This is a police matter. I'll handle it."

He stepped back and she shot out onto the highway, her tires squealing on the asphalt.

When Ben returned to his dad's Chevy, Jo had turned off the engine and slid over to the passenger side. "All things considered, I'd say this is turning out to be a pretty interesting dinner date," he said.

"I thought you said it wasn't a date," she said.

"I lied," he answered, cracking a smile.

As they headed back, he glanced over at her. "You're good company, Jo."

"So are you."

He saw the interest in her eyes as she watched him a second longer than was necessary. He'd always been able to sense when a woman was attracted to him, and that was the case now. Then again, maybe she was playing him. It couldn't have been easy to get under his dad's thick skin. Yet Jo had a way about her, a softness that called to a man.

Ben found himself wanting to know more about her, but he was no longer sure that his motives were as straightforward as he needed them to be. Jo was a complex, fascinating woman, and most of all, a heartbreak waiting to happen.

Jo walked around the trading post, stretching her legs. She'd come back to work, but she couldn't concentrate. Her thoughts kept drifting back to Ben. Electricity had sparked the air between them. She'd felt it every time those world-weary hazel eyes had focused on her.

He'd lived several lifetimes to her one, but as much as Ben intrigued her, she was also wary of him. The boy who'd believed that the ends justified the means was still there, buried under the trappings of a man. He'd apologized for what he asked Regina about her, but the fact that he'd asked at all cast a long shadow of doubt. Then there was his interest in overturning his dad's trust. That topic hadn't come up tonight, but if he'd decided against it, she hadn't heard.

Jo had reached the end of the aisle when she heard a soft scratching sound followed by a low thud at the front door. The scratch could have been an animal—a cat or dog—but not the thud.

Jo ran to where Tom kept the shotgun, beneath the counter and out of sight beneath a gunnysack. You'd never see it unless you knew where to look.

"Who's there?" Jo called out, pointing the barrel at the door, her thumb on the safety.

"It's me, Leigh Ann," a voice called out. "You're okay, right?"

"Yes, I'm fine," she said, relieved. Jo was putting the shotgun back under the counter when she heard Leigh Ann curse. "What's going on?" Jo asked.

"I was trying to get my key in the lock when I dropped it somewhere, and now I can't find it."

"Hang on," Jo said, flipping on the porch lights, then opening the door for her. "What on earth are you doing here this time of night? You nearly gave me a heart attack!"

"I'm sorry," Leigh Ann said, picking up a key that had slipped into a crack between two wooden planks. "I was on my way back from visiting a friend when I saw the light in the back still on. I circled the store and saw your pickup out there, and that's when I got worried. I thought of how you'd found Tom, and then of those guys who tried to break in the day of his funeral, and today's robbery. . . . I scared myself half to death."

Jo nodded. "I appreciate you coming over, but what if you'd

been walking into trouble—me tied up or something, and held at gunpoint?"

"At least, like in the produce locker, you wouldn't have been alone. And I had the phone ready. Once punch and presto—911. But enough of that. What are you doing here? It's almost ten thirty."

"I have to get the inventory software ready for tomorrow. I haven't been able to sleep lately, so I figured I'd use my time productively."

"You mean walking in on a murder victim, interrupting a burglary, becoming the surprise owner of your own business, getting robbed and locked up with the nuts and veggies, and then having your old troublemaking boyfriend show up at the door—all those little nonevents are actually keeping you awake? What's gotten into you? No, don't answer that. Just let me brew some fresh coffee for the one of us who might actually get sleepy, then I'll give you a hand," Leigh Ann said.

"It wouldn't be fair. I can't pay you overtime and I don't want to take advantage."

Leigh Ann smiled. "I volunteered, and the fact that you're worried about taking advantage of me is why you deserve the help. Besides, no one has ever succeeded in taking advantage of me since the night of my senior prom. Don't give it a thought."

Working together, they set up a coding system for all the noncomputerized inventory, complete with electronic folders for each category—silver jewelry, pottery, rugs, and so forth.

It was one thirty in the morning when Jo finally dropped down into one of the empty chairs. "We've done all we can for tonight. Thanks for all your help. Go home now, and don't worry about coming to work on time tomorrow."

"Will you be in late, too?"

"Nope. Until this trading post's back on track, I'll be putting in a lot of time here. First thing tomorrow, I'll start entering inventory into the system—make that today."

"I'll be heading north toward the Ute Mountain Rez at day-break. Melvin lives just south of the line and he's an early riser. I'm going to catch him at home."

"While he's still groggy?" Jo asked, smiling. "But will he be in a better mood or worse?"

She laughed. "No, it's not like that. Melvin tends to follow certain routines when he gets into one of those moods, but I can't go into it. Those aren't my secrets to share."

"I can respect that," Jo said. "Thanks for your help tonight."

"Glad to do it," she said happily. "You take care and watch out for strangers on your way home."

After Leigh Ann drove off, Jo remained in her chair. She could have slept right where she was without any problem, but to really decompress, she'd need a shower and time away from the trading post.

After locking up, Jo walked quickly to her truck, which was parked beneath one of the two light poles in the rear. On the way she automatically glanced at Tom's home. It was Ben's property now, but he hadn't moved in yet. Though he wasn't a Navajo concerned about the *chindi,* painful memories would work against him and block his way.

Even though her own father had passed away at the hospital, she'd considered moving out of her house for that same reason. Eventually deciding to stay, she'd changed the entire look of the place. She'd painted, then traded the old furniture for other pieces that more accurately reflected her own tastes. Her home had soon become haven for her, a place where all the cares of the day were left at the door.

She sighed. She'd sure be glad to see her own bed tonight. She'd crawl deep under the covers and, with luck, finally get some sleep.

※

Leigh Ann heard the alarm clock, and groaned into her pillow. It was six thirty in the morning and time to get going. She grudgingly opened her eyes and reached for the tiny lamp on her nightstand.

As she stretched in the king-sized bed, she became aware of its emptiness. For most of her adult life, she'd proudly defined herself as a good wife, or Kurt's better half. Theirs had been one of those traditional, conservative, deep-in-the-heart-of-Texas marriages—except for one small detail. They lived in northwestern New Mexico.

Throughout their fifteen-year marriage, she'd kept house for Kurt, cooked, and laughed at his sexist jokes. She'd made love even when it was the last thing she'd wanted, and served up chile burgers and beer to him and his out-of-shape buddies all football season. Then, one day, another hunter's stray bullet ended his life.

Leigh Ann walked across the bare hardwood floor to the bathroom. After Kurt's death, everything that had defined her vanished. Determined to put the past behind her and begin anew, she'd given all his things away and even voted Democrat for the first time in her life.

Yet memories were tenacious little things and remained, waiting in every corner of the house. She'd loved Kurt, but no matter how hard she tried to please him, he'd always complained about one thing or another. His one constant gripe had always been her performance in bed, claiming she was frigid and inhibited. She'd tried hard to make things exciting for him, playing cheerleader, doing embarrassing lap dances, and even letting him tie her up. That quickly became his favorite thing, but he'd get too rough when they played those games and he'd scared her more than once.

Right to the end, she'd done her best to make him happy. She'd always cooked him good, man-sized breakfasts, and fixed herself up for him. She even made it a habit to greet him with a smile and a tight sweater each time he returned from one of his business trips.

Leigh Ann stood naked before the mirror, assessing herself. The pretty high school cheerleader who'd lured the high school fullback and been homecoming queen twice had faded away. At thirty-five, everything was still where it should be and hadn't traveled that far south, but she'd drawn into herself after Kurt's passing, not wanting to let another man into her life again.

Kurt had broken her spirit beyond repair, or so it had seemed until the day she met Melvin.

There was something very special at work between them. Melvin could tell it was her approaching just by the sound of her walk. He knew when she was feeling sad or happy, but most important of all, he treated her like someone who mattered.

Her job at The Outpost had helped her heal by showing her that she had something of value to offer the world, but Melvin had reminded her what it was like to feel like a woman again. There was nothing between them except occasional flirting, but maybe it was better that way. She stared at the place where her wedding ring had once been—a hollow groove worn smooth, which summarized it well. Dreams didn't disappoint, but reality all too often sucked.

Choosing a pair of comfortable jeans, boots, and a loose-fitting blouse, she went outside and climbed into her ancient Jeep. It was the only thing of Kurt's she'd kept, mostly because selling it wouldn't have brought in much, and she needed a way to get around. Her pearl white Lexus was long gone, repossessed within three months of his death because she hadn't been able to make the payments.

With a thermos filled with iced water and a box of her special cinnamon cookies to share with Melvin, she set out. At least driving west and then north, she wouldn't have the sun in her eyes.

Melvin's home wasn't at the end of the world, but with a little imagination, one could see it from there. The first few times she drove out there alone, she'd been scared to death that she'd get lost and her body wouldn't be found until spring. On a map, this area of New Mexico was called the Meadows, but there wasn't really much grass, just rolling hills, a few trees, and few landmarks. If you were in a low spot and couldn't see the mountains to the west or the Hogback, it was easy to get turned around.

These days she knew how to change a tire, add oil if necessary, check the battery and radiator, and her cell phone worked—if she could get a signal. Fear was no longer such a big part of the equation.

Anticipation was, and the drive took forever. As the sun rose higher in the sky, she finally saw Melvin's gray, scratch-stucco home in the distance. It was on a gentle slope, surrounded by shrub-high junipers and a few more distinctive piñon trees. It looked so isolated, she couldn't imagine not being lonely out here. Yet that didn't seem to bother Melvin.

Leigh Ann parked, went to his door, and knocked. She waited several minutes, listening, but didn't hear any sound inside. Stepping back, she studied the ground and spotted what looked like a fresh set of vehicle tracks. Melvin didn't drive, of course, but had friends in Fruitland who routinely drove him places too far for him to walk.

Knowing Melvin's schedule by heart, Leigh Ann returned to her car, placed the Jeep in gear, and headed back toward the highway.

Just after 9 A.M., she arrived at Valley Elementary School. The slender trees clustered in the dirt parking lot made the place look like a desert oasis.

After stopping at the office to be cleared, Leigh Ann, with a visitor's pass on a lanyard around her neck, followed the assistant principal down the shiny new hall. Colorful turquoise tiles mixed in with reds and tans formed a wonderful pattern on the floor, and colorful murals depicting local history and landmarks lined the walls between classroom doors.

She breathed in the interesting scent of sweaty little bodies and the trace of paint and glues of new construction as she strolled past the open doors. Finally they reached Mr. Tsosie's room, according to the name on the door. Inside, the children were busy, active, and a little quieter than she remembered from her early years—much earlier, it suddenly occurred to Leigh Ann.

"Go right in," her escort whispered, waving to the young Navajo teacher.

Leigh Ann inched into the room. Nobody looked up except for Mr. Tsosie, who smiled and gestured an invitation with a wave of his hand. Fifteen or so children, half of them Navajo and all about eight or nine years old, were seated or standing around three long tables. Their hands were busy smoothing and shaping lumps of red-, brown-, and yellow-colored clay into various shapes—except for one long-haired Anglo boy. He was pounding his clay flat with his palms.

Standing behind one very enthusiastic young girl with long black braids was Melvin. He was guiding her hands over the figure of a four-legged something—maybe a horse, or perhaps a pig. It was hard to tell.

The room grew silent as Melvin spoke—even the boy with the flat clay stopped his work. "Feel the length and position of the head, ears, snout, legs, and tails. By using gentle pressure and smoothing the clay, you can change its size and shape. The clay's still soft, so if you need to pinch off a piece, or add a little more, there's no problem."

"Mr., ummmm, Melvin. What's a snout?" one of the boys at the end asked.

A few of the children laughed.

"The nose, dummy," another called out.

"Frogs don't have noses, do they?" the first boy asked.

Melvin grinned. "A clay frog can have a nose. Let's see what you come up with. See with your hands *and* your imagination."

Melvin stepped back, then moved down the line. One student reached out, grabbed Melvin's hand, and pulled it gently toward the mysterious glob she was working on.

"What do you think of my chicken?" she asked. "I tried to open its wings, but they kept falling off, so they're next to its body now."

Leigh Ann chuckled, but stayed well back, watching how the children responded to him. Melvin had a way with kids. Being around them made him come out of his shell, too. She'd never seen him looking more at ease. As she moved toward the Anglo boy, who as it turned out, was making a butterfly, Melvin stepped past her.

"Hello, Miss Vance," Melvin said.

"How on earth did you know I was here?" Leigh Ann asked.

"The kids always act a little differently when we have an observer. I thought it might be a parent, then I caught the scent of your perfume."

"Wow. Here? Even with all the clay and paints?"

"I can filter out the interference," he said, then leaned closer to her and whispered, "I'll be finished here in another fifteen minutes or so. Maybe you can drive me home? Mr. Tsosie was going to give me a ride, but he can't leave until noon."

"I'll be glad to take you home," she said. "And Mr. Tsosie won't have to give up his lunch."

Art class finished ten minutes later—with five minutes added for cleanup—and Melvin quickly found his way to where she stood. It never ceased to amaze her how he could orient himself. He'd told her once that he could see deep gray shadows where obstacles stood and that helped him navigate without a cane. Yet, to her, the way he compensated for his lack of sight seemed to hold an almost magical quality.

She led him to the Jeep, helped him inside, and switched on

the engine. The motor roared, cut out for a second, then settled with a more or less even idle. She laughed. "Doesn't exactly inspire confidence, does it? It's like the engine's telling me, 'What now? I'm old. Go away and leave me alone.'"

"If this is just a '98, it's got a lot more miles in it. Are you still taking it to Gilroy Pete?"

"Yes, I am, and thanks so much for the recommendation. He's an amazing mechanic and charges a fair price."

"He's a good man. Right now, he's tuning up my Harley."

"Your—" Seeing the mischievous smile on his face, she laughed. "Why am I the only one you tease? You're always so serious around people—well, adults."

"I don't like being patronized or pitied. With kids it's different. They never see me as a blind guy for very long. I'm just a guy who makes cool stuff."

"You sure do," she said.

"Thank you," he said. "So what brings you here today? Is this a friendly visit or are you here on business?"

"Both. I came to offer you conversation, a job, and I even brought a bribe. I have some cinnamon cookies with me," she said.

"I thought maybe you'd come up with a new Jeep scent—cinnamon oil. So what's the project?"

"Let's wait till we're at your house. I'll tell you more then."

"Always mysterious," he said with a trace of a smile.

"No, I just need to concentrate on my driving. There's too much glare coming off the windshield. I picked up some bugs along the highway last night."

"Yeah, and you also have a serious sales pitch you want to try out on me," he said. "What are you doing, rehearsing in your mind?"

"Busted," she said, laughing.

A half hour later, she pulled up to his home and parked. "We're here."

"I'll get us some iced tea to go with your wonderful cookies," he said, climbing out of the Jeep.

Once they were in his kitchen, Leigh Ann sat at his small round table and watched as he brought out two glasses and a plate for the cookies.

Melvin heard her set the cookies on the plate and reached for one. "These are great," he said after a big bite. "If there are at least a dozen on that plate, consider me bribed."

She smiled. She did a lot of that around Melvin. As she told him about the job, she watched his expression change, growing in intensity. He was interested.

"The money's acceptable—very much so—but I'll have to think about what I'll be making before I begin. It won't be a quick turnaround. I'll need time to come up with the right idea first."

"I love your animal sculptures. Maybe you can make another cougar like the one we sold on consignment at The Outpost last year. The way you fashioned the animal's mouth and muzzle in a growl, even the hunching of the body and extended legs . . . it was as if the sculpture had a life of its own."

"I can't see the animal, but I know its spirit," he said in a quiet voice. "The cougar is a master of his own destiny. He hunts with grace and strength and doesn't waste a single stride. He sets a goal and follows through. I try to mold those qualities into the sculpture."

"They were all there and more. It was amazing piece. If I'd had the money. I would have bought it myself."

"You should have told me you liked it that much. I would have given it to you."

She hesitated. "I appreciate the thought, but that wouldn't have been right. You're no starving artist, but money's hard to come by these days for most of us."

"I hear uncertainty in your voice again. It makes you uncomfortable whenever I offer you anything. If the cougar could have taken that away, it would have been worth the price."

"No one else listens like you do. It's like you hear what's in my heart, not just my words." As she looked into his dark, sightless eyes, she saw a gentle soul who walked a solitary path, like the cougars he liked to sculpt.

"When my sight was taken from me, the universe gave me other ways to see. Finding the path of harmony isn't always easy, but if you open your heart and listen to its whispers, you'll be led there."

"I hope you're right."

Melvin never asked her any personal questions beyond what she volunteered and was willing to share. Their friendship had limits, and that's precisely what made it safe.

"Last time we spoke, you mentioned that your sister was coming to live with you," he said.

"Rachel offered to move in with me after she found out that I was looking for a boarder, and I took her up on it. The rent I'm charging is modest and far more affordable than the exorbitant one she was paying in Farmington. But now that she's moved in, I'm not sure Rachel's the right choice for me. We've never been close."

"Give it a try for a month or two. Just make sure there are rules, like with a stranger. If it isn't going to work out, you'll both know before too much longer."

"Yeah, that makes a lot of sense," she said.

After going over the details of their business transaction one more time, Leigh Ann stood. "I wish I could stay. I love visiting you."

"Then don't go yet. Tell your boss that I was being difficult. Considering my rep, no one's going to question it."

She chuckled. "Good point, but I should get back. I'm needed at the trading post."

"I've heard stories that there's a fight brewing over ownership of The Outpost. Word is that Tom Stuart's son thinks Jo Buck conned his dad into putting her in his will. I have to say that doesn't sound anything like the woman I've dealt with."

"Jo didn't con anyone. That's just nonsense. The problem between those two goes all the way back to high school. They dated back then and it ended badly. That was a while ago, but hard feelings can linger for a long time," she said, speaking from experience. "Tell me something, Melvin. How on earth do you keep up with the latest gossip all the way out here?"

"I hear things down at the Laundromat. Almost everyone this side of the highway goes there to do their wash. Water's scarce and laundry soap and softener can clog up the septic tank drain field. Then you have to call the *chaa-man* and he charges extra for having to drive way out into the county. I usually take a seat by the washing machines, make myself comfortable, and listen. People sometimes forget that blind and deaf aren't the same thing. You'd be surprised at all the things I overhear," he said, laughing.

As they passed through the living room heading to the door, she saw the ever-present bottle of whiskey on the table next to his chair. It was always half full. She wasn't sure if that was because he got drunk every night and she somehow always managed to catch the bottle halfway down, or if it was the same bottle, there for another reason entirely.

She glanced back at him, but resisted the impulse to ask. That was part of the line that stood between them, the one neither would cross.

Respecting his privacy, she walked outside, said good-bye, and got into her Jeep.

"Come back soon, Leigh Ann," he said, stepping out onto the porch.

"I'll do my best," she said. "And whenever you have an errand to run, give me a call. I'll be glad to help."

"I know," he said softly, then went back inside.

As Leigh Ann drove back toward the highway, Melvin remained in her thoughts. Although the rest of the world would probably define them both as damaged goods, around him she felt whole—and maybe even desired. It was all part of the special magic Melvin Littlewater had brought into her life.

—NINE—

A noise outside stirred Jo awake. She opened her eyes slowly, forcing them to focus. She wasn't expecting visitors. What time was it, anyway?

She glanced at the clock and gasped. She'd worked late last night with Leigh Ann and had come home even later. This morning she never even heard the alarm. It was nine thirty in the morning! Sure, it was Saturday, but she hadn't slept this late in years. At least they didn't normally open on Saturday until nine. Jo jumped out of bed and hurried to the window. There, parked beneath the old cottonwood, was Tom's familiar Chevy pickup. As she watched, Ben got out and walked to her front door.

Jo glanced down at herself. She'd slept in jeans and a T-shirt, so at least she was dressed. Jo used her hands to brush her hair away from her face. Loose, it cascaded past her waist in a tangled mess. She smoothed it out as best she could and went to open the door.

"What on earth are you doing here?" she asked Ben.

"Esther asked me to come check on you. She called but you didn't answer. Since bad things have been happening, she got

scared. She's opened up for business. She knows the code and
has a key to let herself into the trading post, but there's no one
else there. Leigh Ann hasn't come in yet either, and Regina
called to say she'd be late. Her baby's sick."

"Leigh Ann and I worked till well after midnight, so I told
her coming in late was okay. But I overslept. I have an alarm
clock that sounds like reveille on steroids, but I never even
heard it. And the phone, what can I say?"

"You weren't just tired—you were exhausted. When I'm that
way, I can sleep through artillery fire—literally—as long as it's
not incoming."

"I'm sorry you had to drive out here, Ben. On your way back,
call Esther and tell her I'm fine. I'll see you at the trading post
in twenty minutes." She started to yawn, then managed to turn
it into a smile—kind of.

"What? Not even a cup of coffee before I get the boot?" he
asked, inching his way into the living room.

"Sorry. I should have been at The Outpost hours ago! We'll
both get coffee at the store."

"That's something that hasn't changed, I see. You'd almost
never invited me over to your place when we were kids either.
You always insisted we go to my house."

She remembered the reason and her throat tightened as
memories crowded her mind. She'd never been able to predict
her father's actions. He would go without alcohol for months on
end, then fall off the wagon for no apparent reason and drink
for several days straight. Every time that happened, her mother
and she would do everything in their power to cover for him. The
instinct to protect a family member had been too strong for them
to do otherwise. Yet, in retrospect, she now realized that they'd
simply enabled him, and the incidents continued for years.

As she thought back to those days, she felt a hollow ache in
the pit of her stomach. Keeping her father's secret had created a
barrier between her family and the community. It had trapped

them all behind a curtain of lies. To make matters worse, back then she'd always been quick to blame herself, at least partially, for her father's drinking problem.

"You're welcome to stay while I get ready for work, but I can't sit and chat."

"How about we celebrate that invitation, such as it is, with a cup of coffee?" he said, stepping closer to her, then with a grin added, "Instant is fine, or even yesterday's leftovers. I could use something to keep me alert on the way back."

Something about that confident smile made a pleasant rush of warmth and awareness course through her. She remembered the last time she'd stood this close to him. They'd been walking back to the bus after a basketball state tournament in Albuquerque. He'd pulled her into the shadows and, as she looked up into his eyes, she felt as if her entire life had been leading up to just that moment. His touch had been gentle and everything . . . so perfect. Temptation now urged her to find out if the feelings—that magic—would still be there.

"I can hear your heart beating. You want me to stay," he murmured.

"You're delusional," she said, moving quickly away from him. "If you want to do something for me, go back to the trading post right now. Esther shouldn't be there alone, especially after the robbery. And if you get restless and want something to do, it would sure be nice to find some fresh coffee waiting," she added, a tiny grin tugging at the corners of her mouth.

He laughed. "Yes, ma'am."

Moments later, Jo went to the window and watched Ben's pickup disappear from view. She was quickly becoming her own worst enemy. Despite everything, she still had strong feelings for Ben, and that was bound to complicate an already impossible situation.

※

Ben made it a point to watch ahead, check passing drivers, and glance in the mirrors as often as possible. Unlike it was with his unit, he was working solo here, and considering what had happened to his dad, and the potential danger to The Outpost still unresolved, he knew he'd have to watch his own back.

To make matters worse, seeing Jo again was scrambling his thinking. As hard as he tried to look at her as his enemy, someone who'd taken away what should have been his, he couldn't do it. For some crazy reason he felt compelled to protect Jo, not bring her down.

For a while back there he'd wanted nothing more than to carry her back to bed and sink into her softness, to see and touch her the way he'd wanted to since he turned sixteen. Being around the girl who'd been his first real love tugged at him, filling him with crazy ideas.

Sometime later Ben arrived at The Outpost and went inside. Esther was standing near the front register, sweeping the tile floor with a dust mop.

He gave her a quick smile. "Jo's fine. She and Leigh Ann worked late yesterday, and Jo overslept. I'd have called you on my cell phone, but it cut out on me."

"Leigh Ann called not long after you left. She'll be in shortly."

He took the mop from her hands and began cleaning the floor. "You like working here, don't you, ma'am? You always have a smile on your face."

"I love my job. It's not just because of the money either, though that's important too. My husband's home all the time these days—he's retired—so we're together a lot. We both enjoy that, but I like knowing that I can still get along on my own if need be."

"What was Dad like here at work? At home he was a bear to live with," he said with a grin. "Everything had to be done his way."

"Your father was always a gentleman," she said after a pause. "As an employer, he expected all of us to work hard, and didn't tolerate excuses, but he was just as hard on himself. The important thing about Tom is that he always treated everyone with respect. That's one of the reasons our customers loved him."

"People say that he hadn't been himself lately," Ben said, deliberately leaving it open for discussion.

The elderly Navajo woman took a deep breath and nodded. "Something *was* bothering him, and he was edgier than usual, but I have no idea why that was. The only time he seemed to shake off his mood was when someone spoke of you. That always brought a big smile to his face. He was really looking forward to seeing you again, Ben."

"I felt the same about him."

Esther paused and grew somber again. "Trouble has an iron grip on this trading post right now. We need to work hard to reverse that. If The Outpost is forced to close its doors, our community will never be the same."

Before he could ask her if that was her way of warning him not to contest his father's trust, Jo walked in, followed by Leigh Ann.

"Ladies, about time. Some work ethic, coming in just shy of noon," Ben teased.

"Quit your howling, youngster," Leigh Ann said with a smile. "I put in twelve hours yesterday, then started up again this morning at sunrise. Some of us have been burning the candle at both ends lately, trying to kick-start this trading post's business."

"Has it been slow this morning?" Jo asked Esther.

Esther nodded. "I was thinking of putting a table out on the porch with some eye-catching merchandise, like that big Two Grey Hills rug," Esther said, gesturing to the one on the display table. The rug was beautifully made, its pattern based on a central diamond shape and geometric borders. It was woven in subtle shades of white, black, and brown wool. "I'd like to take

some pottery, too, and maybe hang up a few of those broom-
stick skirts, something that'll catch the eye of people driving
by on their way to the Indian Market in Santa Fe or the Rio
Grande pueblos."

"That's an excellent idea." Jo glanced at Leigh Ann, then at
Del, who'd just come in through the back. "Let's move the table
and chairs and put out a sign."

While they set out the display table, Leigh Ann put up a
second table with soft drinks and ice in a big cooler, then began
to gather the magnetic letters needed to spell out the message
on the sign over by the turnoff.

"If you guys can take care of things out here, I'm going back
inside to start inventory," Jo said.

"Let me give you a hand," Ben said. "Maybe we can figure
out what, if anything, the robber took—besides the cash."

"Hope you're right," Jo said, wishing that the threat hanging
over them—over her—would go away.

"Once I get the sign ready, I'll handle the register, so don't
worry," Leigh Ann called out.

Jo smiled and gave her a nod, then went back inside, heading for the inventory supplies.

"They're loyal to you," Ben said, quietly following. "That's
why they give you their best effort."

She looked up at him, clearly surprised. "This isn't about me.
Everyone at the trading post has a common goal, to keep things
going, and that's what binds us." She paused, looked away for a
moment, then continued. "The Navajo people believe that everything's connected. No one person exists outside the whole.
What you're seeing here is that connectedness in action."

He didn't answer, wondering if this was all part of her plan
to get him to give up any claims to the business.

"You don't trust me at all, do you?" she asked, handing him a
box with folders, lists, and labels. When he hesitated, she added,
"But why? *You're* the one with the track record for unreliability."

"I think you're suffering from selective memory. You walked out on *me*, remember? When I got arrested for joyriding, my entire world unraveled. I needed you more than ever, but you turned your back on me and walked away."

"What you needed—wanted—was someone to validate your actions, to tell you that your reasons justified your behavior. I couldn't go along with that, and you knew it. Think back. You were purposely getting in trouble to rattle your dad. You told me so yourself, remember?"

"I wanted him to look at me, not through me," he said quietly, remembering how miserable and desperate he'd been. "After Mom died, he shut me out and buried himself in the trading post. The only time he ever paid attention to me was when I got in trouble."

"You were on a downward spiral, and out of control. I couldn't stop you, but I also couldn't let you take me with you. I had no other choice, but walking away from you was the hardest thing I'd ever done."

Her answer took him by surprise. It sounded like the truth, but maybe that was just because he wanted to believe her.

"Let's get started on inventory," she said, all business again. "Leigh Ann and I made up stick-on labels with bar codes. We'll need to place the codes on the right items, then hand-scan everything once we're done with a category."

"My dad never did that?" It seemed odd, considering how compulsive his dad had been. He'd even grouped his shirts by color in the closet.

"Your father was one of the most organized men I've ever known. He used bar codes and electronic bookkeeping on the merchandise that came from our regular suppliers. The problem's mainly with the consignment pieces created by area artisans. He never officially cataloged those. He kept track of them in his head. He'd put a label on them with a short item name and price, then enter that on a ledger under the artist's name.

When the item sold, it went into the computer as miscellaneous merchandise—along with the cost and sale price."

"Every penny counts, doesn't it?" Not waiting for an answer, he continued. "I never realized how close the trading post's profit margin was. I always thought we were rich."

"You were, in comparison to a lot of others around here, but now that you're an adult, you're seeing things in a different light," she said. "The impressions and judgments we make as kids, however lasting, aren't always accurate."

As they worked on inventory, business in the store slowly began picking up. The sign out by the road, along with the activity outside, made weekend passersby curious enough to stop. At least half the customers eventually came inside to browse, too, heading for the sections of merchandise spotlighted outside. For the first time in a week, Leigh Ann was really busy at the front register.

While Jo continued entering the codes, this time ones corresponding to a collection of Zuni squash blossom necklaces, Ben took a break, bought a cold Pepsi, and placed a dollar bill on the counter. Leigh Ann nodded, not even slowing down her conversation with a retired schoolteacher from Cortez. The woman had just settled on the purchase of a hand-painted, hand-etched pot.

Ben leaned back against the wall, watching an attractive Hispanic woman wearing sunglasses and tight jeans. She was now walking up the aisle showcasing their Navajo rugs, looking at everything she passed.

"You've been checking out that tall brunette since she came in," Jo whispered, joining him. "Get back to work, soldier, before she complains."

"Or she hits on me?" He grinned. "I admit she's easy on the eyes, but that's not what's holding my attention. Don't make eye contact, but watch casually out of the corner of your eye. I think she's up to something. Notice the way she's using her cell phone. She holds it away from her for a second or two, then brings it back up to her ear. She's taking photos, not making conversation, and certainly not texting."

Jo glanced in the woman's general direction and saw her looking into the store's convex mirrors, placed in key locations to discourage shoplifting by reducing blind spots. The woman noticed she was being watched and beamed Jo an easy smile. She then picked up the closest item, a brightly colored ceramic paperweight of a roadrunner, paid in cash, then left the store.

"You'll never make it as a spy, Jo," Ben said, heading to the window. Spotting the car, a light blue SUV, he took down the New Mexico plates.

"I wasn't looking directly at her," Jo argued. "She must have a sixth sense or something."

"Did you notice what she seemed most interested in?" Seeing Jo shake her head, he added, "When she took photos, they were of the rugs first, then the layout. At least two of the shots were directed toward the storeroom and the back door. Let's find out if any of the staff recognized her."

"I've worked here longest, and I don't remember having seen her before," Jo said. "Leigh Ann lives nearby and knows a lot of locals, so let's ask her."

Leigh Ann listened, then shook her head. "No, I have no idea who she is. She was pretty enough, though. I guess that's what got your attention," she said, giving Ben a wink.

"I wasn't—," he began, then stopped. "Wait a sec. You just made an excellent point, Leigh Ann. A woman like that is too attractive for any real surveillance work. She'd get noticed by any male over the age of six. That means she wasn't a professional thief."

"Which makes her an amateur—what?" Jo asked.

"I don't know. I'm going to call Detective Wells and see if she'll run the plate."

"Good idea," Jo said. "Use the phone in my office. It's got a better speaker."

Ben made the call. Moments later, Detective Wells answered, and Ben put the phone on speaker. While Jo listened, he described what he'd seen.

"Let me get this right. Unlike it was with the robbery, neither of you actually saw her steal anything or create any problems—vandalism of any kind or like that?"

"No, but why would anyone want to take photos of the security mirrors, layout, and basically the entire interior?" Ben said.

"And you know for a fact that she was doing that?" Wells, countered, sounding bored, or tired. "You said she spent most of her time around the rugs."

"Well, that's true," Ben said. "But she was also working that cell phone camera and trying to conceal the act by pretending to be talking to someone."

"For all you know, she might have been sending photos of what she saw as a quaint old trading post to her friends in New Jersey," Wells said. "Did you catch her doing anything at all that looked like shoplifting?"

"No, but something was off," Ben insisted.

"The woman paid before leaving, correct?"

"Yes, but her behavior was suspicious," Ben said, holding his ground.

"What's normal nowadays?" Wells said. "Let's tackle this from a different direction. What made you notice her?"

"Training. Cell phones are used by insurgents posing as civilians to trigger IEDs and car bombs—and to provide surveillance images."

"You're also a man. Was she attractive, wearing revealing or sexy clothing, anything like that?"

"Good-looking, yes."

"Maybe she knew you were watching her and that altered

her behavior," Wells said. "It's not unusual for a soldier back from a combat deployment to be a little . . . cautious. And after yesterday's incident, it's natural to overthink someone else's behavior. That man parked outside the restaurant last night, for example, was a Farmington salesman making a pitch on his cell phone. All we did was make him late getting home."

Jo spoke up. "Okay, but it doesn't hurt to be cautious, especially after all that's happened. Now let's get back to that woman today. The fact that she was *sneaking* the photos while pretending to be talking is what made it suspicious. Also, when she realized that I was watching her, she was quick to leave."

"She also kept her head down and wore oversized sunglasses to help hide her face," Ben said. "Believe me, Detective. She wasn't just checking out the rug and documenting a trading post, she was casing the place. I gave you the license plate. Will you at least run it for us?" Ben asked. "It was a blue SUV—a Chevy, I think."

"I can't just run a plate just because you're curious. Citizens have a right to their privacy," the detective said.

"True," Jo said, "but keep in mind that the trading post's former owner was killed recently and we don't know if the killer was a man or woman. There have been other incidents linked to this place, too, as you well know. Ruling out this person as a possible suspect at the risk of a little intrusion on their privacy, something they'd never know about unless you tell them, seems like a fair trade-off. But if you're still uneasy about it, I can call the county sheriff directly. Or maybe I should talk to the tribal police. I know several officers there who I'm sure would be willing to help me."

"No need, you've made your case. Just hang on for a minute while I run this on my MDT," Wells said.

Ben raised an eyebrow. "You play for keeps, don't you," he whispered.

Before Jo could answer, the detective came back on the line.

"That plate is assigned to a Dodge Ram pickup. Didn't you just tell me it was an SUV?"

"Yeah, it was," Ben answered. "Maybe the plate was stolen."

"I'll contact the pickup's owner and see where it goes from there. Meanwhile, if your hottie in sunglasses comes back, give me a call."

Once the conversation ended, Ben looked over at Jo. "You handled things with Detective Wells like a pro. At the beginning, she wasn't listening to what we were telling her. I think she resents our involvement in what she sees as *her* case."

"It may be her case, but we all have a stake in the investigation, and so far she hasn't shown us any results, not with your father's murder, the break-in, or the robbery. We did nothing wrong by taking some initiative."

"Now *that* sounds more like the Jo I knew. You never leaned on anyone. Control was always a priority to you."

She stared at him for a moment, eyebrows raised.

"You don't see it?" he asked her after a beat.

"No, not at all. I was forced to rely on myself because there really wasn't anyone else I could count on at home. When something needed to be done, I'd do it myself, not so much out of choice, but out of necessity."

It was clear to him that she believed it, but maybe she didn't know herself as well as she should have. The Jo he'd known had never asked anyone for help, though she'd accepted it from his dad from time to time. Yet when others needed her, she'd always stepped up to the plate.

"There's one thing I see hasn't changed about you," he said. "For you, logic and persuasion work better than confrontations. You do your homework and back your arguments with facts and sound logic."

"Neither of us could force Detective Wells to do anything,

so our options were few," she said, going back to the floor to re-
sume their inventory work.

As he followed her, Ben felt a mixture of admiration and
healthy distrust. Jo was smooth and disarming, and had kept
her cool with Detective Wells. Even as he'd struggled to keep
his own temper in check, she'd never deviated from her goal,
despite the pressure.

One thing was clear. Jo was a formidable woman, and Trouble
with a capital *T.*

etective Katie Wells rubbed the back of her neck. She hadn't been getting much sleep lately. She loved her son, Brent, more than life itself, but he was slowly breaking her heart.

Where had the years gone? Was it really sixteen years since she'd woken up to her baby's cries, and had found Doug Wells's cryptic note on the pillow beside her?

I'm not meant for this. You're better off without me.

With that, he'd stepped out of their lives forever.

At first, she panicked. She'd had no idea what to do. Back then she had no job, no training, and no education past eleventh grade. With one hungry baby to feed, she'd clawed her way out of a bottomless pit of desperation, found work as a waitress, and earned a GED. Eventually, she'd applied to join the sheriff's department, a better paying, often physical job she was equipped to handle. The hours sometimes sucked, but with a full-time law enforcement job, she had health insurance and a retirement plan. Her future seemed assured.

Though her job had plenty of ups and downs, she loved it

from day one. She'd given it everything, and somewhere along the way, Brent had grown up.

Though Brent had never known his father, Katie could still see the similarities between them. Physically, the resemblance was there, and as it had been with Doug, Brent also attracted trouble.

Katie's partner, John Sanchez, an overworked, overweight detective only a few months from retirement, came up to her desk. "Hey, Katie, I'm cutting out early today."

"You don't look so good. Are you okay?"

"Sure. I just haven't been getting much sleep. Bobby's had a hard time of it lately."

That reality check put things back into perspective for her *pronto*. John's son, Bobby, had leukemia and waged a life-and-death battle each day. "I'll cover, don't worry about anything. How's the little guy doing now? Are the new meds helping?"

"It looks promising, Bobby's stopped losing so much weight. But right now my wife's away on a business trip. When Ruth's gone, it falls on me. Sometimes sleep's hard to come by."

"If you need anything, give me a call."

"Thanks," he said. "What about Brent? Is he staying away from those punks?"

Brent's gang connection seemed so inconsequential in comparison to what Bobby Sanchez was going through. "For now," she said, praying it was true.

As John tossed his Windbreaker over his arm and headed for the substation door, Katie leaned back. Things could be a lot worse. Although at the moment she had that walking piece of garbage, Roberto Hidalgo, blackmailing her, she'd eventually find some leverage to use against him. He thought he could control her by threatening her kid, but what he'd really done was turn her into an implacable enemy who wouldn't rest until he went down. She'd get his sorry ass and nail it to the wall. All she needed was a little more time.

She reached down, looking at her nine-millimeter Glock. Or maybe she'd find a way to take him out permanently.

Her cell phone rang and the distinctive ring told her who it was without having to look. "Don't *ever* call me here," she snapped. "Leave a text if you must."

"So you can have a record of it? No way."

Roberto always used a prepaid cell phone. She'd tried tracking the calls once, anything to build a case against him, but all she could get was a cell tower in the middle of the city.

Katie stepped outside into the parking lot, where she wouldn't be overheard or have her lips read. "I don't know why you waste your time and mine asking me to help you," she said, her back to the security camera. "I told you all about the layout at The Outpost, but you couldn't let it go. First you had one of your men lock up the employees and rob the place in broad daylight. And the very next day you sent some woman to take pictures. The owners made her within five minutes. Now they not only have a description, they're likely to upgrade their security. Unless you've got what you want now, your people screwed up again."

"Watch your mouth. Just follow orders. Clear?"

"Abundantly."

"What's going on with your investigation?"

"I talked to the ME on the phone. There's no way the OMI is going to list the death as a suicide. The bullet that killed Stuart was fired from at least three feet away, but you probably already know that," she said. "Also there was no powder residue on his hands or stippling around the wound. The ME found abrasions and rope fibers on Stuart's wrists, and toxicology has revealed that he was drugged with sodium thiopental, which is commonly used in interrogations to make the subject talk. The evidence proves that this was no random break-in gone sour, not only that, but whoever went after Stuart had done this kind of thing before."

"I've been told you were the first detective on the scene. Why didn't you clean up the place—do something?"

"How was I supposed to know it had something to do with you and your business? I'm no mind reader. The more you and your people get involved, the harder it'll be for me to bury this situation."

"I have an interest in The Outpost. Do what's necessary to keep law enforcement from digging any deeper. If nothing else, stall."

"It's my case, but if I keep dragging my feet, the sheriff will assign it to another officer."

"Make sure that doesn't happen."

"That's out of my hands."

"Then find someone off the street to take the fall. Just make sure The Outpost doesn't come under any additional police scrutiny between now and the end of this month. After that, you can sell Stuart's death as a robbery gone bad, or whatever. Just keep me and my people out of it."

"Maybe I can blame it on someone looking for drugs," she said, mostly to gauge his reaction.

"That's precisely what you should not do, *guapa*," he said, using the Spanish word for "beautiful."

Katie stiffened. Roberto's attempts to flirt turned her stomach—the asshole.

"Just remember that there are no bad guys in this, *mujer*, just people trying to take care of their families," he said, his voice softened to a whisper.

Katie heard a door open and the sounds of a child running into the room.

"Papi!"

A cold chill ran up Katie's spine as she heard the child's laughter, followed by a click. No bad guys . . . just evil unchecked.

Roberto Hidalgo looked down at the four-year-old girl hugging his leg with both arms. "Marisol, I've told you not to come into my office without knocking first."

"But, Papi, there's ice cream. Mami bought the really good kind."

He lifted her into the air, loving the way she laughed. "Then we have to do our part . . . by eating all of it!" He set her down, then reached to tickle her. She giggled, then twisted away. "Hurry, okay?"

As she ran out, Roberto stared at the throwaway phone on his desk. The police detective thought they were so different, but Katie Wells was only kidding herself. It all came down to love—for family and for lifestyles carved out of nothing but dreams, and paid for in blood—in his case, that of his enemies.

As he always did when the walls began to close in on him, Roberto went to the bookshelf and reached for the hand-carved wooden box he kept there. Inside was a small silver Saint Christopher medal. It had belonged to his cousin, who'd been gunned down by a rival gang near the border. His death had allowed Roberto to escape and take the drugs into the United States. With that delivery, he'd started down a path that had eventually brought him every comfort money could buy. The death of Primitivo had become his own salvation.

He was now respected by the community and feared by his enemies—those who were still alive. He was no longer a beggar, stealing bread and fruit from vendors to fill his stomach. He didn't follow the rules—he made them. That's the way it was going to stay. He'd earned everything he had the hard way, and he'd fight to the death to keep it. Everything came at a price, power most of all, but he'd made his peace with it.

Katie sat in front of her captain's desk. Frank Tafoya was tall, middle-aged, and as hard as they came. He also had a stare that could tear holes through you. Katie forced herself not to react.

"I know that you've been carrying both your share of the work and Sanchez's, Katie, but incidents along the tribal boundary are on the rise, and that trading post is getting more than its share lately. Are you sure you can handle the load?"

"I'm fine, sir. Sanchez is there when I need him, and after he retires, I'll have a new partner to break in." That delay would work in her favor, too. Right now she didn't need an experienced deputy looking over her shoulder. She had enough trouble covering Hidalgo's ass.

"With the hiring freeze, I may not have anyone I can assign to you right away after Sanchez leaves," Captain Tafoya said, sorting through a folder while he spoke. "Get used to watching your own back out in the field. Don't go into situations where you're likely to get your nuts shot off." He'd been looking down at the paper, then stopped, looked up and smiled. "Or other crucial parts."

She smiled and waited. There was a reason she'd been called in and, with luck, he'd get to it sooner rather than later.

"We got some intel from the DEA this morning." He slid a printed dispatch across his desk for her to read. "Activity among known dealers suggests that there's a big shipment of cocaine on its way in from Mexico. If they follow previous smuggling routes, it'll be passing through the New Mexico conduit into the Denver area. The feds are hoping to intercept the load, so keep your eyes and ears open. If you get a lead, it'll need to be passed on to the DEA. They want to handle it."

Katie nodded, knowing now why Hidalgo was feeling the

pressure. "I haven't heard a word about this until now. Any idea how they plan to smuggle it in? Mules, low-flying aircraft?"

"No one knows," he said, and shrugged. "You're working the Stuart murder case and the break-in attempt the day of the victim's memorial servicel? Correct?"

"Yeah," she said. "Other than a possible robbery gone sour, I haven't found any motive that might explain why the trading post owner was killed. The guy was well liked and he apparently wasn't dating anyone. Stuart's record is squeaky clean, too, no gambling or drug problems. The break-in's probably unrelated to the murder—a target of opportunity, considering everyone at the business was supposed to be at the memorial service."

"You said robbery is a possible for Stuart's death. Do you have any idea what was taken?" the captain asked.

"No, unfortunately, which doesn't make sense unless somebody's lying. Yesterday, too, a punk with a toy pistol locked the staff up and stole the contents of a cash register."

"That's all he took?"

Katie nodded. "He also found some cash in a back office, but gave up before attempting to break into their cash box. All he got was around two hundred bucks."

"And that's not connected to Stuart's homicide?"

"I'm not ruling it out, but at this stage I don't see a link." She deliberately left out the fact that the robber had gained access to the safe, not wanting to speculate on how he knew the combination. That fact alone provided a good link, one she wasn't supposed to make.

"Do you have any other leads on that homicide?" Tafoya asked.

"Since the door to Stuart's home—the murder scene—wasn't compromised, I suspect that Stuart knew his killer and let him in. That's why motive's so crucial to this case."

"You're a good officer, Wells. Stay on it," he said, dismissing her.

Katie swallowed the bitterness at the back of her throat. She'd been a damned good cop once. Now . . . It was strange how something intrinsically good like love and loyalty could lead to corruption. It also grated on her pride, having to play stupid to her boss.

She was on her way back to her desk when she got a call on her cell phone from her next door neighbor. Katie identified herself.

"It's Doris," the caller said. "I thought you might want to know that Brent's out in your backyard, drinking and fighting with another boy. They're just wrestling right now, but it doesn't look like they're playing. I yelled at them to stop, but they didn't even slow down. Brent's got blood on him, too. Should I call 911?"

"Did you see any weapons?"

"No. You think they're just play-fighting to get a rise from me?"

"Maybe, but stay out of their way. I'll be there in a few minutes and put a stop to it. Thanks, Doris." Katie hurried to the parking lot, jamming the phone into her pocket. At least it wasn't drugs this time. Brent was acting out, determined to find trouble. She just wasn't around enough to keep him in line. Her job kept her on the go, and the hours were far from regular, but someone had to pay the bills.

Katie switched on her emergency lights as she flew down the highway, going code one—silent approach. She wanted to take the boys by surprise, and that meant no siren. It took her less than ten minutes to make the fifteen-minute trip home.

As she pulled into her driveway, she saw Doris on her own front porch, pointing toward the back of the house. Katie raced around the corner and found the boys on the ground, bloodied, their shirts in tatters. Brent was on the bottom, blocking round-house punches with his forearms, but the bigger kid was clearly wearing him down.

"Break it up!" Katie yelled, grabbing the kid by the collar. He turned to look, his face covered with dirt, sweat, and spit, his left eye swollen. It was doubtful he could see worth a damn, and she could smell booze all over him.

Brent punched up, catching the big teen in the gut.

"Let go, bitch!" the kid said, swinging his arm around and trying to grab her leg.

Katie kicked the boy in the side just hard enough to get his attention. As he doubled up, she grabbed his forearm and spun him around, flipping him onto his back.

Katie put her boot down on the big kid's crotch. "Stay down sweetie, or I'm crushing your jewels."

The boy looked up at her with glazed eyes, then turned his head and puked on the grass near an empty bottle of cheap whiskey.

Brent rolled over, then rose to his knees, panting.

Katie glared at her son. His nose was bleeding, and his lip was cut, but it didn't look like he needed stitches.

"You promised me you'd stop screwing around—and drinking—but I can smell the whiskey from here. Your word isn't worth shit anymore, Brent."

"Ma, okay, I screwed up. It won't happen . . . again. You can tell that narc Dora, Dorix, it's okay. You're a detective. I'm busted. Throw me in jail if you want. But first you may want to turn off the camera." He pointed toward her digital recorder, sitting on the picnic table and aimed right at them. The green light was on.

"You were filming this?" She walked over, grabbed the camera, and switched it off. A quiet rage filled her as she ejected the cassette and jammed it into her pocket.

"Get up," she said, turning to Brent.

"I'm trying," he said, wobbling as he tried to stand. He began to giggle.

"Shut up," she ordered, and hauled him to his feet. Katie had him by the collar so tight, she scared herself, but at least he'd quit snickering. Stepping back, she lowered her hands to his shoulders, holding him steady. "I'm too angry to deal with you now."

"What about Ralph?" Brent said, pointing to the kid who'd been atop him only a few minutes before. "He's still . . . ralphing," Brent added, chuckling at his own joke.

Ralph was, indeed, still on his knees, gagging and wiping his mouth with his tattered sleeve.

Katie looked at the kid. "I could take you in on a variety of charges, but all you are to me is extra paperwork. Get the hell out of here—right now. If I ever see you near Brent again, I'll haul you in for . . . being a pervert child molester or whatever comes to mind. You read me?"

The kid nodded, wiping his bloody lip with the hem of his shirt.

Katie knew the kid's dad—John Harmon. That piece of walking garbage beat the crap out of his wife whenever he was drunk—which was most of the time. "Get out of here. Now!"

The kid took off, stumbled, got back up, and hurried to the back gate.

Katie glared at Brent. "In the house."

"Ma, give me a break. We were just making something to put up on Facebook. I guess we got carried away."

"Don't push me," she said in a deadly voice.

Brent took the hint and scurried inside. He had some problems opening the screen door, but soon was out of her sight.

Katie felt a pounding headache coming on. She'd never felt so trapped in her life. Drugs, drinking, and hanging with the wrong crowd had been Brent's downfall—and her own. He would have gone to jail months ago if she hadn't stepped in.

Reacting as a mom, not a cop, had cost her dearly. She'd removed damning evidence during a bust because it had implicated her son. Brent's photo had been on the dealer's cell phone—a client list of sorts—and she'd been lucky enough to have seen it first. Yet by removing the cell phone, she'd stolen the necessary evidence that could have been used to put the dealer in jail.

The dealer's boss, Roberto Hidalgo, had put the pieces together and linked Brent to her. Moving fast, he'd found other evidence that tied Brent to previous drug buys and had used that information to blackmail her. Katie soon found herself creating diversions for the smugglers whenever a drug shipment came through their corridor. It was only a small favor, Roberto insisted each time, one that wouldn't get her hands too dirty.

The weight of what she'd done wouldn't have been quite so unbearable if Brent had actually turned his life around after that incident. Yet except for switching from drugs to booze, it hadn't even slowed him down. She'd done everything she could to reach him, to make him see that he was throwing his life away, but her kid had one thing in common with his father—both were great with promises, not so good on follow through.

Despite it all, she'd never given up on Brent. She knew that he'd straighten out if she could just find a way to get through to him.

Hearing a call come over the radio, she answered.

"Farmington PD called," dispatch said. "They nabbed a burglary team—two brothers—suspected of using the obits to target homes. Their MO is to strike on the days of the funerals. It's possible the pair carried out the burglary attempt at The Outpost."

"In that instance, there were three individuals seen in the vehicle. Any news on the third perp?"

"Nothing so far."

"I want a chance to question the two they've got ASAP," Katie said.

"Roger that. Captain Tafoya cleared it for you."

Katie glanced back at the house. She was still too pissed off at Brent to talk to him now, and it wouldn't do much good anyway considering the shape he was in.

Returning to her cruiser, she drove east on sixty-four. She still wasn't sure what part Hidalgo had played in Stuart's murder, so she'd have to be careful. These bozos were probably working for Hidalgo, and if his name came up during questioning, the drug dealer would drag her down with him.

The brothers had already been separated, and as she joined the interview, the Farmington detectives were applying the heat.

"We caught you with the Petersons' big-screen TV and sound system, Frankie. Make it easy on yourself," Joe Medina, the Farmington PD case detective said while Katie stood back. "Tell us about your other jobs—like that business over by Hogback you tried to hit the other day."

"I stole stuff before, okay? I served two years' jail time for that, then rehab. Now I'm clean and strictly legit. I never saw any of that stuff you guys say you found at my house, and I don't know nothing about The Outpost."

"I never mentioned the name of the trading post, Frankie. Tell me about that, and why you were working way out of your turf? And who was your driver, the third man in the car? Either you or Adam put a bullet hole in that yellow pickup. That adds firearms enhancement to the charges and can double your jail time. Give us the name of the driver. Cooperate and we'll recommend a deal."

"How can I deal when I don't know nothing?"

"We've got you on several counts right now. The stolen electronics were covered with your prints," Joe snapped.

"Yeah, well, somebody set me and my brother up," Frankie said, and shrugged.

"How'd they get your fingerprints, then?"

"They must have put the stuff in my house while I was gone, then transferred my prints from a mirror or something with tape, maybe, like on CSI. Somebody hates me."

"Adam tells a different story."

"Nice try. My brother wouldn't say anything against me.

We're flesh and blood. Go ahead and keep wasting my time, and yours. Meanwhile, the real burglars are out there, stealing stuff."

Medina turned away, rolling his eyes.

᛭

After having no better luck with a second pass at Adam, Frankie's brother, Katie met with the two detectives in the bullpen.

"I don't get it," Medina said. "Neither of these guys is exactly a Mensa candidate, and they know we've got them dead to rights on three different burglaries. So why not cut a deal and name their partner?"

"Frankie slipped up with the trading post. The name of the business they tried to hit never made the papers. They're protecting the driver, the guy who first waved around the handgun. They're running scared; otherwise, they would have given him up to get a few years knocked off their sentence," Detective Henry, the other FPD detective said.

"I wouldn't rate either of these guys as violent, but their boss might be," Katie said, thinking of Hidalgo. The driver probably worked for the drug kingpin and that connection was undoubtedly known to the two burglars. The danger of naming names was as clear to them as their desire to see the next sunrise.

"We'll keep working on these jokers and let you know if we get something you can use," Detective Medina said.

As Katie pulled out of the Farmington station sometime later, she reached into her pocket for more antacids. Hidalgo. If only she could get something on that bastard. She should call in Ben Stuart, who might be able to ID one of the brothers. But if he did, she still wouldn't have enough leverage on their boss. All she would do is piss him off. She'd have to sit on this for now and hope Stuart wouldn't find out whom they had in custody.

With a frustrated sigh, she flipped open her cell phone and dialed the number Roberto had given her.

"This is my family time. It better be important," Hidalgo snapped.

"The low-IQ pair you hired to break into The Outpost have accomplished the opposite of what you intended. They're in custody and they're calling way too much attention to the place. So far they haven't given up the name of the third man. Is he one of yours, maybe the same guy who robbed the store and locked up the employees?"

"Don't know what you're talking about."

"Of course you don't. Anyway, I figured you'd want an update. The Farmington cops aren't through with those two yet."

"They won't talk, they want to live. Just do *your* job." Hidalgo spoke to someone else, then came back on the line.

"Listen carefully, *guapa*," Hidalgo said a moment later, his voice a low growl. "The only reason your son's not rotting in jail right now is because you've looked the other way each time I've asked. Keep your end of the bargain and we'll all stay out of prison, your son included."

Katie hung up. She hated Hidalgo. Even if she managed to nail him, nothing would ever be the same for her again. With each passing day, she became more like the ones she'd joined the police to fight. Too much dirt clung to her now, but once it was over, she'd leave the department and start a new life with Brent elsewhere, far from here.

That one hope was all she had left, and the only thing that kept her going.

—ELEVEN—

Inventory was well under way at The Outpost. Earlier this morning, Regina found merchandise in the back room Jo had never even known they carried—high-end Navajo-created dry painting reproductions that were breathtakingly beautiful. Although Jo had been able to find the items listed on the handwritten ledgers, they'd never been displayed for one reason or another. She wondered if they were worth killing over.

Jo could feel Ben watching her as they worked. Those searing looks sent ripples up her spine and brought back high school memories of romance. The man he'd become wanted her just as much as the boy he'd been once.

She stopped that thought in its tracks, knowing she'd somehow have to keep her romantic fantasies at bay. Ben was still her biggest weakness. Although she hated the way he always put her on the defensive, he could also make her feel things no one ever had, before or since.

"Did you hear what I said?" Ben asked her.

"Sorry. I was thinking of something else. Say again?"

"You're not just taking inventory, Jo, you're looking for the reason why Dad was killed—contraband, stolen, illegal merchandise, or smuggled goods. But you know Dad was a straight arrow. He'd never deal in anything even remotely questionable."

"Tom was an honest man, but he bought from many different vendors. What if something he took in was stolen and the thief was willing to kill to get it back? Have you considered that possibility?"

"Everything here has a history we can trace."

"That's assuming the people who brought the merchandise to us didn't lie about its origins. But we've also discovered things here that were never fully documented, like those dry painting reproductions. Where did they come from, originally?"

Ben said nothing for several long moments, then at long last, spoke. "It's not knowing *why* Dad was killed that frightens you most, isn't it?"

"The enemy you don't know poses the biggest threat," she said.

"You'll be fine, Jo. You always are."

"Was that a dig, or a compliment?" she asked.

"It's a fact. You're a strong woman who goes after what she wants—well, almost always," he added, a grin tugging one corner of his mouth.

His voice felt like a caress that teased and enticed all at the same time. He wanted her, and was man enough to sense her attraction to him. Danger surrounded Ben. She wondered if he'd be rough or gentle in bed, or if he'd be equal parts of both. Tempting what-ifs mingled with another dozen if-onlys.

Yet common sense prevailed. "You and I need to keep our minds on business, Ben."

"Nobody spends all their time working. You need to give yourself some time to play, to indulge the other side of you."

His words lingered provocatively in her imagination. "A personal life is a luxury I can't afford right now. The Outpost's my priority," she said. "I've set everything aside for it, my *hataalii* studies, which mean the world to me, and even the marketing course I'm taking at night school. I had to drop it."

"Practical Jo. You always set goals and achieve them, but you've never really needed anyone else, have you?"

She turned her back to him, afraid she'd somehow give herself away. She wasn't the unassailable, formidable woman he thought she was. Far from it. She ached to have someone love and comfort her so she wouldn't have to be strong all the time. Sometimes in the middle of the night when her thoughts refused to be still, she thought about Ben. Back in high school, hanging around him had made her feel almost invincible. His willingness to take chances, to risk it all for a few moments of fun and excitement, had drawn her like a moth to the flame. Yet it was knowing what happened to the unwise moth that eventually gave her the courage to walk away.

No, that wasn't true. She hadn't walked away—she'd run. The intensity of feelings she couldn't control had made her feel too . . . vulnerable. Navajo ways taught that everything had two sides, and she'd seen the flip side of love. It meant carrying another's burdens—as her mother had done for her husband, and as she'd done for her father once her mother had passed.

Life had always forced her to be strong, and she'd played the part to the hilt, but she'd paid a price. No one ever bothered to look past the illusion she'd created to see what lay beyond.

"Am I wrong about you, Jo? Is it really that you don't need anyone, or have you forgotten how to reach out?" He turned her around to face him.

She started to speak, but no words came. It was as if he'd read her thoughts.

"Tell me what you want," he said, his voice rough and low, his eyes traveling to her breasts like a slow caress, then back up. "When you're silent, it sparks my imagination."

She drew in an unsteady breath. "Your imagination doesn't need a spark—it needs a bucket of water."

"Ouch."

She moved away and forced herself to focus on the elaborately made silver and turquoise cuff bracelet she'd found in a small box. "Tom must have taken this in recently. I don't remember it and there's no tag, but I recognize the design, so I can link it to the artist."

Before he could say anything, Leigh Ann came up. "Detective Wells is here. She wants to speak to both of you—in private."

Jo glanced at Ben. "Let's go."

As they walked to the front of the store, Jo saw Detective Wells's gaze shift to Ben and stay on him. It didn't surprise her. Ben had something that could only be described as "presence." Women were naturally drawn to him, even when logic and common sense demanded the exact opposite.

"Good morning, Detective. Can I offer you some coffee?" Jo asked, noticing the dark circles under the woman's eyes. She looked as tired as Jo felt.

"Yes, thanks. Black and strong with two sugars, if you have it. Then let's go someplace where I can speak to both of you in private."

Jo led them into the break room and closed the door. The informal setting would hopefully set everyone at ease. She poured coffee from the corner pot into three cups, grabbed some packets of sugar, and brought them over.

Ben took a seat on one of the chairs, sitting up straight, and wound as tight as a drum.

Jo sat down last. "All right. You've got our full attention, Detective."

"As the new owner of The Outpost, have you come across anything that could explain why Tom Stuart was attacked and killed?"

"No, and I've been searching for just that, too," Jo said.

"We're not looking at this right," Ben said. "Whoever killed my father has been manipulating us from the beginning. You said there were no signs of a fight at home, but as I told you before, Dad was a former marine. There's *no way* he would have just sat there while someone pointed a gun at his head. He would have put up a helluva fight. It was his nature. The room would have been trashed."

Katie nodded slowly. "We know more now, and I can tell you he didn't have an easy death."

"I need to know how he died," Ben said.

"The autopsy report is in, but it might be real hard for you two to hear the details."

"I'm a crewman on a medevac team, and I've already served two combat tours in Afghanistan—the first as a sniper. I've seen more than most people can even imagine. Don't hold back on account of me."

Jo watched Ben. His face was set; his eyes gleamed with an edge of steel. He was holding on to anger, relying on that to give him the added strength he needed. Yet, without balance there was only chaos, and nothing good could ever come from that.

Katie turned to Jo, eyebrows raised.

Jo swallowed hard. "I'm staying." She clasped her hands together in front of her on the table to keep them from shaking.

As Detective Wells gave them details, Jo felt bile rise to the back of her throat. Without a word, she slid her chair back and walked quickly to the employees' small bathroom. After splashing cold water on her face, the urge to vomit passed. She took an unsteady breath, then went back in.

Ben was pacing like a caged tiger. "My father was *tortured.* That's what it is, plain and simple. I should have seen that before now. It's the only way he would have given up that safe combination."

"To catch whoever did this, I'm going to need your help," Detective Wells said, looking directly at Jo. "You knew Mr. Stuart better than anyone else who worked here, according to what I've been told by the staff. Think hard. Who were his enemies and what kind of information could Stuart have had that might have led to his death? Why break into the store safe, and not even try to crack open the cash box? What's more important than that to a thief?"

The chills that preceded a cold sweat gripped Jo; then her hands began to tremble. It always started with her hands; then her entire body would follow. Fighting the symptoms, she clasped her hands so tightly, her knuckles ached.

"I have no idea what they were looking for. I also don't know who his enemies were or even if he had any. Ben's dad didn't talk to me about things like that."

Wells never took her eyes off Jo. "Did he recently conduct business with anyone new, maybe someone not quite trustworthy?"

"Not that I know about, but there's something you need to understand," Jo said. "My boss held himself to a very high standard, and in his book, things were either wrong or right—black or white. If he knew someone was dishonest, he wouldn't have anything to do with them."

"I'll second that," Ben said.

"Anyone can be tricked. Maybe he inadvertently got involved with the wrong people, or refused to deal with someone who wouldn't take no for an answer. It might have also been a personal matter that escalated," Wells said, watching their reactions. "And it had to involve something that was bigger than a cash box and could end up stored in a safe, if there is a connection between those events."

"Your guess is as good as mine. I wish I had more of an answer to give you," Jo said. She'd been ordered not to tell anyone about the threat made over the phone, and maybe keeping that secret had kept her alive. Without knowing exactly what the killer wanted, there was no way to point a finger at a suspect anyway, so why add to the danger she was already facing?

"You told me once before to stay out of police business, but it seems to me you could use some help," Ben said.

"The situation *has* changed, so to work the case effectively I'm going to need your cooperation. If you hear anything I can use, or get any vibes, or notice anything that seems out of the ordinary, call me immediately. You have my number."

Jo nodded and Ben did the same.

"What will you do next?" Ben asked. "You've got a plan, right?"

"Yes, but investigations don't benefit from rigid thinking. I take things one step at a time and change directions as needed. Right now, I'm going to dig hard into your father's personal life—his activities and contacts. The motive's out there and I need to find it. I'm also going to need you to give me a list of everyone who has worked here in the past, say, two years."

"You think one of our people killed him?" Jo argued. *"No way."*

"Last year we had a feed store that was burned to the ground with the owner still in it. One of the clerks he'd fired for theft came back to get even," Katie said. "The suspect took a plea for manslaughter and is serving time right now."

"No one's been fired here, but we had two people who quit last year. I'll get you their names and addresses."

"What about shoplifters?" Katie asked Jo. "What's your policy for handling that?"

"Our losses are usually small. Since our high-end merchandise is under lock and key, the items targeted by thieves are normally food and drink. Most of the time that's the work of a kid, so we call the parents, square things, and let it go. If the shoplifter is in his late teens or beyond, we always press charges. There have been exceptions to that, but they're rare. The last one I remember was about six months ago. A homeless woman was caught stealing some food. Instead of having her arrested, my boss allowed her to work here to pay for the things she needed."

"Is she still here?"

"No. She moved on with her kids, but I have the information on her." Jo brought out a journal, showing her the records, kept by hand. "As you can see, we write down every name and incident, including staff and other witnesses."

"This isn't locked up, maybe in the safe?" Katie asked, speculating.

"Not at all. We keep it here on a shelf," Jo said.

Katie nodded, then wrote down the names of the adults entered on the list. "You mentioned that high-end merchandise is kept in locked display cases."

"It is," Jo said. "It's an added precaution."

"Where are the keys kept?" Katie asked.

"After hours in the safe. It's a new model that's all but impossible to crack unless you know the combination," Jo said.

"If my father was drugged so his killer could get the combination," Ben asked, "then why didn't the robber go looking for those keys the other day when he opened the safe?"

"Were they there?" Katie asked.

"No, they were in my pocket, but he never asked for them and I wasn't about to volunteer," Jo said.

"This just keeps getting stranger and stranger. Now it's sounding like some kind of revenge motive. For now I want your list of employees, particularly any who aren't currently working here. I'll follow up on those names," Wells said, looking at Jo.

"One more thing, Detective," Ben said. "My father didn't get to finish his fight, so I intend to do that for him. I'll never let this go until his killer is behind bars. If you can't track him down, I will."

Katie met his gaze, and for several seconds neither moved. "I know you're angry and in pain, but I'm telling you right now— stay out of it unless I come to you with a question. Nothing good can happen if you interfere. Screw up just once, and the killer or killers could walk, or worse, you might target an innocent man."

Working hard to appear cool and collected, though at the moment she was neither, Jo glanced over at Ben. "All the employee names and addresses, former and current, are in your father's computer in the folder labeled 'Personnel.' Why don't you print out whatever Detective Wells needs."

As Detective Wells and Ben left, Jo remained seated. The cold medical terms for what Tom had gone through had shaken her to the core. She couldn't move. If she stood up now, she was sure her legs wouldn't hold up and she'd crash to the floor. At least she hadn't fallen apart in front of the others.

Alone, she felt the tremors spread through her. She didn't want anyone to see her like this, so she concentrated on keeping her breathing even. With her hand around her *jish* she fought hard to pull herself together.

"You okay?" Ben said, coming back in after several minutes. "You're shaking like a leaf."

"I should have pushed your father until he told me what was wrong," Jo said, her voice unsteady. "If I had, he might still be alive."

"This wasn't your fault. My dad made his own decisions," he said, gently pulling her out of the chair and into his arms.

The warmth of his body melted the iciness inside her. She wanted to lean against him and allow herself to forget everything but him, if only for a moment. Yet afraid of where it would lead, she reached inside herself for strength, and moved away instead.

"If I'd been more of a friend, I would have found a way to help him. He shouldn't have had to go through that hell."

"Don't second-guess yourself, not now. Take it from someone who has been there." His voice dropped and darkened. "We all have regrets, but should-haves and could-haves will destroy you one inch at a time. Clamp a lid on those thoughts before they suck the life right out of you."

Jo sensed the undercurrent of pain behind his words. That

hadn't been just the observations of a man who'd been to war. They'd been the echoes of a boy who'd lost his father long before the man's death—a loss that couldn't be reversed now.

"Dad could have gotten help anytime if he'd asked, but he chose to handle things on his own because that's who he was. He went down fighting, and my guess is that his killer didn't get what he wanted either, even with the safe combination. A small victory."

Jo took a steadying breath, feeling calmer now. "He was a strong man. He never fell apart." She glanced down at her hands. At least she wasn't shaking. "Unlike me."

"You have your own brand of strength," he said. "And you also have me."

Once again she felt the stirring of desire. She didn't want to need him like this . . . but she did. More than anything she wanted to follow her heart and stop being careful. She wanted to lose control, to walk on the wild side without worrying about regrets—but that just wasn't her.

Jo once again put up the familiar walls that kept her safely out of his reach. "I need a chance to decompress. Let me do some office work, then we'll continue inventory."

An hour later she was still at her desk, transferring funds and trying to figure out which bills to pay and which to put off until the last minute. No matter how she looked at it, she needed to step up the cash flow. The trading post's grocery and dry goods wholesalers would stop delivery if they didn't get paid on time, and if that happened, their regular customers would stop coming, too. They'd go out of business in a hurry after that.

Jo called Mike Broome, and the attorney answered after she'd spent several minutes on hold. "It's good to hear from you, Jo. I heard about the robbery. How are things going?"

"Not so good, that's why I'm calling. Unless business picks up, I'll only be able to stay open another couple of months. Is there any way you can make more capital accessible to me?"

"You've got every penny of Tom's business assets. The rest of his funds went to his son. Maybe Ben—"

"No. I'll figure something out," she interrupted. "Once the transfer of ownership paperwork is complete, I should be able to take out a bank loan, if necessary. In the meantime, I'll cut back on my own salary a little more. That'll help stretch things out."

As she hung up, she saw Ben at the door. "I overheard what you said, and I've got an idea if you're open to another solution."

She suspected he was about to offer her a loan, but what strings would come attached to that? She waited for him to continue.

"It's clear from what I've been seeing and hearing since I arrived that Dad made the right choice, picking you to continue his dream. I'm not going to stand in your way."

She smiled. "Thanks for trusting your father, and me."

"I do. That's why I want you to let me get more involved. Dad left me with a home that's already paid off and a fairly large amount of money, so here's what I propose: Let me buy a share of this place, say a one third partnership or whatever percentage I can afford that's less than half. You'll still have controlling interest and can run things on your own when I return to my unit."

She considered it for a moment. Letting Ben join her would ensure that the trading post would stay open at least for the immediate future. Yet, like the Navajo Way taught, everything had two sides. If they failed to save The Outpost, would he blame her? There was also another matter to consider. Was he making this offer because he believed in the place his father had built from scratch, or did he just feel sorry for her?

"You know our profit margin is . . . variable. Why are you risking your capital?"

Ben didn't answer right away. He stared out the window for several moments, then finally glanced back at her. "A lot of GIs have a hard time adapting to civilian life once they leave the service. I don't want to be one of them. Dad made a place for himself here at The Outpost after serving his country, and I think I can, too." He managed a quick half smile. "Does that make sense to you?"

"Yes, it does." She belonged to her tribe, and that connection gave her strength and comfort. The Outpost was Ben's link to his father, and as that, a symbol of continuity. "It makes perfect sense."

"So do we have a deal?" he asked her.

"We do." Although it wasn't a custom she favored, she reached out and shook his hand. "We'll have Mike Broome work up a contract. And you know what one of best things about our business partnership is?"

"That you get to have a normal paycheck?"

She laughed. "I think your father would have been pleased by the arrangement."

—TWELVE—

J o woke with a start as a door slammed shut. It was still dark, and the clock said 5:30. Hearing the wind blowing hard outside and feeling a draft inside her bedroom, she sat up. She must have left a window open somewhere. Last time she'd done that, the curtains had tipped over a vase, and the water damage on her rug had been irreversible.

With a groan, she tossed back the covers and got out of bed. As her senses came to life, she picked up an odd scent. Traces of tobacco seemed to linger in the air, but she didn't smoke.

Her heart beating faster, Jo forced herself to remain still and listen. Over the whistling of the wind she heard a car engine in the distance. The sound receded, then faded away.

She reached over to turn on the light, and the sudden brightness blinded her momentarily. Squinting, she looked around the room and saw that her closet door was open. Someone had been in her room!

As she took a step, something shiny at the foot of the bed caught her eye. It took her a heartbeat to recognize Tom's silver money clip.

She jumped, stumbled backwards, and nearly fell, bouncing

off the side of the bed. Seeing her *jish* within arm's reach on the nightstand, she picked it up and clutched it tightly. Jo evened her breathing, struggling to stay calm, and said a short, carefully worded Navajo blessing. Her visitor was probably the same man who'd killed Tom, and the one who'd ordered her to return what was his. He'd promised to contact her once she was ready to give him what he wanted, but she'd been careful not to park out in front of the trading post, the signal he'd asked for. Maybe he'd lost patience. Was this his way of issuing a final warning?

At least he hadn't harmed her—yet. She turned to get her cell phone from the nightstand, but it was gone. Her heart beating faster again, she looked for it on the bed. Last night she'd decided to keep it close, and 911 was on speed dial.

Finally she saw it on the floor, halfway down the hall. She ran over and picked it up. There was a waiting text message.

If u thnk Im mesng w/u, rmembr he wz shot n rght tmpl. Fnd wht yr ded boss hid. Yr runin out of tme

The guy was for real. None of the news reports had revealed Tom had been shot in the right temple. She saved the message, then inched down the hall toward the living room, phone in hand. The entryway closet door was open a foot, and in the living room the sofa cushions had been tossed to the floor. She glanced in the kitchen, and saw that the cabinet doors were all open as well. She'd been so tired, she hadn't heard a thing.

Jo dialed 911, reported the intruder, and was told to remain inside and leave her cell phone on. A tribal officer would be there as soon as possible. It was still dark, so she turned on the porch light and looked out at her truck, hoping it hadn't been vandalized.

As she stood by the side of the window, she noticed car headlights down the lane. They weren't moving. A chill enveloped her. Was the intruder waiting for her to come out now? But that didn't make sense. He'd been in her room and could have done whatever he wanted then. Shaking, she tried to clear her thinking. She needed to update the tribal police.

"There's a vehicle down the road, sitting there with the lights on," she told the dispatcher.

"Stay inside, Jo. Our officer will check it out."

"Okay, but hurry," she said.

She remained behind the curtain as the minutes passed, watching the brightness of the lights down the road fade as the approaching dawn pulled back the darkness. She didn't know what to do. Should she tell the police about the caller? They needed to know, but would she be risking her life by doing that?

After about five more minutes, she could see well enough to make out some details. Her heart started beating overtime as she realized the vehicle was a green pickup. From this distance, she couldn't see anyone inside.

Jo lifted the phone to her ear. "It's a green pickup, like the one burglars used when they tried to break into my trading post three days ago."

"Stay calm and remain inside your home. A patrol officer is nearby and should be arriving soon," the woman dispatcher said.

Jo hung up and, as she looked back toward the highway, saw flashing emergency lights. She reached for the door handle and dead bolt, then realized it was unlocked. He'd come in that way. Maybe the tribal police would be able to get the man's fingerprints.

She'd go out the back door, but first she needed to put on some clothes.

Two minutes later, Jo was standing by the kitchen window, watching the tribal officer moving around by the green pickup. Her cell phone rang and she heard the dispatcher's voice. "Ma'am, the officer would like you to walk over to meet him. Are you armed?"

"No, I don't own a gun, though I'll be buying one real soon. Why you asking?"

"Our officer just needed to know. Walk down the road to his vehicle, keep your hands visible, and make sure you identify yourself," the dispatcher said. "Stay on the line until you get there, please. It's for your own safety."

Jo went out the back door and walked toward the green pickup and the tribal patrolman's SUV.

The officer was standing atop the back bumper of the pickup, taking photos.

"I'm Josephine Buck, Officer," she called out as she drew near. "Someone broke into my home. I called 911 and when I went to the window to check my truck, I spotted this pickup parked down here. Could it be the same truck involved in the burglary attempt on The Outpost last week?"

"Can't say. I'll have to check with county. But neither one of the two men inside this truck broke into your house tonight. Trust me."

A sharp, all-too-familiar smell drifted in her direction. "They're . . . dead?"

"Yeah, Don't touch anything, but take a look and see if you recognize either of them."

Jo peered over the side of the pickup bed, gagged, and almost threw up. She took a step back and fought the urge to run away as panic surged through her.

"You okay?"

Joe sucked in a breath, and tried not to cry. Bracing herself, she went to take another look. One man had been decapitated, and the head wasn't in the bed of the truck. She gagged again. Trying not to vomit, she focused on the second man's face. She didn't know him, but he hadn't had an easy death. Blood-caked stumps were all that remained of his fingers. His shirt was covered with dark, dried blood. From the condition of the bodies and the smell, she guessed they'd been dead for hours.

This was clearly a warning from the man who'd killed Tom. By coming here, he'd violated her own personal circle of safety, and let her know that no matter where she went, she'd never be out of his reach.

Jo returned home and answered a second officer's questions. A crime scene van with more officers was down the road, dealing with the dead bodies. They'd found little evidence inside her house except for the money clip, and there were no fingerprints on it. The intruder had apparently worn gloves. The front door's lock had been picked by an expert, too. She had intended to put more secure locks on, get an alarm guaranteed to wake her, and buy a gun. The Outpost would also get new keyed locks, and the combination changed on the keypad.

The one thing this latest incident told her for sure was that whoever had killed Tom still didn't have what he wanted. The two mutilated men were probably part of the robbery team that had struck the day of the memorial service—at least based on their vehicle, but why they'd been killed still wasn't clear.

After being assured that Detective Wells, who was working with the tribal officers down the road, would be given a copy of the report, Jo left the house via the old, bumpy back road and went in to work.

It was still early, but the trading post's serene silence comforted her. She checked to make sure the shotgun was still in place and loaded, then went to her desk in the break room. From there she left a call on Mike Broome's machine and called the locksmith. Finally she tackled the volumes of paperwork that awaited.

After a while, a cup of freshly brewed coffee in hand, Jo accessed the business account online. The balance there took her by complete surprise. The bank had made a mistake. According to them, a large amount of money had been transferred into the store account earlier.

The bank wouldn't open for a few more hours, but the day began early at the trading post. Jo opened the doors, and Leigh Ann and Esther got busy while Jo went back to her office. She'd just sat down when she heard a knock. Glancing up, she saw Ben at her door.

"I'm going to the hardware distributor to pick up a few things Dad had on order," he said. "I'll be taking the Expedition. Is there anything else you want me to get while I'm there?"

"No, and be careful not to order anything extra without giving me a call first. Garrett's always pushing those new pellet stoves," she said.

"Don't worry about cash reserves for now. You won't have any money problems, at least not right away."

She glanced back at him quickly. "Wait—what?"

"I had Mike Broome arrange a cash transfer from my inheritance into the trading post's account earlier. It's an advance, pending the partnership agreement. I figure that payment will protect my new investment."

Leigh Ann walked in, and before Jo could thank Ben and warn him about what had happened last night, he was gone.

"I overheard," Leigh Ann said. "So money's one less thing you need to worry about now. Just be careful around Ben."

"Why do you say that?"

"Heaven knows I'm the worst judge of character on the planet, but there's just something about Ben. . . ."

"What?" Jo pressed.

"He's done a complete about-face when it comes to the trading post and you," Leigh Ann said. "He now also has what he wanted all along. It's not just your business anymore—it'll be his, too."

As Jo thought about it, she couldn't decide whether or not she'd been skillfully played, though what he'd said earlier about trusting his father and her had seemed real. All things considered, however, Leigh Ann had made a good point. Ben had been right there, ready to make his move.

"Either way, I didn't have much of a choice, so it makes little difference," Jo said, for her own benefit as well as Leigh Ann's.

"I know, honey, and I'm not saying you could have done anything different. I just think you need to be careful when dealing with Ben. I see the way you look at him sometimes, but you're not on a level playing field, you know? That's one guy who knows his way around women."

Jo knew Leigh Ann's advice was right on target, but it had been such a long time since she'd felt this alive. The attraction, the longing, the heat . . .

"Ben's not an easy man to ignore," Jo said. Danger was all around her now, yet the biggest threat of all lay inside herself.

The first big job of the day had been telling the rest of the staff about the break-in at her home the night before, and the gruesome discovery inside the green pickup. It took a while for everyone to settle down after that, particularly Ben, who'd been informed upon his return. He wanted to hire a guard to watch over her, but she'd refused. With the promised increased tribal police presence around her home, it wouldn't be necessary. The man wouldn't be back. After all, he'd already delivered his message.

Jo had warned them all to be careful at home and while on the road. They were already on high alert at the trading post, particularly after what had happened the other day.

What seemed to help most was activity and hard work, so they all remained busy. The locks were changed—a simple rekeying and reprogramming of the keypad code was all that was necessary. Meanwhile, the store inventory continued.

After closing, with everyone gone, Jo finally took a moment for herself. She went outside and walked around the parking lot for a bit, stretching her legs. It wasn't dark enough yet for anyone to sneak up on her, so it was safe.

Standing alone, she stared at the dark outline of Tom's home. She missed him so much. His absence had left a huge hole in her heart and in her life. So many were now looking to her to do the right things. There was no room for mistakes. Tears ran silently down her cheeks. If only she could be the woman she pretended to be—the one made of cold steel who always faced a challenge head-on, no doubts, no second-guesses.

As she remembered the bodies, a sight that would haunt her until her dying day, she felt her tremors begin. Jo reached inside the *jish* at her belt for the token and as she surrendered to its power, her breathing slowly became more rhythmic. Seconds passed, and feeling more in control, she closed the *jish*.

She was on her way back inside when she heard a big vehicle coming around to the rear parking lot. It was Ben in The Outpost's Expedition.

"I've got a surprise for you!" Ben said, exiting the big white SUV.

She wiped her face with her hand, hoping he wouldn't be able to tell she'd been crying. "Time for the iron lady to surface," she muttered under her breath as she went to meet him.

"I've got some state-of-the-art cameras for the trading post," he said, reaching inside the rear door of the vehicle. The second and third row of seats had been removed long ago to create a large cargo area, and there were two big boxes inside.

"I thought it was time we had some of this stuff here," he said. As his gaze focused on her face, he set the box back down. "What's wrong?"

"Nothing. I was just out getting some fresh air," she said. "Long day."

"Either it's the outside lighting, or you're the palest Navajo

I've seen in a long time." He tilted her chin up so she'd look at him. "What's going on?"

"I came out here to take a break, then I looked over and saw your dad's house, sitting there, dark. It's hard to accept that he's really gone."

"I know." He tried to pull her into his arms, but she moved away, glanced back at the store, then at him.

"Everyone at the trading post looked up to your dad. There was no crisis he couldn't handle. He was the owner, but he was also a leader. I try, but I don't have the business skills he did," she said in a weary voice.

"You've been doing this for, what, a week? Don't be so hard on yourself. You're doing your best, and think about it, Jo. Even if The Outpost closes its doors, it won't be the end of the world. People here will move on and eventually find new jobs," he said.

"You don't understand. Your dad used to say that The Outpost finds its own crew, people who need more than just a job. Are you really aware of what you've bought into? The trading post will tie you to this community in ways you never dreamed."

"Those ties were always there, even though I spent a lot of years denying it." He reached into his pocket and pulled out his wallet. "Let me show you something."

After a quick search, he drew out a well-worn photo. The edges were bent and crinkled, and it was clear that it was a treasured memento.

Jo looked at the photo and suddenly smiled. "Your dad, you, and me after that district basketball tournament victory. We went to state that year."

"There have been few perfect moments in my life, but that was one of them."

"And you've carried this with you all this time?" she asked, surprised.

"We had each other's back in those days, remember? My dad never could understand what you saw in me, but he thought you were darned near perfect and figured you were a good influence."

"That's not true. You were his son. I was just a kid you brought home." Her eyes lingered on the photo. "I'm surprised you didn't throw this away after we broke up."

"I wanted to hate you, I really did, but deep down I knew you'd made the right move. I was bad news for everyone around me back then," he said, his voice gravelly. "But those days are behind us. It's time for us to stand together again. Whoever murdered my father isn't through with the trading post yet."

"Is that the real reason you've decided to become my business partner, so you can put yourself in the line of fire, too? Is this your way of facing down your father's enemies?"

"You want to know the truth, but are you sure you can handle it?"

"I've never run from the truth. It's lies I can't stand."

"Then here's your answer." He tilted her chin upward, and kissed her. His lips were tender at first, coaxing hers to open, but as the kiss deepened, fire blazed to life between them.

Feelings she'd kept bottled up for far too long came rushing to the surface, but this time she didn't fight them. Instead, she surrendered to the sensations, wanting and needing more. Even if it was for only a few precious minutes, she wanted to stop being in control of herself . . . or of him.

She drank in his taste, wanting to memorize every detail, every feeling. She was desired by the man she wanted. That knowledge sent a thrill all through her. His roughness, that sign of needs barely kept leashed, enticed her. She wanted to love him and feel him go wild.

The heat became too intense much too fast. Suddenly afraid of who she'd become in his arms, she broke contact and stepped back.

"I care about you, Jo. I never stopped," he said, breathing hard.

She swallowed, still tasting him, her body throbbing in deep and intimate places. No one else had ever been able to make her feel this way. She wanted to lose herself in that heat and those yearnings again.

"I . . ."

He placed a finger on her lips. "No, don't say anything. You've already told me everything I needed to know."

She struggled to even her breathing. Had she reacted too wildly? What had her kiss told him—or not told him?

As he reached for one of the boxes inside the back of the SUV, Jo shook free of those thoughts. She was seeing way too much in what had happened. She wouldn't let longing and imagination trick her into believing it had been something more than just a kiss.

Clearing her throat, she reached out and touched his shoulder. "Ben, something else happened that you need to know about. Remember the money clip your father always carried in his pocket?"

Ben arrived to work early the following day. He hadn't slept much, unable to get Jo off his mind. She'd been crying when he found her outside last night in the parking lot. Seeing her vulnerable and alone had made him crazy inside. No way he could have just walked away.

Then she told him about finding the silver money clip that had belonged to his dad, something he was sure the intruder left for her to find. Someone wanted Jo scared, but whoever that was had now made a deadly enemy. He wouldn't stop until he knew who was behind what was happening.

He'd always thought of Jo as the girl of steel, one who never let anything get to her. Yet seeing her standing there, tears in her eyes, made him realize that the face she put on for the world wasn't who she was inside.

That knowledge had shaken him to the core and reminded him that no matter how strong you were, there were times you needed someone to lean on. He thought back to the incident in Afghanistan that had changed his life. The memory had become a shadow over his soul, something he'd never outrun.

Seeing Jo's pickup parked in the back alongside an old Jeep, he pulled in an adjoining space. The loading dock door was locked, so he knocked and Leigh Ann let him in. She flashed him a smile, and wished him a cheery good morning in her Texas twang.

There was something familiar in her eyes. It was the same wary look he'd seen on the faces of the children who lived in the Afghani villages halfway across the world, the ones who'd seen too much for their years. He had a feeling that, like them, Leigh Ann was a survivor. Maybe someday he'd find out more about the monsters she'd battled.

Ben entered the short hall and went to the break room, still Jo's office. Inside, she was surrounded by paperwork. He looked at her curiously for a moment, wondering how she'd spent the night alone in her home. Had she managed to get any sleep? Had she taken extra precautions?

"I'm okay, if that's what you want to know," she said, looking up. "I had the locks changed at home and an alarm installed that's guaranteed to wake me up. Leigh Ann knew someone who took care of both for me, a former deputy with his own business. He also handled things here for me." She gave him a new key to the trading post's door, and the keypad code, written on an index card. "Here you go. You'll need these."

"Along the lines of security, if there's nothing else you need me to do this morning, I'd like to hook up the surveillance cameras we carried in last night."

"Go for it," she said, then added, "I'll be leaving around noon and be gone most of the day. I have to visit some of our silver-smiths and artists. The Navajo Tribal Fair will begin in two weeks, and that always means an increase in walk-in traffic and out-of-state visitors. I'll need to make sure we have plenty of quality pottery, rugs, and merchandise on hand."

"So basically you're going off for a day of shopping," he teased. "Sounds like the female version of a day in paradise."

"That's the fantasy," she said with a tiny smile. "The reality is having to drive endless miles across the Rez, then doing some hard bargaining on behalf of the trading post."

"You're going to be out in the middle of nowhere most of the day. You should consider taking along Dad's shotgun."

"I'd feel safer knowing it's here where you and the staff can get to it."

"How about taking someone along with you—like me?"

She smiled, but shook her head. "I'll have better luck if I take Esther. She puts people at ease."

"And I don't? I'm the soul of charm."

"You have your moments," she said, unable to suppress an-other smile. "But I need to inspire confidence when I'm bar-gaining, and that's not going to happen if I bring a stranger with me. Many Traditionalists are reluctant to trust Anglos they don't know—and besides, Esther also speaks Navajo."

"Right now I know more Pashto and Dari, so I guess I'll have to make myself useful here," he said, noting that Jo seemed ill at ease around him today. It didn't surprise him. Last night he'd seen a side of her few ever had, and vulnerability was some-thing you showed only a trusted friend. Clearly their new rela-tionship hadn't reached that level yet. "I'll get the cameras up and running."

Leaving Jo, he went into his father's office. Using a split-screen monitor to help with the aim, he placed the first camera up in a corner. From there, it essentially covered the entire room, including the floor safe positioned against the inside wall.

Next, he installed two cameras in what his dad had always called "out front." This was, of course, the customer area. He made sure the entrance, cash registers, and jewelry section were well covered. Lastly, he positioned a fourth camera in the storeroom, arranging it to catch both the back door leading to the loading dock, and the passage door leading down the short hall and out front.

Once Jo stepped out of her office, he transferred the monitor to her desk, hooking it up and confirming camera coverage. If after he returned to his unit she decided to move her desk into his dad's old office, she could take the monitor with her.

As he checked his work, making sure all four cameras were operational and recording onto the hard drive, he watched Jo go into his father's office. Her back to the camera—he'd planned it that way so whoever was watching the monitor couldn't pick up the new combination—Jo opened the safe, brought out a handful of cash held together by a rubber band, and placed it on the desk.

Curious, Ben zoomed in and watched her count a total of two thousand dollars into five piles of fifty-dollar bills. Jo placed a rubber band around each four-hundred-dollar bundle, then put one in her boot, two in her pockets, and the other two in her purse.

The amount of cash she was taking took him by surprise. Considering the lack of tribal police protection in the outlying areas of the Rez, checks would have been a lot more secure.

Ben sat back, trying to make some sense out of what he'd just seen. Jo hadn't realized the cameras recorded what she'd done. Had she known, would she still have taken that much cash out of the safe? Maybe there was more going on at the trading post, things Jo had deliberately chosen to keep under wraps. Two thousand was a king's ransom in this part of the world. Did it have anything to do with the person who'd sneaked into her home just yesterday? Maybe a shakedown she was afraid to report?

Lost in thought, he watched Jo leave the office. Following her on the monitor as she left one viewing field and entered the other, he saw her stop at the register. She said something to Leigh Ann, then walked out the back door.

Ben left Jo's office and went to join Leigh Ann, who was busy helping a Navajo woman pick out some cooking utensils. When both women looked up at him at the same time, he realized he wasn't needed—or wanted.

"Ladies." He nodded, passing by them and pretending to check out the small stock of fishing gear and supplies.

After the Navajo woman paid for her items, Ben joined Leigh Ann at the cash register. "I wanted to let you know that the surveillance cameras are working and recording," he said, pointing out the ones she could see, then telling her about the other locations and coverage.

"That's great," she said. "The mirrors are helpful, but I like the idea of having that added bit of security, particularly after all that's happened."

"I figured it was about time for more state-of-the-art equipment," Ben said. "You know, the trading post has been a part of my life for as far back as I can remember, but I never realized how much work it took to keep things on track."

"Nothing in life is as simple as it seems on the surface," she said. "The Outpost is a prime example. Look around you. Things may look the same as always, but in reality, everything's changed."

"Until my dad's killer is caught, the appearance of business as usual is the best we can hope for." He looked around at the jewelry, Navajo art, and even the glass-faced refrigerators with milk, eggs, and baking goods. "The person who killed my dad was looking for something he never found. It could be hidden here someplace, or maybe it's staring us right in the face. You've had the chance to think about it, too. Any idea yet on what my father had that might be worth killing for?"

"I wish I knew," Leigh Ann said in a whisper-thin voice. "It would take so much pressure off of Jo. She must have told you what she went through the night before last. Someone in her house while she was asleep, then those dead men all carved up and left for her to find. I don't know how she can stay there now, alone. And we all know it's connected to the murder somehow."

He nodded slowly. "There are too many questions and very few answers."

"Since the morning Tom was killed, I've done nothing but try to figure out why it happened. He wasn't the kind of man who made enemies. Everyone liked him. The only guy your dad even argued with was Ethan Sayers, but those two went at it for fun. Ethan's the largest distributor of farming supplies in this area."

"I know him well. My dad and Ethan loved giving each other a hard time."

"Exactly. Those two men really understood each other."

He had a hard time seeing Ethan as a suspect, but he'd follow up on it anyway just in case that rivalry had turned sour over the years. He had just a little more than two weeks left, so he had to look hard and fast into every possibility. But before he left the trading post this morning, there was one more thing he needed to do here.

"I think you're going to like these cameras, Leigh Ann. Just remember everything going on will end up being recorded by the system."

"Which means Del is going to have to stop scratching his itchy place, and I'll have to stop sneaking a grab at the produce man's tight little butt," she said, looking him straight in the eyes.

Ben laughed out loud.

"I bet those cameras weren't cheap. How'd you manage?"

"I got a great deal from that camera shop on East Main in

Farmington. It's going out of business, and I had to pay cash, but I got them for a third of their list price," he said.

"A lot of businesses in this area are cash or check only, especially the ones with a low profit margin. Credit cards always take a percentage from the merchants and some mom-and-pop businesses just can't afford that," Leigh Ann said.

"I think what gives The Outpost an edge is that we take all forms of payment, including layaway. Dad always put the customers first," he said. "But what about the artists and silversmiths—those not working on consignment? Do they take checks?"

"I don't have anything to do with purchasing, so I can't tell you for sure, but I can't see why they wouldn't. This is the twenty-first century."

Just then a customer came up to the register with several items in her small metal cart, and Leigh Ann got to work.

Ben returned to his father's office, sat down, and tried to think of what else Jo could do with that cash besides pay an artist or vendor. The community had changed since he enlisted, so did merchants here pay protection, like in nearly every Middle Eastern country he'd been through?

His father never would have consented to that, but Jo was more vulnerable. Maybe someone was shaking her down. One way to find out was to learn more about the other businesses in the area. It was time for him to talk to Ethan Sayers.

Twenty minutes later, Ben walked through the doors of Ethan's giant farm equipment and supplies warehouse. As he did, he nodded to the older, though still familiar faces working the pallets and stacking sacks of feed.

"Good to see you back home safe, boy," Ethan Sayers said, coming out of his office to greet Ben.

"Thanks. It's good to see you, too," he said, shaking Ethan's rough, callused hand.

"Saw you at the memorial service but never got a chance to

tell you how much I respected your pop. Sure wish you could have come home to happier circumstances." Ethan looked Ben over and smiled. "Danged if you didn't become a man when no one was looking."

"How's Artie doing these days?" he asked, referring to Ethan's son, one of Ben's former school friends.

"He screwed around in college for three years, dropped out, and took a few dead-end jobs. Then he got into a fight with a state cop who pulled him over for DWI and did a few months' jail time."

"I'm sorry to hear that. Where's he now?"

"Arthur's got an apartment in Farmington now, along with a decent job. He's finally getting his shit together." Ethan gestured to his office. "Come in. Let's talk. How about something cold to drink? No beer, but I've got Cokes and cream soda."

Ben smiled. He hadn't had a cream soda in forever. "Cream soda."

"Here you go," Ethan said, handing him a bottle.

They twisted open the caps and took long swallows. "I know things are tough for you right now, son, but if you need anything, just say the word. Your dad and I always butted heads like two old goats, but we were still good friends."

"I know. That's why I'm here."

"Whatever you need—just name it."

"I've heard here and there that my dad wasn't quite himself these past few weeks, that he was moody and distracted. Is it possible that someone had been shaking him down, maybe blackmailing him for some reason?" he said, mostly to gauge Ethan's reaction.

"Your father wouldn't have taken crap like that lying down, boy. He would have turned on them and gone for the jugular. But what reason could anyone have had to blackmail him? Most of us cut a few corners here and there in business or taxes, but not your dad. He played it straight all the way down the line. Tom was one of the last honest men, and as good as his word. These days, that's saying quite a bit."

"True. By any chance did Dad ever mention any business plans that might have made him some enemies, like a price war with another merchant, for example. Or maybe he was planning to buy someone out, or had a beef with a customer or vendor?"

"No, nothing like that. Tom and I talked a lot about business, and I would have heard if he'd been thinking about anything along those lines." Ethan paused. "But there's something you need to keep in mind. A lot of things have changed around here since you left for the army. Gangs have moved into our area from the cities, and with them have come a slew of other problems we've never had to face before."

"Like what?"

"Punk criminals involved with drugs—making, selling, or using, sometimes all three, especially meth and crack cocaine. Burglaries and violence are way up," Ethan said. "These days I think we all get visits from people we'd rather greet with a shotgun."

"Have you been pressured by some of those hoods?" Ben asked. "Whatever you tell me won't go any farther than you and me. You have my word."

"I get cased from time to time by some druggie looking for a quick score, but basically, I'm not worth the effort. I've got nothing on hand they can steal and sell fast." Ethan let out his breath slowly. "The problem, according to the newspapers, is that there's a big pot and cocaine smuggling corridor that originates in Mexico and runs right through the middle of the state. That business brings the kinds of problems we've never faced here before."

Ben nodded, recalling his own experiences overseas. In 'Stan, drug production and trade accounted for the bulk of the economy. Corruption and crime were the norm. Some things never changed, regardless of where in the world you went.

He continued, still probing for the answers. "There's something else that might explain what happened, Ethan. Was there anything at all about Dad's personal life, or business, that might have targeted him, and maybe The Outpost's new owner, Jo Buck?"

Ethan paced around the office for a few seconds before stopping and looking back at Ben. "Danged if I know, but if you want, I'll ask around, discreetly of course. I won't say anything that might come back to embarrass you or that Navajo girl. She's a peach, isn't she?"

"She sure is. And I appreciate your help, Ethan," Ben said. "Out of curiosity, what kind of questions did Detective Wells ask you?"

"I know who you're talking about, but she hasn't been here, nor any other deputy either."

The news took Ben by surprise. "It's hard to believe that no one from the sheriff's department has been here yet. You knew Dad better than almost everyone."

"I'd like to think so."

He stood and shook Ethan's hand. "Thanks for the information, and if you hear anything that might help me figure out what happened to Dad, and who might have been responsible, let me know."

"I will. Your father might have just got into the wrong person's face, but like the Navajos say, everything's connected. Be careful what you stir up, son."

—THIRTEEN—

Ben returned to the trading post after lunch. Needing time to think things through, he remained outside, sitting on the loading dock and staring off into the distance at Shiprock.

"You feeling okay?" Regina asked, coming up from behind him.

He looked up at the tall Navajo woman in Western-cut jeans and blouse and nodded. "Yeah, I'm just trying to get a few things straight in my head. The way The Outpost does business sometimes doesn't make much sense to me," he said, deciding to press and see how much she knew. "Why would Jo head out into the middle of nowhere carrying a wad of cash? What's going on?"

"You think she's involved in something illegal? Is that what you're saying?"

"Not that exactly, but could someone have been shaking down my father and now her?" he asked.

"No, that's silly. Like with Tom, the money goes out to our silversmiths, not some thug," Regina said. "Don't worry. She'll be safe where she's going, safer than in her own home, as you've no doubt heard. Jackrabbits and crows don't generally carry guns, and she'll see more of those than people where she's headed."

He laughed. "That bad, huh?"

"Depends how you look at it. I wouldn't want to live outside town, but some of our best tribal artists live in Traditionalist areas, and those are isolated communities. Take Rebecca Bidtah, our most popular potter. She's a Traditionalist, and lives over by Crystal. She doesn't have a bank account or credit card. She deals only in cash. It's the same with a lot of the artists and silversmiths, especially over in eastern Arizona."

"It sounds like our buyers have their work cut out for them."

Hearing a noisy vehicle coming up the drive, Regina turned her head and smiled. A restored old Ford pickup painted candy apple red pulled up and parked. "You're about to meet one of our tribe's most gifted turquoise and silver jewelry makers. We sell everything he brings us almost as fast as we get it in. Every jewelry outlet from Flagstaff to Albuquerque wants to carry his pieces. That's why we all go out of our way to make him feel comfortable here, but bargaining with him takes a skill all its own. If you go in too low, he'll walk off in a huff and it could be months before he comes back."

Ben smiled, taking it as a challenge. "Let me see what I can do," he said, going back inside. "I'll catch him out front."

Ben was standing at the back of the room when a tall, very muscular Navajo man came into the trading post. He wore a white, *camisa*-style, open-collared shirt that was squared off at the bottom, and tan, casual cotton slacks instead of jeans. His hair was long and loose, old warrior style, and fell nearly to his waist. He walked up to them confidently, carrying a tooled leather briefcase.

Ben watched as the man went directly to Leigh Ann.

"It's good to see you, Ambrose. It's been quite a spell," she greeted.

"I have some new designs I thought Jo might be interested in seeing," he said.

"Jo's not here right now, but I'd love a peek, Ambrose. I can't make you an offer, but I could tell Jo about the pieces and whet her appetite for you. It'll give her something to look forward to."

He considered it for a beat. "No thanks. Jo and I have a history. When I started out in this business, a lot of shop owners were afraid of gays—like it was contagious or something. I caught a lot of crap from the good ole boys. But Tom and Jo respected me and my work. Tom's gone now, so Jo's at the top of my list. She gets first look."

Ben came out from behind the counter and gave him a nod. "Thanks for your kind words about my dad. I'm Ben, Tom's son."

"*Ben?* I thought you looked familiar!" he said, then laughed and added, "Aw hell, you don't recognize me, do you? I'm the tall, skinny Navajo kid who never could make it up the rope climb."

Ben smiled slowly. "A.J., is that you underneath all that beef?" He reached out and gave Ambrose John a cracking loud fist bump.

"Yeah, man, I got tired of having my ass kicked, so I took mixed martial arts classes and started working out. It paid off. Things are pretty much okay for me these days, even in redneck country. Nobody gives me any . . . crap," he said, glancing at Leigh Ann.

"You two know each other?" she asked.

Ambrose grinned. "In high school, Ben had my back whenever anyone tried to use me as a punching bag. We gave as good as we got. He kept me out of intensive care, that's for sure."

"Now you're *the* master silversmith around here," Ben said, grinning. "I should have known! You were head and shoulders above the rest of us in Mr. Ortiz's art and crafts class. Remember making those leather belts and billfolds?"

"Yeah. I bought my first swivel knife here at The Outpost. Good times." Ambrose replied. "Wanna see what I'm up to these days?"

He placed the briefcase on the counter, then brought several handcrafted necklaces, earrings, and bracelets out of his briefcase. Each piece had been carved, tooled, cut, and polished with exquisite precision, designs too intricate to fully make out at a glance.

Leigh Ann sucked in her breath. "Oh, wow! Look at that cuff bracelet. Those stones are a perfect match, and not just color. Each matrix is like a spiderweb."

Ben turned to her, chuckling. "First you tell him he does perfect work, *then* you try and negotiate, Leigh Ann?"

Ambrose laughed. "That's okay. Hell, I know I'm good."

"And modest," Ben said, grinning.

"Screw modesty. When you're good, you should flaunt it."

"Man, you haven't changed," Ben said, laughing. "That 'I'm great' attitude is what got you into trouble back in high school."

"Good thing you were there."

"Hey, if you think you owe me, bro, how about a good deal on these works of art?"

Ambrose burst out laughing. "Works of Ambrose, dude. Keep dreaming."

"At least give me some room to bargain. Let's go back to my dad's office and talk it over."

Ambrose returned the jewelry to the briefcase and they walked toward the back. As Ben went past the women, he saw that Regina was smiling and Leigh Ann nodded slightly.

Respect. It was earned in degrees and he was making headway. Closing the door, he gestured toward the chairs.

"Man, it's good to see you," Ben said. "You're one of the few pieces of my past that doesn't still haunt me."

"You had your wild days, so what? Your father was all about control, so you went in the opposite direction." Ambrose stared across the room at nothing in particular. "Looking back, I'd say you and I were both trapped, each in our own way. I was different and lived in a small Anglo community where anyone who didn't march to the beat of the same drummer paid in blood. Your war was waged at home. Your old man never seemed to give a damn unless you got into trouble, so you started to oblige. Did things ever change between the two of you before—?"

"I think we were finally starting to work things out, but we never got the chance to follow through," Ben said quietly, and brought him up to date.

"So you're thinking he was being blackmailed or shaken down, and there was a confrontation?"

"It's one possibility. The problem is that I have nothing to go on."

"I'll see what I can find out for you," Ambrose said, opening the case again.

"I'd appreciate it."

An easy silence fell between them as Ben looked down at the jewelry A.J. had brought. "I learned enough from my father to know this is top-of-the-line work." Ben studied each piece, then looked up. "Buddy, I can't offer you the price you deserve for these. The Outpost doesn't have the available cash right now. You'd do better taking this to Albuquerque, maybe Old Town, or one of those tribal operations near a pueblo."

"Talk about a lousy negotiator," Ambrose said, shaking his head.

"You're a friend, and business shouldn't trump that."

"I'll tell you what. I don't generally sell on consignment, but there's always a first time. Sell it here for the best price you can get—I've already placed a suggested retail amount on each tag. Keep your usual percentage and give me the rest."

"Can't ask for more than that, bro. Done."

They shook hands, sealing the deal, and A.J. laid out the jewelry on the desk pad. "I'm your friend, Ben. Remember that. To me, that comes first, too."

"I'm returning to my unit in a couple of weeks, then shipping out to theater for a six-month deployment. But I'm not reupping, so when I'm back for good, let's get together. You still like to fish?"

"Yeah, and there's some great fly-fishing in the quality area below Navajo Dam. You and I can spend a few days out there taking it easy."

"Sounds like a plan, bro," Ben said. "Keep in touch."

After A.J. left, Ben placed the jewelry in a box and brought them out for Leigh Ann. "We should keep these suggested prices if you think they'll still sell," he told Leigh Ann. "They're on consignment."

"Ambrose agreed to that?" she asked, her eyes wide. "Until now, Ambrose has always insisted on getting paid in full up front."

"I had an advantage."

Regina came over, and she and Leigh Ann set up a special display in the center case of the jewelry section.

As they worked, Ben realized that although he seemed to have made some headway with Regina, he still wasn't on solid ground with Leigh Ann. She clearly hadn't trusted him, at least in the beginning.

As Regina left to hand-calligraphy a special sign and labels, Ben returned to his dad's office. He was trying to figure out some of the passwords on his dad's computer. Several files still remained out of reach.

Though they'd listed it for just under four figures, the cuff bracelet Ambrose brought in sold less than an hour later to a couple passing through from Scottsdale, Arizona.

"Jo's going to be thrilled," Regina said, coming into the office to tell him. "But it's always like that with Ambrose's pieces. They're never here more than a few days."

Ben went back to the floor and checked out the display. Five pieces remained. He had to admit that it didn't take much of an eye to see that they were worth the price.

Although they'd had only a handful of customers, three more pieces sold by midafternoon.

It was around four when Leigh Ann stepped into the break

room and Ben joined her. "It must feel strange to you coming to work in the mornings and not seeing my dad," he said.

"Sure does. Tom was like the mountains. Just knowing he was there made you feel safe somehow. Not having him around is a constant reminder of how quickly things can change."

He took the cup of coffee she offered him. "I was hoping the sheriff would catch his killer before I rejoined my unit, but I don't think that's going to happen. Detective Wells isn't making much progress, and neither am I. Nothing really adds up."

"Maybe it does, and we don't want to see the answers."

Her voice had been as soft as a whisper, but he caught every syllable. "What do you know, Leigh Ann?"

"Know? Not much. But here's what I think. Your father wasn't the chatty sort. We knew that and figured he'd eventually work out whatever was bothering him," she said. "Now, looking back, I believe we all should have paid more attention to what he *wasn't* saying."

The words struck him hard. She was right. To know what his father had been thinking, he'd have to focus on his actions, not his words. All the clues he'd need lay there.

Jo returned to work early the next morning, right after sunrise. Although she was safe at home now, with sturdier locks that were much harder to pick and a burglar alarm that was enough to wake anyone with a pulse, she still didn't want to linger there. The house just didn't feel like the haven it had been once, but she wasn't going to move—no one was going to run her out.

For now, there was plenty to keep her busy here at the office, even though the trading post itself wouldn't be open for another hour and a half. Today she'd have to reconcile her purchases with her remaining cash, add the new pieces to the inventory system, and get displays set up. Fall and state fair time usually signaled the start of their best quarter, and she had to get The Outpost ready.

Jo walked down the tiny hall past Tom's old office. Now, seven days after his return, Ben had already added his stamp with the new surveillance camera. The desk had been cleared of all mementos, and the files were in perfect order near one corner. As she caught the citrusy scent of Ben's aftershave, she said a silent good-bye to the past. Tom had always been an Old Spice man.

Once inside her office, Jo looked at the camera now set to monitor her every move. It was a necessary concession, though she hated the idea of always being watched, even electronically. Making a face at the camera, she sat down before her low-tech adding machine and began totaling the receipts. Most of the artisans who lived in the outlying areas weren't big on paperwork. Some with limited English had no writing skills. A list of items, a witnessed X, and the name she printed beside it were sometimes all that formalized a payment.

As she worked to reconcile the amounts, she heard footsteps in the storeroom. She knew she'd locked up after coming in, and it was still too early even for Leigh Ann.

She started to pick up the phone, but talking now would only give away her location. Frantically she searched for a weapon. Her scissors were the small aluminum kind with round tips, and her ruler was plastic. The stapler—that was a joke, as was the legal-sized clipboard. The only real firepower was the shotgun behind the counter, but she'd have to go past whoever was inside to get to it.

She looked around, seeing only the half-height refrigerator, microwave oven, and an empty glass Coke bottle. She grabbed that by the neck. It was thick at the bottom and would have to do.

Holding the Coke bottle like a club, Jo flattened against the wall. She could hear the intruder's footsteps just outside her office door. She waited, her whole body shaking, ready to clock him the second he stepped in.

Jo saw the knob turn and then the tip of a boot. As a leg and an arm appeared, she stepped out and brought the bottle down.

His arm shot up instantly, blocking the blow while using his free hand to grab the bottle in mid-swing and wrench it from her grasp. Something else hit the floor with a crackle.

"What the hell?" Ben said, looking at her. "You trying to ambush me?"

Shaking, Jo glowered at him. "*Why* were you sneaking around the trading post?" she managed through clenched teeth. "It's barely six thirty."

"Sneaking? Are you nuts? I came in early to set out some treats for the staff." He pointed to the clear plastic storage box on the floor. The lid had popped loose from the fall, and two dough-nuts had spilled out. "Made 'em myself. I was going to leave some on your desk."

She blinked. "Huh?"

He pulled out a tissue from the box on her desk, picked up both doughnuts, then set them on her desk pad. "You follow the five-second rule on floor spills, don't you?"

She nodded, glancing at the sugar-covered doughnuts atop the Klcenex. "You . . . cook?"

"I like to eat; ergo, I cook. What about it?"

"Nothing," she answered quickly. "I'm just . . . surprised."

"Why?" he asked with a half smile. "Not macho enough for you?"

"No, it's just not the Ben I knew once. You used to spend all your time outside."

"Yeah, 'cause the house was a war zone after Mom died."

"When *did* you learn to cook?" she said, picking up the clos-est of the two doughnuts and taking a bite. They practically melted in her mouth, and tasted wonderful.

"After I came back from my first tour, I needed to reconnect with life, so I bought a deep fryer and a microwave oven. Cooking turned out to be good therapy."

"These are really good," she said, taking another bite. "I'm sorry for the way I greeted you, but you took me by surprise. I never heard you drive up."

"That's 'cause I didn't. My dad's Chevy is back over by the house, but I guess you didn't notice because you got here pretty early. I spent the night at home and walked over."

"I didn't know you'd moved back in. I'm so used to seeing that pickup there, I guess I didn't think about it."

"A.J. came over to the motel last night and helped me transfer my gear and get set up at the house. He also brought medicine bags that he said would help me. There's one for you, too."

"A.J.?"

"Ambrose John."

She stared at him. "You two are friends?"

"Yeah, he and I hung out senior year. You'd graduated by then."

"Guess we still have a lot of catching up to do," she said.

"I'm ready whenever you are," Ben said. "In the meantime, have another doughnut." He placed another on her desk, then turned toward the door. "I'll go make coffee."

The trading post was open now, and Jo had just finished reconciling yesterday's expenditures when Leigh Ann came in holding a fresh cup of coffee for her.

"Hey, boss. I forgot to tell you earlier, I've got some good news," Leigh Ann said, and told her about the jewelry they'd sold yesterday. "That bracelet was worth every penny."

"It sounds like things went incredibly well," she said, surprised and maybe just a touch jealous.

"There's something else," Leigh Ann said, her voice dropping to a conspiratorial whisper. "I think Ben believes that someone was blackmailing his dad, and maybe you, too, now. Regina told me about a conversation she had with him yesterday, but she doesn't know how he came up with that theory. I thought we were supposed to be looking for some mysterious merchandise or inventory that led to Tom's death."

"Ben's desperate to identify his enemy—Tom's killer—and is going down every path," Jo said. "But there's no blackmail, or sign of it, that I've seen, at least so far. He and I discussed that possibility once before. No money has left the business that isn't well documented. Unless he's found something in Tom's private accounts that I don't know about, there's no basis for it."

"Maybe he just needs closure."

"So do I," Jo said. "If he'd let me, I'd work right alongside him to find out why his dad was killed."

Leigh Ann didn't answer right away. "He's got a soft spot for you, but Ben's a man of secrets. Distrust comes easier to him than trust."

"What makes you say that?" she asked, wondering if Leigh Ann knew something she didn't.

"It's that haunted look in his eyes. My cousin Chris's wife used to call it the thousand-yard stare. When Chris came home after combat in Iraq, he'd space out like that sometimes. What he'd seen in battle changed him forever. Coping was very hard for him, particularly at first. To this day, he still struggles with those memories."

"That's why my people have special ceremonies. Sings restore the *hózhó*, the balance and harmony necessary to keep evil and sickness away." Jo said, then after a pause, added, "But Ben's beliefs are different from mine."

"Everyone has to find their own way. Some people carry secrets for so long, they end up becoming a part of who they are. Getting involved with a man like Ben means accepting the part of him you'll never reach, or know."

"We all keep secrets," Jo said softly, thinking of the killer who'd been stalking her. She was no closer to finding him than before and had no way of knowing when he'd strike again. Yet that was a secret she'd have to keep, at least for now.

"Maybe some secrets should stay that way—hidden so they never see the light of day," Leigh Ann said with a nod.

Jo watched her walk away and couldn't help but wonder how much she knew about her late husband's infidelities. Trying to spare her feelings, everyone had chosen to keep silent after Kurt's sudden death. Jo had joined that conspiracy, too, but she still wasn't sure if they'd made the right choice. Now the fact remained, and it was too late to turn back the clock.

That was the problem with secrets. They gained strength the longer they stayed hidden.

FOURTEEN

Tony Gómez was inside within twenty seconds. Even though the tall, good-looking gringa woman's front door had two locks, they were like the ones at the Stuart and Buck houses—easy to pick. The ones at the trading post, on the other hand, had been a bitch, and he still hadn't had a chance to search the dead man's shed, with the son coming and going. At least on this job he could work alone. Roberto had allowed him to get rid of Frankie and Adam. Hopefully, Jo Buck would get the message this time and deliver the goods.

He still wished he could have come right out and told her what he wanted. It was possible she didn't know what the hell he was talking about and would need to look around for it, but the boss ordered him not to specify.

Closing the door behind him, he moved quickly to the alarm panel, having seen the ADT sign outside. The unit was dead, deactivated probably. Roberto had said that she was a widow, and if the woman's only source of income was that trading post job, she probably couldn't afford the security service anymore. Playing it smart, she'd left the sign outside anyway to discourage people like him.

He looked around, not moving at first as he surveyed the interior of the large living room beyond the foyer. He'd grown up with six brothers and sisters in a mud shack half the size of that room. Back then, he and his family had lived in a constant state of fear. His father had been a real bastard whose fists were worse than his backhand.

Tony dismissed those memories with a quiet curse and focused. There was less furniture in the house than he'd expected. The living room contained a worn sofa, a matching chair, a lamp, and coffee table—nothing else. On the wall opposite the sofa there was a dusty rectangular outline about the size and shape of a big-screen TV. There were also impressions on the thick carpet where more furniture had rested at one time. The kitchen had what looked like marble counters and one of those islands, but there was empty space where the table should have been, and two tall stools against the island instead of chairs. She'd probably sold off what she could after her husband died to make the house payments.

Tony stood absolutely still and listened, hearing only the vague hum of the shiny stainless steel refrigerator. After a while he could even hear the ticking of his watch, it was so quiet.

Good, nobody was here, not even a cat or dog. He'd been watching the leggy blonde come and go for a few days now and knew her routine, and that of her roommate. They always left the house no later than 6:45 A.M., and didn't return until six thirty or so in the evening.

He took another look at his new watch, with its fancy turquoise and silver watchband. Tony never let it show around Roberto. He'd know where it had come from, and there'd be hell to pay.

Taking it and that money clip had been stupid and risky. No one with a brain ever kept a souvenir from a man he'd killed. Yet he'd acquired a taste for the finer things. The dead didn't need a watch anyway. They had all the time in the world. He might as well enjoy it. The police would never be able to use it against him, because they'd never catch him alive. He'd go down fighting before he spent a day behind bars.

He glanced around, trying to decide where to start. It was 9 A.M. and he'd be here for hours, if necessary, searching for that special rug, the one with the distinctive design. He hadn't found it in the trading post, not yet, nor at the Indian woman's home—not that she'd be stupid enough to hide it there. More likely it had been placed in the care of someone who had no idea of its value. Here, maybe.

He decided to start upstairs, in the woman's bedroom and work his way down, but he'd have to be extremely careful not to leave any trace of the search. Roberto had insisted on that and if he messed up here, Roberto would cut off his *cojones* and jam them down his throat.

Tony had his pocket flashlight out and was looking under the bed when he heard a car pull up outside. Jumping to his feet, he looked out the window, careful to stay behind the thin curtains. A tall, slutty-looking red-haired American woman in tight shorts was climbing out of a red BMW parked in the graveled driveway. The roommate. Except for her hair color, she resembled the owner, close enough to be her sister. Both women had small breasts but great legs, and with this one, they were out there for anyone to see and admire.

Tony put away his flashlight and reached for his long folding knife. If long and leggy came inside, there was no way he could race to the end of hall, then downstairs and out the back. The open space between the two doors left little cover except for that kitchen island.

As he heard the sound of the front door opening, Tony inched down the hall, hoping to find a hiding place in a spare room.

"I'm at Leigh Ann's, Mona," the woman below said, her heels clicking across the oak floor.

Guessing she was on her cell phone—most Americans had one glued to their ear nowadays—Tony tried the first door to his left. He peered inside but all he saw there was carpeting and deep impressions that revealed where a bed and furniture had once stood.

Stepping back out, he closed the door, but he moved too quickly and the mechanism clicked loudly.

Shit! Tony nearly said aloud.

"Hold on, Mona. I think she's here. Leigh Ann! You up there, sis? It's Rache."

Hearing footsteps on the hardwood stairs, Tony moved back into the bedroom, closing the door halfway. Taking a quick look around, he decided on the closet, which had louvered doors.

He stepped inside the lavender-scented enclosure, pulling the door shut, and brushing up against the woman's garments. One silky blouse caught against the rough stubble on his chin and he brushed it away.

He could see out into the room through the angled slats, but hopefully, because it was dark in the closet, Rache—probably Rachel—couldn't see him.

"Leigh Ann?" the woman called out again, this time from down the hall. The clicking of heels came closer, and Tony saw mostly hips and legs as the woman stepped into the bedroom. Rachel was tanned and beautiful, at least the parts he could see. Cheap but expensive, he thought, knowing she'd have never given him a second look on the street.

"Damn," the woman muttered. "It smells like a locker room in here." She sniffed the air, then opened the window.

"There. That's better." The woman walked over to the dresser, opened the top drawer, and looked inside. After a moment she shut the drawer and checked the next one down.

"Sis, where *do* you keep your scarves? The closet?"

Tony's mouth was dry, but his body was covered in sweat. If

she opened the door, then what? Kill her? He'd never hurt a woman, though he'd never hesitated when a man needed to be killed.

It had started with his father. He'd been sixteen back then, and his youngest sister, María, twelve. People had always claimed that María was *loca*, but she'd never hurt anyone. She'd sit for hours playing with the dancing shadows cast on the floor by sunlight filtering through the leaves of the tree outside. One evening his father, drunker than usual, had kicked her out of his way, then kept on roughing her up, forcing María into a corner. Then he'd touched her.

For the first time in his life, Tony snapped. He'd pushed his father away from her, grabbed a pencil off the table, and stabbed him in the neck. He'd enjoyed seeing the son of a bitch die. The feeling of power that act gave him had been more of a high than what those druggie idiots got from their heroin or cocaine. He'd known then where his future lay.

The family had stood back and watched until the old bastard stopped twitching. Then they'd all helped dig a hole and dropped him inside, wrapped in an old blanket. They'd walked back and forth over the surface of the makeshift grave, packing the ground, then left and never looked back. To this day, Ramón Gómez was probably still buried in the alley behind their house next to the trash.

Tony had left home the following morning with twenty U.S. dollars in his pocket and never returned. He'd known a guy who knew another guy, and with his particular skills he had risen to the top of his profession in no time at all. It was easy, the pay was great, and he liked it. What more could a man want?

The American woman came right up to the door, close enough for him to smell her perfume. His heart was beating so hard, he was afraid she'd hear. As she reached for the doorknob, he held his breath.

Suddenly she turned away. "I remember, the bottom drawer,

next to the bed!" Rachel walked over to the nightstand, opened the drawer, then pulled out a yellow scarf with lavender butterflies—or maybe they were flowers.

Tony watched as the redhead put the scarf around her neck, then stood in front of the dresser mirror, adjusting it in several ways. He watched her eyes, afraid she'd see him there, frozen like a statue. But her focus was on the image in the mirror. From the heels, the heavy makeup, and her well-toned body, Tony decided the woman thought a great deal of herself.

"Perfect!" She closed the drawer, checked herself once more in the mirror, then walked out of the room, leaving the door in the half-closed position.

Tony didn't move a muscle until he heard the car driving away.

❈

Jo sat back and finished her last doughnut. She'd had a total of four today. She'd have to jog and maybe skip lunch to get rid of those calories.

After she finished copying the accounting records into the flash drive, she walked over to Tom's old office and placed the backup into the safe. She was just closing the handle when she caught a whiff of a familiar citrusy-scented cologne. Startled, she jumped halfway out of her skin as she turned to look. It was Ben.

"You scared the hell out of me. I'm going to put a bell around your neck," she said.

"Didn't mean to sneak up on you. Moving quietly helps keep my head on my neck overseas." He plopped down in his dad's desk chair, then glanced at the large shoe box on the desk filled with handwritten receipts. "Please tell me that's not the way we do our bookkeeping around here."

She laughed, sitting down in a second chair against the wall.

"It seems insane, I know. The problem is that too much paper-work, or fiddling with a BlackBerry makes our Traditionalists nervous. They don't trust those business rituals, and that could cost us some of our best artists."

"Carrying around a couple thousand in fifties isn't a good idea either. You could get robbed and killed out in the middle of nowhere."

"How do you know how much cash I was carrying?" she asked, her eyes narrowing.

He pointed to the ceiling corner. "Cameras, remember? I was working on the field of view when you pulled out that wad of bills."

"Then you also saw me divide it into smaller amounts and noticed that I don't carry it all in the same place. Your father did the same thing."

"Considering that we're low on cash reserves, should we be making any big purchases right now?"

She sighed, a bit annoyed that her judgment was being questioned. Then it occurred to her that maybe he had something else in mind. Either way, she owed it to him to explain.

"Ambrose's jewelry is great for our high-end customers, but we need more midrange merchandise on hand for local traffic and impulse buyers. With the state fair just around the corner and the weather cooling off, we'll get lots of people passing through, and we need to have a wide selection on hand. Otherwise, they'll wait and go to the big pueblo shops or to the Plaza in Santa Fe, or Albuquerque's Old Town."

"Yet I heard Leigh Ann mention to Regina that you didn't buy that much this time. How come?"

"Business has been slow, but let me save you some time in case I've guessed where you're headed with this," Jo said. "I understand you think someone was blackmailing your father, but that's just crazy. Your dad wouldn't have put up with anything like that."

"Okay, then let's say someone was demanding protection money, and threatening The Outpost. I've seen that racket at work all around the world. If that's what was going on here, they'll try to squeeze you, too."

"So you still think I was making some kind of payoff?" When he didn't answer right away, she sighed. "First of all, I came back with nearly a thousand in cash, which I returned to the safe. Secondly—and addressing your point—I'm definitely *not* paying protection or any other kind of blackmail. If someone *were* leaning on me, I'd call the sheriff. I've got them on speed dial now, as you can well imagine. I've been on edge ever since your father died."

"Which brings me to another point. There's very little progress being made on his case, including everything that's happened to us since then—you mostly. Just how much do you trust local law enforcement?"

She drew in a breath and let it out slowly. "The deputies are spread out a little thin, but I think the department as a whole does its best, and the deputies have been sharing reports on the incidents, apparently. Has something specific happened that bothers you?"

"I spoke to Ethan Sayers yesterday. It turns out that Detective Wells hasn't even spoken to him. In my book, interviewing one of my dad's oldest friends should have been one of her top priorities."

"Maybe she had other leads."

"Something about this is just . . . off. I feel it in my gut."

"Why don't you pay the detective a visit?"

"Yeah, maybe, but the direct approach won't work. If I'm not sure I can trust her, everything she says is going to sound like just another excuse. She's also paranoid about anyone else getting involved in the investigation."

"It's possible she only wants to make sure no evidence is compromised. Give her the benefit of the doubt for a while longer."

"I've learned to stay alive by doing the opposite. Besides, I'm running out of time. It won't be long before I'll be heading out for more mountain training, then Afghanistan a month or so later."

"I know that you've been under a lot of stress since you got home, Ben. Things aren't at all what you expected them to be, but don't automatically assume everyone around here's your enemy," Jo said.

"'Enemy' might be too strong a word, but I'm not completely among friends either," he said. "Let's face it, Jo. Even you don't really trust me."

"In some ways, you're still a stranger to me. You're not the kid I knew anymore, and I don't really know the man."

He gave her an outrageous grin. "Know me in the biblical sense? I can fix that."

"That's *your* Bible, not mine," she said, laughing.

"I thought Traditionalists believe that sex is like any other human need. It's not bad or good, it just is," he said.

"First, I'm not a Traditionalist, I'm a New Traditionalist, but more to the point, your needs and mine are obviously different. I see no reason to get all hot and sweaty just for entertainment purposes."

"Think of the fun you're missing."

"What you really mean, is think of the fun *you're* missing." She stood up. "How did we get so sidetracked? I've got business to take care of."

"I'm going to the station to see if Detective Wells has come up with any new leads. I'll also try to talk to people there and see if I can get a better handle on her. I'll let you know how it goes."

Jo went back to work at her desk in the break room. Paperwork—who knew there'd be this much to contend with?

❂

Hours passed and Jo made progress. She was almost ready to take a break when Leigh Ann came in.

"Hey, you've been doing paperwork all morning. How about a coffee break and some good old-fashioned gossip?" Leigh Ann said.

Jo smiled. It was weeks since she'd had time to just talk, and she missed being part of the good-ole-girl network. Sometimes women just needed other women.

They took the last doughnut and split it.

Leigh Ann licked her fingers. "That hunk of manhood can sure cook."

"Yeah, who knew?"

"Ben's got a lot of layers to him, doesn't he? I saw him as a tough guy when he first arrived—strong and silent. Now I'm not so sure."

"You mean because he cooks a mean doughnut?"

Leigh Ann laughed. "No, not just because of that." She paused for a long moment. "You should have seen him with Ambrose. They were like long lost brothers. A lot of straight men are uncomfortable around Ambrose and go out of their way to act like pigs. For some reason, they think it makes them less manly if they show him any respect."

"Ben's always made his own choices when it came to friends, and if he liked you, it didn't matter what other people thought or said. He'd stand up to them."

"From what I saw, he's still that way, just more so."

"By the way, how much did we pay for Ambrose's jewelry? I didn't see any paperwork, except for the receipts on his pieces," Jo said.

"Ambrose left the merchandise with us on consignment."

"No way!"

"It was because of their friendship. You should have heard Ben and him laughing and talking over old times."

Hearing the phone at her desk ringing, Jo reached for the receiver. "Looks like our break is over."

Jo answered and heard Ethan Sayers's voice on the other end. She greeted him warmly, and before he asked, explained that she'd written his check a little late, but that the money was on its way.

"Ben and I had a long talk the other day, and I understand you're having cash flow problems right now. Tom and I go back a lot of years, so if you need me to extend you some credit, just say the word. We'll work something out."

"Did Ben ask you for that?"

"Ben didn't have to, and neither do you, little lady. Just remember the offer."

As she placed the phone down, she stared at the wall, lost in thought. Ben had made several business decisions without consulting her, but at the same time had managed to get great results. The trading post could certainly use some extended credit, and, clearly, Ambrose hadn't gone away unhappy.

Yet she still didn't like the fact that Ben hadn't consulted her, or even told her about it afterwards—and that wasn't just her bruised ego talking. The trading post was primarily hers, and she needed to be kept current on all its business dealings.

They needed to talk—soon. As much as she appreciated Ben's help, to work together harmoniously, they'd have to find balance. Serving as a sergeant in the military, Ben was used to a chain of command and the responsibilities that went with it. Hopefully, he'd see her point or, at the very least, respect it.

Deciding what she needed to do next restored her harmony. Jo left her office and joined Leigh Ann, who was standing behind the counter, checking out a line of customers. "Once Ben comes back, let me know, okay?" she whispered.

"Sure, hon. No problem."

Jo smiled at the customers, two of whom she recognized as regulars. She was happy to see that there were more people in The Outpost today than there had been since Tom's death.

The rest of the day became a blur as Jo pitched in to help at the registers, then restocked perishables along with Del and Regina. New seasonal displays were set up, too, between surges in traffic, showcasing their pottery and Navajo-made rugs.

At closing, Jo thanked each staff member for their tireless efforts. As she went around, locking up, she wondered what had happened to Ben and how his meeting with Detective Wells had gone. The only thing she'd noticed today was the big truck from a local charity group parked in Tom's driveway, apparently hauling away some of the furniture. It made sense that Ben was making the place his own now.

She'd just returned to her desk when she heard a pickup circling around the back of the building. Jo went to the window and saw Ben pulling up in his dad's white Chevy. Maybe it was a good thing that he'd taken this long to come back. With the staff gone, she'd be able to talk to him without feeling rushed.

Jo went out onto the loading dock, intending to call him over, when a big red Dodge Ram pickup loaded with chrome and testosterone came to a sliding stop beside Ben's truck.

"Hey, butt-wipe! Was that you who cut us off back there?" a man wearing a cowboy hat yelled, sticking his head out the passenger-side window.

Jo recognized Danny Vaughn, one of Ben's pals back in high school. With him, sitting behind the wheel, was Artie Sayers, Ethan's son. The trio had raised hell all the way from Kirtland to Shiprock back in high school.

"Hell, yeah, it was me. Wanna step outta that pussy truck and do something about it?" Ben yelled back a second later, recognizing the pair.

"Damn, straight, dickhead. But before I kick your ass, let's grab dinner and a couple pitchers of beer," Danny said, throwing open the door and stepping down.

"Now you're talking, Danny," Ben said, jogging over. They exchanged fist bumps, then vigorous handshakes. "Hey, Artie.

Long time," Ben added, stepping over and fist-bumping the driver next.

"Climb in, Danny," Ben said. "I'm not riding between you two ladies," he said, pointing at the seat.

"You duck down while we're rolling, and I'll throw you out, bro," Danny said, laughing as he climbed back in.

"Dream on, Dan," Ben said, joining in the laughter.

They never saw her standing on the loading dock, and before Jo could step down and get Ben's attention, he was in the truck heading out. She watched as Artie whipped the Dodge around, burning rubber as they raced down the highway and out of sight.

Though she'd looked forward to talking to Ben, she was glad to see him finally catching up with old friends. He deserved some downtime. Ben had fought in two brutal wars, and all he'd found stateside was more sorrow and death.

What she had to say to him would wait. She had plenty of work still waiting inside.

FIFTEEN

S orry about your dad, bro," Danny said, nodding to Ben as they raced east toward the community of Kirtland.

"Me, too," Artie added. "Everyone around here respected Tom Stuart. He was a good man."

"Yeah, and he did the right thing, throwing me to the wolves and making me choose jail or the army," Ben said quietly, knowing that would be the next thing to come up in the conversation. They hadn't really talked about it at the time, and he hadn't seen these guys since graduation night.

"'Tough love,' my mom called it," Danny said.

"I was a real screwup back then, and it took the army to straighten me out," Ben said with a nod. "Danny, did anyone ever figure out you were with me the night we went joyriding?"

"If they did, they never said," Danny answered. "You saved my ass, bro, throwing me out just before the deputies pulled you over."

"You were already on probation. Add joyriding in a 'borrowed' car to that, and you'd have served time for sure," Ben said. "I got off lucky. I was given a choice. Serve your country or serve time."

"That night scared me straight," Danny said. "I've been clean since then, not even a frickin' speeding ticket. Got a good job at Valley Auto. Four years now, and I'm shop foreman—salary and commission."

"Hey, all this touchy-feely shit is making me thirsty," Artie said, jumping in. "Where we going, the Palomino?"

"You said dinner. They have a kitchen now?" Ben asked. That bar had been pretty rough. He'd been thrown out the only time he tried to get served. Of course, he'd been seventeen at the time, carrying a really bad fake ID.

"You *are* out of touch, bro. They're practically a family restaurant now," Danny said, elbowing Artie. "Right, Artie?"

"Exactly. And there's a dress code. All the waitstaff are required to wear tiny tops and the tightest shorts in the county. They make Hooters seem like Sunday school. You still remember women, don't you, Ben?"

"Oh, man, Ben's back in the saddle for sure. You seen Jo lately?" Danny laughed.

"So are you and Jo catching up on old times?" Artie asked. "Jo's sure filled out. Short but stacked, and those jeans . . ."

Ben just shrugged, feeling uncomfortable and growing more annoyed by the minute. "Jo and I haven't gone out since high school, and our only connection now is The Outpost. So let's talk about *your* fantasy love lives, guys. Those are bound to be more interesting than what's not going on with me and Jo. Artie, what ever happened to you and Etta Mae, that band chick with the button-popping chest? You ever stop drooling long enough to ask her out?"

A half hour later, Ben was sipping a Coke at the Palomino Tavern, trying not to make eye contact with the leggy blonde waitress who kept looking his way. She had wonderfully tanned legs that went all the way up to those tight jeans shorts, but he'd always preferred women who advertised less. He was partial to someone like Jo, who made a man's imagination do the work.

"Ben, you sure you don't want to tap into a brew?" Artie asked, holding up his bottle of Coors.

"He's watching his figure. That right, bro?" Danny smiled, raising his own beer bottle toward the center.

"Nah, that's not it." Ben brought up his Coke, and they clicked their drinks in a toast. "To Mexican Cokes, with sugar, not corn syrup. When there were no locals around, we had beer up to our asses, even at the most remote outpost you can imagine. But Mexican Cokes? Hell no!"

Danny nodded. "Ah well, I'd still take beer," he said after a long swallow. Then he lowered his voice. "Ben, I hear you went to sniper school. You were always good with a rifle. Tell me something. What's it like to kill a man at a thousand yards?"

Ben put down his Coke and glanced around the room. It was so strange hearing that question here, as far away from combat as you could get.

"How'd you know about my sniper work?"

"I'd come by and talk to your old man every once in a while. He liked to brag about you, showing me photos of you in uniform, getting that Silver Star and all. I read the citation. You bailed your unit out of an ambush by taking out, what, twelve bad guys with twelve rounds?"

"Tom told everyone who'd listen, Ben," Artie added. "So why did you switch to medevac duty for your second tour? It sounds like something out of Jo's playbook, keeping the balance and like that."

"Guess it does," Ben said with a shrug. He had no intention of talking about that now. Seeing the waitress approaching with three big plates, he took the opportunity to change the subject. "Here comes our Navajo tacos. It's been a damn *long* time."

"Sorry about that, honey, we're a girl short," the tall blonde whispered, giving him a big smile. "How can I make it up to you?"

"Whoa. I'm eating here, too, Barbie," Danny joked, reading the name tag perched atop a sloping chest.

"It wasn't the service, ma'am," Ben said, trying to suppress a laugh. "It has just been a long time since I've had this particular meal."

"Then you've got to come here more often, handsome. I work Monday through Thursday nights," Barbie said.

"Good to know," Ben said, returning her generous smile.

"Must be your aftershave," Danny grumbled after the woman stepped away.

Ben chuckled, then hearing loud footsteps on the hardwood floor just to his left, turned his head. An ugly but familiar face from his not-distant-enough past, Roger Ferrell, was coming toward him. Last time they'd met, Ben had stepped in and traded punches with Ferrell, who'd been roughing up A.J. They were both suspended that last week of their senior year.

"Well, look at you, Smart-ass Stuart. You've finally lost your baby fat. Did the army give up trying to make a man out of you?" The big, former high school tackle weighed maybe 250 now, and it looked to be all muscle.

"Farthead Ferrell," Danny muttered under his breath, and Ben couldn't help but smile.

"Good to see you again, Roger," Ben answered pleasantly enough. This evening was about catching up with old friends, and there was no need to rekindle old grudges. "Buy you a beer?"

"I don't drink with pussies, Stuart," Roger growled, loud enough now for half the room to turn their way.

Artie and Danny both set down their beers and started to rise to their feet. "Stand down, guys," Ben ordered. "Roger's just giving us a hard time, right, Rog? No harm, no foul."

There was no way he was going to let this idiot ruin their dinner. Two years ago, he would have gone for the guy's throat, with or without a KA-BAR. Tonight was going to be peaceful.

"Hard time? Hey, Stuart, hear you've been trying to get back into Jo Buck's panties again. Wonder if your hard time is as big as your old man's hard time? Now we know how she convinced him to leave her your trading post. Down on her knees a lot, was she?"

Ben went hot before the big guy could throw up a fist. His chair flew back, there was a blur, and suddenly he was on top of Ferrell, who was flat on his back like a thrown steer. Ben never even felt Ferrell's few desperate punches as training took over and he gripped the big man's throat, pressing in with his thumbs.

Artie and Danny moved in and pulled him off Ferrell. "Whoa!" Danny said, his arms still locked around Ben, who was on his feet now.

Artie glared at Roger, his boot a foot from his head. "Haul ass out of here before you really get hurt. In case you haven't noticed, this place is on Ben's side."

The bar owner strode up, holding a baseball bat in his burly grip. "Out of here, Ferrell, or I'm calling the cops—after I clock you one myself."

After Ferrell left the tavern, Danny eased his grip and Ben relaxed. He ached in a few places, but the son of a bitch had deserved what he got.

"Man, you're going to have some shiner tomorrow," Danny said, looking back at Ben.

Ben felt the cut over his eye and realized he'd been hit probably two or three times. Head wounds—they always bled like crazy. He glanced at his Navajo taco, which had managed to survive the carnage. "Damn. I was really looking forward to that," he said, trying to button up his torn shirt.

Barbie was suddenly right there. "Somebody'll keep your meal warm, hon, don't worry. Come with me into the back room. I can patch you up. We've got some skin glue."

"Go for it, bro," Danny whispered. "We'll wait out here. Maybe we'll have another beer in your honor. It was about time someone dropped that jackass."

Ben had to smile even though it hurt to do so. "I'll take you up on that patch job, Barbie, and I'm definitely staying for dinner."

The owner gestured toward one of the side rooms. "You're Tom Stuart's boy, right? You've fought for our country and deserve more respect than what you got here tonight. Dinner's on me."

Jo looked up at the clock and noticed that it was nearly midnight. Ben and his friends had obviously decided on more than dinner and a few beers.

Jo leaned back in her chair and glanced at the shotgun she'd brought into her office. There'd been too many incidents for her not to take precautions, and having it within arm's reach made her feel safer.

Reaching into her top drawer for the peanut butter chocolate cups she loved, she wondered if Ben would come home sober. A boys' night out around here usually went hand in hand with a case of beer and a wobbly ride home. She hoped one of them had held back so he could take the wheel.

Jo walked to Tom's office and placed the flash drive with the accounting records back into the safe. As she reached to close the heavy metal door, some papers propped flat against the side wall of the safe caught her eye. Jo reached in and pulled out a handful of newspaper clippings encased in the type of plastic sheets usually found in photo albums. Curious, she placed them on the desk and took a closer look.

A cursory glance at the first article from a Manhattan, Kansas, newspaper gave an account of Ben's heroism under fire. A sniper, he'd saved his platoon, part of the First Infantry Division, from being cut off and wiped out. Though hit by mortar shell fragments, he'd taken out three machine gun positions and kept the remaining enemy pinned down while the wounded were evacuated. He'd received the Silver Star as a result.

Another headline told how soldiers from Ben's brigade had been treated for PTSD, post-traumatic stress disorder, after returning home two years ago. Reading how their heroism in the villages and mountains of Afghanistan had come at a cost, Jo once again thought about the Enemy Way Sing. It was the Navajo way of restoring the *hózhó*. The ceremony was lengthy— one of the prayers done was 399 lines long—and required nothing less than perfection both in intonation and wording.

The Sing concluded with the words, "It is normal again. This day may I go invisible to evil. . . ." That set the patient free, and beauty was once again restored.

While there were prayers in Ben's world, there were no such ceremonies and no way of releasing contamination from evil, fear, and death—the by-products of war.

She read the headlines and opening paragraphs of the last two articles. The first reported Ben as having been in a serious vehicle accident off base, a short time after his last return stateside. He'd been driving drunk and skidded off a cliff. Miraculously, he walked away with only minor injuries. Ben had been cited, then disciplined by his unit commander.

She remembered that time. Tom had driven all the way to Kansas to see Ben, but she never knew the details, only that Ben had been injured off base.

The last, most recent article featured a medical unit Ben had been assigned to during his last deployment. Judging from the headline, Ben had distinguished himself there, too, risking his own life to recover and evacuate wounded soldiers while under fire.

Although she wanted to read each of the articles carefully, gleaning as many facts as she could, she resisted the urge. Even by glancing at these articles, she'd probably done more than she should have, intruding on both Ben's and Tom's privacy. Ben, in particular, had told her he wanted to keep his past a closed book.

She returned the articles to the safe, placing them back in a way that would make them easier to spot in hopes that Ben would find them on his own. They'd all known Tom was proud of his son, but this was tangible proof. The way he'd kept track of Ben and the manner in which he'd preserved these articles said it all.

Yet after seeing these, she found Ben to be more of an enigma than ever—a man wrapped in contradictions. As a soldier, he'd distinguished himself many times. Yet now he wanted to leave that world and come back to one that had never satisfied him before. She still had difficulty seeing him settling down to a life of predictability and routines.

Jo stood and stretched. She was beat. It was time for her to go home.

Turning out the office lights, she entered the storeroom and reached for the final switch when she heard a pickup roaring up out back. Cautious, she turned out the light and went to the back door, opening it slightly and peering out.

As Ben stepped out of his friend's truck into the glow of the overhead lamp, a beer bottle rolled out the door with him and fell to the ground. Disappointment washed over her. At least part of the bad boy she'd known once was still alive and well— or at least still standing.

Ben bent over, picked up the bottle, and tried to hand it back through the window, but someone inside rolled up the window, almost catching his hand. Ben dropped the bottle. Jo heard Danny and Artie laughing, and Ben had to jump back as the pickup lurched forward.

As they drove off, Jo went outside to help Ben, who'd picked up the bottle again. He was fumbling in his pocket with his other hand, probably for his keys. Close up, beneath the bright cone of the parking lot light, he looked like crap. There were bruises on his face and his left eye was almost swollen shut. The only plus she could find was that he didn't appear to be drunk, and didn't smell of booze either.

"I thought you'd finally grown up. This reminds me of high school, when you were always getting into a fight over something or another."

"Yeah. It really pissed you off back then."

"I'm not overly impressed now either," she snapped. "Come on, let me give you a hand. You're not too steady on your feet right now."

"I took a few punches, no prob. At least I wasn't dodging RPGs."

She blinked, suddenly regretting her words. He'd been in foreign, hostile lands fighting for his country and saving the lives of fellow soldiers. She could, and should, cut him some slack. "So what happened tonight?"

"I had the best Navajo taco in the world, and the first Mexican Coke since—forever. You can't believe how much I've missed the little things in life."

She took his arm and draped it around her shoulders.

"I like this," he said.

"Don't get used to it. I'm just helping you walk home. What happened?"

"Just a guy with a big mouth. Remember Roger Ferrell?"

Jo nodded. "He's still a jerk after all these years. You were saying . . ."

"He started it, I finished it. End of story."

She rolled her eyes. "Couldn't you have just walked away?"

"I did—right after he hit the floor."

"Before that," she said.

"No, sometimes you have to stand your ground."

"I don't understand you. *I* would have found a way to walk away."

"Are you really so sure?"

She saw something flash in his eyes. Was it a warning? She couldn't tell. "I wouldn't have put myself in a position where I couldn't back out, or chosen a place where I'd be inviting problems just by being there."

He didn't argue the point, and she took it as confirmation. He'd gone out with his pals and found trouble—his specialty. She considered letting go and pushing him in the right direction, but she owed Tom more than that.

"Have you considered going to the hospital and getting yourself checked out?"

"No need. I'm a medic now, I know what symptoms and problems to look for. Tonight was more like full-contact football practice, without the gear. Trust me."

She'd walk him home anyway. She wasn't sure how much of what he was saying was "man talk" or reality.

"Get cleaned up," she said. "I'm sticking around until I'm sure you're okay."

"Sounds thoughtful. Are you going to tend my wounds?"

"You wish. For now, just take a shower. You smell . . . ripe."

He burst out laughing. "Ow. That hurt," he said, grimacing as he touched the side of his face. "But thanks for the laugh."

"What the hell's so funny?"

"You haven't changed a bit. Like with this morning and my aftershave, you could always pick up a scent all the way across the room."

"This morning you smelled great, but fistfight perfume isn't my idea of a turn-on."

"Speaking of turn-ons, what does get you excited these days?" Ben placed the empty beer bottle he'd been carrying atop the fence post, produced a set of keys, and let them through the gate, which was now equipped with a new lock and chain.

"You're supposed to be injured. Act the part or I'm leaving," she snapped as they passed through.

"Hey, I'm hurt," he said, reaching back to retrieve the bottle. "Why don't you come inside with me and undress my wounds?"

"Are you kidding? You look like day-old roadkill," she said, trying to undermine his weak attempts at flirting.

"Yeah, yeah, okay," he said with a sigh.

As they entered the house, she realized just how much of Tom's old furnishings had been removed earlier. The sparse, utilitarian interior reflected more of Ben's personality, though it was a work in progress. His mother's salt and pepper collection was still in place, but Tom's Western memorabilia were all gone. The old Western-style sofa with the wagon wheel pattern had been replaced by a brown leather contemporary love seat and chair with a matching hassock.

Feeling much more comfortable with the new look, she took a seat as Ben stepped over to the kitchen and dropped the bottle in the trash.

"One last chance. Wanna go green and save water?"

"Either you bathe now, by yourself, or step outside so I can spray you down with the garden hose. You clearly need a cold shower."

"It's a hot summer evening, and two former almost-lovers are together again after so many years. Yet all you can think about is soap and water. You're not much for romance, are you?"

She ignored him, and soon he disappeared from view. Once she heard him turn on the shower, she finally dropped her guard and sighed. Even scuffed up and bloodied, there was something about Ben that made her a little crazy inside. It wasn't just his looks, particularly in this case. What really drew her were his confidence and that unholy aura of danger that encircled him.

Whenever she was with him, emotions she thought she'd conquered ages ago came to life inside her. He made her long to be loved, to be protected and cared for. But the stability she yearned for and needed just wasn't Ben's to give. He was unconquerable, a man whose spirit demanded nothing less of him.

Restless, she turned on the TV. After a while, Jo saw a reflection flicker in the TV screen and turned her head. Ben stood in the doorway barefooted, wearing low-slung jeans and an open shirt that fell loosely around his shoulders.

She didn't want to feel anything. He was trouble of the worst kind. Yet the scent of soap mingled with aftershave teased her senses. He smiled slowly at her, and her heartbeat quickened.

She forced herself to look at his bruises, not the tight muscles that defined his chest, and tried to see him only as a man who still needed to prove himself with his fists.

Illusion and testosterone. That was all Ben was, and could be to her. She deserved more than that. It was time for her to go.

—SIXTEEN—

eeing the flicker of desire in Jo's eyes, Ben narrowed the gap between them. He'd waited a long time for this day, and he had no intention of wasting even one more precious moment.

"Now that I know you're going to be okay, I've got to leave," Jo said quickly, a hitch in her breath.

He stood in front of her a moment longer. He was man enough to know when a woman wanted him, and her words didn't match what her body was telling him.

She hesitated, then lowered her gaze and stared at the bruises that were starting to form around his ribs, and the three-inch scar an enemy sniper's bullet had left as it grazed his right arm. "I can't stay," she said again.

"So you still bail when you see something you can't handle, or that upsets you," he whispered. "Scars and bruises are part of a soldier's world, darling."

"I'll give you the scars, but barroom brawling . . . maybe that's something you'll never outgrow," she said.

He opened the door for her, and Jo hurried out without looking back.

Ben remained where he was, watching her as she got into her pickup and drove out of the graveled parking lot. She'd made up her mind about him, and wasn't even willing to give him the benefit of the doubt. She wasn't worth his time. She could go straight to hell, for all he cared.

He kicked the door shut and cursed. The problem was he did care. He'd wanted to make love to her tonight more than he'd wanted anything in a very long time.

He'd taken one punch too many, that's all there was to it. Tired and sore, he lay down on the couch. Even with the TV going, he quickly fell into a deep sleep.

⚹

Jo stayed busy the next day. She'd accepted Ethan Sayers offer of credit and placed an additional order. Livestock supplies were a large part of their daily sales, even now. She'd also redone the sign up front with Leigh Ann's help, made room in the attached loafing shed for more alfalfa hay, then helped restock grocery shelves.

"You've got lots of energy today," Leigh Ann said, offering a soft drink when they finally took a break midafternoon.

"I need to stay busy. Otherwise, I'll overthink things."

Leigh Ann smiled. "Sounds like you've got Ben Stuart on your mind."

"Yeah, but not in a good way."

She laughed. "The bad ways are always a lot more fun to think about."

Jo glared at Leigh Ann, then suddenly laughed. "Okay, you've got a point, just don't let him hear you say that."

Leigh Ann glanced around. "Where *is* Ben, anyway?"

Del came into the room and, having heard the question, answered. "Ben's outside. A buddy of his just drove up."

"Keep an eye on him. We don't need a fight in the parking lot," Jo said.

"So you heard about that throw-down last night at the Palomino lounge? I guess Ben really lost it," Del said. "He was stone-cold sober, too, good thing for the other guy."

"You were there?" Jo asked, surprised.

"No, but my uncle was, and I heard the story after school let out. Apparently, Roger Ferrell decided to give Ben a hard time— shooting his mouth off, trash-talking—like that. Ben tried to walk away, but Ferrell kept pushing. Then when he said that about—" He turned beet red and looked away.

"Go on. It's okay," Jo said.

"Just . . . trash . . . about you, and Tom, and Ben, too. Sex stuff. Ben flew off the handle and dropped Ferrell right there on the hardwood floor. It took two men to pull Ben offa him."

Jo knew Ferrell from her high school days. The man was a classic bully, always pushing people into a corner, itching for a fight. She didn't need a great imagination to figure out what he must have said.

"I hope Ben knocked his teeth out the back of his head," Leigh Ann said.

"He's still got a few," Ben said, coming in from the back.

Feeling guilty, Jo found it difficult to look at Ben. She shouldn't have been so quick to judge him last night. She needed to apologize and right now, but she wasn't sure what to say.

"If I'd have been there, I would have kicked him where it hurts," she said at last.

Leigh Ann looked at Del; then they both hurried out of the break room.

"Is that your way of saying you're sorry?" he asked with a quick half grin.

She nodded. "I shouldn't have said the things I did. I over-reacted. Apology accepted?"

"Yeah, we're cool, but you were right, we should talk. We'll be working together the next couple of weeks until I have to leave, then again in about a year when my hitch is up. We really need to get to know each other—not who we were back in high school, but who we are now."

"Let's set aside some time and do just that."

"So come over to my house tonight. I'll fix something for dinner."

"Not a date, though—a working dinner between partners?"

"Sure, if that's what you want."

"It is."

"After work, then."

Jo watched Ben walk away. He had "it," however you defined the term. He was built to perfection. His butt alone could have jump-started a failing heart.

With a soft sigh, she returned to the floor, and took over for Regina at the front register.

T he afternoon went quickly, and after the drive-time rush between four and five thirty, she coasted to the seven o'clock closing. It was finally time to call it a day.

"I'm ready," she said, finding Ben by the back door.

"I can see now why Dad left you the place," he said as they headed across the parking lot and down the driveway to his house. "You love The Outpost as much as he did. You put in long hours and never give it a second thought. To me, working here was just a way to bridge the gap with my father—if I got lucky. Now that he's not here, it's a whole new ball game."

"Do you think you'll ever see The Outpost the same way he did?"

"No, this was his dream, not mine. When I'm finally out of

the army and return here, the trading post will be part of my life, but not its center. I have other plans, too."

"Like what?"

"I've got some medical training, and I'd like to put that to good use by becoming an EMT," he said as they walked to his front door. "I also plan to write a book about my experiences as a soldier. It'll be my way of coming to terms with everything I was . . . and became. It won't be a story about how many times a man can fall down. It'll be about getting back up and not letting the past cloud up your future."

The Ben she'd known back then hadn't believed in planning for more than today. This was another side of him she'd never seen. "Knowing where you're going will make it easier to get there."

"Yeah, but my plans aren't set in concrete. I've also learned to adapt as I go."

"And that's how you walk in beauty," she said, waiting as he unlocked his front door.

"So, should we do this the Anglo way or the Navajo way?" he asked.

"I don't understand."

"You told me once that according to tradition, Navajo men lead the way into a room in case there's danger waiting. The Anglo way, where a guy steps aside and lets the woman enter first, made no sense to you."

"You remember that, do you?" she said, smiling.

"There are things one never forgets," Ben said, going inside first. He turned on the light, then glanced back at her. "Latch the screen, but leave the door open, will you? There's a nice breeze, and I hate to waste it."

As she followed Ben into the living room, she suddenly re-membered how he'd looked after his shower, shirt open, handsome enough to make her fingers tingle with the need to touch him.

Wanting something to do that would get her mind off him, she asked, "How can I help with dinner?"

They went into the kitchen, and at his suggestion, she began to chop freshly roasted and peeled green chilies. They worked in silence for a while and finally he spoke.

"I'm on your side, Jo."

"I know, and I really am sorry that I jumped to conclusions last night."

As he placed the casserole composed of ground beef, green chili, potatoes, and cheese into the oven, Jo studied the photo of Ben and his father that hung on the wall. Ben had probably been fourteen at the time. "Your father was so terrific, the kind of dad I wished I had. Even way back in high school, I could always count on him looking out for me."

"I know, and sometimes that really bugged me, because Dad and I never agreed on anything. He was always on my case about something. Now I know he was just doing his best, but we were both too stubborn." He sat beside her on the sofa and stretched his legs out, resting them on the hassock. "I'd like to think we would have turned things around if he hadn't run out of time."

"I don't think you realize just how much your dad loved you and how proud he was of who you'd become."

"You sound so sure," he said in a weary voice.

"I *am* sure." She'd wanted him to find the articles on his own, but leaving it up to chance seemed wrong to her now. "Did you know he collected clippings from the Fort Riley area newspapers that mentioned you?" she asked, and told him what she'd found.

"I had no idea," he said.

"They're still there in the safe. No matter what you might have thought, your dad always kept track of you."

"Good thing he never saw all of the mistakes I made along the way. My past in the military is far from spotless."

"Maybe so, but you had some pretty spectacular moments. The headline on one of the clippings I read said you were given a medal for bravery. There was also a more recent one about a car accident. Tom never gave us the details, but I remember when he went to see you."

Ben stared across the room. "That happened after my first deployment. I came back to the States really screwed up. Dad drove to Kansas to visit me at the hospital, and seeing him helped me get back on the right track. What else did you read in the clippings?"

"I skimmed the opening paragraphs, that's all. I wanted to know more, but I felt like I was prying. You'd made it clear to me before that you didn't feel comfortable sharing some of your army experiences."

"I've managed to bury some of those memories, and that's where they need to stay."

"Is that one of the reasons you don't drink? I heard you had nothing but Cokes the other night. And that bottle you picked up was empty."

Ben took a slow, deep breath. He'd forgotten how fast word traveled in this mostly rural community. "Things are seldom that black-and-white, but as I said, some doors have to stay closed."

"Closed doors can isolate you," she said.

"Are you speaking from experience?"

Jo thought back to the days when her father had struggled with his own demons. For years she'd resented him bitterly. Then, as she'd nursed him during the last few months of his life, she finally learned to come to terms with her feelings. The process had taken her down a long, lonely path, but at the end of that road, she found peace. Her only regret was that her father had never been able to let go of his anger and walk in beauty with her.

"We all have our secrets," he said after a few minutes of

silence went by. "Maybe someday we'll trust each other enough to open up."

"I like the man you've become—the bits and pieces I've seen," she answered. "But you're right, trust is hard to give—and accept."

"I hear you."

There were four electronic beeps as the oven timer went off. "Let's eat," Ben said.

A fter dinner, she helped him clean up the kitchen, then they went back into the living room. He walked with her to one of the bookcases and showed her a photo he kept on the shelf there.

"The other day when I was packing up some old books, a photo fell out of one of my high school yearbooks. Remember this night?" he asked.

She looked at the snapshot. They were together beneath a loafing shed in front of some livestock pens. Ben was smiling but she looked somber and miserable.

She sighed. "Sure do. That fluffy *churro* lamb was one I'd raised for the fair, my 4-H project, but when the time came to sell it, I wasn't ready to let go. The bidding began, I realized I was going to lose Cloud forever, and I couldn't stop crying."

"You wiped away your tears each time they appeared, but I could see that it was killing you to say good-bye. So I gave Danny's dad all the money I had and told him to bid on it for me."

She smiled. "You didn't tell me what you'd done until later. When the auction was over and your dad snapped that picture, I thought I was going to be sick."

"Dad got pissed off at me afterwards when he found out what I'd done. He believed that letting go of the animal was part of the lesson you'd needed to learn, since you might have been raising animals for food someday. You weren't supposed to personalize livestock like that, but I couldn't stand seeing you unhappy."

She smiled. "Later that night, you took me to the old barn and there she was."

"You started crying all over again," he said.

"I was so happy to see her alive! That was one of the nicest things anyone had ever done for me," she said.

"I wasn't a total screwup, was I?"

She laughed. No risk, not even his dad's anger, could have deterred the Ben she'd known back then from doing something he'd set his mind on. Judging from the newspaper clippings, he was still like that, only the stakes were higher.

"Cloud had several lambs and my mom and I used her wool for weaving. My father didn't believe in pets that didn't serve a function, but Cloud was perfect, even by his definition."

"I remember something else," Ben said, looking back at the photo. "That night was the first time you and I kissed."

"I was saying thank you in a way any sixteen-year-old boy would appreciate," she teased.

"There was a full moon overhead," he said, pointing out the window, "just like tonight."

Without giving her a chance to protest, he leaned over and took her mouth in a gentle but persuasive kiss.

She'd meant to respond casually—a thank-you and an apology all at once—but the moment his lips covered hers, fiery sensations began coursing through her. Arms around his neck, she melted into him. All her senses went on hyperdrive as the past and present joined in one glorious moment of pure desire.

He gripped her hips and pulled her against him. Instinctively, she rubbed her body against his, but all too soon, the fires became too intense. Afraid of the heat, she pulled back, catching her breath.

"We can't do this, Ben."

He released her and watched her move away from him. As his breathing evened, his expression became impossible to read. "Consider it a way of cementing our new alliance."

Taking a breath, she forced herself to match his expression. "Alliance?"

"You can count on me to watch your back, and I expect you to do the same for me. What binds us now is our connection to Dad, and what that might mean to the person who killed him."

"The danger's far from over," she said with a nod. "Whoever killed your dad will continue coming after us. They still don't have what they want."

"Agreed. I'm not sure what level of danger we're facing, but I intend to find answers before I leave. That'll mean turning over a few rocks and making some noise."

"The sheriff's department—"

"Is sitting on their collective asses. Detective Wells isn't pushing to solve my father's murder. I waited over an hour to talk with her yesterday, and she never even showed up."

Jo stood and paced, mostly to put some distance between them. She didn't want to be distracted, but she could still taste Ben on her lips. She pushed those feelings aside. To him, it had only been a way of cementing alliances . . . or maybe pushing for a meaningless quickie.

She reached for her purse. "I better get going. I have to be at work early tomorrow."

As Ben reached around her to unlatch the screen door, she heard a noise coming from behind the house and froze.

"Something's back by the shed," he whispered.

"Skunk?"

"I don't smell anything. You?"

"Maybe a coyote?"

There was a thump.

"More like the two-legged kind."

He crossed the room, grabbed the fireplace poker, then continued down the hall. The house's back door was solid wood with a small window. As Ben looked out, he saw a figure standing on the small step of the shed. The door was half open, and the guy was aiming a flashlight beam into the interior.

He felt rather than saw Jo behind him, reaching for the outside light switch. "No! Leave it off.

"Stay here," he said, undoing the lock as gently as he could. Then, feeling the heft of the steel poker in his left hand, he inched open the door. Ben saw the man's flashlight in one hand, then a shiny object in the other he recognized instantly.

The man turned in his direction.

"Gun!" Dropping the poker, Ben whirled around and yanked Jo to the floor just as a shot rang out.

There were two more quick, thundering blasts, and splinters rained down on them. Past the ringing in his ears, Ben managed to hear running footsteps.

"Stay low, stay here, call the cops," he yelled, jumping to his feet.

Jo brought out her cell phone, trying to enter 911 and still keep her eyes on Ben as he raced after their assailant. The burglar scrambled over the field fence about fifty feet beyond the shed, dropped to the ground on the opposite side, then turned around.

Ben dived to the left, hitting the ground as the man's pistol flashed in the dark.

Jo heard bullets thump into the house. Staying down on the floor, she spoke quickly to the emergency operator.

Jo heard more running in the distance, and the roar of an engine, followed by spinning tires. By the time she looked up, the sound had faded.

Ben was standing beside the fence, alone, watching red taillights disappearing down the dirt lane to the south.

She ran outside. "What happened? And why didn't you grab

a gun?" she said, her hands shaking so badly, she had to jam them into her pockets.

"The shotgun's in the trading post, remember?" he said.

"But I thought you'd have your own—"

"You mean my military sidearm? That's locked up back in my quarters at Fort Riley."

"Then why did you chase him? Are you crazy? You had no way of defending yourself." Her voice rose an octave.

"All I had to do was stay close. He had a revolver, six shots, then he'd be unarmed again. I could have taken him out."

"If he hadn't already shot you," she snapped.

"Were you worried?" he said with an irrepressible grin.

She narrowed her eyes. "You're trying to distract me from the fact that someone was shooting at us."

"Yes," he admitted. "Did you call 911?"

She heard a siren and nodded toward the highway. "I would imagine that's the sheriff's department now."

A few minutes later, a county patrol car pulled up. Close behind was an unmarked SUV.

The uniformed deputy climbed out and glanced back at Detective Wells, who was just exiting the SUV.

"The burglar's gone. The last I saw were taillights headed in that direction," Ben said, pointing west toward tribal land.

"Did you see what type of vehicle he was driving?" Detective Wells asked him.

"I didn't get a make, it was too dark, and the parking lot glare didn't help. All I can tell you is that it was a dark-colored van."

She gestured to the patrol deputy, who raced off, then looked back at them. "According to dispatch, the intruder fired a total of five shots. Did either of you get a look at the weapon?"

"A chrome- or nickel-plated revolver, with a four- or five-inch barrel," Ben said.

"Any idea where the rounds went?"

"In the wall around the kitchen, maybe the outside wall, too," Jo said, remembering.

"We weren't his target. He was more interested in the shed," Ben said.

"Anything missing?"

"We haven't looked, not yet, but I doubt he had time to pick up whatever it was he came for."

They walked over and Wells aimed her flashlight beam into the interior beyond the half-open door.

"Looks pretty full. When's the last time you had a look inside?" Wells asked him, her eyes still checking out the contents.

"A few days ago. I was in the process of moving in, and decided to store some of my dad's things until I could figure out what to do with them."

"Could this be connected to what happened to his dad?" Jo asked Detective Wells. If the shed hadn't been searched, maybe that was where Tom hid the "property" that had gotten him killed.

"It's too early to know," Wells said. She shifted the light toward the door, where a key was still in the lock.

"You leave this in here?" she asked Ben.

"No, ma'am."

"So the person had a key that fit the lock," she said quietly. "How did he get it?"

"I have a set, and so does Ben, but I thought my former boss's keys were taken by the police, along with everything he had on him when . . . ," Jo said, doing her best to avoid saying Tom's name out loud.

"Whatever he had on him is now locked up at the station. Those items are evidence, and nothing can be taken out of that room without going through a shitload of paperwork," Katie said. "I'll check it out, but maybe the killer got this key from Mr. Stuart."

"Then he already had a chance to look inside the night of the murder," Jo said.

"Maybe not, and with me here, or people coming and going and on the lookout for more trouble, he had to wait," Ben said. "Or maybe Dad just faked him out, trying to buy time by telling the kidnapper that the key would give him access to whatever he was after—but lied about which lock it fit. It's what I might have done, just to piss the guy off. That would also explain why the man waited so long to get to the shed. Remember the burglars the day of the memorial service? They couldn't get past the keypad and dead bolt and had to resort to the crowbar. One of them, the killer, knew that once inside, he could use the safe combination Dad must have given up. But after not finding what he was after in the trading post, the house, and your home, the shed was the next logical place to search."

"That's a good theory," Katie said with a nod. "From what I've learned, your father was tough and smart. As a former marine, he would have kept his cool and played it anyway he could."

"*Hooah*, ma'am," Ben said.

"I'm going to save some time and dust for prints myself. The forensic techs will be here ASAP and recover any slugs they can find."

O nce she'd processed the lock, key, and the area around the handle, Detective Wells pushed the shed door open all the way. "Now let's take a good look."

"I can tell you right now that my dad wouldn't have left something of value in a relatively unsecured place like this," Ben said.

"Or maybe he did, and the safe was just a diversion. Hiding a valuable item among everyday things can be a good strategy.

How thoroughly have you searched this shed?" Detective Wells asked.

"Not very. I gave some of the house furnishings to charity—Jo might have noticed the truck the other day. I also shifted things around to make room for other stuff I took from the house. Most of it is on the left side."

"Let's take a look now," Wells said. "I just wish I knew what we're looking for."

Jo brought two emergency lanterns from the trading post and the interior was soon brightly illuminated. They searched inside the boxes and trunks, including those Ben had recently taken from the house. Unfortunately, there was nothing of obvious value among the used clothing, furniture, and household items.

The forensic van pulled up just as they finished, and two techs stepped out of the vehicle.

Wells turned the key and fingerprint evidence she'd gathered at the shed over to them, then gestured to the house. "Rounds impacted inside and against the outside of the structure."

"I think at least two came into the kitchen," Jo said.

"I'll start there, then," the blond-haired tech said.

As they entered the house, Jo placed her hand on the *jish* at her belt. She opened the top and reached inside, touching the bead token with her fingertips. Slowly, she pushed back the terror she'd felt when she heard the shots. So much violence in such a short time . . .

Concentrating, she forced herself to stop trembling. She wouldn't give in to this now.

Detective Wells spotted a bullet hole in the refrigerator and studied the impact point. She turned and looked through the open door toward the shed. Then she stepped aside, allowing the tech full access.

"First Tom and his house, then the store—twice, my house, and now the shed. It's got to be the same guy, the one who locked us up in the freezer. So we already know something about him, like his build, general age, and the fact that he has an accent. What will he do next when he runs out of places to search for whatever it is he's after?" Jo said.

"Then everything changes," Wells said. "He'll come for one or both of you. You'll need to be especially careful."

"This man is dangerous, but so am I," Ben said. He'd given his words no particular emphasis, but there was no mistaking their deadly intent.

Ben was a soldier, trained to fight. Jo hoped that would help them stay alive.

"If we could figure out what he's after, we might be able to uncover a motive for what's been going on," Wells said.

Jo looked at Ben, then Detective Wells. Maybe it was time to speak up and tell them both about the mysterious caller and the threats made. Yet if she did and the man found out she'd told the officer, her own life would be on the line. The police and the others already knew the important points—what was going on and that they were being threatened. Maybe it was better to let law enforcement just concentrate on trying to find this man. Except for the call itself, they already knew everything she did—at least all that counted. It was more important to figure out what he was after, and once that was clear, a trap could be set.

Ben looked at her strangely, apparently waiting for her to speak. When she remained silent, he shrugged and spoke to the detective. "We've searched the shed, and everything in the trading post has been carefully inventoried. I've gone through the contents of the house, too. There's nothing here of significant value—not worth killing for anyway," Ben said.

"Same with my house," Jo added.

"You're both thinking in terms of money, but what it means to someone may not have anything to do with dollars and cents," Wells said.

"You mean like a figurine with a map or something very valuable hidden inside it, or maybe an object that would implicate someone in a crime? If that's the case, I'm not even sure how to begin looking for it," Jo said truthfully.

"Those examples are strictly Hollywood—but, yeah, like that. Look among the victim's papers and the ordinary things he kept close. Try to find something that doesn't seem to belong or that appears out of place."

"I'll do my best," Jo said.

"I'll help," Ben said.

"You might also consider closing the trading post and leaving the Four Corners area for a few days. We'll stake out the place and hopefully catch the suspect when he tries to break in again. If nothing was taken tonight, the intruder might give the trading post another go when he thinks he has more time."

"Sorry. I can't do that. The trading post's business has already taken a serious hit. We can't close up on the off chance that the burglar might come back. In fact, I'm considering staying open longer hours on Sundays, at least for a while."

"How many suspects with breaking and entering records are on your list?" Ben asked her.

"Several. There were two who looked like good candidates, at least for the attempt on the day of the memorial service, but obviously, neither one was responsible for tonight. They were brought in for questioning, made bail, then turned up dead— murdered," Wells said.

"The same men that were found in the back of the green pickup, right down the road from my home?" Jo asked, not really surprised.

"Yeah, the two had previous convictions for burglary, and they often struck residences and business sites when they knew the people would be elsewhere—weddings, funerals, you name it. I'm still waiting for the Office of the Medical Investigator, via the tribal police, to make a positive ID on one of the victims,"

Wells added. She brought out two photographs from her jacket pocket and handed them to Jo. "Have you ever seen either of these men before?"

Jo looked at them carefully, and handed them to Ben. "I saw the dark-haired man in the back of the pickup, but can't say for sure he was one of the burglars. Ben got a good look at one of the men, though I was too busy ducking."

Ben looked at the photos, then returned them to Detective Wells. "The man in the top photo was the person in the green pickup who fired a shot into the yellow pickup. He also aimed the pistol at us, and I backed off. I'm positive that's him."

She nodded. "They're brothers, so my guess is he's the one who was decapitated. DNA tests won't be coming back for a few weeks, though. The tribe has agreed to give me those results."

"What about the third burglar, the driver? Has his body been found—elsewhere?" Jo asked.

"Not that I know of."

"So you don't who he is?" Ben asked.

"Maybe he killed the brothers—so they couldn't identify him," Jo suggested. "That makes sense, doesn't it?"

"Could be," Wells answered. "It's not my case, though, unless it turns up showing a connection to Mr. Stuart's homicide."

"What about tonight's incident?" Ben asked.

Detective Wells looked down at the small notebook she carried, then made a few notes before answering. "Depending on the condition of the slugs we find here today, it's possible we'll be able to link the caliber and the type of bullet to a suspect, maybe even the actual firearm. It's all we have right now. But it won't help us in any of the other incidents. The only time we've actually recovered a bullet was when your father was killed, and the weapon used has been in the evidence locker for more than a week now."

"Give me the names of some of your suspects, and I'll help cut down on the legwork. They might tell me something they'd never tell a police officer," Ben said.

"No chance. I can't get someone outside of law enforcement involved in a police investigation," Wells said, staring at him intently for a few seconds before placing her notebook back into her jacket pocket. "I've got to get rolling on this. If you think of anything that'll help, call my cell."

Jo watched Detective Wells leave. "You made her . . . uneasy," she said after struggling to find just the right word.

"That was my intent," Ben said. "So far she's got nothing, but she's right about one thing. We need to figure out what my father's killer wants. Once we do that, we'll have a better idea of what we're up against."

"We'll find the answer," Jo said firmly, glad that the secret she was keeping would not interfere with the investigation. "Evil and good exist side by side so each can balance the other. Evil made its move. Now let's make ours."

SEVENTEEN

Jo was at the trading post early the following morning. Despite the new locks at her house, she'd scarcely slept. Too many worries clouded her mind and the lack of rest was starting to wear her down.

Esther, who'd also come in early, entered Jo's office holding a large paper sack. "I've brought some fresh vegetables from our garden. You're here before the others, so that means you get first pick," she said with a bright smile, setting the bag on the table and removing tomatoes, cucumbers, and summer squash.

Jo looked at the summer squash, noting how beautifully tended they'd been. She loved thin sliced, pan-fried summer squash with a smattering of butter.

Almost as if reading her mind, Esther picked up three of the summer squash and set them in front of her. "Here. I know you love these. Take them home and cook them up as a treat. You won't find balance if you neglect yourself."

"Although you adopted the Anglos' religion, you still respect the ways of the *Diné*," Jo said with a gentle smile.

"They're part of me, too."

"I know you're living mostly on a retirement income, Esther. Why not can or freeze these vegetables?"

"This year, the weather and the pests have been kind and we already have enough to meet our needs. As for the rest, it gives me pleasure to be able to share them with my coworkers, my friends."

"I'll fry these up in butter," Jo said. "Or grill them, maybe."

"Good. Relax and stop trying to carry the mantle of responsibility for the trading post all by yourself. We're in this together, you know."

"But what if I can't keep the trading post going?" The words slipped out of her mouth before she could stop herself. Horrified, she clamped her mouth shut. Words had power, and saying things out loud was sometimes enough to make them happen.

"You want to be a Singer, so you already know that some things take time and demand effort—a lot of effort. It's the same with the trading post."

"I feel so overwhelmed sometimes," Jo said softly, walking to the window and staring outside for a moment before speaking again. "Does anything ever come easy?"

"Giving up is easy. Fighting for what you want is a struggle that requires persistence and the ability to stand your own ground." Esther grew silent, then after a beat, added, "But the biggest battle we wage is always inside ourselves."

Jo heard the echo of pain woven through Esther's words. "Is everything okay with you?"

"I think my Truman has the beginnings of Alzheimer's," Esther said. "He's become very forgetful. We spent half of yesterday evening looking for the car keys. Eventually, we found them in the refrigerator."

"Maybe he had them in his hand when he tried to grab a carton of milk, set them down, then got sidetracked," she said, then wondered if that sounded lame.

"I'm not sure of anything yet, but for now, like you, fear's my biggest enemy. That's a battle *I'll* have to fight—and win."

"If there's anything I can do, just let me know," Jo said, giving her a hug.

"Please don't say anything to the others yet. I'd like to get a better handle on things myself first."

The sound of Leigh Ann and Regina coming in through the storeroom interrupted them. As Esther left the office, Jo leaned back and took a breath. Esther feared what she couldn't change. If Truman had Alzheimer's, there would be little she could do except work with the diagnosis. Esther felt trapped, and fear was a natural result.

She, on the other hand, had some power over the situation she was facing. Someone had definitely targeted the trading post, but her enemy was human and could be defeated.

"You okay, hon?" Leigh Ann asked, stopping by Jo's office door.

"I'm fine," Jo said, rubbing her temples, then reaching for a bottle of aspirins in her desk drawer. "I'm just tired of having to tough things out."

Leigh Ann went around the desk and gave Jo a hug. "Sweetie, it's okay to be upset, you have good reason. I heard on the radio about the shooting last night."

"So now the whole world knows, and that could come back to haunt us like before," she said, then expelled her breath in a slow hiss. "One way or another, I'm going to have to figure out what the person who killed our former boss wants. This won't stop till then."

"Ever since that break-in the day of the memorial service, we've all been trying to find the answer to that."

Regina came in next, knocking on the open door as she entered. "The tribal rodeo is less than two weeks away now, and we're going to need some of those inexpensive Mexican rugs that Tom stocks this time of year. They're perfect for those who can't afford a Navajo rug but are looking for Southwest-style accents. They always sell fast."

"Tom placed his regular order with the Juárez wholesaler, and I know we're due to make a pickup soon. I remember seeing the paperwork. A third of that inventory is already presold," Jo said.

As the women stepped out, Ben came in carrying his father's desk calendar. "Dad wasn't big on iPhones or electronics, but everything on his schedule is written here."

"Does he have a pickup scheduled there with León Almendariz, by any chance?"

"Here it is—Juárez, Mexico," he said after a moment. "It's listed for anytime this week. I remember Dad always drove down in the SUV to get those rugs himself. I rode with him on a few of those trips. Why don't you let me go get the rugs? I'm getting restless. The lack of progress on the sheriff's department investigation is really eating at me, and I need a change of pace before I do something stupid."

"Thanks, but I should go down there myself. I have to tell León that we'll be cutting back on our orders, and as the new owner that should come from me."

"Why cut back, particularly under the circumstances? Didn't you tell me once that those rugs sell fast?"

"Yeah, they do, but they also undercut our local weavers," Jo said. "Your father and I were always at odds about this. I wanted to carry a wider range of sizes crafted by locals. The smaller rugs that usually sell for less might become more attractive to those who'd ordinarily buy the cotton-blend imitations."

"But in the interim, we might lose sales."

"Not if we do things gradually—testing the strategy before we get burned. For instance, the next order I'll place with León will be for about twenty-five percent less product. León probably won't like that much, which is why, as the new owner, I

258 Aimée & David Thurlo

wanted to speak to him personally. It's a matter of respect. Do you understand?"

He nodded. "I follow, but let me go with you anyway. I need to get away from here, if only for a day. Consider me your security detachment, or your driver, whatever it takes to change your mind."

"No problem. It's a long drive and we can take turns behind the wheel. The company will also help keep me alert. Just let me finish a few things here first. I'll need to ask Leigh Ann to take over while I'm gone and give her a complete set of keys. I'll also have to pick up a few things at my house. After that, I'll be ready to leave."

Like Ben, she wanted—needed—to get away from the trading post, even if only for a bit.

Leigh Ann, in charge of The Outpost for now, took her place behind the front register and watched a couple of customers sorting through bolts of fabric. Esther's ready smile always managed to convince them to buy an extra yard, or maybe some contrasting material.

Regina was across the way, talking to another customer—an Anglo woman looking for a present for her granddaughter. Regina was good with people, and Leigh Ann could tell that she really enjoyed her job at The Outpost.

Yet as happy as the young Navajo woman seemed, Leigh Ann sensed another side to her. She'd often wondered if Regina saw her job as a way of getting away from problems at home. She'd heard Regina talking to her husband on the phone more than once, and Regina always seemed to be apologizing for one thing or another. It had reminded her of her own marriage.

Although she and Regina had never confided in each other,

Leigh Ann sensed the special kinship between them. It was clear to her that Regina was going through her own version of hell at home.

Regina came over after the customer left. "She didn't buy anything, but I have a feeling she'll be back for Ambrose's necklace—unless someone else gets to it first."

"Good. Jo will be gone till tomorrow, probably, and once she's back, I'd love to be able to greet her with the news that we've sold the last of Ambrose's pieces."

"Jo's really been tense lately," Regina said, "but after what happened last night, I'm surprised she's kept herself together as well as she has."

"She's still pretty edgy, which is why she needed to get away for a day or so."

"Nothing ever goes according to plan, does it?" Regina took a shaky breath.

"I'm a good listener, if you need to talk," Leigh Ann said softly.

Regina sighed. "It's Pete. He took off again. Last time this happened, he didn't come home for three days. He says that the baby, Mom, and me drive him crazy, and sometimes he gets so angry, he loses control. He can be really scary when he gets like that."

"Does he hit you?" Leigh Ann asked in a whisper. She'd never told a soul, but Kurt had often come home from his business trips tired and cranky. He never actually hit her, but he'd fly into a rage over some little thing, cuss her out, then force her to have sex, holding her down until he was done. The next day, she'd be sore and covered with bruises. At least most of those hadn't been in easily seen places.

Remembering, Leigh Ann suppressed a shudder. Nobody should ever have to go through that kind of hell alone. "You can trust me, honey. It'll be our secret."

"It's not really bad—not now, anyway. Pete slapped me once,

but then my mother started hitting him with the broom. She told him that if he ever raised a hand to me, she'd shoot him while he slept and he'd never see it coming. That was the last time it ever happened."

"Damn straight!" Leigh Ann said with a smile. "Good for her! You don't have to take that crap from anyone."

"I still love him," Regina said softly, "and sometimes it's my fault, getting him upset."

"No, that's what abusive men *want* you to think. Putting the blame on you is their way of excusing their own behavior," Leigh Ann answered quietly. "The problem is that our hearts won't turn themselves off, and being alone seems scarier than staying with our man."

"Yeah, it's like that," Regina said. "Thanks for listening, and don't worry. Pete and I will work through this."

Leigh Ann recognized the tone. It was the same one she'd used whenever her sister Rachel had asked too many questions, and she'd wanted the subject dropped. Respecting that, Leigh Ann didn't press her any more.

Regina quickly switched to business. "I know how you want things to go smoothly while Jo's gone, so I should probably tell you what I overheard. Del's mom stopped by earlier and chewed him out. He's off his meds again. There's a prescription waiting for him at the Walgreens, but he hasn't picked it up."

Leigh Ann knew about Del's medical disorder, attention deficit hyperactivity disorder, ADHD. Without his medication, he became unstable under pressure. He would have a hard time getting along with other people, finishing tasks, organizing— all the qualities a stock boy needed.

"I'll go speak to him. If he ran out, maybe one of us can take him to the pharmacy."

Leigh Ann found Del in the storeroom, arguing with a deliveryman who was trying to unload a pallet of canned goods. "Come on, man. I haven't got all day!" Del said.

"I'm pacing myself," the man in his late forties said. "I've got a bad back."

"You're just jacking around," Del snapped. "You shoulda been done and outta here ten minutes ago."

"If you're in such a hurry, Del, do it yourself."

"It's not my fricking job, old man."

"Then get out of my face," the man growled at him. "You young dickheads are all the same. Who put the rocket up your ass, anyway?"

Del threw down his work gloves. "You wanna piece of me? Come on, bring it. You're not too old to have your ass kicked."

The delivery man dropped the case of peaches right at Del's feet and put up his own fists. "Happy now, you punk?"

"Delbert Hudson, what in the *hell* do you think you're doing?" Leigh Ann stepped up, placing herself between the two men and crossing her arms across her chest. "This is no high school locker room. It's a place of business. You're here to do a job—and it's not picking fights with our vendors. Apologize this instant, then get your sorry butt over to the produce locker and clean it from top to bottom."

Del lowered his fists, slowly, but didn't move.

"Get on with it, Del," Leigh Ann demanded, her hands on her hips now. "I don't have all day."

"Sorry—old man," Del mumbled. His head lowered and a scowl still on his face, he whirled around and hurried out of the room.

Leigh Ann breathed a sigh of relief, then turned to the deliveryman. "John, just leave the boxes there on the floor. We'll take care of them later on."

"You need to control that kid before he gets in some serious trouble. You're gonna get sued if he keeps it up."

"I'll take care of it, don't you worry. If he causes any more problems in the future, just back off, pick up the phone, and call me or Jo."

As soon as the deliveryman finished emptying the pallet and drove away, Leigh Ann went to find Del. He was in the cooler, wearing a jacket and sweeping.

"Nice job so far," she said, noting that the boxes of fruit and vegetables were neatly stacked on the metal slats of the cooler shelves.

"But you're not yourself today, Del. You're not taking your meds, and you know you have to keep a close watch on that," she said quietly.

"Yeah, yeah."

"Don't you *dare* take that tone of voice with me! Now, you answer me. Did you ever pick up your pills?"

"Yeah, well, no."

"It can't be both."

"I was going to do it on the way to work, but I was running late. Jamie left her book bag in my pickup, and I had to go back by her house. I guess I forgot."

"Let's go. You're on break. We're going to pick up that prescription right now."

"I don't have enough cash on me."

"I'll make up the difference and you can settle it with me on payday. Now, get moving."

Leigh Ann walked out to the customer area and stopped at the rear register. "We'll be back in fifteen," she said to Regina. "I'm taking Del to the Walgreens. Call me on my cell if there's a problem."

As the day marched on, Leigh Ann came to the conclusion that she'd never worked so hard in her entire life. The crisis with Del had passed. Although the meds would take a while to get into the boy's system, at least he was now trying his best to make it up to her. Then, just as things settled down, the plumbing had decided to act up in the employees' bathroom sink. Good with a plunger, she'd managed to clear the drain after a struggle. Now she needed a break. Desperate for some coffee, she went to the break room.

Esther was there, finishing a cup of coffee. "You've done really well today, Leigh Ann, taking care of problems and getting everything else done at the same time. Three more hours till closing, and we're still standing tall. You should be proud of yourself."

Leigh Ann sat down and sighed. "I just wanted everything to go smoothly so Jo could see I can handle things."

"A lot went on and you took care of it all—successfully. That qualifies," Esther said.

As the thought registered, Leigh Ann smiled. "Yeah. You're right. Everything has turned out okay. Thanks for reminding me."

By the time Leigh Ann returned to the front register, she felt better than she had all day. Esther was the calmest person she'd ever met. Of course, at her age, with social security and her husband's pension, she probably didn't have a care in the world.

For a moment, Leigh Ann wondered what it would have been like to be Esther's age and not have so many worries anymore. After seeing so much of life, did anything ever rattle Esther? She supposed she'd find out someday—if she lived that long.

Regina appeared at the door. "We've got the wrong shipment. John, the deliveryman that squared off with Del, left us the wrong pallet. I guess in the confusion nobody noticed. When I opened the first case, I found out the cans are private label. The only places around here that carry that brand are the Smith's stores in Farmington," Regina said.

"Wonderful," Leigh Ann said with a sigh, rising from her chair. "Let me find the telephone number."

Fortunately, John readily agreed to stop on his way back from Shiprock and make the switch. By the time Leigh Ann straightened out that mix-up and was back at the register, another hour had gone by.

Just as she took a seat on the stool, Ambrose John walked in. "Hi, there, Leigh Ann. Jo around?"

"Nope. She's gone to a wholesaler to pick up a scheduled order. She won't be back till tomorrow."

"And Ben?"

"He's her driver. They're picking up a shipment of rugs south of the border."

"That *tourista* crap?" Seeing Leigh Ann nod, he grimaced. "I thought Jo wasn't going to carry those knockoffs anymore."

"You'll have to talk to her about that," Leigh Ann said with a shrug.

"I know business has been tough for The Outpost lately, so I came up with an idea that might benefit us both. How about letting me do some of the finish work on my latest pieces here? We could set up a table out front under the covered porch. I've brought some nearly completed pieces with me. My working right out in public might attract some customers. Old school advertising, like with the historic Hubbell Trading Post, way back when. With drive time coming up, a lot of commuters will be passing by in the next two-plus hours."

"That's a *great* idea!" Leigh Ann said. "I'm sure lots of people will stop just to see what you're doing! I'll put a sign out at the end of the drive ASAP."

"While you're doing that, I'll set up a table. I'll also need an outlet."

"There's one outside just below the window. If you want one of our evaporative coolers out there with you, just say the word."

"It's not really that hot outside today. It's in the mid-seventies, really nice."

As he walked out, Regina came over. "If we're lucky, he'll

get just a little warm working outside. Then maybe he'll unbutton his shirt, roll up his sleeves, and we can enjoy the view."

Leigh Ann laughed. "It's a shame he's not interested in women. He's sure nice to look at, rugged and a bit on the wild side. That long, warrior hair just adds to the package."

Ambrose came back inside and went to the soft drink machine. "Ben was always scrappy, but skinny as a rail back in high school. The army's really filled him out. Have you ladies noticed?"

Leigh Ann smiled. "Big wide shoulders and a great butt—not that I've been checking him out, of course. If I were a few years younger . . ."

Ambrose laughed. "I'm glad to see you're finally doing some window-shopping. For a while there . . ."

"Yeah, I know. It's taken me a month of Sundays to figure out that I'm not over the hill yet."

"It's tough to start again, sweetheart. My partner and I were together for almost five years, then he moved out one afternoon without so much as a 'Go to hell.' The house feels real empty."

"The problem with changes like those is that sooner or later we end up having to take another giant leap into the unknown," Leigh Ann said. "You seem to like stability as much as I do, Ambrose. So how on earth did you end up becoming a silversmith? Though you're a true artist, that's got to be a very uncertain business."

"I knew from day one that it would be tough to get established, but I was sure that I'd always be able to sell enough to keep food on the table and a roof overhead," he said. "These days, people know my name and my work, so it's a lot easier."

He stopped at the door and turned around. "So what do you think? Shirt open and cuffs rolled up? Red headband and the stereotype silversmith look? The ladies might like that."

"You're definitely eye candy," Regina said, smiling.

"Thank you, sweetheart."

"Sleeves folded halfway up your forearm, and no more than two shirt buttons undone," Leigh Ann said. "It's more fun when you leave a little to the imagination."

"You've got it."

"Now, let me get that big folding sign," Leigh Ann said.

A half hour later, the rate of cars pulling into their parking lot had almost tripled. Ambrose was very well known, easy to talk to, and women, by and large, just loved him. They'd sold the pieces almost as soon as he finished them.

It was long past regular closing time when Leigh Ann began locking up, starting with the back door. There were no customers with Ambrose now, so it was a good time to call it a day.

Leigh Ann was crossing the store toward the front entrance, intending on thanking Ambrose and helping him gather up his things, when she glanced out the window. Three high school boys in baggy pants and T-shirts were standing beside a double cab pickup parked in front of one of the six-inch-high concrete barriers along that side of the building. Their body language suggested trouble, and as she stopped and listened, Leigh Ann realized they were yelling crude obscenities at Ambrose.

Leigh Ann picked up an axe handle from hardware and went out onto the porch. It was time to run off the vermin. She walked past Ambrose, who'd come out from behind his table. He was standing at the top of the wooden steps, ready for a fight if it came. His huge fists were curled and ready.

Although she knew he could take out half a dozen guys like these without breaking a sweat, she wasn't going to let things get that far. There was no way she was going to have a call to the sheriff's department create more bad publicity for The Outpost and undermine all their hard work.

"You boys can take that trash-talking right off this private property. I won't have it, you hear me?" Leigh Ann hollered.

"We're just trying to toughen up the faggot," one of the boys wearing a studded leather vest yelled.

The other teens with him laughed and jeered. "You stay out of this, Mama Cougar," the guy in the vest added. "Unless you're looking for a ride—if you know what I mean."

Leigh Ann heard the door open behind her. Esther stormed outside, holding her Bible out like a sword. "Now, you all listen, and listen good. You, Charlie—I know your father. I taught him in Sunday school when he was half your age. He'd beat your butt with a razor strap if he ever heard you sassed me. And you, Petey," she said to the kid in the vest. "Your mother works two jobs keeping you and your three sisters fed. You want to be a real man? How about helping your family by getting a job instead of driving around making trouble? And you—" She moved toward the smallest of the three, a boy about seventeen with a black eye. "—your father's a pastor—a man of God. What would he say?"

"Dad says all fags go to hell."

"Then I'll be praying for him to see the light. The good book says, 'Judge not, lest you be judged.' Hatred's not part of the Lord's teachings." She waved the leather-bound volume at them. "Now, you all git, *right now!*"

Seconds later, the parking lot was empty, and not one blow had been exchanged. "Esther, you're really something," Leigh Ann said.

"Sometimes a little guidance outside the home does wonders for children who need to learn to treat their fellow man right."

As Esther went inside, Ambrose looked at Leigh Ann. "For a moment, I thought she was going to smack someone with that Bible."

"I've got to say she sure got their attention. That's the thing about Esther. When she gets mad, you're not just dealing with a five-foot senior. You're dealing with the wrath of God."

"Amen to that."

"Let's wrap it up," Leigh Ann said, smiling. "It's been one *very* long day."

—EIGHTEEN—

Ben and Jo had been on the road for close to five hours and were now passing along I-25 through the Bosque del Apache Wildlife Refuge south of Socorro. Most of the preserve to the east along the river provided food and shelter to everything from deer and coyotes to many species of migratory birds.

As the interstate took a more southwesterly turn, Jo looked in Ben's direction, now watching him rather than the scenery beyond. "It's good to have someone share the all-day drive to Juárez and back. It's easy to zone out."

"The desert's beautiful this time of year. Did you notice all the birds back there? Early migration, maybe?" He gestured toward the river with his right arm.

She nodded, noting the jagged scar that cut a path along his powerful biceps. "That looks like it might have been a nasty wound. What happened, you get caught on some barbed wire?"

Ben glanced at her, then back at the road. "It's my lucky bullet wound. Another foot to the left, and I would have been history. The sniper who fired that bullet hurried the shot and revealed his position. Before he could correct, I was able to reduce the threat."

"To do what?"

"I killed him."

"Oh." The use of jargon and the lack of emotion in his voice told her that there was a lot more to that story. As with his father before him, the more detached Ben sounded, the more involved he actually was. Over the years, she'd learned that sometimes, men outwardly expressed the exact opposite of what they were feeling.

"Was it difficult doing that kind of work for the army?"

"You mean being a sniper?"

She nodded.

He shrugged. "A lot of people think that a sniper's just a highly trained killer, but that's not it at all. Our mission is to take out the enemy before they can harm our own. We're there to save lives. Often, we're the only real-time eyes on a target, but a battlefield is in a constant state of flux and things can go wrong in a hurry."

"Like you getting shot?"

He didn't answer.

"It's the memories that work against you, isn't it?" she asked softly, wishing she could help him see the value of an Enemy Way Sing.

"There are some things in life you can't outrun or forget," he said.

Seeing the lack of expression in his eyes, she yearned to do something. "Is there any way I can help you deal with this?"

He glanced at her in surprise. "What could you do?"

"I don't know. I was asking *you*."

He shrugged. "It's all part of combat—war. Most soldiers come back with baggage, and some of us handle it better than others. The army also makes shrinks available to anyone who chooses that option. Either way, once I'm out of the army for good, I'll move on and let time bury those memories."

They approached the port of entry at Ciudad Juárez around three in the afternoon. Ben stretched in his seat as if working out the kinks while they waited in the traffic line.

"You've been at the wheel since Albuquerque. Want me to drive now?" Jo asked him.

"I've got it," he said.

"It's easy to get sleepy on long drives."

"I don't sleep much. Don't need it," he said. "Infantry's trained to do most of the fighting at night, and that tends to turn your day around. I sleep when I get tired—and when it's safe enough to do so."

"I tend to wake up at around three in the morning, then stay up thinking."

"About what?"

"My life, my goals, wishes," she said, her voice thoughtful and far away. "Sometimes, no matter how hard we work, some doors refuse to open and the things we want most end up falling by the wayside. Walking in beauty means seeing there's harmony and balance even in plans that fail, but knowing when to let go of a dream . . . that's always the hardest part."

"What do you wish for, Jo?" he asked softly.

"To go with blessings before and behind me," she said, remembering and repeating the words of the Creation Chant. "But until I figure out why someone is targeting the trading post, that's not going to happen."

After paying their toll and passing through the checkpoint, they drove away from the crowded port of entry area into Juárez's business district. Halfway down a hot, wavy asphalt street was a large cinder block and metal warehouse covered with graffiti.

"Does León still have his apartment on the second story?" Ben asked, looking up at the barred windows.

"As far as I know. If he asks us up, accept the invitation," she said. "After we go through the customary rituals, I'll take León aside and break the news to him that The Outpost will be carrying fewer Mexican-made rugs in the future. That'll be hard for him to hear, but don't interfere. I'll handle it."

He watched her. "You're testing yourself? You want to see how well you deal with things like this."

She nodded slowly. "Your father would have done what was necessary without making an enemy or losing a supplier. I don't know if I've got the same gift, but I'm about to find out."

"Once the warehouse door is open, keep a lookout for anyone who appears to be watching us from passing vehicles. There's a drug war going on here, and they sometimes take it out on U.S. citizens," Ben said.

"And here I was thinking you'd be relaxing today. Is this the real reason why you wanted to come along?" Jo asked.

Ben nodded. "Except for IEDs, it's probably safer in Baghdad or Kabul right now than it is here."

"I'll be careful."

They found a parking place along the crumbling concrete curb just a few feet from the big metal overhead door, which was closed and padlocked at the bottom. The entrance, just to the right, was locked, too, to her surprise.

Jo rang the bell, and León answered a few minutes later. Despite the heat, he was wearing a long-sleeved, sweatstained cotton shirt.

Seeing Jo, he gave her a quick smile, then looked up and down the street. "Once I open the door, pull inside quickly," he said, using a key on the padlock. He then called out in Spanish for someone to open the warehouse door. "We've been having problems with thieves lately."

As soon as Ben drove into the bay, León lowered the door,

then signaled to a young man who looked like he was sixteen at most. *"Las alfombras,"* he said, ordering him to bring the rugs.

The boy nodded and hurried off toward a pallet covered by an old blue tarp.

"It's good to see you again, León," Jo said.

He nodded absently. "Until you called a few hours ago, I'd been wondering who'd be picking up the shipment," he said, hurrying into the office, a partitioned cubicle open to the warehouse from the waist up.

Something wasn't right; Jo could see it in the way León was acting. He was wary and nervous. Normally, his wife would have come down to greet them and ask them about the trip. They'd then go upstairs for Mexican Cokes and *pastelitos*. Business was usually conducted in a leisurely manner here in Juárez. Yet the outbreak of violence, like a festering wound, destroyed everything that surrounded it. Times had changed.

"León, is it safe for you to do business with us?" Jo asked.

"I'm as safe as anyone else is these days," he said, then looked at Ben. "I was sorry to hear about your father's passing. At first I was told it was suicide, but when I called the trading post a few days later, *Señora* Leigh Ann said he'd been murdered."

Ben told him what they knew. "We *will* get to the bottom of it. I won't give up until I have answers."

León's face went one shade paler. "Be careful. Sometimes knowing too much isn't a good thing. People who see or say too much often end up dead."

"I'll risk it. My father deserves justice, and that means exposing whoever killed him."

León nodded absently and looked away. "Miguel, what's taking so long? Get the rugs into the back of the Ford. *Ahora mismo, muchacho.*"

Jo recognized the words "right now." It was clear to her that León was worried. His wife, Teresa, continued to remain out of sight.

She considered asking León about his wife, but coming from her, someone he'd met only a few times, it would be seen as an intrusion.

She waited until all but a few of the rugs had been loaded into the back of the Expedition, then brought up the subject of future orders.

"Almendariz Imports and Exports has had a long association with The Outpost," she said, handing him the check for the rugs.

He jammed it into his pocket without a glance. "Over the years, Tom and I became good friends. I'll miss him. When he and I first started doing business, things were less . . . complicated. These are very bad times."

"Business at our end is changing, too. The economy has hit all small businesses hard. That's why I'll be reducing our next order by twenty-five percent."

He stared at her. "I thought the last order sold very well. What's wrong? You haven't received any advance orders?"

"Yes, we have. All the Chinle-design rugs in this order have been presold. That's why we'll continue carrying those for a while longer. Eventually, my plan is to phase out imports and carry Native American rugs exclusively. Of course, if that doesn't work out, we'll adjust our orders."

He nodded, then hurried to the window and glanced outside through the heavy welded steel bars. After exchanging some quick words with his young assistant, he returned to join them.

"Traffic is light right now. You should leave before people start getting off work. We'll see you next time."

León's good-bye was so quick and devoid of the warmth he'd shown Tom and her in the past that it left her at a loss for words.

"What's wrong? Is it the drug gangs?" She hadn't meant to pry, but the words slipped out before she realized it.

"Very much so. It's dangerous in Juárez right now. People

are getting killed for no reason at all. You need to go," he said, handing her the bill of sale and the paperwork they'd be needing for customs.

With Jo at the wheel, they soon left Ciudad Juárez. At the port of entry checkpoint on the El Paso side, they were motioned out of line for a customs search. She gave them her driver's license, the paperwork for their cargo, and waited while the inspectors verified the number of rugs and looked around for contraband.

One of the border guards approached Ben and asked for his ID. Seeing the military ID, the man smiled. "I'm ex-army too," he said. "You're a long way from Kansas, soldier. You with the First?"

Ben nodded.

"*Hooah,* soldier. I served with the Seventh Field Artillery," the older of the guards said after having checked the underside of their SUV with a long-handled mirror. "Saw a lot of action during Tet."

"Vietnam is ancient history, Chuck. I served a tour with the Tenth Mountain, First BCT in Afghanistan," the younger, Hispanic-looking guard said. "No jungle, but the insurgents are harder to spot and it's colder than camel shit in winter. Snipers are everywhere, but I'd still rather walk into an ambush than be sitting on my ass and drive over an IED."

"I remember passing through Kunar Province," the young guard added, nodding toward Ben. "Saw some of your people. What unit were you with?"

"Third BCT," Ben responded.

"Heard that the First took a lot of casualties during their first deployment. You going back this year?" he added.

Ben nodded. "In about six weeks, give or take."

"Stay safe, soldier," the older guard said, waving them on.

"Yeah," Ben said. "You, too."

They drove into El Paso, one of the safest cities in the

Southwest, though ironically, it was adjacent to the current murder capital of the world.

"That wasn't so bad," Jo said. "By the way, did you notice anything unusual about our visit to León's? Other than the paranoia, that is."

"Yeah. I've never been there without being invited for a *merienda*, a Spanish version of an afternoon tea. Their dinner hour is around eight or nine at night, so they eat midafternoon to help tide them over."

"Something really felt wrong back there, and I don't think it's just the danger from the cartels either." She closed her eyes for a brief second, took a long, deep breath, then expelled it slowly.

"You do that with your breathing when you're feeling tense, usually right before your hands start shaking," he said quietly, not looking directly at her.

"I've had plenty of reasons to get the shakes these past few weeks, Ben," she said, not apologizing or denying it.

"You'll get no argument from me on that one."

"You've lived through your own version of hell. How do you cope?" she asked him.

"It isn't easy. There was a time when I almost drank myself into an early grave. I tried counseling for a while, but talking about it endlessly—well, that didn't work for me. If anything, it just kept the memory alive."

Jo immediately noted that he'd used the word "memory"— singular not plural. From what she'd put together on her own, she had a feeling that whatever haunted him was tied to his days as a sniper. Though it was one of the hardest things she'd ever done, she didn't ask him anything more about it. She wanted to respect the boundary he'd set.

They rode in silence for several miles. "I really expected León to try to bargain with me," she said finally. "I replayed the scene in my head dozens of times, trying to decide how to best present my position and hold it without making an enemy. Yet when it came down to it, he never even countered."

"The look on his face—I've seen it before on the faces of shop owners and villagers who live in the disputed areas," Ben said. "They would talk to the marines or GIs if they knew nobody else was around, but they were always looking over their shoulders and locking doors. It's all about survival."

"It's hard to imagine León, or anyone in that section of town, having problems with the drug cartels. They're just people trying to make a living."

"I think the gang influence is everywhere in Mexico these days. Armed confrontations get the press, but the greatest danger lies in what you don't see."

"It's not a war zone, not like Afghanistan or Iraq."

"In a way, it is. There aren't blown-out bridges or destroyed villages, but the violence or threat of violence is always there. León may worry that his association with the 'gringos' could bring him major trouble," Ben said.

"I hope not. He's a good man who works hard. In that respect, he's no different from you and me."

"Troubles come to everyone, rich or poor. It's part of life."

Jo thought about the Navajo Way. Everyone and everything was connected, and that slender thread that bound them all could bring chaos or harmony.

—NINETEEN—

They stopped for dinner in Albuquerque, choosing a family restaurant in the city's north valley. Though it had cost them close to an hour of travel time, he'd needed the break and something to eat.

Behind the wheel again now and much closer to home, he recognized the area of dry juniper hills from their earlier drive south. There were lights from isolated houses in the distance, though they were few and far between along this stretch.

Jo had grown steadily quieter since they stopped for gas in the forested area around Cuba, the biggest community for seventy miles. In the darkened interior, he could see her dozing, her eyes closed, and her head moving with the motion of the big SUV. She'd stuck her Windbreaker behind her head as a pillow and looked as peaceful as an angel at the moment.

Though Jo tried hard to look as tough as the devil himself, he could tell that the events following the murder of his father had hit her hard, and that something had been bothering her. Of course, there was the obvious—the threat to her and the business coming from the killer or killers, and the search for whatever had led to his dad's murder in the first place.

He wished he could have taken her someplace safe, away from the trouble that had remained half a step behind them. Yet even as the thought formed, he knew the only way he could have done that was to kidnap her. No matter how scared, she'd never run away from the trading post or the ones who were counting on her.

Most important of all, Jo didn't need, nor want him to protect her. He stole another glance at her as she shifted. For a brief moment, he envisioned her beneath him, crying out his name over and over again.

Yeah, that was going to happen—the day after hell froze over.

As they left the Jicarilla Apache Indian Reservation, he slowed to navigate a curve and saw a pickup ahead, blocking the right-hand lane. Its headlights weren't on, but he could make out a man in a jacket waving a flashlight. A deer hunter orange–colored plastic triangle was in the center line, indicating a hazard.

Ben fought the GI training that told him to either come to a full stop while still some distance away or race past at full bore. Ambushes, IEDs, or suicide bombers weren't part of daily life here in the States. Then he noticed a second person by the raised hood of the pickup, staring in his direction.

Ben took his foot off the gas and eased down to thirty. This wasn't Afghanistan, it was Sandoval County, New Mexico, USA, and somebody needed a mechanic or a replacement fan belt—or whatever.

"What is it?" Jo asked in a groggy voice. "An accident?" she added, her voice rising an octave.

"No, it looks like a breakdown. I'm going to stop and help them get that pickup off the road. If one of those oil company eighteen-wheelers comes hauling ass down the highway with a load of well casings, things are going to get ugly."

Ben stopped on the shoulder of the road about fifty feet

away, highlighting the pickup with his headlights. "Need a hand?" Ben yelled, sticking his head out the window.

"Sure do. Maybe you can give us a jump. I called triple A, but nobody can get here from Bloomfield for another hour or so, and it's dangerous as hell stuck out on the highway like this," the man with the flashlight yelled back, walking slowly in their direction.

Ben climbed out of the SUV and Jo did the same.

"I thought there were two of them," Jo said, putting on her Windbreaker. "Where'd the other guy go?"

"Right here," a deep voice came from the darkness behind them. "Turn around slowly."

Ben tensed his body, ready to strike at the first opportunity.

Ten feet behind them stood a man holding an M16 clone, the barrel pointing at Jo. "If you try and make a move, dude, I'll kill your girlfriend."

"And I'll kill you," flashlight guy added, pointing a pistol at Ben's midsection. "Keep your hands where we can see them, tough guy."

A third man, the one who'd been in front of the hood, came over, waving a short-barreled pump shotgun back and forth. "Give me your cell phones."

"Haven't got one. Search me," Ben said, hoping to draw him in. He'd left his in the SUV.

The guy with the flashlight looked over at the shotgun man, who then waved the barrel at Jo. She brought the phone from her pocket and dropped it onto the sand.

"Now, get over there by that rock," he said, pointing the shotgun to a spot about twenty feet downslope from the highway shoulder.

"We're being robbed, right?" Jo said, sounding almost hopeful.

"Shut up, lady," the man with the shotgun said, then turned to the guy they'd seen first. "Karl, hand me the flashlight, then get the pickup off the highway before a car comes along." Glancing at his other companion, he added, "Don, pick up the cell phone, then keep an eye on them. Shoot them if they make a move."

The man with the shotgun, clearly the leader, took the flashlight from Karl, walked to the back of Jo's SUV, and looked inside.

"You can take the rugs," Jo offered, her voice wavering slightly.

"Shut up, bitch," the man guarding her snapped, jabbing Jo in the back with the barrel of his assault rifle as he reached down for her cell phone.

Ben's move was lightning fast and straight out of hand-to-hand. Grabbing the weapon in the forestock and magazine, he swung the butt upward with a quick twist of his wrist.

The man's head jerked from the blow to his chin and he staggered back. Ben, in control of the weapon now, swung the barrel around and caught the man across the neck. He gagged, clutched his windpipe, and sank to his knees.

"Run!" Ben pointed to an arroyo. "Down there."

Jo bent down to pick up her cell phone, then raced over to the gully. As she jumped down into the blackness, she tripped over something and landed flat on her face on the damp earth. For a moment she just lay there, disoriented.

Ben, who'd slid down behind her and kept his balance, grabbed the back of her Windbreaker and hauled her to her feet. "Keep moving."

They raced upslope, running blind in the mushy sand. Somewhere behind them, Ben heard the dull thud of someone jumping down into the wash.

"Don't slow down," he whispered, trying to make out the terrain ahead.

Ben aimed for higher ground. There was a good chance they could make a stand there. Defensible terrain was all they needed. He could pick them off as easily as Pepsi cans on fence posts.

Though they were making good speed, he could hear someone racing along above the arroyo, paralleling their escape route
and with better visibility. He had to find a way to slow them
down.

"Keep going," he said again, then turned and snapped off
two quick rounds in the direction of the sound.

"Shit! Take cover!" one of the men yelled.

As Ben raced to catch up to Jo, the arroyo grew shallow,
blending into the hillside. "Up behind that rock," Ben said, running around an outcrop of hard sandstone.

Jo, breathing hard, looked back and nodded.

There was a loud blast, and buckshot whistled past them like
angry bees. Ben whirled, saw the shooter, then returned fire,
aiming a foot over the man's head and forcing him to dive to the
ground.

Ben caught up to Jo just as she reached the eroded formation
of sedimentary rock. It was steep here, and there was only a narrow ledge to stand on, but they had a three-foot-thick wall of
solid sandstone between them and the arroyo below.

"Keep your head down," he said.

"Want me to call for help now?" Jo asked, gasping for air.

"Good a time as any," Ben said, drawing a bead on his end of
the arroyo.

As Jo tried to contact the police, he kept watch. His night
vision was good and the moon was out, but he couldn't see anyone moving around. Any of the men hoping to approach unseen
would have to use the arroyo, but three men had been in on the
ambush. That meant he'd have to watch for eventual flanking
moves, though their assailants would have to climb like goats to
get behind or above them.

Three minutes went by; then he saw a head poking out from
the arroyo, moving right into his sight picture. There was no way
he was ever going to kill again, not unless it meant saving Jo's
life, but he could, and would, scare the hell out of these assholes.

He sent the bullet downrange. The round struck just to the left of the target, breaking off a large chunk of clod from the arroyo bank. The man ducked back out of sight.

"State police are on their way. An officer is at Counselor, north of here. That's not too far," Jo said.

Another two minutes passed; then Ben saw movement on the left side of the arroyo. Somebody was trying to climb out and flank them. He sent a round that direction, close enough to scare the idiot back inside.

"You are—were—a sniper. Did you hit him?" Jo whispered.

"No, but I've got a twenty-round magazine, and I'll do whatever's necessary—if they come any closer." Ben heard the faint wail of a police siren in the distance.

"Here comes the cavalry," Jo said.

"The officer knows these men are armed?" Ben asked.

"Yeah, and that there are three of them."

"He'll need some backup. You stay here," Ben said, moving out from behind cover, the rifle still pointing toward the arroyo.

"No, I'm going with you. I'm the only one here who's not armed. No way I'm staying by myself," Jo said.

As they inched down the slope, they could see three figures in the distance racing across the highway toward the truck and their Expedition. Ten seconds later, both vehicles raced off to the east.

"They're gone, along with our wheels," Ben said.

"And a thousand dollars' worth of merchandise," Jo grumbled as they ran toward the road.

The state police officer, who'd slowed to a crawl, aimed his spotlight in a wide sweep and caught them in the beam.

"Come out with your hands where I can see them."

Ben placed the assault rifle on the ground and stepped out into the clear. "We're the ones who called you."

"The three men who robbed us are gone, along with our 2006 white Ford Expedition. It's loaded with a shipment of

Mexican rugs for my trading post," Jo added. "The license plate is ALO-566."

"I appropriated one of their weapons and used it to keep them at bay. The guy I took it from wasn't wearing gloves, so he probably left fingerprints. Mine are on file, so you can rule them out." Ben waited as the officer in the black uniform climbed out of his unit. "You got a description of their vehicle, right?"

"A dark Ram pickup, right?" As he responded, the tall, slender officer picked up the weapon by the trigger guard.

Jo nodded. "Yeah, it's dark blue or black."

"You two okay?" Seeing them nod, he continued. "Roadblocks are being set up outside Cuba. Hopefully they won't get far." He looked at Ben, then at Jo. "Can you describe the merchandise you were carrying?"

"Sixty inexpensive, Mexican-made cotton-blend rugs with Southwest patterns and colors. They're all in tight clear plastic wrap. We just picked them up in Juárez. The Expedition, our company vehicle, has over a hundred thousand miles on it. It has two seats and a cargo area. There's a sign on the door that has our business's name—The Outpost."

The state police officer, a man in his mid-forties with very short cropped hair, spoke into the radio clipped to his shirt, then turned back to them. "Maybe they thought you'd have something more expensive onboard, like jewelry," the officer said. "Mexican silver, maybe?"

"Or maybe *we* were their target," Ben said. "I'm sure they planned on killing us."

"What makes you think that?" the officer asked.

"They used names and didn't bother to hide their faces or avoid leaving fingerprints," Ben said.

"But all we had was an old four-thousand-dollar Ford loaded down with cheap tourist rugs! Surely lives are worth more than that," Jo said.

"The value of a life . . . I'd say that depends entirely on who you ask," Ben said. Seeing the shocked look on her face, he wondered what she would have thought of him had she known about the incident back in 'Stan that had turned his life inside out.

One thing was clear. No possible relationship between them would survive that knowledge. He'd saved the lives of many that day, but it had come at a high price.

Like his dad, Jo lived in a world of black-and-white answers, but *his* world was shaded in grays and bloodred. There was no way Jo could live with what he'd become. Some dreams just weren't meant to be.

✳

The following morning, Jo woke early. After offering her prayers to the dawn, she got ready to drive to Hosteen Brownhat's place. She and Ben had caught a ride, courtesy of the state police, and when she arrived home late last night, she found the note Hosteen had left pinned to her door. He wanted to know if she intended on continuing her apprenticeship.

Since inheriting The Outpost, she hadn't been able to help her teacher prepare for upcoming Sings or meet with him other than at the Blessing rite he'd done for the trading post. The Navajo Way demanded that Hosteen Brownhat and she, as his apprentice, walk the path of beauty, but her life had changed drastically. Fear had her in its grip, and without inner peace, she'd never be able to bring harmony to anyone else.

Jo was locking her front door when an unmarked but easily recognizable sheriff's department car pulled up beside her pickup. It was Detective Wells.

"Good morning, Detective," Jo said. "I guess you heard what happened last night and that's why you're here so early?"

Detective Wells nodded. "According to the state police report I found on my desk this morning, you were only transporting several dozen cheap Navajo-style rugs. Your SUV isn't exactly last year's model either. I know you were coming in from Mexico, so what else did you have in the vehicle?" Detective Wells looked at her closely.

"Nothing but Ben and me," Jo said firmly. "And anyone out to steal rugs would have known the low value of those knockoffs. I find it very hard to believe that those men were willing to risk their lives and jail time just for the Expedition and our cargo."

"But you still can't add anything new to what you've already told the state police?" Wells looked skeptical.

"Sorry, no, but talk to Ben. Maybe he can remember something helpful."

"I'll do that, and in the meantime, watch your back."

Jo watched the detective as she drove away. What happened to her and Ben the night before seemed to finally have lit a fire under the detective. Hopefully, Wells's renewed efforts would pay off.

As the county police's unit disappeared from view, Jo climbed into her pickup. She still had time to visit her mentor before work.

K atie knew that what had gone down last night was far more than a simple carjacking and robbery, but she wasn't getting the answers she needed. Stuart's son didn't trust her, and Jo Buck either didn't know anything, or was holding back. Either way, what she needed now was an informant.

She'd done the dirty work before sunrise. Among all the trading post's employees, Del Hudson appeared to be the one most vulnerable to intimidation. The teen was also in a great position to watch everything and everyone at the trading post. With some luck, she'd get answers—and maybe she'd also find the leverage she needed to finally slip out of Roberto Hidalgo's clutches.

Although she hated the thought of setting up a seventeen-year-old kid, she had no choice. The boy was in no danger from her, of course. The trick would be to make him believe that life as he'd known it would come to an end unless he helped her.

Katie waited alone at the end of the road Del would have to drive down on the way to school. Before long, she saw his pickup approaching.

Katie waited until Del pulled out onto the highway, then followed several car lengths behind. After about a mile, she flipped her siren and pulled him over.

As she walked up to his driver's-side door, Katie noted the tension on his face. "You're Del, right? You've got a busted brake light. Did you know that?"

"No, ma'am," he said. "I'll get it fixed right away."

"Let me see your proof of insurance and registration."

Del leaned over to reach the glove compartment and fished out both.

"What's in that plastic bag, son?" she asked, pointing to the "evidence" she'd slipped in through the crack in his window just before sunrise.

He reached down to the passenger's-side floorboard and picked it up. "I dunno. I never saw it before," he said, holding it by the top and bringing it closer to her.

Katie opened the bag, then made a show of checking the contents. "Get out of the vehicle, hands on top of the hood," she said, slipping the bag into her jacket pocket.

"What? What's wrong?" he asked, his eyes as big as saucers.

"Just do as I say. Get out of the vehicle and place your hands on top of the hood."

He stepped out, his body shaking, and did as she asked.

"I'm taking you in for possession," Katie snapped, patting him down.

"Of what? What's in the bag?"

She reached for the handcuffs in the keeper at her belt. "Either you're a powdered sugar freak, or it's cocaine."

"No way!" he said, turning his head around, fear in his eyes. "That junk's not mine. I don't do drugs, not even pot! You've got to believe me!"

"If it isn't yours, then how did it get there?"

"I don't know. Someone set me up. It wasn't there last night, I swear!" His voice was suddenly two octaves higher.

"So who's your enemy? You dis someone lately? Been in a fight?"

He stared at the ground, desperately searching for an answer. "You know I work at The Outpost part-time. Well, I got into a delivery guy's face the other day because he was just dicking around. He was an old guy, at least forty. I bet that son of a bitch did this!"

Katie waited, letting the fear build until he was squirming so hard, she thought he'd pee his pants. "This is a felony, Hudson. You know that?"

"Oh man, oh man! It's *not* mine. You've got to listen to me! I was set up."

"Why should I believe you?"

"I get decent grades in school, I have a job, and I work my ass off. Ask Jo Buck and the others at The Outpost. I've never been in trouble with the police—not ever."

"Hand me your truck keys, then get back inside and give me a moment to run a check," she ordered.

Once she had the keys, Katie went back to her unit and let the kid sweat it for a while longer. When she returned, Del was nearly in tears, his face as pale as chalk.

"I ran a check and you're clean. Not even a moving violation."

"See? I told you!"

"But we still have a problem—that bag of coke. Where did it come from?"

"I have no idea. Just take it!"

"It's not that simple," she said, pretending to be wrestling with the problem.

"You've got to let me go! I didn't do this. Honest. I'm not a drug dealer, and I don't use. Give me a drug test, you'll see."

"Not necessary. I believe you, Del. You sound like a good kid who just happened to screw with the wrong person," Katie said, then after a pause, continued. "I'll tell you what I'll do. If you help me with a problem I've been having, I'll help you out, too. Are you willing to do me a small favor?"

"Yeah, sure. What do you want me to do?" he asked eagerly. "Just tell me."

"I'll take this and pour it into the closest irrigation ditch," she said, patting the bag of baking soda in her pocket. "No one needs to know."

"Thank you!" he said, almost in tears. "I really mean it."

"Okay, now here's what I need you to do for me. I'd like you to keep your eyes and ears open when you're at work. Tom Stuart's killer is still out there, and I need to know if Jo Buck or anyone else at the Outpost is covering up or hiding something. Tom Stuart was murdered for a reason, and if I find out what that was, it'll lead me to his killer. Can I count on you to help me gather information, Del?"

"Yes, ma'am. I work after school today, so I'll start then."

"One more thing. Our deal has to stay strictly between you and me. You'll be my confidential informant on this case. I'll keep you out of jail, you help me find a killer."

"Tom gave me my first job, so I'll do my best. I owe it to him."

"Good."

Katie watched Del drive away. *Now* she had a chance. All she had to do was wait and watch.

⁜

Jo arrived at Hosteen Brownhat's small woodframed home
west of Shiprock as the long shadows of early morning
gave way to the climbing sun. The home was a faded white, and
the wood trim needed paint, but the gray shingle roof was new,
replaced just last spring. As she parked, Rudy came out of his
hogan accompanied by an elderly man.

While Jo waited to be invited to approach, Rudy's visitor, a
man with long white hair, jeans, and a plaid shirt, walked to a
horse grazing on the clumps of yellow grasses scattered about,
took up the dangling reins, and mounted the old pinto gelding
with surprising fluidity.

Rudy was dressed much like his patient, wearing jeans and a
long-sleeved green flannel shirt. His hair was jet black and woven in a long braid down his back. He wore a white headband,
and canvas running shoes rather than boots.

The *hataalii* watched the older man ride away toward the
bosque for several seconds, then finally turned and waved, inviting her over.

"You got my note, I see," he said as Jo drew near.

"Yes, Uncle," she said.

He gestured with his lips toward the medicine hogan, a six-
sided pine log structure with a single entrance covered during
the winter season only by a heavy wool rug woven in shades of
red, black, and gray. "Come inside."

The interior was stark, with a small added wooden shelf, a
fire pit in the middle, and sheepskin pelts for sitting. A kerosene
lantern sat in one of the several corners along with boxes of ceremonial items. She sat on the north side, as was the custom for
unmarried women.

"You've come very far in your training, but you still have
much to learn," he said after a brief silence. "Although you've
shown dedication, you're now letting other things interfere with
what you set out to do. To become a Singer, you have to want it
more than anything else; otherwise, you won't succeed."

"My life has changed, Uncle. Others are depending on me. I won't be able to continue my training until things are more settled at the trading post."

He stared at a small black beetle making its way across the dirt floor of the hogan. "Your trembling, is it still troubling you?"

"At times, yes," she admitted.

"When it does, do you reach for the token as I recommended?"

"That helps me," she said, nodding, "but a killer's still out there, Uncle, and he's threatened me personally. Until this is resolved, I can't go forward with my apprenticeship. To do that, I have to be able to walk in beauty, free from fear."

He lapsed into a long silence, then finally spoke. "It's very difficult for a woman to become a Singer. I told you that the first day you came to me. The situation you're facing now will eventually be resolved, but by then, your focus might have shifted. Do you still have feelings for the murdered man's son?"

Her previous relationship with Ben had been common knowledge, so the question didn't come as a surprise. "It's complicated," she said after a beat.

"The problems women Singers face go beyond not doing certain Sings while pregnant. Their focus tends to shift to family sooner or later. Will becoming a Singer have your heart, or only a piece of it?"

Jo stared at the packed dirt floor of the hogan. "Becoming a Singer is the path I choose to walk. The rest of the pieces will fall into place if they're meant to be."

He nodded, approving of her answer. "I'll do a brief pollen blessing over you before you go." The *hataalii* picked up a basket, turned it over to use as a drum, and began to Sing.

Jo repeated each line of the prayer, matching his intonation. It was important to show respect but not humility before the gods.

"On the trail of beauty, I walk," he said, finishing.

Jo repeated the words, feeling the power of the spoken word

wash over her. The blessing had renewed her strength. "Thank you, Uncle."

Jo slipped off her cuff bracelet. It wasn't of great value, but it was all she had to give. "Take it, Uncle. When you're ready, bring it to me at the trading post and I'll trade it for anything we have at the store."

He nodded once. "I accept your gift."

On her way to work minutes later, Jo heard the old pickup squeaking and rattling as it traveled over uneven ground. Once she finally made it to the highway, the ride became easier.

As she thought about things, Jo wondered if that's the way it would be in her life, too. At first, bumps would be all she'd be able to see and feel. Then, sooner or later, the way would finally clear.

Jo spent the next two hours calling customers who'd prepaid and were waiting to receive their Mexican-made rugs. She'd assumed some would cancel after being told of the delay, but no one did, though several seemed more upset than she'd expected.

Ben walked in just as she placed the phone back down again. He hadn't shaved this morning, and the stubble made him seem even more masculine somehow. As she looked up at him, she felt a stirring inside her. That awareness wouldn't go away, no matter how hard she fought it.

"You came in later than usual this morning," he said. "I hope you got some rest after what happened last night. Are you feeling okay?"

"I'm fine. I needed to make a stop this morning." Although she saw the questions in his eyes, she didn't elaborate.

"Any idea what you want to do about replacing those presold rugs?"

"I've spoken to almost all of the customers who placed those orders and it's clear they still want the rugs, so I'm going to call León next. I'll ask him to get another shipment ready for us," she said. "León should be happy to make the extra sale, so I don't expect any problems, and insurance will cover most of our loss."

"We're also going to need an SUV or van to pick up the replacement rugs. Have you contacted the insurance company yet?"

"No, but I have the policy information right here and the state police will be faxing a copy of the report later today." She swiveled around in her chair, opened the file cabinet, and brought out the insurance folder. "If you can call our insurance agent and give her the details, I'll contact León."

"Roger," Ben said, taking the folder and leaving for his own office.

After quickly confirming León's number, Jo placed the call. His wife, Teresa, answered, but instead of their usual friendly exchange, she immediately placed Jo on hold.

León answered a moment later. "Miss Buck, this is León. How can I help you today?"

She told him about the hijacking, leaving out the details. "Some of our customers are upset, so I'm going to need a duplicate order as soon as possible."

"Did I understand you right? You said you were robbed?"

"Yes. We were about a hundred miles from The Outpost when it happened. They got the rugs and my old SUV."

"At least you weren't hurt," he said. "I can find you some more rugs from my supplier, but you'll have to stay on your guard. This isn't business as usual, not anymore."

"What do you mean? What's going on? Is there something else I need to know?" He sounded afraid, as if he'd been the one nearly killed last night instead of Ben and her.

"I've told you too much already," he said in a low voice. "I'll make some calls, then let you know how soon I can have a replacement order ready for you. Is that acceptable?"

"Yes, that'll be fine."

The next thing she heard was a click, then silence. Jo placed the receiver down and stared at it for a minute longer, lost in thought. She was still trying to figure out what was going on with León when Ben strode into her office, his face flushed with anger. He crossed the room, noisily pulled out a chair, and sat facing her.

"You wouldn't believe the crap I just got from the insurance agent, the same woman who has been getting yearly checks from us for probably fifteen years. Nothing but bureaucratic runaround. The bottom line is that the van was still in Dad's name, so the claim must be handled by the trustee. I called Mike and he said he'd take care of it, but it'll probably take a week to get everything sorted out. The one bit of good news is that Mike told me he expects everything connected to the trading post will be transferred to your name soon. There are a few legalities he still needs to clear up."

"Will the insurance cover the purchase of a new van?"

"No. They'll reimburse us market value, so we'll only have enough for another used one. In the meantime, we'll need to rent another set of wheels. I called around, got the best deal I could get, but it won't be cheap."

Jo leaned back, suddenly feeling exhausted despite the fact it wasn't even noon yet.

"What happened with León?" he asked. "You looked worried when I came into the room."

She gave him the highlights. "I don't get it. He should have been a little more upbeat. He didn't lose a client, we weren't hurt, and he gets twice the sale."

"Don't overanalyze it. He's like my dad, old-fashioned. He may be trying to protect you in his own way because you're a woman."

"Maybe," she said, unconvinced.

"I'm going to go to Farmington to pick up the rental van. I'll be riding in with Del, if you're okay with that."

"Sure."

After Ben left, Jo answered two calls from clients checking on special orders they'd placed. Then, as soon as she hung up, Leigh Ann came in.

Jo looked at her and sighed. "Please tell me that everything at least went well *here* yesterday."

"We had our ups and downs, but everything turned out fine. We also had more customers than we've had in a long time," she said, describing the day and Ambrose's cooperation.

"That's all good to hear. You did a great job yesterday."

"Now for this morning's problem. Regina hasn't shown up yet. Should I call and find out if she's coming in?"

"Give her a little more time. We all have complicated lives."

"You know she's having trouble with Pete, right?" Leigh Ann asked.

"Just that he'd hurt his arm, and was having problems finding work. But if it's also hurting their marriage, that would explain why she hasn't been very talkative lately. I knew something was wrong."

"Women—we can feel each other's pain. Maybe it's intuition, or maybe we just don't close our eyes as much."

Jo smiled. "Maybe so."

The rest of the day, including the afternoon, went by without any hitches. It was seven thirty, a half hour after closing, when Jo finally took a break. Her stomach was growling loudly, and she realized that the only thing she'd eaten today was a Snickers bar and a half dozen cups of coffee.

Jo stood and walked around a bit, stretching her legs. The store was silent and empty. Ben had gone home about ten minutes ago, and he'd been the last to leave. Although the front door was locked, the loading dock was still open a crack. They usually kept it propped open with a rock to create a good air flow and make the evaporative cooling more effective.

Jo had walked down the hall to the storeroom, ready to lock

up, when she caught a faint whiff of tobacco in the air. For a minute she didn't move. Tom had smoked off and on all his life. Was it his *chindi*? No one else here smoked.

Suddenly an arm snaked around her chest, and a rough hand clamped her mouth shut. "Don't fight me!" he ordered in a harsh whisper.

Out of the corner of her eye, Jo saw a second figure, wearing a rubber clown mask, step out from behind a stack of wheelbarrows, holding what looked like a pillowcase. "You're going with us. Then you're going to tell us where Old Man Stuart hid that shit."

The voice sounded familiar, especially that pronounced Hispanic accent. This was Tom's killer, the man who'd threatened her over the cell phone. It didn't take a genius to figure out what these men were planning for her. They'd torture her and she'd be unable to save herself, because she still had no idea what they were after. Eventually, when they realized that, they'd kill her. Her only choice was to fight back now and catch them off guard.

Jo bit down hard on the fingers covering her mouth, then kicked up with her heel.

Her attacker yelped and pulled his hand away from her mouth. He grabbed her around the waist and leaned back, lifting her off the floor.

As the clown with the pillowcase rushed forward, she bent her knees, then kicked him in the chest with both feet.

Recoil from the collision knocked her and her captor back. As he stumbled and fell, she twisted free. Jo landed on the hardwood floor butt first, then rolled away, jabbing her side into the handle of an overturned wheelbarrow.

"Get the bitch!" clown face yelled, regaining his balance and advancing.

Jo rose to her knees. The man who'd grabbed her was wearing a werewolf mask and was struggling to his feet as he adjusted the eyeholes, trying to clear his line of sight.

Jo was still on the floor, caught in the middle, when she heard Ben's voice.

"Whose van—what the hell?" Ben yelled, standing in the back doorway.

In a heartbeat, Ben dived at werewolf guy. Jo jumped to her feet and kicked the clown in the chest, sending him staggering away from Ben.

While Ben had the shape-shifter wannabe on the floor, she swung at Bozo with a clenched fist. He ducked her round-house, slipped past her, and tackled Ben, knocking him off the other guy.

Ben fell against the wall, knocking several empty gasoline cans off the shelf above and down on himself with a horrible racket. By the time he was able to stand, the two intruders were out the door. The werewolf slammed the door behind him, and Ben, too late, bounced off the metal with a loud thud.

Jo yanked the door back open just as the men jumped into the van. As she rushed outside, Ben at her heels, the steel blue or gray van raced off, throwing dust and gravel out in two big rooster tails.

"New Mexico plates, CAX-845," she called out, then pulled a marker pen from her shirt pocket and wrote the code on the metal door trim.

Ben was already gone. He'd jumped off the loading dock and raced after the van, but all he managed to do was get lost in a cloud of dust and flying gravel.

Shaking, Jo groped for the cell phone in her pocket and dialed 911.

—TWENTY—

Detective Wells was the first officer to arrive, not that it made much of a difference, considering the van had raced in the opposite direction fifteen minutes earlier. Detective Wells soon confirmed that the plates had been stolen from a car parked at a Farmington mini mall.

After taking the brief descriptions Ben and Jo could give her of the men, she asked for a copy of the surveillance camera feed. Although they didn't really cover the area of the struggle, Wells said she hoped they'd find images of the men casing the place prior to closing.

After Wells left, Jo went back to her office. Ben came in behind her and began to pace, his face red and his eyes still afire.

"Ben," she said.

He never even slowed down.

"Ben!" she snapped, and he stopped and glared at her.

"You're acting like a caged tiger, and anger isn't going to get us anywhere. We need cool, rational thought."

"What we *need* is to figure out what they're after and why they want it so badly."

"How did you know that I was in trouble? I never got a chance to yell for help," she said.

"I noticed you'd turned off the lights, but still hadn't come out. I was waiting because I was going to ask you over for dinner. When I saw the van with the rear doors open and the motor running, I knew something was wrong."

"Good thing for me," she said. "Help me lock up the place, and let's get out of here."

"Then come over to the house and have dinner with me. Right now I'm real tempted to pour myself a stiff drink, and if I'm alone. I just might."

She'd faced the results of alcoholism most of her life. Her father would go for six months or more doing just fine; then one drink would send him on a desperate downward spiral.

"Are you cooking?" she asked with a smile.

"You bet," he said as they walked across the parking lot. "You're pretty good in a fight, Jo. From what I could see, you were holding your own."

"They didn't expect me to resist and that gave me an advantage, but my goal was just to get away. I'm glad you showed up. In the long run, I wouldn't have had much of a chance against two men."

As they went inside his home, the scent of pot roast greeted her. "Wow, that smells wonderful."

"I left it in a slow cooker all day. I also added some freshly roasted red chile." He went to the cupboard and brought out some plates. "Are you still into cream sodas? There are some in the fridge."

She smiled. "My mom got me hooked on those when I was ten. I introduced you to them, remember?"

He nodded and went to set the table while she poured the sodas into glasses. "You have no idea how much I envied you when we were growing up," he said in a quiet voice.

"*Me?*" She almost choked. "Why? You were the one who

had everything—money to spend, a car, a nice house, plenty of clothes."

"That wasn't what really mattered. My dad and I . . ."

She nodded slowly. "After your mom died, you two stopped getting along."

"For a long time I tried my best to work things out with him, but it was like talking to someone who didn't even know I was there—unless I screwed up. The only time he ever really spoke to me was to compare me to you. You were the lucky one. It was like you had two dads, mine and yours."

She averted her gaze, afraid he'd see too much.

"Yeah, I know you and your dad had problems from time to time, but you always seemed to work it out."

"He was a good father, when he was himself," she added quietly.

"He had health issues, right? I always suspected that was why you never asked me over."

She didn't answer right away. "My mom and dad are gone, so I don't have to keep this is a secret anymore, but I'd still like your word that what I tell you stays between us."

"You have it."

"My dad had problems with alcohol, and he'd go on binges. When money got tight or there was too much stress at home, he'd fall apart and drink himself into a stupor. Sometimes he'd lock himself in his office for days. It would only happen once or twice a year, but when it did, he'd get mean. Mom told me it all started when she got pregnant with me and he had to quit college to make a living. Dad never stopped resenting the fact that he had to give up his own dreams to take care of his family."

"So that's why he'd disappear like that? I just figured he had some kind of recurring illness, like malaria, you know, from Vietnam."

"My dad battled demons all his life."

"You didn't want me there, because you never knew when

he'd start hitting the bottle, right?" Seeing her nod, he continued. "That never even occurred to me. I thought you had the perfect family."

"Dad's drinking was something we kept secret. It was Mom's way of protecting him—and us, I think."

"Now I understand why you were always making plans. That was your way of regaining control and adding a little predictability to your life."

"Working toward a goal, and always having a plan B in case things went wrong became part of everything I am."

"And now one of your goals is to become a medicine woman—a Navajo healer."

"Yes. It's my dream, and I have to follow my heart."

Ben invited her into the den. "I'm glad we had a chance to talk this evening."

"I've been the one doing most of the talking," she said, sitting down beside him. "You have secrets that weigh you down, too. If you'd let me, I could help you shoulder some of that burden. Let me be your friend in more than just name," she said gently, and covered his hand with her own.

He said nothing for several long moments, entwining his fingers around hers, and just holding on.

She allowed the silence to stretch, hoping that the warmth of her touch would soothe the pain he carried. She could almost feel the battle raging inside him. "The best thing about a good friend is that they're not there to judge. No matter what you say, it won't change what we are to each other."

He gave her hand a gentle squeeze. "I want to tell you. I'm tired of secrets." His voice was quiet now. "You know I was a sniper. What you probably don't know is that I was one of the best. I took pride in my missions and accomplishments—until one morning. In a matter of seconds, my entire life changed."

He stood and began pacing. "Our patrols were being hit hard by an enemy sniper. He was positioned in a neighborhood we'd been ordered to occupy—but there were hundreds of civilians living there, so we couldn't call in artillery. What we needed was a surgical mission, so my spotter and I were sent in after dark. I'd studied the pattern of victims and had an idea where our target was hiding—in an apartment building near the center of town. We selected a home near the site as a base and waited for hours, watching and listening. A security team covered our backs."

She watched him pace, but didn't interfere. The best way for her to help him now was simply to listen and let him get things out in his own way.

Ben finally stopped pacing, his fists clenching and unclenching as he leaned back against the wall, eyes closed. "It was dawn when my spotter located the sniper, about three hundred yards away. He was inside a second-story one-room apartment with a large open window. As we watched, he brought up his rifle and took a bead on a patrol advancing up the street." Ben took an unsteady breath.

Jo saw the shudder that ripped through him. She started to go to his side, but as he began speaking again, she stopped and remained where she was.

"Mike, my spotter, verified the firing solution and I took the shot." His voice wavered. "The sniper went down. Then I saw a little boy across the room slump to the floor, blood shooting from his chest. The same bullet that took out the insurgent struck a child who came into that room at just the wrong time."

"Oh . . ." The breath was sucked from her lungs, and she couldn't speak.

"Mike put his head down, swearing a blue streak, but all I could do was watch through my scope. A woman came into the room next—probably his mother. She fell over the child, covering him with her body and started screaming. We could hear her all the way back to our unit."

There were no words of comfort she could possibly give him.

Following her heart, she threw her arms around Ben, absorbing the shudders that tore through him into herself. His skin was ice cold, so she pressed herself against him, warming him with her body. "You didn't know, you didn't know," she repeated. "You're a good man, Ben. What happened wasn't your fault. Do you hear me?"

Ben's arms tightened around her. In a move fueled by a need to make that never-ending pain stop, he bent his head and took her mouth. His kiss was hard and rough, but she didn't pull away.

"You make me feel . . . human," he managed with a groan.

She cupped his face in her hands and forced him to look at her. "What happened that morning turned you into the man you are today—one who won't hesitate to protect another, even if it means placing your own life in danger. When I needed you tonight, you stepped up, though you weren't armed and you knew you were outnumbered."

"I'll defend myself, and you, but I'll never shoot to kill again, not unless it's to protect an innocent and there are no other options."

"Don't you see? You turned your pain into lifesaving compassion, Ben, and that's how a man walks in beauty."

He kissed her again, but his time his lips were gentler and more persuasive than demanding. This new, gentle man before her, a warrior whose wounds remained raw, needed her . . . and that felt wonderful. Her heart opened naturally, inviting him in.

"I want you," she whispered. "I always have, but . . ."

"Don't think, just feel," he murmured, kissing the base of her throat. "No promises, no lies, just now."

She tugged at his shirt and kissed his chest, enjoying the ripple of muscles and hard planes. Feeling the rapid beat of his heart against her lips, she left a string of moist kisses down the center of his body.

He groaned. "Slow down." He lifted her into his arms and

carried her to his bed. "There are hours and hours ahead of us. The night's still young," he whispered in her ear. "Let's make it one we'll remember forever."

He undressed her slowly, kissing the places he exposed, his gentleness and patience stoking the fires within her. Slowly, her body flowered open to him. She invited everything, refusing him nothing.

"More," she begged.

He took her over the edge time and time again, but even after she lay spent, he didn't enter her.

Needing more, she whimpered, her hips rising, ready for him. "I need to feel you . . . inside me."

Unable to hold back anymore, he pushed into her warmth. "Move into me . . . like that," he said, and groaned. "With you, I'm not a man with half a heart. I'm just . . . a man."

She lost herself in the passion. In that textured warmth there was healing, and power, and most important of all, an awakening. She came apart with an overwhelming rush, then felt him shudder in a final release of his own. In the midst of imperfection, they'd found perfection.

After a brief eternity, he rolled over and placed her on top of him, holding her there.

As she lay in his arms, thunder rumbled in the distance. "Is a storm brewing?"

"Oh yeah," he murmured. "The sky will light up for us again tonight. Outside, too."

She chuckled softly as he began kissing her again.

—TWENTY-ONE—

Leigh Ann sat at the old kitchen table that served as the desk these days and stared at the balance in her checkbook. Then she glanced over at the tiny stack of just-paid bills on her right. Unlike last month, she'd have enough to cover everything, and maybe even buy that cute pair of shoes she'd found online. Having Rachel move in as her roommate had sure helped her finances.

"I'm going to the store for some diet soda and snacks. Do you need anything?" Rachel yelled from her room.

"No, hon, but thanks for asking!" she yelled back.

Leigh Ann heard her sister hurry down the hall, her three-inch heels clicking on the hardwood floor. At first, she hadn't thought they'd be able to live under the same roof. After she'd married Kurt, Rachel and she drifted apart. Kurt had been attracted to Rachel, and knowing that had made it impossible for her to feel comfortable around her own sister.

The clicking of heels grew louder again; then Rachel popped her head into the study. "I forgot to tell you. While I was looking for some roach powder, you know, for under the sink where I found the dead one, I found an old box of Kurt's in the garage.

It was in one of those cabinets next to the breaker box, and it's labeled 'tax records.' I set it down on the floor. Do you want me toss it into the trash?"

"No. Kurt wasn't the most organized person, and there's no telling what else is in there. I'll sort through it. I'll also need to keep the forms in case I get audited in the next few years."

"Yeah, better safe than sorry. If you need help moving any stuff around in the garage, just let me know. Meanwhile, I'm off."

"I know," Leigh Ann said, chuckling, but Rachel never heard.

Alone, Leigh Ann pushed her chair back and stood. She hated to have things hanging over her. Today was trash day, so she'd take a look at the box, see if there was anything in it that she wanted to keep, then throw away what was left. Anything with personal information would be shredded, of course. That was something she'd learned from Tom at the trading post.

On her way to the garage, Leigh Ann stopped to answer the house phone. How wonderful to finally be able to pick up the phone without first looking at the caller ID and making sure it wasn't a bill collector. The rent money Rachel was paying had really turned things around.

"It's me, Regina," Leigh Ann heard the familiar voice.

"What's up, hon?"

"I'm going to be late to work this afternoon, and I was wondering if you'd cover for me. You can add it to your own hours and take home the extra," she said.

"What's going on?"

"I've got to take the baby to the doctor's. She's running a fever."

"No problem, hon. I'm happy to help." It wasn't like she couldn't use the money. Maybe she'd have enough to buy herself the shoes *and* a matching purse. It was practically forever since she'd been able to buy anything that she didn't absolutely need.

After reassuring Regina, Leigh Ann walked out to the adjoining two-car garage. Rachel, predictably enough, had placed the box right in the pathway between the wall and Leigh Ann's car door.

As Leigh Ann picked it up, something shifted inside, making a clunk. Curious, she set it on the garage counter, turned on the overhead lights, then opened it up. The top layer was composed of spiral notebooks small enough to fit in a jacket pocket. She picked them out and set them on the lid, revealing a layer of old newspapers beneath. Not seeing anything important, she lifted up the stack and found three compact video cassettes, the TV VHS adapter cassette, and an old movie camera and battery charger packed in foam peanuts.

Kurt had loved everything electronic. She remembered him walking around the house with the camera, making a visual record of their belongings for insurance reasons. He'd even taken the camera with him on a few business trips for sightseeing opportunities that had never materialized. She'd never used the camera and had forgotten all about it until now.

Wondering if it was still operational, she put everything else back into the box. After looking around for more tax records, she dusted away some spiderwebs with an old broom, then carried the camera gear and cassettes with her back into the house. She'd see if anything was on the tapes, and if not, maybe she could sell them and the camera, providing it still worked.

Leigh Ann plugged in the camera to recharge, loaded a cassette into the adapter, then started up the TV and VCR, a leftover from her early married days. After hitting the Play button, she stepped into the kitchen for some coffee, but the odd sounds coming from the TV quickly brought her back into the room.

She'd expected footsteps and comments about household items, not grunts and groans. Maybe the VCR was falling apart. It was old and obsolete. The only reason she'd kept it was because she could still record TV programs and movies to view on it. She definitely couldn't afford a new DVR.

She peeked into the living room, and as she saw what was on

the screen, all the oxygen in the room suddenly vanished. She couldn't breathe; she couldn't move. The mug slipped out of her hands and crashed to the floor. Scarcely aware of the scalding liquid that splashed onto her feet, she remained rooted to the spot, staring at the images on the screen.

Kurt and she were making love atop their big bed. Once, not long after he'd bought the camera, he'd decided to film them in bed, but she'd refused to allow it. He'd argued that it would be a real turn-on, and had called her a prude when she'd continued to say no.

Leigh Ann crossed the room, furious. She'd burn the tape, that's what she'd do, and hope Kurt's sorry butt would burn in hell right along with it.

By the time she found the remote, Kurt was done and had rolled over onto his side. Endurance had never been his strong point in bed. As she reached for the Stop button, the image suddenly changed. All she could see clearly of the redheaded woman on the screen was her backside as she mounted Kurt, impaling herself with a gasp.

Leigh Ann stepped closer. Kurt had wanted her to role-play, but she'd never worn a wig in her life. Who the hell was that woman?

As she watched closely, Kurt laughed, then rolled the redhead onto her back, moving away from the camera. He picked her up, then shifted them toward the center. After looking over at the camera, probably making sure they were still in the picture, he began his usual routine—hammering his partner into the mattress. He continued until they were both covered with sweat, then collapsed with a loud whoop onto the mattress, out of breath. Another lack of endurance record. The woman laughed and threw her hands up against the headboard. It was then that Leigh Ann saw Rachel's face clearly for the first time.

Leigh Ann covered her mouth with one hand, ran into the bathroom, and threw up. By the time she returned to the living room, another clip of her sister and Kurt was running, this time with Rachel sitting astride him, pumping away, her head toward his feet.

Leigh Ann was trying to find the remote to turn it off when she heard the front door slam.

"I'm back in record time. Got some extra snacks for you, too." Rachel came into the room, glanced at the screen, and gasped. "What the hell?"

"You tell *me*, little sister."

"Oh . . . I . . ."

Leigh Ann found the remote, turned off the TV, then held up one hand. "No excuse could ever explain this. Don't say a word."

She couldn't stand looking at Rachel anymore. Leigh Ann grabbed her purse off the coffee table, ran out to the garage, and jumped into the Jeep. The possibility that maybe they'd made love here, too, on these seats, made a bitter taste rise to the back of her throat. She pushed the button on the garage door opener, turned on the engine, and nearly hit the rising door backing out.

Leigh Ann raced out of the neighborhood and headed west. No one had ever felt comfortable speaking of Kurt even when she'd be the one to bring the subject up. At first she'd assumed that it was because he'd been killed in that hunting accident and it made them uneasy. Now she saw another, more disturbing reason. Something assured her that they'd all known he'd been sleeping around.

Humiliated, she wondered if everyone at the trading post had also known. They'd wanted to spare her, she was sure of that, but she couldn't bear the thought of facing them now.

Then she noticed the direction she'd automatically taken as she left the house—the route led to Melvin's home. He was the only person she really wanted to see now. Just being around him made her feel like a woman, not one who'd failed as a wife, but one who was desired and respected.

Wiping the tears from her face, she settled down to the

speed limit, easing pressure on the gas pedal. There was no need for recklessness. Her life was far from over. Looking ahead for the turnoff, she suddenly remembered that she'd promised Regina she'd fill in for her.

Leigh Ann swallowed hard. She'd be there. Unlike the sex-crazed pervert she'd married, *she* kept her promises. But first she'd visit Melvin, if only for a little while. Being around him would help her more than anything else could right now. Afterwards, she'd head in to work.

Driving the rental van, Ben circled the Juárez neighborhood. He'd made the trip alone. Jo had been swamped with last-minute paperwork transferring ownership of The Outpost to her, so he'd volunteered to do the return run to León's. According to Jo, León had promised to have at least forty replacements available; all Ben had to do was pick them up.

As he studied his surroundings, Ben noted that sidewalk vendors and foot traffic had all but disappeared from this area. The lack of activity in what had always been a busy street sent warning signals to his brain. It was like Iraq on his first deployment—during the Surge, when danger lay everywhere.

As he approached León's warehouse, Ben spotted a pale blue Toyota pickup parked across the street. It felt like a stakeout, so he decided to drive by and get a better feel for what was going on. The two men inside the cab watched him pass; then the one on the passenger's side raised a cell phone to his ear.

Somebody was definitely watching the warehouse, but he had no idea if they were good guys or bad. The line between them was getting more blurred with each passing day. Many police officers were being paid off by the gangs here—and if they refused to be corrupted, that usually meant their gruesomely staged death.

León was obviously expecting him, but instinct told him that a little extra caution was called for, along with an indirect approach.

Ben parked in an open slot at the busiest market he could find, about a quarter of a mile away, then got out. His day-old beard, inexpensive old sneakers, cheap ball cap, baggy tan slacks, and short-sleeved sweatshirt wouldn't automatically label him as a *gringo*, a *tourista*.

At least one skill he'd learned in sniper school was transferring to the private sector. Knowing how to find his way through an urban combat zone filled with hostiles was, hopefully, about to pay off. If everything was okay at León's, he'd go back for the van—assuming it hadn't been vandalized or stolen—then pick up the replacement rugs and head for the closest port of entry.

Ben strode past local civilians without much notice, adopting their strides and walking at their pace to fit in. Everyone here avoided eye contact and remained as invisible as possible. He'd seen the same behavior in Afghanistan, where nobody knew when or where violence would erupt next.

Fifteen minutes into his "mission," Ben went up to León's side door and knocked. There was a distant voice—he couldn't make out the words through the sturdy metal door, then silence. Ben took off his sunglasses and cap and looked straight at the one-way glass window behind the metal bars to show León who he was.

Another minute went by, but Ben heard nothing but the sound of traffic in the distance. Finally he reached out and turned the knob. To his surprise, it wasn't shut and actually moved back a few inches.

"León?" Ben called. The door should have been locked. He remembered that from his last trip.

Putting on his hat again, Ben stepped inside. The small entryway led down six wooden steps to the concrete floor of the warehouse. No lights were on, but enough illumination came through the two high, barred windows to show that the warehouse had been thoroughly trashed.

Cardboard boxes and wooden packing crates were ripped or smashed apart and strewn across the floor. Their contents, bolts of fabric, rugs, curtains, and metal hardware, were everywhere. Packing peanuts were scattered like snowflakes from burst shipping containers. Oily footprints stained the merchandise, and the acrid stench of bleach told him why many of the darker items were spotted with white splotches and stains—ruined deliberately.

Ben took out his pocketknife, an old four-inch Craftsman lockback blade his father had given him for Christmas way back when they were still getting along. It wasn't much of a weapon, but his training would give him an edge if things got up close and personal.

Halfway across the floor, right below the long staircase leading up to León and his wife's living quarters, Ben found a familiar sight in his line of work—a blood trail. It began with splatters, those seen when someone was struck enough to bleed, then became smeared in places where shoes and boots had slid on the slippery stuff.

Wary of a concealed assailant, he glanced quickly from side to side, listening for movement as he searched for victims. There weren't any within view. Then he saw more blood on the stairs. Taking them two at a time, careful not to step on the drippy places, he climbed up. "León?" he whispered.

There was a grunt that sounded like his name.

Ben took another step, high enough to see onto the second story. León was slumped against the closed door leading into the private quarters—bedroom and bath. The older man's face was bloodied, almost unrecognizable, with a torn lip, blackened eyes, and a nose that had to have been broken in at least two places. There was blood on the front of his shirt, mostly dried, and he was holding a rosary in his broken fingers.

"Ben," León whispered, struggling to speak. "Go, before they come back."

Ben rushed to León, pushing aside the tipped-over wooden chair that was now missing a leg. Even at a glance it was clear the man needed urgent medical attention.

Ben brought out his cell phone. "An emergency medical team. What number do I call?"

"No. Even if I made it that far, they'd finish me off at the hospital, and maybe kill the doctor and nurses, too."

"Your wife—where is she?"

"Dead. They killed her. They made me watch."

"Who are *they*? Tell me, and I'll make sure the police go after them."

"No police, no justice . . . not for me, not for your father."

"My dad? What did he have to do with this?"

"Your father wanted to know, and the answers killed him." He coughed, paused, then began again. "He wanted to force them to let us both go. He had evidence that would hurt the cartel."

"Cartel? Where did he hide this evidence?"

"In a rug? I don't know for sure. He had all he needed to stop them . . . but they came to take it back."

Ben heard the sound of a siren in the distance, but instead of growing hopeful, León looked away. "They own the police. Go while you can."

"Not yet. What were they after?"

"They were using us . . . to take drugs into the U.S." He paused, gasped for air, then continued more slowly. "Tom threatened them, so he had to die. Now it's my turn." León started to cough, and blood came up from below, coating his tongue. For a moment, his eyes began to fade, but then he inhaled sharply.

Gripping Ben's forearm, he struggled to speak, English and Spanish mingling in his mind. "Find rug, *muchacho*, and the *prueba* . . . need both. Let everyone see and hear. That's your only chance. *Corre,* run . . . ," he managed, switching back to English. "They're coming."

"What *prueba?* You're talking proof, but what is it? A video?"

The sirens were getting louder. As Ben watched, León's eyes glazed over and the rosary fell out of his broken hands.

Ben hurried down the stairs and looked out through the barred window, keeping well back and to the side. A police car passed by the warehouse slowly, then parked just within sight. The officers didn't jump out immediately, obviously expecting trouble.

His shirt bloodied, Ben looked around for another way out. Seeing a back door, which opened onto an alley, he moved quickly in that direction. On a hook by the door, he found an old cloth jacket and a straw hat and put them on, tucking his cap into his back pocket. He unlocked the door's heavy latch, then slipped out into the shade of the overhanging roof. Pulling the straw hat low over his eyes, he walked purposefully down the alley in the opposite direction of the border crossing.

Moments later, he crossed the street at a jog, right behind a smelly city bus throwing out clouds of smoke. A white police car turned the corner, but Ben slowed to a walk, never looking in their direction. He knew from the screech of brakes that the police had pulled into the alley leading past León's warehouse.

Moving as quickly as he dared, Ben circled around and walked toward the market where he'd parked the rental van. While still a block away, he spotted two more police cars staking out the market. Knowing they were probably watching the van, he veered away casually.

He deliberately avoided the logical, closest crossing and headed farther down. He stayed off the main streets and encountered no one curious enough to approach him.

Two hours later, it was dark. Ben approached the Mexican

side of the border, crossing as casually as possible. He'd already ditched his cap, sunglasses, and bloody shirt, and bought a cheap T-shirt to wear beneath the borrowed jacket. Finally he stopped at a liquor store just a street over and purchased a bottle of Bacardi, which he carried in a paper sack. If he tried to pass through empty-handed, it might have led to questions, especially because he was on foot.

The uniformed Mexican guard, a woman, seemed more interested in his ass than anything else, though her male border guard had insisted on looking inside the bag.

After fifteen seconds, they waved him on. Forcing himself to stroll at an unhurried, even pace, he walked across the bridge's walkway above the river. He was in no-man's land now.

Just as he began walking downhill, the halfway point, and was closing in on the El Paso guardhouse, he heard rapid footsteps behind him. Ben turned his head and saw three men making double time, narrowing the gap. They weren't in uniform, but they were focused on him.

Knowing this was no time to take chances, Ben jogged toward the American border guards and reached the U.S. side first. When he glanced back casually in the men's direction, he saw they were suddenly very reluctant to make eye contact. Suspecting that the danger hadn't passed, Ben remained on the alert. If they were on his trail, he could be jumped anywhere from here to The Outpost. He'd have to find a way to lose them—and the sooner, the better.

He held out the paper bag to the tall, fit Dallas Cowboy-look-alike guard, knowing he'd have to pay duty on the rum. He paid in cash, but when he was asked for his ID, Ben pretended not to know where it was. He set his wallet down on the counter, searched through his jacket, then his pockets. Eventually the three guys behind him were waved on to the next guard and the man processing him grew annoyed.

"You got some ID or not, boy?"

Ben looked down the line. The three men were walking slowly away from the checkpoint, but one was looking in his direction. He glanced away when he saw Ben watching.

"It's here somewhere. Maybe it's with my cocaine, in my boot."

"Shit, boy, now you've done it. Come with me, we're going to have a talk and maybe a strip search."

Ben smiled. "Whatever you say, sir."

An hour later, Ben was in the backseat of an air freshener–scented cab on his way to an El Paso hotel. He'd confessed to having a few drinks, then produced his military ID from a compartment in his wallet and volunteered to be X-rayed. He then allowed a drug dog to come in and give him a good once-over.

The guard he'd given a hard time to had a nineteen-year-old son stationed in Kuwait and they'd shared a few anecdotes. Hearing that Ben was scheduled to be deployed to Afghanistan, the guard wished him a safe return and let him go.

Ditching the men he'd suspected were on his tail had been worth the delay. Once inside his El Paso hotel room, an inexpensive place east off Highway 62 rather than I-25, his most likely travel route, Ben used his cell phone to call Jo.

Jo answered within two rings. "Hey, it's me," he said immediately. "I had to leave the rental van across the border. I'm temporarily stranded in an El Paso motel now, but I know a lot more now about what happened to my dad. I'll fill you in when I see you, but there's something you need to know right away. We're both in danger, I'm talking about our lives now, and that might extend to the rest of the trading post staff."

"If they came after you before, they'll be watching for you to rent transportation. Stay where you are, Ben. I'll come and get you."

"No."

"People are watching *you* at the moment, Ben, not me. I'll be careful and watch my back, but I'm coming, so stop arguing."

"Okay. But don't rent a vehicle unless absolutely necessary or drive anything connected to The Outpost. Make sure you don't tell anyone where you're going. Well, maybe you should confide in Leigh Ann, but insist she not tell anyone else, especially Detective Wells or anyone else in law enforcement. León said that there were cops involved on his side of the border. I'm thinking there may be dirty cops on our side as well. Once we get a chance to talk about this, we'll decide how much Detective Wells needs to know. I want to make sure I don't end up in the hands of the Mexican police, accused of killing León and his wife. My fingerprints are there, and I have no idea how hard the Juárez cops are going to be working on this case."

"Probably not very. They've got enough to do staying alive. Just listen to the news."

"Yeah, you're probably right."

"Stay where you are. I'll be there in about five or six hours," Jo said.

"Watch your back—and bring the shotgun—just in case. We're targets for sure now, and we're in this together."

"We always were. We just didn't know it," Jo said.

Ben was reading a newspaper, watching from the farthest corner of the small lobby of the Mesquite Motel, when Jo drove up. She came in a car, a good thing since it would throw others off who might have expected a van. He hurried outside and grabbed the passenger door handle. It was locked.

"Sorry," Jo said, unlocking the door with a click from the console next to the stick shift.

Ben slipped in, fastened his seatbelt, and she put the car in gear.

"It's good to see you—alive," she said, pulling out into traffic and driving west toward El Paso.

"Whose car is this?" he asked, looking in the rearview mirror.

"It's a rental—but under Leigh Ann's name. She paid cash."

"Good thinking." He leaned back. "Did you notice anyone following you?"

"No, and I kept one eye in the mirror all the way south."

Tense, they drove in silence until they entered New Mexico. "Okay, how about telling me what's going on," Jo said at last. "Coming down, I heard on the radio that two bodies were found inside the burned-out Almendariz Imports/Exports warehouse. The El Paso station picked up the story because of all the smoke. Officials in El Paso are speculating that it's related to the violence between the drug cartels, but the Mexican authorities aren't giving out any details except for the deaths."

"León and his wife were murdered, and the fire was set after I'd already left his warehouse. I imagine it was used to cover up the crimes," he said, but didn't go into the details of the murders. Instead, he told her what León had said before he died.

"What about that *prueba*? Do you have any idea what he was talking about?" she asked.

"I suspect it's a video—well, digital recording—because of his emphasis on seeing and hearing, but I can't be sure," Ben said. "The only rugs that connect León and my dad are the ones sold at The Outpost. Logic tells me that the proof is in one of those, but it would have to have been one from a previous order dating back to when Dad was alive."

"If what León said is true, then we need to find the rug he mentioned and this *prueba* to put a stop to what's been happening to us. But are we talking drugs, money, or guns, and what does any of that have to do with rugs anyway?"

Ben tried to guess what was so special about cotton rugs that sold for less than fifty dollars apiece, but drew a blank. "Maybe somebody had drug money hidden inside those rugs. They were rolled up tight and sealed in thick plastic wrap."

"Or maybe small packets of drugs. But where do we look? There aren't any rolled-up rugs from León's previous orders in the store. I know what they look like."

"We have to find the evidence Dad hid. Otherwise, these people might decide to set the trading post on fire, hoping to destroy the evidence."

"And do to us what they did to León and his wife?"

"Yeah. We're a threat to them because they aren't sure how much we know. They need to get us, or the stuff, or both."

"How much should we tell the staff at The Outpost and the police about this?" Jo asked.

"Let's find the evidence first. Then we'll go from there."

Jo sat there silently for several miles, then finally decided it was time to give up her secret. Now that she knew what the killers were after, and that she could no longer protect anyone by keeping quiet, Ben deserved to know the rest of the story.

"I got a phone call from your father's killer the day of our grand reopening," she began.

Ben looked over at her. "So that's what you've been keeping to yourself for so long. Let's hear it."

It took less than a minute to explain, but the questions Ben had lasted almost a half hour. Unfortunately, she had no more answers beyond what they already knew. They rode in silence after that.

Finally Jo's cell phone rang, and she motioned toward the cup holder on the center console. "Will you get that, Ben?"

Ben picked up the phone and identified himself. A second later, he put it on speaker.

"This is Lieutenant Gary Ramirez of the New Mexico State Police. We've found the bodies of three men who fit the description of the ones who jacked you and your cargo. They're suspected of running guns for the drug gangs in Mexico, and all three have long records. We need you to stop at the OMI morgue in Albuquerque and see if you can identify them." He gave them the address.

"We'll be there inside two hours," Jo answered, looking over at Ben, who nodded.

As the call ended, Ben looked at her. She was gripping the steering wheel so tightly, her knuckles were white. "Are you sure you're really up to this?"

"I've got protection," she said, gesturing to her medicine pouch, "but I don't want to hang around that place any longer than absolutely necessary."

There were no surprises awaiting them at the morgue. The three bodies belonged to the men who'd carjacked them. Word had come from the DEA that the killings were believed to have been retaliatory in nature, but that was all the police were willing to tell them.

Jo had been allowed to verify Ben's ID of the victims by looking through a window. That had spared her having to approach the bodies, as she had before with the men in the pickup. When it came to bodies, most Navajo had been raised with the rule of three—don't touch them, don't look at them, get away from them. Lately, she'd been forced to do too many things that were counterintuitive to her, and it was taking its toll.

At the wheel, Ben glanced at her, then back at the road. Jo still looked paler than pale. What she'd been through lately would haunt her dreams for a while. Violent deaths had aftereffects on the living, and the trio at the morgue had died hard.

The men's apparent leader, shotgun guy, was full of bullet holes, and Don, the guy he'd decked with the assault rifle, was nearly decapitated, though still recognizable. The third guy, Karl, was clearly the victim of torture.

Ben called the rental company and told them about the van he'd left back in Juárez, explaining that he'd left it behind, fearing he was about to be hijacked. Silence stretched out between him and Jo, but as the minutes passed, Ben saw that Jo's color was returning to normal. Although he tried to hold her back at the station and get her to talk to him, Jo had just shut down. All things considered, maybe she'd been right not to lean on him. In a little over two weeks, he'd be gone again and out of her life for at least a year.

Ben glanced over at Jo. Her seat was reclined and her eyes shut. Her hand remained over the medicine pouch on her belt. He'd rediscovered just how much she meant to him, and that connection wasn't because they'd had sex. It was much more. Once he was gone, he'd miss her more than she'd ever know.

—TWENTY-TWO—

Safe. That's how Leigh Ann felt when Melvin held her. There was something reassuring about his touch, and best of all, he never pressed her for more than she wanted to give. He'd never even kissed her. Now, standing on his front porch in the cool breeze, she rested her head on his chest, listening to his heartbeat.

She remembered the few times she'd asked Kurt to hold her. He'd get all hot and bothered and end up wanting sex. She'd learned quickly to stay away from him unless that's what she wanted, too.

With Melvin, everything was different. In his arms there were only gentleness and a wonderful sense of peace. His touch was light, but still all-encompassing and strong, a tree in the desert.

Reluctantly, Leigh Ann moved out of his embrace and stepped away, still holding his hand in hers. "I have to go. I need to get to work."

"I wish you could stay longer," he said. "I don't know if I've helped you."

"You have," she said, pressing her palm to the side of his face. "I'm stronger just having been next to you."

"I know you're hurting right now, but I still think you should let Rachel stay with you, at least until you can get another boarder," he said, squeezing her hand. "That rent money is helping *you*. This isn't about her or your late husband. That's over, done and gone—in your words. Think about what's good for you now. That's all that really counts."

"I'm glad you're my friend, Melvin," she said, and stepped closer, kissing him on the cheek.

"Come by anytime," he said, and smiled. "You're always welcome."

Five minutes later, Leigh Ann was on her way to work. Had her marriage been a sham from day one? In the beginning, Kurt had seemed larger than life to her, the tall Texan with the easy smile and sexy walk. Yet as the years wore on, reality had systematically shattered each one of her illusions.

She took a deep breath. Melvin was right: no more looking to the past. Kurt had broken her heart, but she'd never again have to listen to his put-downs or crude, sexist jokes.

She had a brand-new life now and was free to live it as she saw fit.

Katie pulled up in front of the trading post well past closing time, gambling that Jo Buck would still be around. Noting a light on in the back office, she smiled to herself. Jo clearly loved this place almost as much as she'd loved law enforcement . . . a lifetime ago.

She thought back to the days when she'd first joined the department, eager to start her career. She'd had so many plans for herself, ready to change the world. Then the world changed her.

Katie got out of the cruiser and walked up the stairs to the main entrance. "It's Detective Wells," she announced loudly.

There was a short pause. "Hang on. I'm coming," a voice that sounded like Jo's called out from inside.

Katie watched through the glass, spotting two individuals inside moving toward the door through the darkened interior. When the latches were turned and the door opened, Ben Stuart and Jo were standing there. "I'm glad to find you both here," she said. "I've got some news."

"We have some information for you, too," Jo said, motioning for her to enter. "I was going to leave a call first thing tomorrow. I didn't think you'd be working this late." She glanced up at the clock, noting that it was close to 10 P.M.

"Looks like neither one of us works normal hours these days," Katie said, nodding to Ben, who nodded back.

Jo led them to her office and offered her a seat. Ben straddled a folding chair and reached for a half full mug of coffee.

"Would you like something to drink?" he offered.

Katie shook her head and opened the manila folder she'd brought with her. "I'd like you to take a look and see if these look like the rugs that were stolen from you."

Katie set out several photos. The rugs pictured there were a muddy, stained mess. "A farmer with land adjacent to the San Juan River west of Bloomfield found these along the bank, caught on the branches of a fallen tree. There were a few more farther downriver, hung up on an irrigation gate."

Jo studied them, and then glanced up at Katie. "These *look* like the rugs we purchased, though obviously they've been removed from their packaging and unrolled. But why on earth would anyone go to the trouble of stealing five dozen rugs, then ruin them like this?"

"Drugs are sometimes dissolved and soaked into fabric, in this case, the rugs. When the cotton dries, the drugs are hidden within the porous weave. Later, after being smuggled past the authorities, the rugs are soaked in water and the drugs dissolve back out. When the water evaporates, you have the drugs, in crystal form, which is then packaged and sold," Katie said. "Got it?"

Katie watched Jo and Ben carefully. When she'd first seen these photos a few hours ago, she realized instantly how Roberto Hidalgo had imported his drug shipments and what part The Outpost had played in that. What she still didn't know was if Tom Stuart had been a willing part of the operation, or an innocent man who'd found out too much and become a liability.

Either way, she now had a motive for his killing. What she needed to figure out next was how much these two had already guessed, and how she could use the information to bail herself out of the mess she was in.

She reached down and tapped one of the photos. "So you'll verify that these rug designs and colors match the stolen ones?"

"Yes, and the tags should identify them as Mexican made—the Desert Mirage brand," Jo confirmed.

"They have that product name—and 'Hecho en Mexico' on the label," Ben said, looking more closely at two of the photos.

"Do you have a regular clientele for your Mexican rugs?" Katie asked, looking at Jo.

"I'm not sure if they're 'regular' customers or not. This was the first time I was responsible for the Mexican imports. My boss was the one who arranged the buys and handled the sales. But I do know that the rugs sold well. All of the Chinle-style rugs from this last shipment were presold. The remaining rugs would have gone to walk-in customers. If you'd like, I can give you the telephone numbers of all the customers who placed advance orders."

"I'll need that, yes. Do you happen to have any more Mexican rugs here from the same vendor, or any other Mexican source?" Katie asked.

"We just completed a storewide inventory a few days ago. We're completely out of Mexican rugs," Ben said. He turned to Jo. "Right?"

Katie saw Jo nod, but she also saw what looked like a visual signal pass between the two. Neither of them had a reason to lie that she knew of, but Katie had a gut feeling they were holding out on her. Del, her informant, had already said that Ben had seemed very frustrated by her lack of progress on the case. Maybe Ben had put other things together on his own, too. If he suspected that she was on the take . . .

She needed a new game plan. "You said that you had something to tell me?"

Ben nodded. "We have reason to believe that my dad kept some form of evidence that will point back to his killer. That's what they've been searching for."

"What kind of evidence?"

"I don't know."

"How did you get the information?" Katie pressed.

"From a man on the telephone who wouldn't give me his name," Ben said.

"What can you tell me about him? Where was he calling from?" Katie asked. This was the kind of information *she* needed to break Hidalgo's hold on her.

"I agreed not to say—for his own protection. If I find out anything more, I'll pass it along."

Now she was pissed. "I can detain you right now for withholding evidence," she snapped. "Or have your phone records subpoenaed."

"Probably, but it won't get you anything but a list of times and places. I've already given you all I know."

Katie reached for the cuffs, planning to bluff, but then Jo spoke up. "There's more. We've recently learned that the Mexican vendor The Outpost uses may have been involved with the drug cartels."

Ben gave Jo a sharp look, and that was enough for Katie. She was nearly certain that was where Ben had gotten his information. Even using her informants, Katie had never been able to get anything on Roberto's Mexican drug connections. This was just the opportunity she'd been looking for, but in order to identify the supplier, or at least the conduit, she'd have to back off and give these two a little more room. "Okay. What's your vendor's name?"

"León Almendariz. He has—had—a business in Juárez. We understand that he and his wife died yesterday in a fire," Jo said.

"But you have no idea what it is your dad hid, or where it might be?" she asked Ben again.

"No, and we've searched everywhere," he answered. "We believe that this evidence is what the murders, break-ins, and incidents have all been about, and why they keep coming back at us. The people who killed my father are worried that this can do them serious harm."

Katie nodded. There was something else going on here just beneath the surface, but suspecting she wouldn't get any more answers tonight, she said good-bye, then drove away.

A few miles east of the trading post, Katie pulled over to the side of the road and called Roberto. "I have some news."

"Come to my home," he said. "Park a block away, then walk up the alley and through the back gate to my office."

Katie arrived at his estate fifteen minutes later. An armed guard—a slender, tough-looking Mexican thug about her age with a Bluetooth at his ear and a cigarette in his mouth—let her through the eight-foot-high, stout electronic gate. Then he swept her for bugs with a hand scanner. Ignoring her handgun, he pointed toward what looked like a mother-in-law house about fifty yards from the Mediterranean-type McMansion with a terra-cotta tile roof.

Moments later, Katie identified herself in a soft voice as she knocked, though she knew it wasn't necessary. The guard had already called in.

Roberto opened the door and invited her inside. "What do you have for me?" he said, waving for her to take a seat on a white leather sofa. He sat down beside her, a little too close for comfort and within arm's reach of her holstered sidearm.

Katie turned to face him, placing the weapon farther away, then told him about her meeting with Ben and Jo. "They've made a connection between the Mexican rugs and a drug-smuggling operation, but they've got nothing that leads to you."

"I know. If they did, I'd have the DEA and state police parked across the street. The list of telephone numbers they gave you leads nowhere. Those people are fictional, just names. But Stuart Sr. and Almendariz gathered names and dates they hoped would link me to the wrong people, and that could be a problem. They also kept one of the rugs. Then Stuart, that crazy *pendejo*, actually had the *cojones* to threaten *me*. If his son and that Indian *puta* think they're going to do the same, they're as good as dead."

"There's no need for more violence," Katie said firmly. "If you let *me* handle this, you might still be able to get what you need without attracting the attention of the INS, DEA, Homeland Security, and the FBI. Otherwise, this could blow up in your face and I'd be helpless to stop it."

"So, what are you planning to do?"

Roberto didn't have to know about her informant. "As I said, the less you know, the better. Now, tell me about the rug— the one you don't want them to find or use against you."

"It's what they call Chinle style, in black and reds and whites. It's cheap cotton, not wool. Nothing about it will be remarkable— except what it contains."

"Which is?"

"Like you don't already know? It's pure cocaine, dissolved

into the fabric. Get me that rug and the list of names Stuart made. If you do, your service to me will be complete. I'll turn over what I have on your boy and you can forget that you and I ever met. If not—there's no place you can ever hide that will make you safe from my partners south of the border."

She nodded and stood. Roberto was lying, of course, about letting her walk away. The only reason she was still alive was because killing a cop would mobilize every law enforcement agency in the state. But if she could get that list *and* the rug, there was a chance she could use them to buy her way out, or at least get a really good head start.

She'd check in with Del tomorrow. Maybe he'd heard something else she could use. If not, there was still another way. Plan in mind, she left Roberto's and drove home.

☀

T he next morning, Katie walked into her kitchen. She hadn't slept much at all last night, nothing new. Pouring herself some coffee, she glanced over and saw Brent sprawled out on the sofa. He must have gone to sleep watching TV, because the set was still on.

"Wake up, Brent," she snapped. "You've got school today."

Brent opened his eyes. "Huh? What time is it?"

"It's six thirty. Hustle off that couch and jump into the shower. I need you awake and alert today. Something's going down."

"Huh?"

"Listen up, Brent. I want you to pack a bag with things you'd take on an overnight trip and keep it handy in case we have to leave town in a hurry."

Brent sat up quickly. "What's going on, Ma? You in trouble with the department?"

"We're both in a shitload of trouble, Brent. I don't have time for questions right now, just remember to keep your mouth shut around your friends. If we have to split, nobody can know about it. Before the bus comes, get your stuff together. Pack only what you can carry in your backpack so it won't tip anyone off."

"We're leaving *today*?"

"I don't know yet. I've got a plan, but if things go wrong we'll need to move fast."

"Is this about the drug thing?" he asked in a whisper. "I've been clean, honest. You told me that I wouldn't go to jail."

"Jail is the least of my worries right now. If we screw up now, we could both end up dead. Come straight home, don't bring any friends over, and be ready to leave."

"I'm so sorry I let you down, Ma. I mean it. Where are we going?" His eyes were as wide as characters in those Japanese cartoons, and she saw real fear in her child.

"I can't say, because I don't know yet, but it'll be as far from here as we can go with the money I have on hand. We'll also have to change our names, our identities. The whole nine yards."

"Then we'll be safe, right?"

"We can't count on it, Brent. The people we're running from have long memories. As long as they're alive, we'll have to look over our shoulders."

"But you're a cop. You've got friends who'll watch our backs."

"Nobody can be trusted now, Brent. All we've got is each other. I'm depending on you, so please don't screw up now." She grabbed him firmly by the shoulders, looked into his frightened face, then eased up, giving him a big hug.

"I've got your back, Ma," he whispered. "Be careful today."

Katie released him and strode out the door before he could see her tears.

⚜

Ben paced like a caged tiger around his father's office. "If my dad hid a rug, then it's here in the trading post. He wouldn't have taken it home. There aren't any secure hiding places there, and, besides, this is where he spent most of his time."

"We've already looked everywhere."

"Then we've missed it. Think about it, Jo. It makes even more sense if you factor in the woman we discovered taking photos of the interior of the trading post with her cell phone. She may have been working with them, and mapping out possible hiding places. Her vehicle plate was stolen, remember? And the deputies never found the blue SUV—or her."

"I hear you, but facts are facts. We've inventoried everything here."

"We inventoried the things we could *find*. This time let's try to put ourselves in Dad's place. If he'd wanted to hide something, where would he have put it? A three-by-five rug could be stashed in any number of places, and my dad could hide things better than anyone I know."

"A rug has two minimizing shapes—rolled up like a tube, or laid flat. That should help us narrow down potential hiding places," she said.

Jo went to the front and told the staff that Ben and she would be in the office, but didn't want to be disturbed no matter what they happened to hear. She hadn't considered how that sounded until she saw the surprised look on Esther's face, Leigh Ann's mischievous smile, Del's grin, and Regina's raised eyebrows.

"No, no, guys," Jo said quickly. "We're just looking for something that belonged to Tom and we may have to move some things around in the office. We wanted to make sure everything ran smoothly here while we took care of that other business."

"Do what you have to, and don't worry," Leigh Ann said.

Moments later, Ben and Jo began searching the small eight-by-ten room. Working together from the bottom up, they left nothing unturned. Jo searched each drawer while Ben looked at the desk itself. They then tipped the safe and other furniture and looked underneath. Despite their hard work, they found nothing.

"We've searched behind and beneath everything in this office, Ben. If it's in the trading post, it's got to be in another room," she said at last.

"No. This was *his* space. It's here." He looked up at the ceiling. It looked solid, and they'd already checked the long fluorescent light fixture. "Let me think."

"Be reasonable. The only place we haven't searched is *inside* the walls."

He looked at her and smiled. "Brilliant. Try tapping the panels. Maybe one will slide or come loose. There's a framework inside, which means spaces between studs."

Once again they started on opposite corners. Jo worked her way downward toward the baseboard, tapping and listening for changes in density. As she passed the file cabinet, she heard a hollow sound. "Here—maybe. But how do we get in there?"

He tried to pry the baseboard loose, but it was nailed shut. Ben studied the paneling and found faint, vertical scratches in a few spots. "We need to go up higher, behind the wainscoting."

"I always thought it was weird putting wainscoting in a trading post office, but your Dad said it added class to the place," she said.

Ben brought over a chair. "These are all lightweight sections he got as payment from one of his contractor customers once." Ben looked along the top trim, tested a small section with a tug, and it lifted right off. "It's not nailed or glued. A dado has been cut so the trim will fit in place atop the panel."

"A dado? You mean the notch in the bottom?" she asked.

"Yeah, sorry. Shoptalk. Woodworking shop—ninth grade."

"So, where does that get us? The panel is screwed into place."

"Screws and not nails? Interesting." He tapped the panel,

and one of the screws started to come loose. When he pulled at it, it came right out. "No threads. It's a dummy." He tugged at the one farther down and it came right out, too. "So what's holding the panel in place, glue?"

He tugged and the panel suddenly came loose, drooping forward slightly.

"Are those magnets?" Jo pointed toward the two-by-four studs that constituted the uprights in the frame.

"Yeah. And there are metal strips glued to the inside of the panel. Here we go," he said, lifting the thin wood panel up and out from behind the baseboard.

Beyond that were the wall studs, a lot of cobwebs, and a colorful rug wrapped in clear plastic, standing on end inside the gap. "It's the right color and size," Ben said, bringing it out.

Using a pair of scissors, they cut the clear tape that held the clingy plastic wrap in place. Ben held it at one end as Jo slowly unrolled the small rug. "There's nothing in it, but it sure smells funky and feels a bit stiff and heavy."

"I bet it's full of cocaine," Ben said.

"I hate to say this, but by itself, this isn't proof of anything. They could just as easily accuse your father, or arrest *us* for possession of illegal drugs. Judging from the weight, there may be enough cocaine inside the weave to send us to prison for, say, twenty years," Jo said.

"You're right—so was León. He said we'd need that *prueba* too," Ben said.

"But if it's something small, it could be *anywhere*. We could search for years and never find it."

"Let's wrap the rug and put it back into its hiding spot. Then we'll look around a little longer."

Once the rug was out of sight and the panel in place, they searched Tom's office again. An hour later, they'd found nothing else and no more secret panels.

"Time's slipping away from me. I don't want to go until

things are settled here, but I've only got sixteen days left, seventeen tops if I can reschedule my flights. For the first time in my life, I wish I could stay—for good."

Yearnings too powerful to ignore filled her. Attachments . . . she'd avoided them, even though the Navajo Way taught that only by pairing could a male and a female be complete. Harmony demanded a woman's promise and a man's strength and power.

For the first time, she truly understood what that meant. In his arms, she'd found a place where the what-ifs of life couldn't reach her. Nothing mattered except that incredible feeling of being wanted, of loving, and knowing there was someone who cared enough to stand beside her, no matter how rough things got. All she needed to let their future unfold was the courage to reach out to him.

Jo's thoughts quickly melted away when she heard Regina and Leigh Ann talking just down the hall. "We need to get back out there before they start to wonder what else we've been up to."

"You're right, but not a word about what we know," Ben warned, opening the door.

K atie pulled off to one side of the road and parked, ready to wait. She knew Del's schedule. He took a break from work around this time of day and went home for an early dinner. Del Hudson was the key, and her only hope of finding out what was going on at that damned trading post before it was too late. Today she was going to squeeze the kid till he bled.

Katie thought back to the days when she'd been one of the good guys. If things went her way these next twenty-four hours, she'd be free of Hidalgo once and for all. Then maybe she'd be able to carve out a new life for her and Brent. Her son, for the first time, was showing some maturity, and she knew they had a chance as a family—if they could get through this last crisis.

It took over an hour, but she finally saw Del coming down the road. She ducked down, waited until he passed, then sat up, switched on her emergency lights, and pulled him over.

She climbed out of the vehicle and walked toward the operator's side, noting the frightened look on his face. She didn't blame him for being afraid. Things were about to get a lot worse for Del.

She stepped to the driver's-side door and motioned for him to roll down the window. "I gave you a chance, Del, but you've let me down."

"You can't arrest me. Where's the evidence?" he asked, a weak smile on his lips.

"Hey, smart-ass, did you really think I'd let a drug dealer completely off the hook? That bag is still in a safe place—with your fingerprints all over it. I can make your life miserable in more ways than you can count," Katie snapped.

"You lied to me! That's illegal."

"No, it's not, and don't try to weasel out of our deal. You haven't given me jack since our last meet—not even a call. I'm running out of patience. I've got a son of my own, and that's the *only* reason I'm going to give you one more chance to save your ass. Give me something I can use, and I'll square things with you."

"But I don't know anything!"

"Tell me, what's been happening over at the trading post? Anything strange, or maybe just different from the routine," Katie pressed. "Think hard, kid. This is your last chance."

"Tom Stuart's office," he said after a pause. "Ben and Jo were in there most of the morning. They told us they were looking for something of Tom's. I think they found it, too, because now they're keeping the door locked, something they never did before. When I left, they'd gone back in there again, and I could hear a lot more noise."

"What kind of noise?"

"They weren't getting it on, if that's what you're thinking—not unless hand tools are sexual aids these days."

"Any idea what they found, or what they're still looking for?" Katie pressed, ignoring his comment.

"No. There aren't any windows in that room, so unless the door's open, it's not like I have X-ray vision."

"You've just bought yourself another few days, Del. Good job. Keep your eyes and ears open, and if you find out what they've been looking for, call me."

"Yes, ma'am."

"And, Del, don't go home for dinner. Turn around and get back to the trading post. Buy some cookies and pop if you're hungry, but don't leave again until quitting time. You're my eyes and ears, and I need you in there. Got it?"

"Yes, ma'am." The kid put the truck in gear and was gone as quickly as the speed limit allowed.

Katie watched him disappear down the highway in the direction of the trading post. Her instincts so far had been right on target, and it looked like things were about to come together.

After reaching for her cell phone, Katie dialed Hidalgo. "Ben Stuart and Jo Buck have found something they're trying to keep hidden," she said, explaining. "I can haul them to the station with me on one pretext or another right after closing time tonight. While the store is empty, you and your men can go in and get whatever you need. Take your time and go through Stuart's old office piece by piece if you need to do that. I'll keep Jo and Ben with me and make sure no deputies are in the area. Your men will have free access as long as they stay out of view from the highway."

"I've got a better idea. Come to my office, same as before, and we'll talk." He hung up before she could respond.

Katie felt a tingle going up her spine. As long as Hidalgo needed her, she'd be safe enough, but the clock was ticking and she was running out of time—and hope. She'd been preparing for this moment for months now, and she was as ready as she could be.

Katie checked her watch. Knowing he'd be home by now, she dialed her son next. "Get your things ready, Brent. Put what you want in the Jeep, then go get the bag tucked under my bed."

"Mom, what's going on?"

"I can't tell you now," she whispered. "Just get the license plate I've been saving for emergencies and switch it with the one on the Jeep. Understand?"

"Yeah. When are you coming home?"

"I'm not sure yet. A couple of hours, maybe more. No calls to anyone—and, Brent, stay home. If any strangers show up at the door, hide. Don't let them see or hear you."

"But, Mom—"

"We've talked about this before. We have the fake plate so we can't be traced so easily. Just do it, and be ready when I get home."

"I won't screw up, Mom," came the hurried reply. "I swear. And, Mom, take care of yourself."

Katie hung up. Maybe, just maybe, if she played her cards right, she and her son would come out of this alive.

Ben leaned back in his father's chair. They'd run their hands over the leather and even removed the armrests, but so far they'd found nothing. "I think we should dismantle each piece of furniture in here before we move on."

"Okay, but let me go out front and check on things. It's past closing time, and the staff will be getting ready to leave."

"Before they go, reassure them that nothing's wrong."

"In other words, lie to them," Jo said. Before he could answer, a knock sounded at the door.

Jo opened it and found the trading post's staff all standing there. "What's going on, guys?" she asked, surprised.

"We know something's up, and that it has something to do with Tom's murder and this trading post," Leigh Ann said. "Whether you two like it or not, that affects all of us and we want to help." She glanced at Del, then looked back at Jo. "Del has something he needs to tell you, too."

Del stared at his shoes.

"Go on. Tell her what you told me," Leigh Ann said.

"I really didn't have a choice," he began.

"He was being blackmailed," Leigh Ann said.

"It's Detective Wells," Del said, then told them what had happened with the drugs and why he'd come back early from dinner. "I didn't want to rat you guys out, but I didn't know what else to do!"

Esther stepped forward. "This isn't your fight alone, Jo. Whatever happens, we need to stand together, but you have to tell us what's really going on."

"You're right. You deserve to know." Jo told them what they'd learned about the cocaine, the rug, and the other evidence they'd yet to find. "But we've looked and looked, and there's nothing else here."

Ben invited them into the office and removed the panel. Esther gasped and Del whistled low.

Leigh Ann stepped up to the opening. "I've learned many things from Melvin, and one is that we should all go beyond what our eyes can see." She reached into the hiding place and closed her eyes. "If a spider gets on me, y'all get ready, because I'll be screaming my head off." Leigh Ann ran her hands slowly over the interior, checking the backs of the adjoining panels and the studs.

Several moments later, after stopping once to remove a splinter, she looked over at them. "There's something on the other side of this two-by-four." She kept her right hand in place on the beam. "I hope it's not a wasp's nest, but it doesn't feel like dried mud. It's more squared off."

Ben reached into the dark interior, touched Leigh Ann's hand, then felt the blind side of the wood in the right spot as she pulled away. There was a solid, plastic object there held in place with tape.

"Where's the flashlight?" he asked.

Del grabbed the light from atop the desk, and aimed the beam toward the spot.

After probing around with his fingertips, Ben found the end of the tape and pulled it loose. A tiny memory card inside a plastic case fell into his palm. He brought it out, and saw it had the word CANON in the upper left corner.

"This is for a pocket-sized digital camera like the one my dad sent me last Christmas. It stores videos with audio as well as photos," Ben said.

"Your dad also had a Canon, but it was taken in to be examined as possible evidence," Jo said. "I don't know what it contained."

"Well, this was hidden for a reason, so he must have switched the memory card long before he met up with his killer," Ben said.

"There are some Canon pocket cameras on display next to the jewelry cases," Leigh Ann said. "I'll go get the demo model."

A few minutes later, with the card in place, they watched the short video of a frightened León Almendariz naming the ones who were behind the drug operation and revealing crucial details.

"Roberto Hidalgo," Esther said in a horrified voice. "I know that name. He's a deacon for one of the Farmington parishes— Saint Mark's, I think. He's also on the board of directors of the Valley Senior Center. If this is true . . ."

"Mr. Almendariz paid with his life for giving this information to my father, and Dad died because he wouldn't give it back, or tell his killer where it was," Ben said. "This is what they've been looking for all along."

"I wish Tom had just given it to them," Esther said.

"Dad knew he was a dead man anyway. The only thing he could do was make sure they didn't get what they wanted."

"What do we do now?" Leigh Ann asked, her voice shaking as she looked around the room at the others. "Call the sheriff?"

"No, that would put everyone here on the witness list—and in danger. You should all go home like it's just another day. But don't go out again or open the door to anyone until you hear from me," Jo said. "Ben and I will take the evidence to the state police. We can't trust Detective Wells or the sheriff's department. We don't know what side they're really on."

"Wait a minute. Nobody should leave until I do some checking," Ben said, realizing it was nearly dark outside now and the parking lot lights had just come on. "Del, when did you say you spoke to the detective?"

"During my dinner break—around four thirty."

Ben considered it. That was more than enough time for the drug dealers to react and get an operation under way, especially if they'd known they were about to be compromised.

He went to the front window of the trading post, which had the best view of the highway. Most of the interior lights were off now, so he knew he'd be hard to see from outside. He stood to one side of the glass, back far enough to be lost in the deep shadows that followed sunset. Beside the highway, a hundred yards away, he could see a dark van parked in the middle of the lane that led to The Outpost.

"We're already blocked off," Ben said as calmly as he could. "Everyone stays here and away from the windows. Don't let them know we're on to them. We need to call the state and tribal police right now."

"My cousin works for the state police. I'll call them," Leigh Ann said.

"I'll contact the tribal station in Shiprock," Esther said. "They should be able to respond in twenty minutes or less if they have patrol officers close by. We're right outside tribal jurisdiction here, but I know a few people, and should be able to convince them to back up the state troopers."

"Tell them we can't call the sheriff's department, because one of their people is involved in the murder of Tom Stuart," Ben said. "We don't know that for sure, but it might help speed things up."

"And in the meantime?" Jo asked.

"We need to find ways of protecting ourselves," Ben said. "My guess is that they'll make their move once it gets completely dark—earlier, if they think we're on to them. We have about ten minutes, so let's get to it."

TWENTY-THREE

Del, get that pallet with the cases of canned goods out here and place it against the front of the door. Then block the back entrance with the other pallet, the one with the lard and baking goods," Ben said.

"But both doors open out," Jo said. "Wait—I get it. They'll have to crawl over the top of the cases to get in."

Ben nodded. "We'll also have another way of slowing them down. Jo, get a length of rope for us from the tack supplies. Once Del gets those pallets in place, we'll loop it through the base, top to bottom, then tie everything to the door handles. If they manage to break the locks, they'll still have a hell of a time opening the door."

"On it," Jo said. "Remember the shotgun, Ben," she added, moving toward the saddles and animal supplies.

"Still behind the counter?" Ben asked, moving quickly toward the main cash register.

"Yeah. It's loaded, too, but we don't have any extra shells."

"Everyone else—get something you can use as a weapon," Ben said as Esther and Leigh Ann came over. "Use an axe handle, a shovel, whatever you can find that'll force them back."

Jo returned with the rope, and Ben reached out to give her the shotgun. "You'll need to use this."

"No, you know guns better than I do," she said. "I've only fired a shotgun twice in my entire life."

"I've got some hand-to-hand skills you don't. Once everything else is set up, I want you to duck down below the counter, and if anyone tries to force their way inside, shoot them. Aim low, there's a natural tendency to shoot high when taking a quick shot."

"What about us?" Leigh Ann asked, coming up holding a pitchfork at quarter arms. Esther had her Bible under one arm, and a rubber mallet in the other.

"What are you going to do with those?" Del asked Esther as he passed by, pulling the jack back for the other pallet.

"I won't be spilling any blood, but I can pound those animals to sleep with these babies," she said.

"Did you ladies call the two police departments?" Ben asked.

"Yes, but the tribal police doesn't have any units in the Shiprock area right now, and the closest state patrolman is on the east side of Farmington," Esther said. "No one will be able to reach us in less than thirty minutes. That's why the tribal police dispatcher is contacting the Farmington cops. They might be able to help."

"Let's get a rope through that pallet by the main entrance," Ben said. "Leigh Ann, Esther, make the rope tight. Jo, keep watch. If you see anyone approaching on foot or that van start to move, let us know ASAP. I'll help Del secure the back door."

Five minutes later, they met behind the counter at the rear of the front room. Jo, still by the window, looked back at each of them. Esther was now praying, and Leigh Ann, wearing heavy leather gloves, was trying to decide whether to hold the pitchfork tines up, or down. Del had put on a thick denim jacket, gloves, and was holding a heavy roofing hammer he'd picked up from the hardware section.

"If I'm going to be protecting the front door with the shotgun, who's watching the back?" Jo asked Ben.

"Del will be keeping watch from the passage door leading into the storeroom. He's got soup cans to throw if anyone manages to open the door even a crack. If they get inside, he'll lock the inner door and head to the produce locker."

"Where are you going to be, son?" Esther asked.

"Close to the front entrance, hidden from view," Ben said. "But I'm also armed." He held up a long hunting knife taken from the sporting goods display. The curved blade gleamed in the low light, and Esther drew in a breath.

Knowing he had to keep everyone busy or panic would seep in, Ben called to Jo. "What's going on outside?"

"Nothing, I think. Not yet anyway," Jo said. "In the headlights of passing cars, I can see at least two figures in the front seat."

Ben glanced at the Coke machine by the entrance and pointed to the doorway. "Anyone want to help me with the refreshments?"

Three minutes later, as the black van crunched across the gravel of the parking lot, lights out, the refrigerator-sized drink dispenser rested against the pallet of canned goods. The front door was completely blocked now.

"It'll take a tank to bust through," Ben told them with a grim smile.

"Here they come," Jo called out.

"Flip the main breaker, Del," Ben called. "And watch that back door."

As the teenager turned off the main power to the building, the small battery-powered lamps in the four corners of the main room came on. With the aisles piled high with merchandise, they didn't make much of an impact. It wasn't much brighter than a full moon inside, and anything below the top few rows of merchandise remained in deep shadows.

Esther and Leigh Ann made their way back beside the produce locker—their keep, Esther had called it. The big room, cool as it was, offered the best practical protection from gunfire. The freezer was too small for more than two people, and clearly too dangerous for other reasons.

Ben, hiding behind the shoulder-high stack of canned food cases on the wooden pallet, watched the van come to a stop. A woman, clearly visible beneath the glow of the closest pole light, climbed out of the front passenger side of the vehicle. It was Detective Wells. She wasn't wearing a belt or carrying a weapon, so he wasn't sure if she was a hostage, or just trying to pass herself off as one.

✳

Jo, looking out from beside the front cash register, watched Detective Wells walk up the steps and across the porch. She stopped at the front door and knocked loudly, identifying herself as she did.

"I know you're there, guys, so open up," Katie said, her voice strained. "I'm here to pick up what you've found. If you don't give up that evidence right now, we'll all be killed. The people who forced me to come here are prepared to do whatever it takes to get it back."

"Don't bother pretending, Detective Wells. You're working with them, and we know it," Jo called out. "We're not letting you in, and we're not giving you anything."

Jo looked over at Ben, who never took his eyes off the door. He had the big hunting knife in his right hand, and the thought of what he might have to do with it made her shiver.

Jo kept to the plan. She was supposed to stall as much as she could. Every minute put friendly forces just a little bit closer.

"Jo, I'm trying to save lives," Katie called out. "Give me that rug and the other evidence. Just throw them out onto the porch and this will all be over. Or break the window, climb up on the shelves, and dump them outside if you want. I'll stand back out of the way."

"No deal." Jo gripped the shotgun tighter, checking again to make sure the safety was off. She'd never shot anything except for tin cans, and the way her hands were shaking, she doubted she'd be able to hit the side of a barn, much less a moving target.

She had to find a way to keep Detective Wells busy. That's when she remembered the woman's constant antacid diet. How long had she been fighting on the wrong side, and why? It was clearly eating her from the inside out. Maybe there was still hope.

"Why are you working with these people? You're no murderer or drug dealer. Are you being blackmailed? Did they force you into something, like they did Tom Stuart?" she asked.

"There's no time for talk. If I don't give them what they want—now—we're all going to die!" she yelled. "Don't you get it?"

Jo didn't answer. She heard what sounded like Detective Wells kicking the door with her boot, then silence. The sound of men's voices eventually carried over to them; then the van's headlights came on.

Blinded, Jo looked away as the vehicle came closer. To try to ram those doors was just plain stupid. Tom had six-inch-high concrete barriers all along the front, and they were staked into the ground with rebar. If they tried to drive over those, they'd kill their speed and high center before they ever reached the porch. Then they'd still have to come up the steps. The wheelchair ramp on one side was too narrow for a vehicle.

As she peered out from behind the end of the counter, she heard the van's sliding door open, followed by a thud and running footsteps. The rumble of people on the wooden porch told her they'd decided to target the door using manpower.

Jo saw Detective Wells stand back, her hands by her side, as a big Hispanic man with wavy hair held a pistol to her back.

"Break it down, *muchachos!*" he yelled.

There was a loud thump, metal against metal, and the entire doorframe shook. Jo inched out from behind cover for a better look. Two men were holding a battering ram composed of a pipe and welded-on handles. When they swung it forward again, the door shook, and something popped.

After that, it was quiet for a minute. The next sound was an electric whir. She inched to one side and saw a man pulling a cable from the front of the van.

"They've got a winch. They plan to yank the door off," she whispered.

"Be glad they don't have explosives," Ben said. "Get into position and ready to fire. If that door flies open, they'll still have to crawl over the top of those cases to get inside."

The van's engine got louder, the winch whirred, and Jo heard a metallic twang as the cable drew tight. The doorframe shuddered, actually bowed out on the left side, then suddenly something snapped and the front door flew open.

She crouched on one knee and raised the shotgun. Her knee and her hands were shaking and, unfortunately, so was the shotgun's barrel. She kept her finger off the trigger, afraid she'd pull it by accident, but continued to aim at the space above the boxes.

"Jo, if you see anyone coming over the top of that stack, shoot," Ben whispered. "Make them afraid to come in."

Nodding, Jo looked back down the barrel and swallowed several times, almost sure she was going to throw up.

"Get that shit out of the way, *pendejos,*" the man outside said.

When Jo saw a hand reach up and a cardboard case move, she fired. The shotgun kicked into her shoulder painfully, but that was nothing compared to its flash and roar. For several seconds she froze, stunned.

Aware that someone was cursing in Spanish, she pulled herself together, worked the slide, and loaded another round into the chamber. She had five shots left. Each had to count.

"Move to a new position. *Now*," Ben said in a harsh whisper.

Jo scooted down the counter several feet, then inched up, hiding behind a candy display.

She heard shuffling in the gravel outside; then an explosion of bullets flew into the store. Splinters exploded off the wood and laminate where she'd been just a few seconds ago.

"Kiss my ass!" Del yelled from the back of the store, and a metal soup can flew over her head. It struck the side of the doorframe and bounced outside onto the porch. "Come and get it!"

Leigh Ann tried next, hurling a can from somewhere on Jo's right. It bounced off the Coke machine, though, nearly hitting Ben.

"Sorry," Leigh Ann whispered in the subsequent silence.

As Jo looked down the barrel of the shotgun, she saw the winch cable, fastened into a big loop, fly across the entrance. It slid across the boxes atop the pallet, then wrapped around the stack about halfway down.

"They're going to pull away some of the boxes to give themselves more clearance. Then they'll rush the door," Ben whispered. "Get ready."

The winch began its electrical whine again, and the cable looped around the stacked cases tightened. The cases were yanked outside, tumbling onto the front of the porch with a racket. Then the winch stopped.

She heard footsteps on the wooden porch; then a shape appeared just outside the door. Jo fired again and the figure ducked back. Once again, the flash blinded her for a second. Jo pumped the slide to reload as someone dived across the remaining cardboard cases and landed on the floor, below her line of sight. Ben leaped toward the attacker.

A gun went off and a light fixture shattered on the high ceiling, followed by the sound of bodies rolling along the floor. Ben was in a fight for his life, and she had to do something.

Just then someone jumped onto the pallet from outside. Jo

pulled the trigger and the shotgun roared. Terror gripped her as she heard a groan and realized she'd just shot someone.

Her heart in her throat, Jo ran around the counter. Ben and another man were locked in battle, rolling on the floor. She couldn't shoot or she might hit Ben.

Metal flashed between the men, and Jo heard an agonized cry. The man fighting Ben thrashed for a second, his feet knocking over a newspaper stand; then he stopped moving.

Ben rose to his feet, bloody knife in hand. "Watch the door," he whispered.

Out of the corner of her eye, Jo could see Del and Leigh Ann moving up the canned goods aisle, crouched low. Leigh Ann had the pitchfork's business end leading the way, and Del held his hammer like a club.

"Stay back," Ben warned, turning toward the entrance.

Jo swung the barrel around. Outside in the glare of the headlights, she could see a man facedown on the ground, and Katie Wells struggling with the wavy-haired guy. Katie clamped her hand on his wrist and twisted it, trying to force him to drop the weapon. The man kicked out and caught her in the stomach, knocking her back.

Jo stepped sideways, trying to get her sights on the guy, but before she could, Ben leaped onto the pallet and slid out onto the porch. She jerked the barrel away, her shot blocked.

The man shot Katie Wells twice in the chest, then whirled around to meet Ben.

In a heartbeat, Ben grabbed the man's wrist with both hands, knocking him to the ground. The pistol flew into the gravel ten feet away. As Ben rolled to his feet, Jo scrambled up onto the pallet, angling for a shot.

Suddenly the sky lit up as a brilliant flare exploded overhead. Spotlights flooded the front of the store and the van. The man who'd just shot Katie started reaching into his jacket. Instantly a half dozen tiny red dots covered his chest and Ben's.

"Hands up" came a powerful voice over a loudspeaker. "Reach for a weapon and we'll shoot."

Four heavily armed and armored officers rushed up, the dots from the laser sights on their assault weapons dancing around on Ben's and the other man's chests.

Ben held his hands out away from his body to show he was unarmed.

While one officer kept his weapon trained on Ben, the others grabbed the wavy-haired man, removed a second handgun from his inside holster, then forced him to the ground, face-first.

Slowly Jo set the shotgun down on a cardboard case of green beans. Tears were streaming down her face, but it was over. Turning to look inside, she could see that everyone from The Outpost appeared to be alive and unhurt.

Jo looked back just as Ben was being handcuffed. There was blood all over his torn shirt.

For a moment her heart stopped. "He's Ben Stuart, one of us!" she called out, scrambling over the cases of canned goods and onto the porch. "Ben, are you hurt?"

"No. I'm fine," he said, turning to look at her. "How about the others?"

"They're okay, thanks to you," she said as the cuffs were removed.

Jo gave Ben a shaky smile just as more officers arrived. While medics began to check the wounded, she turned to Leigh Ann and the others, who were all staring at the body lying on the floor beside the Coke machine.

"See his wrist?" Esther said. "He must be the man who killed Tom."

Jo stepped onto the pallet and looked down. The slender, wiry-looking, dark-haired man lay in a growing pool of his own blood. On his wrist, where Esther was pointing, was Tom's silver and turquoise watch.

A week later, as the trading post's new door and frame were receiving their final coat of paint, Detective John Sanchez of the sheriff's department stopped by. Ben, in uniform now, led him past the construction area into Jo's office.

She was working at the computer terminal and looked up as she heard them approach. "I thought we were finished with all the paperwork, Detective. Do we still have forms to fill out?" she asked.

"No, we're all done. The district attorney and every branch of government involved in investigating this incident finally agree that the death of Hidalgo's bodyguard, Tony Gomez, was a clear case of self-defense. There's nothing to keep Sergeant Stuart from returning to his unit. I'm just here to fill some gaps in the case for you," he said, taking the offered seat.

"Detective Katie Wells was my partner," Sanchez said. "Her involvement took me by surprise, but I've now learned that her reasons for working with Roberto Hidalgo were far more complicated than they appeared to be on the surface. I thought you'd want to know the backstory," he said, then told them about Katie's son, the blackmail, and how her plan to protect him had backfired.

"But in the end, she put her life on the line to protect you two and the other employees here," Sanchez said. "With the information she was able to provide, and the rug and memory card we got from you, a drug network is now out of business."

"How's Detective Wells doing?" Jo asked him.

"She's still recovering from the two broken ribs, but her ballistic vest saved her life. The man who was wounded in the neck by the shotgun pellets is out of intensive care and scrambling to make a deal by testifying against Hidalgo. The man who died, Gomez, turned out to be an illegal. His immigration papers were forged. He'd been Hidalgo's bodyguard for years, and fits the description of a drug cartel thug linked to a dozen murders. We're trying to get more on him, and have contacted Mexican authorities, but don't hold your breath. The cops down there already have their hands full."

"What will happen to Detective Wells and her son now?" Jo asked.

"Her attorney is pushing for witness protection in exchange for her testimony, Ms. Buck. My bet is that the feds will come through on that option."

"Detective, you know where to reach me if necessary, right?" Ben asked him.

"Yeah, we do. Good luck, Sergeant Stuart," he said. "Hope you're safer in Afghanistan than you've been here."

Sanchez stood, then held out his hand to shake Ben's. He nodded to Jo, who didn't offer hers.

After Sanchez left, Ben looked at his watch, picked up his travel bag from against the wall, and placed it on his chair.

"Sorry I couldn't get a later flight. I wish I had more time," he said, looking at her.

"I know," she said, struggling not to get misty-eyed. She wanted him to remember her smiling, not all teary. "You'll be back."

"That, you can count on." Ben took her in his arms and kissed her slowly and gently, wanting to imprint the memory in her mind and his own. When he finally released her, he smiled, seeing the look of passion there. "I love you, Jo."

"Ayóó ninshné," she said, speaking the words in Navajo. "I'll be here when you come home."

Suddenly the office door swung open, and all the employees were standing there. Leigh Ann was holding a huge cake. "And so will we!"

He looked down at the cake, which said, HURRY HOME.

"Thanks, guys!" he said, then gave Jo a wistful smile. He'd had other plans for his last hour with her, but appreciated the sentiment anyway.

"If you blow out the candle, then you'll be back safe even sooner than you expect," Leigh Ann said.

"Is that local lore?" Ben asked.

"Hell no. I just made it up, but it sounds good, doesn't it?"

He laughed, and blew it out. "You never know. Wishes sometimes come true," he said, looking at Jo.

"Amen to that," Esther said.

"Now, let's eat!" Del said.

As slices were passed out, Ben's gaze locked with Jo's. In those gentle brown eyes he saw his future, one filled with endless possibilities.

ML   5-13